I0763322

Insatiable

Books by David Dvorkin

Fiction

The Arm and Flanagan
Budspy
Business Secrets from the Stars
The Cavaradossi Killings
Central Heat
The Children of Shiny Mountain
Children of the Undead
Damon the Caiman
Dawn Crescent (with Daniel Dvorkin)
Earthmen and Other Aliens
The Green God
Pit Planet
The Prisoner of the Blood series
- *Insatiable*
- *Unquenchable*

Randolph Runner
The Seekers
Slit
Star Trek novels
- *The Trellisane Confrontation*
- *Time Trap*
- *The Captains' Honor* (with Daniel Dvorkin)

Time and the Soldier
Time for Sherlock Holmes
Ursus

Nonfiction

At Home with Solar Energy
The Dead Hand of Mrs. Stifle
Dust Net
Once a Jew, Always a Jew?
Self-Publishing Tools, Tips, and Techniques
The Surprising Benefits of Being Unemployed
When We Landed on the Moon: A Memoir

INSATIABLE

PRISONER OF THE BLOOD I

David Dvorkin

Paperback edition published by Zebra Books in 1993
Trade paper edition published by Wildside Press in 2000

Editing, print layout, e-book conversion,
and cover design by DLD Books
Editing and Self-Publishing Services
www.dldbooks.com

ISBN: 978-1-7345636-9-6

ONE

Venneman dropped the coffee carafe in the sink as he was filling it with cold water. It smashed into flying slivers. One sliver hit him on the knuckle. He sensed as much as saw one fly past his eye, just missing him.

"Damn!"

His knuckle was bleeding. He held his hand under the stream of cold water, washing the cut until the blood stopped flowing. It stung deeply, but he kept his hand there. He deserved some pain for such carelessness.

It was a small cut, but Venneman was worried that the piece of glass might still be in there. Years ago, his mother had warned him that cuts from broken glass were the worst kind, because often one could not feel the glass in the wound. Unlike a splinter of wood, glass didn't always give its presence away. The image of a glass splinter under the skin, cleanly slicing away the very nerve endings whenever the wound was touched and thus preventing telltale feelings of pain, had stayed with Venneman ever since.

He shivered and told himself not to fret about such things. Surely the fact that the cut had already stopped bleeding was a good sign. He should expend more energy worrying about the invisible pieces of glass he had just scattered all over the kitchen.

Venneman spent the next quarter-hour sweeping the floor carefully and wiping off all the counters. Then he stepped outside and wiped his shoes on the wet grass just in case there were some slivers in the soles. It was still dark outside, and cold and drizzling, a prelude to the snow predicted for the day. Venneman took his time anyway and did a thorough job before going back inside. Finally he was ready to get the spare carafe from the cupboard and start the coffee-making process all over again. Once the coffee had started dripping, he took the shopping list off the refrigerator door and added to it *Coffee Carafe—12 Cups.*

Jill came into the kitchen as he was pinning the list back on the refrigerator door with a magnet. She was wearing only her bra and panties, and she was toweling her hair. "Did you yell, Richie?"

"Yeah, I yelled." He held up his hand, knuckle toward her, and told her what had happened. "Better not walk around in here until you get your shoes on."

"Right. Bring me a cup when it's ready, will you?"

He watched her as she left the kitchen, still rubbing the towel over her hair. The wetness made her hair look dark, but when it was dry, it was a light brown, almost blonde, shining and healthy. It reached almost to her shoulders, turning under at the end. It was naturally fairly straight hair, with only a slight, soft wave. Jill had always avoided permanents, preferring her hair's natural beauty. It complemented the aristocratic beauty of her face—high cheekbones, firm jaw, straight, slender nose, pale skin. Her eyes were brown and her eyebrows almost black, a startling contrast to her hair and skin color. She stared at people fixedly, sometimes; it was an unconscious habit. Venneman had seen its effect: uneasiness followed by fascination.

Jill was tall for a woman, only a couple of inches shorter than Venneman. She was slender and firm, despite a sedentary job and lifestyle and a large appetite. She had always seemed unaware how blessed she was by heredity.

Venneman knew that Jill Kennedy in her underwear would have excited most other men, but she no longer had that effect on him. Living together, he thought. It's as good as marriage for suppressing libido.

Not that he had found her as arousing even in the beginning as he was sure other men would have. Their lovemaking was certainly pleasant, though, and Venneman would rather make love to Jill than not do so, most times.

In the early days of their living together, he remembered, Jill had always taken care not to appear in front of him naked, or even so nearly naked as she had just done. He had always assumed that that was due to her shyness about nudity and her uneasiness with her own body. For the first time, it occurred to him now that she might have been afraid of exciting him too much. She had had as many unpleasant experiences with the libidos of others as he had, and she must have feared his. For a moment, the idea amused him.

Later, they had breakfast, drank the last of the coffee, and went to church. Then they came back and read the newspaper, did their various housekeeping chores, and went out on a brief shopping trip. After all of which, it was time for Jill to prepare their lunches for the next day, for Venneman to make sure that all the non–food items he wanted to have in his lunch pail were in there, and for both of them to go to bed.

They were both very tired. They gave each other a quick kiss, said goodnight, lay down back to back, and fell asleep quickly. Despite his fear that it would wake him, the cut in Venneman's hand didn't bother him at all during the night, and by the next morning, he had forgotten about it.

The young woman at the front of the bus kept watching him. Venneman tried to keep his eyes glued to his newspaper, but he could not avoid looking up now and then. Whenever he did, his eyes met hers and she smiled warmly at him. Even Jill's presence in the seat beside him was no deterrence to the young woman.

Predators, Venneman thought. The world's full of them. He had always hated being stared at, especially when the look had in it that element of sexual interest that he had learned to recognize and fear even as a child.

The bus went all the way downtown, but Venneman and Jill normally got off at an earlier point, at one edge of the university where both worked, Venneman in the basement of Currigan Hall, the building housing the physics department, and Jill as the receptionist for the history department. Today, Jill had an appointment at a doctor's office along the way.

"Here's my stop," Jill said. "'Bye."

Venneman offered his cheek, and she gave him a peck on it. Then she hurried from the bus into the grey light of a winter morning.

Quickly, Venneman slid his lunch pail from his lap onto the seat Jill had just vacated. He tried to watch the young woman at the front of the bus without actually looking at her. She had half risen from her seat as Jill headed for the exit. Now, seeing what Venneman had done with his lunch pail, she sat down again. She was watching him, though, still trying to catch his eye. Venneman stared at his newspaper again, pretending to read it.

The bus reached the university, and the young woman stood up. This was Venneman's normal stop, but he decided to stay on the bus for a while this morning. After a long look at Venneman, the young woman shrugged and got off. Venneman relaxed for the first time since boarding the bus and managed to finish the main section of the newspaper before the bus reached its next stop, which was downtown. Venneman left the bus and began the trek back toward the campus.

Walking carefully along the wet, slippery sidewalk, Venneman wondered when it would end. Age would do it, he supposed. At some point, he'd be old and wrinkled enough that women would no longer want him. He had once tried taking up smoking in order to hasten that day, but Jill had objected strenuously. Possibly he would one day get used to the unwanted invitations and learn to ignore them, but he doubted it.

He got to work five minutes late instead of his usual ten minutes early. Not that it mattered all that much. The first supercilious Ph.D. wouldn't show up until ten or eleven o' clock. Of course everything had better be ready by then, and both lab technicians must pretend to be eager to jump to the lordly one's commands.

He and Dale did all the work, but the faculty members got all the credit. No doubt a really good Christian would be able to accept that and even be content with the way things were,

Venneman thought. He had never pretended to be a particularly good Christian, though, much as he thought he ought to be. Instead, he was sure he was one of the most sinful ones.

Faculty members and students were already roaming about in the hallways, but none of them paid any attention to Venneman. He was beneath the notice of the faculty members except when they needed his help in the lab, and the students ignored him because they knew he was of no use to their academic careers.

Oh, ease up, Venneman told himself. Less bitterness and more understanding, please.

He went down the main stairway, down to the basement level of Currigan Hall, trying to put a spring in his step, as if doing so would in turn affect his mood and make him feel happy and carefree.

At the bottom of the stairs, the way was blocked by double glass doors. A box was attached to the wall beside the right-hand door. A small light on the box glowed red. Venneman unclipped from his shirt pocket the badge which functioned as a cardkey. He inserted it into the slot in the box and pulled it out again. The red light changed to green, and Venneman heard the faint click as the door was unlocked. He reclipped the badge to his shirt and pushed the door open. "Home again," he muttered.

In fact, though, he had always liked the cleanliness and order of the lab.

Upstairs, there were other labs, the ones where first- and second-year physics students did what were grandly called experiments as part of their course work. No matter how often the students were preached to about the importance of neatness in a lab, those rooms were always a mess—in Venneman's opinion, anyway. He had started out up there, setting things up for the kids beforehand and then cleaning up after them. It had seemed a hopeless and endless task. At least he had done it, unlike his successor, who was really little more than a glorified janitor, and not a very good one.

Down here, matters were different. This was Dale and Venneman's domain. Oh, not in the view of the physics faculty, but in the view of the two lab technicians, who knew the truth of the matter far better than the part-time visitors with doctorates did.

Although the truth of the matter, Venneman knew, was that he was still little more than a glorified janitor. And this was Dale's domain if it was anyone's.

Dale was there already, seated at her desk, bending forward to concentrate on the screen of her computer. Venneman could see that she had on her usual Serious Graduate Student expression, but the blue light from the screen made her look like The Graduate Student from Another World.

Venneman was not surprised that Dale had arrived before him. She was as punctual as he, and frequently worked even later.

She had a future to work for, which could not be said for him. She had chosen this way to pay her way through graduate school, preferring it to teaching undergraduate courses or grading papers for one of the faculty members. From what Venneman had heard, Dale was highly respected in the department and was doing very well. She'd be gone all too soon, off to her no-doubt brilliant career. At which time, Venneman was sure, she would be replaced by someone considerably less pleasant to work with.

He called out across the room to her. "Hi, Dale! How's Dr. Dirtbag's little darling today?"

Dale looked up from her console, gave him a quick smile, and returned her attention to the panel in front of her. "Humming right along. All the little dials keep spelling out 'Nobel Prize.'"

Could Harold Dinsmuir with a Nobel Prize to his credit be any more insufferable than he already was? Venneman doubted it.

He put his lunch pail on his desk, hung his coat on the rack beside the desk, and walked over to Dale's desk. He stood behind her and looked over her shoulder. He realized that he was halfway hoping Dale had found a glitch, some sign that Dinsmuir's project wasn't working. Venneman felt guilty immediately. Don't think about Dinsmuir getting glory out of this, he told himself. Think of the university and the department getting the glory. Think of your job security.

If Dinsmuir succeeded, Venneman was sure, money would start flowing into the department, this lab would expand, and maybe Venneman could even swing a raise for himself. Such a raise would be even more likely if he could bring himself to stay in Dinsmuir's favor, since much of the money flowing into the department would flow to Dinsmuir, whom other universities would be trying to recruit. Should Dinsmuir choose to stay, he would have more money, more prestige, and more power. A pay raise was important to Venneman and Jill. If it were large enough, they could get on with serious planning for the future.

He realized that he had rarely stood this close to Dale before. For the first time, he noticed a few grey hairs in her short, thick cap of black hair.

Poor Dale, he thought. It's a good thing for her she's so good at physics and will be able to support herself. She'll never get a man.

Immediately, Venneman felt guilty for those thoughts. Dale was a wonderful young woman, he told himself sternly, and the man who won her heart would be lucky, indeed.

"What does he have you doing for the presentation?" Dale asked him.

She was twenty–five, the same age as Jill, but that was the only similarity between the two women. Dale was taller than Venneman, her face was plain, and her body was slender, shapeless, and sexless. "I'm the kind of woman every man expects to find in a physics lab," she had once told Venneman. But her face was pleasant and open, and Venneman had always found that looking at her relaxed him inside, made him feel calm and peaceful. Perhaps that was largely due to her being one of the few woman who didn't openly want him sexually.

He said, "I copied and collated all the handouts for Dirtbag. He also told me to double check all the tables and graphs against the original readings. You know, he's terrified that his positive results will turn out to be an artifact of the instruments, and he'll look like an idiot."

"Even more of an idiot, you mean. I bet there are lots of physicists who'd be happy to disprove his results. A lot of them are on the faculty here."

"Yeah, well, they might dream of undermining him, but they're also happy enough to hold onto his coattails as long as he's a rising star."

Dale laughed. "You're mixing your metaphors."

"Dale, I don't even know what a metaphor is, let alone how

to mix one. Anyway, now I have to put the stuff into those glossy binders he bought. And give the place a once over, make it neat and shiny. I'd better get to it. Dr. Dirtbag'll probably be along in an hour or two."

Dale widened her eyes at him and said loudly, "Why, here's Dr. Dinsmuir now. Hi, Dr. Dinsmuir! Everything's swimming along swimmingly."

Venneman pasted a smile on his face and turned toward the door.

"Good girl," Dinsmuir said. The tone of his voice dismissed her. His gaze slid over her and came to rest on Venneman, and his face lit up. Harold Dinsmuir was a tall, athletic man, darkly handsome. Venneman knew that he was past forty, but he looked no more than thirty, and the quantity and quality of his research were those of a young scientist. The current project, the complex of machinery which occupied all of the west end of the lab, was Dinsmuir's most ambitious research yet. It was also his ticket to worldwide fame. Today, Dinsmuir would be showing a group of money men and policy makers what he had accomplished. It would be the first step toward cashing in that ticket.

"Richard," Dinsmuir said. He had the voice of an orator even when he wasn't trying, and now he *was* trying. His voice grew deeper, richer, more commanding. "Let's go up to my office, Richard. We need to talk about what you'll be doing today."

Venneman stood his ground. "We discussed it yesterday afternoon, Doctor. I know what to do, and all the handouts are ready. I've got them stacked over there on my desk."

Dinsmuir's glance flicked back to Dale and away again,

back to Venneman. "Hm. I see. Okay, carry on, both of you. I'll check in later today."

After Dinsmuir had left, Dale said, "I wish I knew your secret, Richie."

"I wish *I* knew, so I could get rid of it."

Dale shook her head. "I don't think it's something you *can* get rid of. Or transfer to someone else, which is what I really wish you could do. You're more than handsome, you know. In an earlier age, you'd have been called beautiful."

"No," Venneman said quickly. "Jill's beautiful. Men are just handsome. But I'm not even that."

Dale said, "Jill *is* beautiful, but so are you. Or handsome, if you prefer. Very handsome. You're about six feet tall, aren't you?"

Venneman shook his head. "Five ten."

Dale laughed. "Okay, let's compromise. Say five eleven. And in good shape. And you've got that gorgeous hair—I don't even know what color to call it."

"Let's call it brown and change the subject. Please."

But Dale persisted. "No, it's not really brown. More like auburn—such a dark red that it's almost brown, but it's much more interesting than brown. It's a color women want to touch, to see if it feels as beautiful and sexy as it looks."

"It feels like hair," Venneman said.

"Of course it does. But you're avoiding my point. And then there are your eyes. They're even larger and darker than Jill's, and hers are killers. But you don't look at people the way she does. You're always looking at the ground, instead of the person you're talking to."

"That's not true!" Venneman said. "I'm looking at you right

now." He forced himself to keep his eyes on her face.

"With an effort," Dale said. "I can tell. Anyway, it's more than just your looks. I think you'd have that amazing sexual attraction, that sexual magnetism, even if you were ordinary looking. Maybe it's pheromones. Every woman wants you. And a lot of men, too, obviously."

"Not every woman, thank God." He smiled at Dale, feeling safe doing so.

"Most men probably envy you."

"They don't know what it's like. Anyway, I'd better get on with making Dr. Dirtbag look good."

Venneman put the handouts for the presentation into the new binders that had "Harold Dinsmuir" prominently printed on their covers. Then he scoured the lab. He found a few stray pieces of equipment and put them back on the appropriate shelves in the appropriate cabinets or in the supply closet, as appropriate. He noticed a couple of crumpled-up pieces of paper on the floor, and he picked them up and threw them away. He dusted surfaces and washed and dried the coffee mug with DINSMUIR stenciled on it. He worked mechanically. He was thorough, but his conscious mind was elsewhere.

He, too, wished that he could transfer whatever it was to someone else—to one of those men who supposedly envied him, perhaps, or to Dale, who obviously also envied him. Whatever it was, in Venneman's opinion it was a curse.

It had been with him for as long as he could remember. It predated puberty, the awakening of his own very mild interest in sex. As far back as he could remember anything, he could remember adults of every age and both sexes stroking him, hugging him, kissing him, and all those memories filled him with disgust. In school, teachers and other children had done the same thing to him.

God, how he hated being pursued! Pursued, desired, the protagonist in others' fantasies. He would sell his soul, he sometimes thought, to be free of all that.

Thank God for Jill Kennedy. She too was beautiful, desirable in the eyes of others. And she too wanted to be free of others' eyes on her body, wanted to be liberated from other people's needs. She and Venneman had found each other with vast relief. Each had become the other's shield against the world's lust.

They had been living together for more than a year. True, they slept together, but the physical side of their relationship was so subdued, so almost chaste, that Venneman was sure God would forgive them for it, especially since it protected them from the temptations of others and since they fully intended to marry very soon—as soon as money permitted, as soon as their financial future seemed secure enough.

Much of that depended on Dinsmuir—unchaste, lust-filled Dinsmuir.

Campus rumor had it that no attractive student in Dinsmuir's classes—male or female—was safe from him. A man of lesser professional ability would have destroyed his career with even half of the escapades that were attributed to him, but Dinsmuir—Dirty Harold, Dirty Dinsmuir, Dr. Dirtbag—had so high a record of achievement in his field that a university administration desperate for national recognition had chosen to hold its breath and ignore his trespasses and hope that Dinsmuir had the sense to know how far was too far.

Sometimes Venneman felt dirty working in the man's lab.

He also had no options. He was lucky to have this job. Were he to lose it, he would have a hard time finding another like it.

He was only here because of Dinsmuir, in the first place. There seemed no end to Venneman's dependence on the vile man.

Venneman's parents had died when he was a senior in high school. He had spent the small insurance settlement on college tuition, books, and room and board. In retrospect, it had been a foolish gamble, and he might have been better off spending the money at the racetrack.

He had reached the first semester of his junior year before admitting that his intellectual abilities weren't equal to his ambitions: he would never be a physicist. He had signed up for a course in Electricity and Magnetism and one in Optics, both required for physics majors, both taught by Dinsmuir, and both acknowledged as killers. They had certainly killed Richard Venneman's academic career.

There was nothing else Venneman had ever dreamt of being, nothing but a physicist. But it had become clear to him that it wouldn't matter if there were anything else, for he was talentless, as inadequate for everything else as he was for physics.

Of all people, Dinsmuir had come to his rescue. Dinsmuir, so vile in Venneman's eyes, had exerted his influence and persuaded the university to create a permanent lab-assistant position and hire Venneman to fill it.

Ten years later, Venneman was still there.

Even in his own eyes, he was just a glorified janitor. He made up for his lack of intellectual ability, his lack of any qualification for advancement, by an obsessive attention to detail. In any lab that was his responsibility, every surface would be spotlessly clean and every item would be in its proper place.

He would be here, he knew, doing this kind of work, until he was an old man. The years that should have constituted his career in science, he would instead spend in this lab or one like it, cleaning up after those with real ability, surrounded by science he could not understand.

The afternoon visit and demonstration went well for Dinsmuir.

Venneman did his part. He was appropriately unobtrusive except when Dinsmuir needed help, and then he was there immediately, handing Dinsmuir photocopies to distribute to the visitors, getting a clean ashtray for the two smokers in the group, refreshing drinks as necessary. Smoking was not supposed to be permitted in the lab, and drinking was outlawed everywhere on the campus except in one restaurant in the student union building. But Venneman said nothing about that. It was understood that laws did not apply to such visitors as these.

He and Dale had an hour of peace after the tour was over. Then Dinsmuir returned, alone.

He came into the lab shouting. "Great job, guys! They loved it. More important, they believed it. Which means money, funding, greenbacks for everyone. Dale, your doctorate's in the bag. I'll see to it. Richard, you still living with that little Kennedy girl?"

"Jill. Yes, sir."

"Yeah, I remember her from back when she was in my Physics 101 class. Hmm. Dropped out of school, didn't she?"

Physics 101, Venneman thought. What other faculty member of Dinsmuir's fame and accomplishments would teach a beginning physics course for non-science majors? But Dinsmuir wasn't doing it out a sense of academic philanthropy. Dinsmuir did it so that he could bask in the awe of a roomful of freshmen and sophomores and simultaneously select his prey for the semester. Jill had described her experience in that class to Venneman. She remembered no formulas from it; she remembered only the constant feeling of Dinsmuir's eyes on her body. Venneman had once overheard Dinsmuir refer to the 101 classes as being "filled with juicy little freshmen with elastic skin."

"Yes, Professor," Venneman said. "That's right. She hopes to go back and finish her degree some day. When we have the money saved up."

"Yeah, money. Everyone's problem. Well, listen, Richard. You deserve a reward for all your hard work on this presentation. You and Jill ever ski?"

"No, Professor." What a question, Venneman thought. As if ski vacations were within his economic compass!

"That's too bad. I've got a couple of plane tickets and reservations for a place in Colorado for next weekend, for me and a friend. But now I won't be able to go, because I've got to follow up with these money men, and my friend won't be able to go because her husband will be in town after all. So, if you and Jill want to use the tickets and the reservation, you can have them. It's too bad you don't ski. But hell, no one really goes out there to ski, anyway. Know what I mean? Maybe if you're really lucky, little Jill won't be able to go with you, and you'll get to go by yourself, you know?" He winked at Venneman.

"I think Jill would love a vacation in Colorado, Dr. Dinsmuir. Thanks."

"Uh huh. Well, then, come on up to my office later. I'll leave the packet on my desk, in case I'm not there."

They watched him leave, and then Dale said, "Good thing you know when he's scheduled to teach, so you can be sure he's not in his office when you go there. You know," she added, "it just occurred to me. I bet I know what he really meant when he said that about Jill not going with you. I bet he was thinking about her being here alone, with you out of town, so that he could get in touch with her and offer to keep her company."

Venneman snorted. "You're probably right. God, what a slimy toad!"

Dale smiled faintly. "Sex isn't necessarily bad, Richie. Just complicated."

Sex. Venneman thought about the word as he finished the few small tasks that remained. Such a small word for something that loomed so large in the lives of so many. What explained their obsession with it? It was the physical process God had designed for the propagation of the species. It was mildly pleasurable, but it wrinkled the sheets. Big deal.

It was a big deal for many, as Venneman knew. People like Dinsmuir risked their entire careers in the pursuit of it. So many people—Dale and Jill being among the rare exceptions—wanted Venneman for sex, even though he tried so hard not to attract them, not to radiate anything. It was as if his broadcasting of sexuality, a broadcast that lied, was another natural force, like sex itself, beyond his control and having nothing to do with his real nature.

In a way, he thought, it was like Dinsmuir's project.

Venneman came to a halt in front of the mass of equipment. It was two cylinders bolted together to form one longer cylinder, turned on their side, sealed at both ends, encrusted with the devices that controlled and measured the progress of the experiment. He corrected himself. This afternoon, it had officially progressed beyond being an experiment to being something else. Being what? A prototype, Venneman supposed. A first stage in something new and strange, something that would unsettle the world. Or so Dinsmuir hoped.

Venneman had read and tried to understand the handouts as he had copied and stapled them. He had, he thought, a vague understanding of the project and its significance.

Somewhere inside that long cylinder, a plasma burned. Venneman pictured it as a slender bar of light, a glowing cylinder within the metal cylinder. Perhaps it was unmoving, unchanging, or perhaps it writhed and twisted as though alive. Atoms tore themselves apart, shedding electrons, becoming naked nuclei. The nuclei rushed together and merged—no, "fused." But what was generated was not heat, but electricity, direct current.

That was where Venneman's understanding broke down. He had read enough popular science articles about fusion power to understand what the giant experimental setups in various parts of the world were working toward. But Dinsmuir, he gathered, had bypassed all of them and leaped ahead. Some new physical principles were involved, principles discovered by Dinsmuir. If Dinsmuir were not really responsible for their discovery, he would no doubt manage to claim credit for them.

Venneman didn't understand the physical principles themselves, but he understood the result obtained by applying them. Dinsmuir had used these new concepts to cobble together a pile of machinery which contained a small plasma in which fusion took place and electricity was produced directly from the plasma. The plasma was small enough, and well enough contained, that there was supposed to be little physical degradation of the equipment inside the cylinder. The entire project was small and fairly simple and required little maintenance by humans. If Dinsmuir had come even close to achieving all of this, then he would very soon be famous and rich, and he would have changed the world.

Dinsmuir planned to run the experiment for a few weeks more, to gather enough data to put his achievement beyond any possibility of doubt. Then he would shut the experiment down and unbolt the two cylinders and pull them apart to see how much damage the plasma had actually done to the equipment on the inside. His hope was that the damage would be slight enough to verify the commercial feasibility of his approach to fusion power. Overnight, giant power projects would shut down all over the world and industrialists would beat a path to his door. Could the Nobel Prize be far behind?

Venneman knew he should be impressed by Dinsmuir's accomplishment, but it was the plasma at the core of the experiment that fascinated him, the fiercely gleaming thread of sun hidden within that silent cylinder. It was all so mundane on the outside, but what must it look like beyond those metal walls?

It was like human nature, he thought. Outwardly, most people were bland, ordinary, quiet. But the glances Venneman always felt on him, the gazes that moved up and down his body, showed what blazed inside, the fascinating, deadly fire that would consume him if he ever dared expose himself to it. The mundane exteriors shielded him and must be maintained.

Only he—and Jill, thank God—lacked that awful inner flame. Only with Jill was he safe.

He wondered, though, what it would be like to have that fire blazing within him.

TWO

First class, of course. What else should he have expected?

Venneman shifted from side to side. First class seats were designed for much wider hips than his; they were designed for the hips of the rich, the kind of rich whose hips are wider than those of the poor. But there's a kind of rich people whose hips are narrower than those of the poor, Venneman thought. People like that would slide around in these seats. They'd be knocked from side to side every time the plane hit some turbulence.

He chuckled aloud at the image. Four free glasses of champagne made it easier to chuckle aloud. Anyway, even here in first class, there was enough noise from the engines to hide the sound of his laughter.

No, they wouldn't slide from side to side. They'd have all kinds of expensive doodads with them on the seat, doodads enclosed in expensive leather. They'd be using the doodads to work as they flew, to increase their wealth and power. "Must be nice," he muttered.

It would be even nicer if Jill were with him. That had been the plan, but the head of the history department had decreed otherwise. At the last moment, on Thursday afternoon, with their flight scheduled for Friday morning, Montfort, the chairman of the history department, had rounded up his office staff and told them that any weekend plans they had were canceled.

"But he knew about that damned conference months ago," Venneman had complained to Jill on Thursday evening. He was packing for the trip. Jill, looking unhappy, was unpacking what she had already packed and hanging it back in her side of the closet. "So why didn't he prepare ahead of time?" Venneman persisted. "Why is he doing this to you now?"

"Who knows?" Jill said. "That's just the way he is. Why didn't you pack your stuff ahead of time, so you wouldn't be doing it now, the night before? Same with him."

"No, it's not the same. The difference is, because I didn't pack ahead of time, I'll end up losing some sleep in order to get it all done in time. But I'm not screwing up someone else's weekend. I'm only screwing myself."

"I wish you wouldn't use expressions like that," Jill said. "Anyway, it's irrelevant, right? I'm stuck here, so you might as well go to Colorado and enjoy yourself."

"Enjoy myself without you? I doubt it. Why don't you just tell Montfort to go scr—To get lost."

Jill's hands dropped to her sides. She felt exhausted, physically and spiritually. "Oh, Richie. We're not making it financially now. Let alone saving up anything for the future, for me to back to school, which we said we'd do. I can't risk my job, especially not with the way the economy is these days, and me without any kind of marketable skill."

"You could be a model," he said impulsively. "You could get rich that way."

Jill smiled at him. "That's sweet of you to say, Richie. But I'm already too old to break into modeling—even if I thought I could do that sort of thing, which I never could. Can you imagine having people looking at you and taking pictures of your face and your body like that?" She grimaced. "Thanks, but I'll stay with the job I've got. Montfort's not so bad. I've heard about bosses who're a lot worse."

"I'd rather not go without you. If you've got to stay here, then I should stay here, too. Just say the word."

"Oh, don't be silly, Richie!" She laughed. "Just because I'll be stuck here doesn't mean you should be, too. I'll feel better knowing that you're enjoying yourself."

"I won't enjoy myself at all without you," Venneman assured her, but he felt relieved that she had rejected his offer to bypass the vacation.

So now here he was, lolling in the luxury of a first-class seat, drinking free champagne, waiting for his lunch, and watching the snow-dusted farmland of the Midwest slide away beneath him. And doing his best to ignore the gaze of the stewardess, who kept trying to make eye contact with him.

Dinsmuir wouldn't ignore her, Venneman thought. Dinsmuir would jump at the chance. Dinsmuir would maybe even grab the pretty young woman and see if these first-class seats were wide enough to hold two. Hell, Dinsmuir would probably grab the pretty young man from the coach class, too. Venneman chuckled again. Dinsmuir would...

Maybe Dinsmuir would drink less of the free champagne and keep his wits about him. And maybe Venneman should do the same.

He sat up straight and put his champagne glass on the fold-out tray in front of him. It was still about a quarter full, and Venneman was determined to leave it that way.

The stewardess took his gesture as a request for more champagne, or perhaps simply as an opportunity to approach him. She came down the aisle with the open bottle. "A refill, sir?"

What a lovely smile she has, Venneman thought. She *is* very pretty. Not quite so pretty as Jill, but that left considerable leeway for prettiness. And she was trying very hard to be friendly. Venneman smiled back. "No, thanks, Miss. I've had more than enough. Lunch is coming, isn't it?"

"Oh, yes, sir. It's heating right now. It should be ready in less than a minute. Traveling alone, are you?"

No, it wasn't a lovely smile; it was a frightening one. The lips wanted to touch him, the tongue to suck, the teeth to nibble and tease. Venneman shriveled within and drew back, shutting himself off, donning his armor. "Only to Denver," he told her. "My fiancée is meeting me there." A lie was surely forgivable in such circumstances as these.

The stewardess nodded. "I see. She lives there?"

"No, we're meeting there. We're spending the weekend in Steamboat Springs."

"That's a nice town. Hope you enjoy yourselves." She paused. "I have a layover in Denver this weekend, and I was kinda thinking of going to Steamboat myself. Maybe I'll see you there. My name's Karen, by the way."

Venneman smiled and nodded but said nothing. It was unlikely that she would see him in Steamboat Springs, since he would not be there. His weekend reservations were for another resort town entirely. He had seen the name Steamboat Springs on the map of Colorado he had been looking at before leaving on this trip. The name had appealed to him, and it had come in handy to mislead this particular predator.

A few hours later, when Venneman was wandering around helplessly in the winter-vacation madness of Stapleton Airport, he bumped into Karen again. Or she bumped into him.

She was pulling a small suitcase behind her on a wheeled metal frame. Amid the colorfully garbed skiers with their bulky jackets, she looked trim and appealing in her dark, form-fitting uniform. "Hi!" she said. "Fiancée didn't show up?"

"Oh, ah, no. Minor change in plans. We're going to meet in Steamboat Springs, instead. If I can find the airline that flies there, that is."

"If you don't, I could put you up for the weekend here in town."

"It's called Rocky Mountain Ski Transport," Venneman said, pretending he hadn't heard her. "But I don't see any signs for it."

"Oh, I know where that is. Come on." She took his arm and steered him through the crowd.

Her hand was small, but her grip was strong. Venneman, despite himself, found that exciting. The feeling frightened him. At last he saw a sign for Rocky Mountain Ski Transport ahead of him, above the heads of the crowd. "There it is!" he said, relieved. "I'm okay now. I can find my way. Thank you, Karen."

She smiled that lovely, predatory smile at him again. "At least you remembered my name. I remember yours: Richard Venneman. Thank you for flying with us, Mr. Venneman. Climb aboard any time."

Venneman mumbled something and pushed his way through the crowd toward the Rocky Mountain Ski Transport ticket counter, thankful when the mass of people closed again behind him and hid Karen from him. He realized that he was sweating. She could not have realized, of course, how she had terrified him. He told himself that, excusing her.

He verified his reservation and then headed for the appropriate gate. He had little time to spare. The small prop-jet would be leaving soon.

After Venneman had disappeared, Karen approached the desk and asked the young man behind the counter what Venneman's destination was. The agent grinned at her. "Better taste than usual, Karen." He told her what she wanted to know.

"I bet it tastes very good," she told him. "And I intend to find out."

This was another world, and Venneman wasn't sure if it was one he cared for.

There was snow everywhere up here in the mountains. And it wasn't dirty from traffic like the snow at home. Colored lights draped the buildings and the coniferous trees along the streets, as though the whole town were already decorated for Christmas. There were people in a party mood everywhere, the same gaudily dressed skiers he had encountered at the airport, and all in frantic pursuit of fun. For the most part, they went in pairs, happy couples bent on enjoying the slopes, the restaurants, and each other. As he watched them, Venneman's mild missing of Jill became less mild.

The biggest difference between this world and the one he knew was the prices. Everything cost two or three times as much as he was used to. It became clear to him suddenly just how generous Dinsmuir's gift really was. The seasonal room rates listed behind the receptionist's desk at the hotel took Venneman's breath away. Dinsmuir, however, had telephoned ahead and made sure that the room cost was covered and that Venneman would be able to eat in the hotel's coffee shop and charge his meals to his room—which meant to Dinsmuir's charge card. If not for that arrangement, Venneman realized, looking at the prices on the menu, he would have had to manage with one meal a day for the whole weekend. If this was what he would have to pay for simple food in a coffee shop, what would he be charged in one of the town's fancier restaurants? He would never find out, obviously.

Well, it would be a very simple vacation. He would spend a couple of days wandering around, watching other people having fun. He would eat only in the coffee shop at the hotel. He might window shop, but he would not be able to buy anything. And then he would go back to the small airport and begin his trip back home. It would not be an escape and it would not even be fun; he could already foresee that.

It was still only Friday evening. He had a long, lonely weekend ahead of him.

I think, Venneman told himself, that I will splurge on a lonely drink in some sleazy bar.

It seemed an appropriate way to kill what was left of his first evening alone in this town dedicated to skiing and sex. He showered with the hotel's fragrant soap, dried himself off with the thick towel, and put on layers of clothing. He had brought with him the warmest clothes he had, but it was scarcely enough, as he had already discovered from his stroll around town in the late afternoon. Now, with the sun long down, it was bound to be even colder. His woolen cap should be adequate, but he wasn't sure about his gloves. He looked at himself in the mirror, contrasting his bulky, drab appearance with the brilliant peacocks he had seen earlier roaming around the town. He felt poor and out of place.

You *are* poor and out of place, he told himself. So, all the more reason for a drink.

One drink would probably be all he could afford. He hoped Jill would understand his spending the money. He would tell her how lonely he had been and how silly he had felt for coming here. She would be sympathetic, he knew.

Venneman need not have worried about his colorless clothes. The revelers on the sidewalks ignored him. They were far more interested in each other.

He walked past the bars the peacocks seemed to be frequenting and kept on going. Eventually he should reach a part of town where the streetlights were further apart and there were no colored lights on the buildings. Even in a town like this, there must be an area frequented by those with less money. There, perhaps, he would find a bar where he could afford to buy a drink. Or maybe even two.

One of the peacocks blocked his path.

"Well, hi, fancy meeting you here! Another change in plans, right?"

It was Karen. She took his arm as she had in the airport in Denver and held on. "Going for a walk?" she asked. "I'll go with you."

"Uh, no, I was just going to head back to my hotel room."

"'*My*' hotel room? No fiancée?"

"A delay. She'll be here tomorrow. Well, 'bye."

But Karen held tight to his arm. "In that case, come on in

here and let me buy you a drink."

Weakly, Venneman let her lead him into one of the bars he had shunned earlier. Inside, the place was a bewildering riot of color and noise and the smells of cigarette smoke, alcohol fumes, and something pungent that Venneman didn't recognize. Karen seemed to know everyone there. They exchanged cryptic greetings with her, and twisted their faces, and it all seemed to be a secret language, communicating whole volumes that were closed to Venneman.

She pushed him onto a bar stool and climbed onto the one next to him. "There, now. What do you want?"

"I shouldn't let you—"

"Of course you should. Hey, Stan, margarita. Okay, Rich, what?"

"Uh, just a beer." The bartender was looking at him with raised eyebrows. "Miller Lite, if you've got it."

The bartender shook his head, but it must have been in disapproval rather than negation, for he opened a cabinet beneath the bar and took out a bottle of Miller Lite beer, opened it, and put it and an empty mug on the bar in front of Venneman. "You gotta watch those things," the bartender said. "Two or three of them, and you're flyin'." He winked at Karen.

"Stan," she said, "you're a killer. Where's my margarita?"

Stan held his hands up, palms out. "Comin', darlin'."

"Stan left his g's behind when he moved out here from Boston," Karen told Venneman. "But if you can get him drunk, he finds them again."

Venneman grabbed his beer with relief and drank a large part of it, from the bottle, without pause. He decided that as soon as he finished it, he would be justified in leaving the bar and Karen and this whole repellent subculture and heading back to his hotel room.

In the dim light of the bar, Karen looked even prettier and younger than she had on the plane. She surely couldn't be spending much of her time in this sort of unhealthy, smoke-filled atmosphere. How old *is* she? Venneman wondered. A kid, for Heaven's sake! What am I doing here, feeling lonely, out of place, with a girl hardly out of high school buying me drinks? I should be at home with Jill.

For the first time, Venneman noticed another woman, seated around the curve of the bar and watching him with interest. She reminded Venneman vaguely of Jill. She was blonde, like Jill, and although her face was only moderately pretty, there was something about the bone structure and the eyes that resembled Jill's. She wasn't as pretty as Karen, either, he decided, after a longer examination. And her clothes were less colorful and flamboyant than those of Karen and most of the others in the bar. But more expensive, he decided, after a closer look. Through all of this, Karen was talking to Venneman, trying unsuccessfully to draw words from him. She was already on her second margarita.

The woman across the bar smiled at Venneman. It was a smile that lit up her face, transforming her from pretty to beautiful. It was also a conspiratorial smile, as if she were expressing her sympathy for his awkward situation.

But behind all of that, Venneman knew, was something else, something old, something he knew too well and hated with all of his heart. He finished his beer quickly.

"Gee, don't drink so fast," Karen told him. "You'll get nonfunctional. Alcohol affects you a lot more at this altitude.

Less oxygen in the air. I think that's the reason. Stan, another one for Rich."

"No, really, Karen, no more for me."

"Hell, yes, Rich. Just accept what you're offered, okay? Now, I've got to go pee. Will you just stay here and sip your beer and wait for me? Really, just *sip* it. Okay?"

Venneman sighed. Perhaps this *was* marginally better than a lonely hotel room. "Okay, I'll wait. Go on."

Karen left. This time Venneman poured his beer into the mug. He sipped at the beer and then stared into it. He told himself that he had not felt so foolish and out of place since adolescence.

Someone slid onto Karen's barstool. It was the woman whom Venneman had been watching earlier.

"I'm Elizabeth," she said. Her voice was low, strong, and pleasant.

"Good grief," Venneman muttered. No one had any shame or self-restraint in this place.

"I said, I'm Elizabeth," the woman repeated. She had raised her voice, and now it was not quite so pleasant to Venneman's ear. She seemed demanding, and she reminded Venneman momentarily of Harold Dinsmuir.

"You're Elizabeth, and I'm leaving," Venneman said. Karen would have no trouble finding someone else to fill her evening, he was sure. He finished his beer in a few gulps, then slid off the bar stool. "Good night."

To his surprise, Elizabeth laughed. "Whoa." She grabbed Venneman's coat sleeve and kept him from leaving. With her free hand, she picked up Karen's margarita and swallowed what was left of it. "Wait for me."

They left the bar side by side, Elizabeth keeping a firm grip on Venneman's coat. Outside, she finally let go of him, and he turned to face her. He put his hands in his pockets for warmth. His gloves were in there, but he felt more protected this way, with his hands inside his clothing. Elizabeth stood there without gloves, without even a coat. For the moment, at least, she seemed unbothered by the cold.

She was taller than he had realized. She was quite a bit taller than Jill—almost as tall as he, in fact. The light from the bar window lit up the right side of her face, and the left side was almost in shadow. For a moment, Venneman wondered how he could have thought her only moderately pretty. She radiated something—sexual power, or perhaps just her desire for him—that affected him despite himself. He was aware that his heart was beating fast and that he had the beginning of an erection. She's a dangerous and unclean influence, he thought.

He said, "Thank you for walking me out, but now that I'm safely here, I'd better get back to my room. I need a good night's sleep. My fiancée will be flying in tomorrow, and—"

"And that's all the more reason to enjoy yourself tonight, while you still can," Elizabeth said.

"This is ridiculous," Venneman snapped. "You people ought to be ashamed of yourselves!"

Elizabeth drew away from him. She frowned and stared at him. "'You people'?" she repeated. "What people are those?"

Venneman waved his hand toward the bar. He was trying to work himself up into a fit of anger to match his words, hoping that the anger would dampen his growing sexual arousal. "All of you. All those people in there, all the people walking around the streets in this town. All of you oversexed people. You all seem to be thinking about nothing except picking each other up and going to bed with each other."

Elizabeth's frown disappeared. She laughed again. Her laugh, like her speaking voice, was strong and low pitched, and it stirred Venneman all the more. "Oh, *those* people," Elizabeth said. She stepped closer and put one hand on his cheek and stroked him gently.

Her hand was very warm. It sent a thrill through him, like a wave of heat. His heart was hammering now. He had never felt anything like this with anyone before. God, she's a stranger, he told himself. I don't even know her last name!

Behind Venneman, someone said, "Why didn't you wait for me, Rich?"

It broke the spell Elizabeth had cast, and he turned around. Karen stood in the doorway of the bar, her coat over one arm. Now she saw Elizabeth. Karen glared at Venneman. "Oh, I see. So much for your shy act, you son of a bitch." She spun around and went back inside the bar.

"Rich," Elizabeth said softly.

Venneman turned back to her.

"Richard, is it?"

"Yes, Richard." He had trouble making his voice work properly. The words came out in a broken whisper.

Elizabeth whispered in response. "Richard," she said, caressing the word with her voice. "Richard." She put her hand against his cheek again. "Come, Richard."

She lowered her hand from his cheek and gently tugged his hand from his pocket. Clutching his hand firmly, she led him from the well-lit street and down a short alley.

Even her hand was almost as large as his, and he sensed

that it was stronger. Her skin was like a flame against his, sending heat into him, kindling something inside him that he had always thought he lacked.

The alley was narrow, a snow-packed walkway between dark building walls. They could just barely walk side by side, and Venneman could scarcely walk at all. His knees were weak and he was gasping for breath. Elizabeth gripped his hand more and more tightly, pulling him along urgently. Her breath came unevenly, too. "I wanted you right away," she said. "As soon as I saw you. All women want you, don't they?"

Venneman said nothing. He was overwhelmed by what he felt growing and burning inside him. Was this how other people felt all the time, whenever they were excited by each other? Was this was he had been missing all his life? It was wonderful and it was terrifying.

"Now," Elizabeth said. "Here."

They were far away from the buildings of the town, at the base of a mountain. Far above them, along a ski run, the mountainside was brightly lighted. Behind them, the town gleamed against the night. Around them, the snow glimmered with reflected light. But Venneman and Elizabeth were two silhouettes, dark figures against the whiteness. They reached for each other, mouths meeting and opening, tongues sucking eagerly.

Venneman wanted to fill her with himself in every way he could. He wanted to touch her everywhere. She was hard and strong through her clothes, large, powerful—different from Jill in every detail.

Somehow, she had stripped her clothes off, and now she was tugging at Venneman's. He didn't think of the cold, didn't notice it. They sank down onto the snow, onto the pile of clothing, bodies glued together.

He was in her, her legs were wrapped around his, her arms around his neck. Her body was like a fire inside. She rolled on top of him and raised herself slightly. She stared into his eyes as she thrust her hips against his. His body responded without his willing it to consciously. He was under her control, or else under the control of this new force inside him.

"Never," Venneman tried to say. "Never, never, never."

Elizabeth's eyes widened. "Never," she whispered. She lowered her mouth onto his and sucked his tongue into her mouth. Even her mouth was fire. She gripped his head with both arms, his legs with hers. He wrapped his arms around her and squeezed as hard as he could, thrusting into her rhythmically, knowing he need not fear hurting her.

His climax began and went on and on, growing more intense, drawing more from him than he would have thought he had in him. Elizabeth was moaning into his mouth. Her eyes were closed. Her eyelids fluttered open slightly, showing only white. She pulled her mouth away from his. "Oh, God!" she whispered. "Oh, God!"

She slid her arms down from his head, past his neck, down his torso until she was embracing him around the waist, trapping his arms. She began to move even more urgently, pounding against him, hurting him. The pain added to his own excitement, lengthening his climax still more. Her arms tightened around him until he could scarcely breathe, and her legs squeezed his still tighter.

She lowered her mouth again, this time to his neck. She kissed him, a long kiss that he felt throughout his body. She opened her mouth and bit deeply into his neck, through the skin, through muscles and ligaments, down to his carotid artery and into it.

Venneman tried to scream, but it came out as a choking gurgle. He tried to pull away, but Elizabeth held him immobile. Her face pressed into his neck, and he could not get away from her mouth. Through the agony, he could hear and feel her sucking at him, drawing his blood in with huge gulps. All the while, her pelvis kept thrusting and rotating against his, and she moaned repeatedly as her orgasm continued, and his own hips kept responding to hers and his ejaculations continued.

Venneman kept struggling, kept trying to free his arms and pull away from her. But she was too strong, and already he was growing weaker. He tried again to draw a breath and scream, but he couldn't quite manage it. He was too weak, and her crushing grip around his waist kept him even from being able to pull air into himself.

Now the pain was fading. All feeling was fading. No, not quite all. He could feel the cold, now. He could hear Elizabeth sucking at his neck, a slurping sound, and he could hear her moans, which were growing even louder. And he could feel his own ejaculations, still going on, becoming more intense.

It would never end, he thought. It would last forever.

His thoughts became more and more muddled and then stopped.

When even her powerful tongue could suck no more blood from him, and her orgasm had diminished to nothing at last, Elizabeth pulled herself slowly off Venneman's still erect penis and pushed herself to her knees.

She knelt above Venneman's corpse for a moment. She touched his cheek as she had before and whispered, "Richard. Thank you, Richard. Goodbye."

She put the corpse's clothing back on it quickly, hurrying while the joints were still warm enough to be flexible. Then she scooped up a handful of snow and carefully wiped away the trace of blood that remained on his neck. She pulled his woolen hat down over his face and turned up his collar. The huge wound she had made was completely covered. No one would notice it—not while it still mattered.

Now Elizabeth put her own clothes on quickly. Sated and happy, she walked back into town. Her strides were long and energetic.

By the time dawn came, and some early-morning skiers discovered Venneman's body, it was frozen stiff. The sheriff was called. He said to himself, "Another drunken idiot frozen to death after an evening in a bar," but he kept his expression grave and reverent. He arranged for the body to be taken to the local funeral parlor, whose director doubled as county coroner, for the inquest required by state law. The coroner promised to get to it as soon as the corpse was sufficiently thawed. Or possibly the following morning, depending on the press of other business.

It was in the funeral parlor, in the early morning hours, that Venneman awoke.

THREE

He was cold. Jill had pulled the covers off him again. He was filled with a slow, sluggish rage. He fumbled toward his right, toward her, to yank them back, and his hand encountered empty space. At the same time, Venneman became aware that he was lying on a hard surface, not the mattress he was used to.

What? he asked himself. This isn't right.

He struggled to wake up. He had been trapped in some dark, deep place. Light shone high above him, and he felt himself rising toward it, toward the world and life.

But even his eyelids felt sluggish and glued together. He rubbed at his face with both hands, numb and awkward hands that felt like someone else's, and managed to open his eyes.

He was in a dimly lit room he did not recognize. A faint light shone through thin curtains covering a window off to his left. Venneman pushed himself slowly and painfully into a sitting position. He was hungry and thirsty, and his joints felt stiff and uncooperative. Suddenly, he remembered drinking some beer and that stewardess, Karen, warning him that alcohol affected people more at higher altitudes. This must have been what she was talking about. You could wake up in someone else's bedroom feeling like hell. And, he realized, looking at himself in the dim light, still dressed in all your clothing. That last was a relief, in a way. It meant he had not done anything for which he would have to apologize to Jill.

Elizabeth. He remembered a woman named Elizabeth, and he remembered kissing her. Had they done more? He couldn't bring any more memories about her to the surface.

He turned and let his legs dangle over the edge of the hard surface he had been sleeping on. Some sort of table, he thought. He had actually fallen asleep on someone's table! I'll never drink alcohol again, he vowed to himself.

It was a long, narrow metal table with a raised edge, and it was cold. His clothes were damp, and so was the woolen cap that covered his head and his forehead down to his eyebrows. He pulled it off and ran his hand through his cold, wet hair. He longed for a hot shower, but even more, he longed for food and drink.

He slid off the table, onto his feet. His knees buckled, and he grabbed the edge of the table just in time to keep himself from falling. He held onto the table. His legs were shaking, his head swimming. His pulse pounded in his ears.

Venneman stood still for a while, bent over, leaning against the table, and breathed deeply. At last he felt able to stand straight. In the dim light, he could just make out glass-fronted cabinets lining the walls and filled with unidentifiable objects. He walked cautiously over to the window and drew the curtain aside. Outside was a snow-covered hillside, gleaming with reflected light. The sky overhead was dark, filled with brilliant stars.

Venneman let the curtain fall back into place and walked

cautiously across the room to the doorway. He began to feel stronger, more his normal self. His legs had regained their strength, he no longer felt dizzy, and his pulse seemed normal again. His hunger and thirst, though, were overwhelming.

Wherever he was, he thought, there must be something to eat and drink in the place. Finding it was his first priority. And then dry, warm clothing.

He opened the door and stepped through it. Some light came through the door from the room behind him, but not enough to see anything. Venneman slid his hand around on the wall beside the doorway and found a switch. He threw it, and a brilliant white light came on overhead, showing him another room much like the one in which he had awakened. In this room, too, there was a metal table in the center of the room. Someone was lying on it. The person was asleep on the table, just as Venneman had been, but was covered by a sheet up to the chin.

Venneman hesitated. The other person might also be sleeping off the effects of alcohol at high altitude. But Venneman's hunger and thirst were becoming too powerful to ignore. He stepped forward and cleared his throat.

Now he was close enough to see that something was wrong with the sleeper's face.

Venneman stepped even closer. The sleeper was a young man. His eyes were closed, and one seemed lower than the other, with the eyebrow where the eyelashes should be. His forehead sagged down on the same side. Above that, his scalp had been sliced open in a line running from side to side across the top of the head, and the skull gleamed through the opening.

Venneman gasped in horror and jumped back. Where was he? What had he gotten himself into?

Elizabeth, the woman in the snow... Something moved beneath the surface of his mind, some nightmarish memory involving her, something this mutilated young man reminded him of.

Hesitantly, Venneman stepped forward again. He couldn't just run away and leave this injured man alone, much as he wanted to. He reached for the sheet. "Listen," he said, "I'm not going to hurt you. I just want to see if you have any other injuries before I go looking for a doctor, okay?"

He peeled the sheet back. The young man had been sliced open from shoulder to shoulder, and from the breastbone down to his genitals. Bone and muscle and skin had been pulled back in two huge flaps, exposing a dark emptiness within.

Venneman stood staring down into the opening, unable to breathe, unwilling to move. "Jesus," he whispered at last. "Oh, God!"

He leaned over the corpse for a closer look. His first impression had been wrong. There were some organs within the opening. Which was which? he wondered. That one, he thought. What's that one? He reached in cautiously and touched something reddish-yellow with a veined surface. It was cold. He had somehow expected it to be hot. The coldness disgusted him. He pulled back and grimaced and let the sheet fall over the corpse.

And then he realized what he had just done. A wave of nausea hit him. It's the cold, he told himself. Hunger. I'm confused because I'm so hungry.

That was *his* excuse. What excuse could the mutilators of this poor young man have?

He had to get out of this place, wherever and whatever it

was, and find the police and tell them what was going on in here.

The room had another door. Venneman went to it and turned the handle. The door was locked. "Damn you!" he shouted. He turned quickly to the corpse. "Sorry." Jesus, he thought, I'm going off the deep end. Apologizing to a goddamned corpse. A sliced-open corpse. He laughed, and stopped short. "I'm going crazy," he said aloud. "Hey! Open the door! Let me out!"

He rattled the handle. "Let me out!" he shouted. He threw himself against the door. It shook on its hinges but remained locked. "God damn you!" Venneman shrieked. He took a few steps back, then ran at the door, hitting it with his shoulder. The door split down its middle, and Venneman was free.

He stood on a sidewalk in the night. At one end of the street, a quarter moon hung above the mountain peaks visible between the low buildings. At the other end, the horizon was almost flat and the sky was turning grey. There were no human beings in sight. Venneman didn't recognize the building he had just escaped from or anything else around him. Where was his hotel? What had happened to him while he slept?

Have to find the police, he thought.

The strength and alertness he had felt before now drained away again. Once again, hunger gnawed at him, and thirst made his tongue stick to the roof of his mouth. He was cold, shivering. He feared he would freeze to death. He staggered down the sidewalk, choosing his direction at random. Got to find someone, he thought. Got to find help. Got to clear my head.

A few blocks along, he saw someone coming toward him on the sidewalk. Venneman stopped and waited, weaving slightly from side to side, lacking the strength to walk further.

For a nightmarish moment, Venneman thought the figure walking toward him was the young man he had seen moments before, cut open and lying on a metal table. Then, as the other pedestrian came closer, he realized that it was also a young man covered in white, but the white was a coat covered with white fur and a white ski cap. There the resemblance ended. This young man was filled with life and warmth.

Venneman held up a trembling hand to stop him. "Help me," he tried to say, but the words came out garbled and incomprehensible. "Police. A body." He couldn't seem to make his tongue work properly.

The young man looked at him warily and kept his distance. "Wrong town for a handout, buddy."

Venneman shook his head. He felt a faint return of his anger. "No, no. Police. Murder."

The young man's face cleared. "Oh, a foreign tourist, huh?" He started speaking slowly and louder. "You tell me what you need, okay? I help you, okay?"

Loud though they were, his words faded away, drowned out by the sound of his beating heart. Venneman could hear nothing else.

The young man's coat was open at the neck, as was the collar of the shirt underneath it. Venneman stared intently at his neck. He could see blood vessels pulsating there. Listening with all his being, Venneman heard the faint whisper of the blood rushing through them.

How young and alive this man was, how vital!

That was what Venneman needed, that vitality. His hunger and his thirst became intolerable, but now they were a force urging him forward, not a weakness holding him back.

He took a step toward the other man, reaching for his neck.

"Hey!" The other man stepped back. "Watch it, buddy! This is America!"

Venneman lunged at him, flinging his arms around the other man's chest, trapping his arms against his side. There was something familiar about this, but he could spare no thought for that. He could think only of the blood now so close to him.

His victim shouted, "What the fuck!" He struggled vigorously, but he was helpless against Venneman.

Venneman seemed to be watching all of this from somewhere outside. He watched Richard Venneman lower his face to the struggling man's neck and sink his teeth in, deep, down to where the blood flowed.

The other man was large and heavily muscled. How, Venneman wondered, watching himself from the side, could the weakened Richard Venneman hope to overpower him? And yet he was doing it. The other man's shouts had turned to weak gurgles, and his struggles were subsiding. He was unable to pull his arms free and unable to wrench his neck away from Venneman's teeth. His kicks against Venneman's legs seemed to have no effect.

Venneman snapped back into his own body, drawn by the rush of blood through his mouth.

It was honey, it was wine, it was electricity. He had never tasted anything like it before. He had never felt such delight. He had never felt so strong. He was possessed by a strength that had come from somewhere outside. No, it came from the blood he swallowed greedily. That strength flooded his body and his being, suffusing his every cell, filling him with the other man's life and heat.

Venneman's victim hung limp in his arms. With some difficulty, Venneman loosened his grip and let the man slide to the ground, where he lay on his back, staring sightlessly up at Venneman. His head was bent to one side, away from the ragged hole in the side of his neck. The edges of the wound were colorless, bloodless. His face was pale.

Venneman's hunger and thirst were gone. He was filled with life and warmth. His clothes were still damp, but that no longer bothered him. His mind was now clear and alert.

With alertness came horror and disgust at what he had done.

With it came memory, too. He remembered everything that had happened with Elizabeth, from their glances at the bar to his death outside in the snow. She had done to him what he had just done to this young man.

Understanding came as well. Elizabeth was a creature that, until now, Venneman had thought was only a myth.

She was a vampire, and she had made him one.

The street was still deserted. Venneman picked up the pale, drained body of his victim and carried it between two adjacent buildings and left it in the narrow, dark space.

How easily he had picked it up and carried it! He was something more than he had been before Elizabeth.

No, he thought, I'm only superior physically. Morally, I've become a beast, a killer, a predator. I've murdered a fellow human being.

But he could no longer speak of fellow human beings. Those old movies he had watched on television as a boy had taught him that much about vampires. He had become a nonhuman, a creature of night and nightmare. He had died and come back as one of the undead—soulless and beyond salvation.

What good had all his years of going to church and believing in God done him? Through no fault of his own, Venneman was now cut off from God, from Heaven, from any hope of an afterlife. This was his afterlife: to lurk in the shadows and avoid the light and kill innocent human beings. This would be his eternal life, until the world ended.

Venneman raised his face to the lightening sky and shouted, "No!" He would put an end to this.

Vampires could be killed. So the movies had told him. He considered driving a sharpened stake into his own heart, but the idea horrified him, and he doubted if even this new vampirish strength filling his body would be sufficient for that. He had felt weakened by his hunger and thirst, so perhaps he could simply starve himself to death, but he couldn't remember seeing anything in a movie about vampires dying that way. Nor was he sure he could exert enough self-control to starve himself. He remembered how little control he had had over himself when his victim's blood had called to him. The blood had been in control, not Venneman. What chance that he could hold back from feeding again, when the hunger and thirst struck, and the blood sang?

That left sunlight. A single touch of a sunbeam was supposed to make a vampire burn and shrivel and steam away into nothingness. He had seen that scene often. It looked like an agonizing way to die, but didn't he deserve a painful death for having committed a terrible murder?

Venneman stepped back out onto the sidewalk and stood still and waited for the sunlight to find him.

Overhead, the grey was turning to blue. On the horizon, the blue was tinged with red. Any moment now, Venneman knew, the first golden edge of the sun would appear, coming over the horizon to destroy him. He felt gripped with panic, with the need to run and seek a place where he could hide until nightfall. That's not me feeling the panic, he thought. That's the vampire inside me. I'll defeat him.

But his panic grew. His body vibrated with the need to move. He clenched his jaws and held himself stiff and still.

His right foot began to slide along the sidewalk, moving in the direction of the dark place where he had left his victim's body.

"No!" Venneman said. He forced his feet together and squeezed his knees against one another, willing his legs not to move.

The edge of the sun glared above the horizon, and Venneman shut his eyes.

His face was on fire.

The sun rose higher, and the furnace heat moved slowly down over Venneman's clothing, seeking a way in, to his skin. It caught his ungloved hands and set them ablaze, too.

Venneman yanked at his coat, pulling it open, trying to expose more of himself.

But it was intolerable. He couldn't control his need to escape any more than he could have ignored his earlier need to kill and feed. He broke and ran, diving head first into the dark, cool space between buildings where his first victim lay.

He landed on the corpse, rolled off it, and lay half conscious beside it.

When the first pedestrians passed by an hour later, their

voices echoing from the walls to either side of him, Venneman roused himself enough to crawl further back into the shadows, dragging his victim's corpse behind him. Well back in the dark, safe from the eyes of the living and the light of the sun, Venneman curled himself into a ball beside the stiffening corpse and slept.

In his sleep, he shivered with fever. He dreamed dreams of blood and fire and pain, of a sea of blood that choked him with its smell, and lakes of fire that burned his ever-renewing skin off him over and over. He dreamed of agony that filled the universe, inescapable, that chewed him and swallowed him and spat him out so that it could chew and swallow him again.

Slowly, the pain and fire disappeared. Only the blood remained. Rivers of blood rushed and pulsated through his dreams, emptying into a sluggish red ocean. The smell was a perfume.

Venneman drifted up into wakefulness.

He opened his eyes and stared into the empty eyes of his victim.

He jerked away and sat up. Above, visible between the buildings, the sky was fading into darkness again. The brilliant stars of the high altitudes gleamed down at him.

Each one is a sun, Venneman thought. Why don't they burn me? Distance. I'm far enough removed from their light. Distance from the light means safety, distance from the light that powers creation.

He rose to his feet. He felt strong again. He ran his hands over his face. The skin felt smooth and unharmed, and he felt no pain from his own touch. But his mouth was dry, and in his stomach once again he felt the beginning pangs of hunger.

"No, please," Venneman whispered. "Not again. I can't do it again."

He brushed the snow from his clothes and walked out onto the sidewalk.

The glow of sunset was still fading in the west, where the mountains were a jagged silhouette against the orange afterglow. Venneman looked in that direction, squinting against the brilliance, and then turned away. He walked toward the darkest horizon.

The sidewalks were alive with vacationers, the same gaudy peacocks Venneman had sneered at before. But now, as he walked, they didn't ignore him. Their eyes seemed drawn to him, and yet they moved aside for him, leaving him walking in an island of loneliness.

And now he saw them differently, too: not as a superior species, looking down at him, but as a herd of cattle, walking repositories of a life that was by natural right his to take when he needed it. Their blood pounded in them and filled the air about them with its sound and smell.

I will not, he told himself. I will not do it again. I will not.

To keep that pledge, he had to avoid these creatures. Their blood and his hunger would overpower him.

Venneman walked as fast he could, desperate to leave the crowds behind.

The street and the sidewalk ended abruptly. The town had been planned and built as a ski resort. Beyond its designed edges, the original landscape reasserted itself. Venneman found himself in a snowy field surrounded by tree-covered hillsides, with the light and life of the town behind him. Here, the snow came up above his knees. Yet the cold didn't bother him, and he had so much more strength than before that he could plough his way through the snow with little difficulty.

Off to his right, he could see a steep hillside. A wide swath running from its top down to its base glowed in the remnants of twilight and the man-made lights strung along its length. Around it, the hillside was dark. It was a ski run, Venneman realized, and a familiar one. He was not far from the place where Elizabeth had made love to him and killed him.

Drawn against his will, he made his way through the snow in that direction. The place of his death was still hidden from him by the shadowy bulk of a snow bank when he heard a last faint, gurgling cry, dying away, and then a slurping, sucking sound that lasted for minutes more.

Frozen in place, his heart pounding, Venneman listened. The sucking ended, and then he heard a sigh of satisfaction.

Then he heard Elizabeth's voice, clear and loud in the darkness. "Come, Richard. Come here."

For a moment, Venneman stood still. Elizabeth must have heard him somehow, but if he didn't move, didn't make another sound, then she wouldn't be able to find him.

"Come here, Richard." Louder, deeper, thrilling through him. His legs moved. Control of them had been taken from him. He pushed his way forward through the snow, breaking through the head-high snow bank as easily as if it had been mist. The powdery snow floated in the air and drifted slowly away. He could feel it faintly on his face, cold little points of ice. He could see it sparkling in the air, reflecting manmade light.

Elizabeth knelt in the snow, looking up at him. She was a dark figure against the white. On the ground before her lay another dark figure.

"Come closer, Richard. Look." She lowered her head toward the still figure on the ground.

Venneman stepped forward. Her victim this time was a middle-aged man. He lay on his back, his head tilted to the right. His heavy coat was pulled open at the throat. The left side of his neck was a huge wound, its edges pale and bloodless. His eyes were open, staring over Venneman's shoulder. His face was slack, expressionless.

"He has his clothes on," Venneman said. "So do you."

Elizabeth smiled. "Of course, Richard. Did you think I make love to all my prey? You have a lot to learn about what you are. I have a lot to teach you. Look." She gestured again at the body in the snow. "He was prey, that's all. A sack of blood, a reservoir of life that I needed. I didn't want him after that. Not like you."

She rose to her feet. She was as graceful and strong, he thought, as a lioness. She stepped over the corpse, not even looking at it. "You came because I called you," she said. "You'll learn to do that, too. You can keep your prey alive for your future use. You don't have to kill them. You can take just some blood from them. You'll learn how to do that, too. I think we must have something in our saliva that stops their bleeding and encourages their wounds to heal fast, even a deep bite that would otherwise be fatal. So they live and become healthy again—and filled with blood again. And then you can call them to you when you need them again. Always, for the rest of their lives."

Venneman stepped back, filled with disgust. "I'm not going to be a parasite like that. I won't live that way."

Elizabeth smiled and stepped forward, stopping inches

away from Venneman. "You can't live any other way, Richard. And you won't want to do anything but live."

He tried to protest, but he couldn't speak. And now he couldn't move. Elizabeth put her hand up slowly and stroked his cheek, as she had done before. Venneman's heart raced and his knees felt weak.

"I can hear your heart," Elizabeth whispered. "I can hear your blood. Oh, Richard, it's so much stronger than it was! Come, Richard."

She stepped back and undressed slowly. She laid her clothes out on the snow and stretched out on them and held her arms up to him.

Venneman pulled his clothes off and fell on her, hungry in a different way, in a way he had felt only once before, and that with her. But now he was stronger than Elizabeth. He could feel strength and vitality surging through him, growing with each thrust into her, each grinding of body against body. He was unaware of the cold snow beneath, of the cold sky above, of the cooling corpse beside them.

But when they finished, hours later, he was drained and weak again. He rolled off Elizabeth and lay on his back in the snow. "I need..." he gasped. "I need..."

Elizabeth raised herself onto one elbow and looked down at him, stroking his face. "You need blood. You need it most at the beginning of your life. You have to feed frequently, now, to build and grow properly, to complete the process. The need diminishes later. I usually feed once a month or even less. Here." She leaned closer. "Just for now, just to give you a bit of strength, take a little sip of mine. Vampire blood is so much stronger than human blood, it only takes a little bit." She bent down over him and pressed her throat against his mouth. She whispered, "Just a tiny nip, Richard."

Venneman tried to turn his head away, to take his mouth away from her skin, but the sound and smell of her vampire blood overpowered him. He bit carefully into her skin, making only a tiny wound, and sucked.

And pushed her away and rolled off the clothing and into the snow, coughing. Her blood was sour and bitter and nauseating. He spat it out again and again, unable to get the disgusting taste from his mouth.

"See how well evolution works, Richard?" Elizabeth said. "We can't take blood from each other, only from our natural prey. I could have told you, but this way, you'll always remember it. We never attack each other. Come, now. Let's go into town and find you someone."

Venneman scooped up a handful of snow, stuffed it into his mouth, and let it melt there. He swished it around in his mouth and spat it out. The taste of Elizabeth's foul blood was almost gone. Only a faint, stomach-churning hint of it remained. He struggled to his feet and stumbled backward. He picked up his clothes and pulled them on clumsily. "Evolution? This doesn't have anything to do with nature! We're not part of nature, we're something unnatural!"

She shook her head. "We're the top of the food chain, Richard. Whether you like it or not, you're very much a part of nature. You've never seen a lion take its prey, have you? Or a bear or a tiger or any of the other great predators? It's magnificent to see, Richard. Thrilling. Now you're the same as they are. And you have to learn how to live the predator's life properly, just as they do. You must have felt that when you encountered humans on the way out of town. Didn't you?"

"No," he lied. "All I could feel was that I was something unnatural and evil and that God hates me now."

"God?" Elizabeth repeated. "Oh, my. Richard, if God exists, and if He's all-powerful, then He created us, too. He's responsible for our needs and our deeds, isn't He?" She thought for a moment. "Perhaps our victims deserve what they get. Perhaps we're their punishment for some sin, and we're helping to fulfill God's plan, whatever that is. If one believes in God."

"I believe in God," Venneman said. "But He didn't create us. The Devil did."

"While God wasn't looking? God must have allowed the Devil to create vampires for some impenetrable reason of His own. So, once again, everything's as it should be, and we should just get on with enjoying our lives. Our very long lives. Richard, this is the sort of theological silliness college boys argue about late at night. We have pleasure to concern ourselves with, and that's far more important than religious arguments."

"There's nothing more important than this," Venneman said. "Because of you, I'm going to spend eternity in Hell." He stopped, struck by a new idea. "I think I'm already there, God help me."

Elizabeth smiled. "You'll change your mind about that. Come. Let's go into town, and I'll show you that for us, this world is Heaven. Your mind isn't working properly because you need blood. You'll see how much better you'll feel after you feed."

"You mean kill another innocent victim?" Venneman said. "I'll die first. I'll die," he repeated. "I'll do it somehow. I'll kill myself."

"You'll try, perhaps, but you won't succeed. Forget the

stake and the cross and the silver bullet. They don't work. And you might as well forget God, too, Richard. If God does exist, He didn't raise a finger to help you, and now He'll shun you. We're immortal, and we have dominion over mankind. That makes us the true gods."

"Damn you," Venneman said. "You and your smooth tongue. The Devil has a smooth tongue, too."

"Come and see again how smooth mine is, Richard."

Venneman snarled at her. "You're going to Hell, but I can still redeem myself." He staggered away from her. His feet were almost too heavy to lift, and he gasped for breath. His belly shrieked with hunger, and his tongue stuck to the dry roof of his mouth.

From the darkness behind him, Elizabeth said, "Don't go too far away, Richard. I'll be calling you later." Then she laughed.

FOUR

Venneman made his way through the town toward his hotel. He avoided the crowded streets because he thought he would have trouble controlling himself when surrounded by so much blood. It pounded in their arteries. It sang to him, called to him.

For a moment, reality tilted, and he thought he was walking, not through a bustling crowd of human beings, but rather through a rushing, pulsating sea of blood, and the humans were figments of his imagination or memories left over from his past life, or at best emptied sacks floating on that red sea.

Venneman turned a corner abruptly and left the busy street behind him. He wandered instead down dark, almost deserted streets, encountering only occasional pedestrians. But this made it even harder for him to resist his urges. Alone with a potential victim, in no danger of being seen by a third party, Venneman found it almost impossible not to give in to his hunger and thirst, and to feed.

He managed to reach his hotel without yielding. He let himself into his room, closed the door behind him, and fell onto the bed. He had a moment to congratulate himself on his self–

control and virtue before he fell into an exhausted sleep.

He awoke a few hours later, just before dawn, pulled from sleep by his hunger and by a nagging thought he couldn't pin down.

He realized that he was still wearing the same clothing he had put on before going out on the town on Friday evening. Did becoming a vampire make one less fastidious? He was able to smile at the thought. He felt better for the small amount of sleep, he realized. Perhaps a shower would make him feel still better. More human, he thought, with conscious irony.

Later, drying himself off, he wondered if that had been entirely ironic. What if he resolved to live as human a life as possible? He could refuse to drink human blood. He could simply eat normal, human food to satisfy his hunger and drink water to satisfy his thirst. I can make myself human again, he thought.

And he could pray.

How simple it all was!

Elizabeth and any other vampires the world might contain could surely do the same thing, if they really wanted to. That she didn't, indicated only a lack of will. One was what one chose to be. Elizabeth was choosing to remain a vampire.

Heartened by this realization, Venneman dressed in clean clothes, combed his hair, and headed for the coffee shop. A sleepy waitress brought him the ham and eggs and coffee he ordered. He stared at it. He could no more imagine eating it, he realized, than he could imagine eating the tablecloth.

"Something wrong?" the waitress asked.

He looked up at her. "No, noth—" Blood pulsed in her smooth neck. He could feel her heart beating, pounding across the small space that separated them, pulsing against his chest. He could smell her skin and knew how it would feel and taste to bite into it, to bite deeply into her, to draw her blood into him. How that blood would suffuse him with its strength and life!

Venneman managed a smile and shook his head. For God's sake, get away from me! he screamed inside.

"Okay," she said. "I'll pick this up whenever you're ready." She put the bill on the table beside his arm.

Venneman shrank away from her, avoiding any possibility of a touch.

The waitress shrugged and walked away, vanishing into the kitchen.

His hands shaking, Venneman scribbled his room number on the bill, adding a very generous tip. He pushed himself away from the table and stood up. His head swam and he felt breathless from even that small effort. He leaned on the table for a few seconds, trying to regain some strength.

Doing his best to appear normal, Venneman left the coffee shop and went through the hotel lobby and out the main door.

Overhead, the sky was grey. In the east, it was already bright enough to hurt his eyes.

Another dawn, he thought. Another barrier shutting me off from human beings. Why, it's Sunday! It's Sunday morning! Jill's getting ready for church at this moment!

But Venneman would never see the inside of a church on Sunday morning again. He could go in only at night, and even then not to pray. Elizabeth was right about that. After his experience in the coffee shop, he knew that prayer would do him no good. According to what she had said, he needn't bother going inside a church to try to kill himself, either.

Assuming she was telling the truth. Could a vampire tell the truth? Weren't all of the Devil's creatures able only to lie? Such ideas seemed less certain and clear cut to Venneman than they once had.

There remained the sun. Venneman's one experience with it had persuaded him that that legend, at least, was true. The sun could kill a vampire. All that had been missing the first time was sufficient will on Venneman's part. Now he had another chance to prove that his will was stronger than this evil which had been imposed on him. What better way to do it than with the glorious sunlight of Sunday?

He headed out of town again, hurrying as the sky lightened further. This time, he would take no chances. He would reinforce his will by finding a place away from shadows, away from refuge.

In the middle of a snowy field covered with animal tracks, Venneman undressed and lay down on his back. He lay with his head pointing toward the sunrise, his arms straight out to the side, crucifying himself on the snow, and awaited the sun.

The shadows of night moved away slowly, retreating eastward toward the mountains above which the sun rose. The first light touched Venneman's feet, bathing them in fire. He gasped but lay still. The fire crawled over his ankles and slowly, slowly up his shins toward his knees. Venneman began to writhe and groan. Then he drew a deep breath and forced himself to lie still.

The agony continued upward, searing his thighs, and then washing over his genitals. He clamped his jaws shut to keep from screaming, but he could not quiet his moans and gasps. It continued—up his belly, over his chest, creeping onto his face. I don't deserve this, he pleaded with God. Why should I burn this way? I'm guiltless.

But he wasn't free of sin. He recited to himself a list of his sins, culminating in the worst: murder of an innocent man. Or was lying with Elizabeth the vampire the worst of his sins? He deserved to burn, and this was just a foretaste of what his Eternity would be.

Venneman opened his eyes against the awful glare and looked down at himself. His skin was steaming. Strips of it were peeling up, standing up to greet the light. The ends of the strips gleamed and steamed in the sun's glow and then turned dark and shriveled away.

He couldn't watch this happening to himself. He clamped his eyes shut, clenched his jaws, and waited to die.

Instead, the agony continued.

Throughout the day, Venneman lay in the field in the full glare of the sun, burning, burning, endlessly burning. He was afloat in a sea of fire, immersed in the eternal torments of Hell. It was never ending.

His will was strong enough to keep him there, but he did not die. He did not even gain the release of unconsciousness.

Eventually, even as his will was weakening, he became too weak to move. He lay on his back, his eyes partly open, steaming tears running down his cheeks, whimpering, begging his God for release. "Why have you forsaken me?" he whispered. "What more can I do?"

The air began to cool. The pain faded slowly. Venneman opened his eyes further. The sky was fading from blue toward black overhead, and Venneman could see stars.

As his pain faded, some strength returned, and he could move again. Groggy, he sat up. His skin was a mass of open sores and cracks. His chest looked like raw meat, stripped of its skin. And yet he was still alive. Awful as his wounds looked, they must actually be superficial. He had suffered so horribly for so many hours, and he had achieved only this instead of self-destruction.

The hunger and the thirst were greater than ever.

He caught movement from the corner of his eye. At first, he thought it was a small wolf, or possibly a coyote, but then the animal came hesitantly closer and Venneman saw that it was a half-grown husky with a collar around its neck.

He held out his hand. "Good dog," he said. "Good boy. Come here."

The husky wagged its tail slightly and crept forward, face averted, looking at Venneman sideways.

"Don't be afraid," Venneman said, his voice low and soothing. "I won't hurt you. It's okay."

The husky gained courage and came close. Venneman let it sniff his hand and then slowly moved his hand to the side of its neck and stroked softly, gently. The husky relaxed. It lowered its haunches to the snow and looked at Venneman and whined.

"Are you lost?" Venneman asked it. "Need a friend? Huh? Just like me. Two lost souls, right?"

He was relieved that he felt no bloodlust. Animals were exempt, it seemed. Or perhaps he should tell himself that he remained to that degree human and not an unreasoning hunter and killer.

But then the hunger and thirst returned, shooting through

him like a lightning bolt. Venneman flung himself on the dog, forcing it to the ground under his weight, and buried his face in the fur of its neck, his teeth seeking the flesh beneath. The dog squealed in alarm, struggled, snarled, snapped furiously at Venneman. But it couldn't get at his face, and Venneman bit into its neck, finding the blood coursing there.

It was strange and unpleasant–tasting stuff. Not as foul and disgusting as Elizabeth's blood had been, but still he could scarcely swallow it. And yet it cut through the dryness in his mouth and filled a small part of the emptiness in his stomach and gave him energy.

When he had finished, Venneman rose from the dog's still body and pulled his clothing back on. He couldn't bear to look at himself, at the oozing sores covering the front of his body. They hurt when his clothing passed over them, but he persevered.

With his clothes on, only his face betrayed him. He walked back into the town, feeling nervous and jumpy. The dog's blood unsettled his stomach and filled him with a twitchy unease that was unpleasantly different from the electric energy he gained from human blood. As he walked, nausea grew in him.

He roamed the darkened back streets and took his second victim toward midnight.

It was a young woman this time. It might have been the waitress who had served him in the coffee shop that morning, it might have been Karen, the stewardess from the airplane, or it might have been some stranger he had never seen before. He neither knew nor cared. The human, whoever she was, was only a vessel for the blood. As Elizabeth had said, the prey was a container for the life he needed and wanted—and to which he had a right.

This time when he was done, he took the drained body of his prey back out into the fields beyond the town and left it there, beside that of the dog he had killed earlier. He hoped that animals would discover both of them and tear at them, making more wounds like the ones he had inflicted.

Venneman tried to dredge up feelings of self-hatred and disgust, but he failed. He was filled instead with a fierce delight. He touched his face and found that his skin was smooth and healthy again. The open sores and cracks inflicted by the daylong exposure to the sun were gone. The blood of one young victim had compensated for all of that damage and had satisfied the hunger and thirst he had felt even before lying in the sun.

He realized that he felt stronger and more alive than he ever had during his previous, human life. He thought that realization should depress him, but it didn't.

It was time to think about the future. If the sun could not kill him, then he would have to continue to live as a vampire. Perhaps in the future he could try some other way of destroying himself, but for now, he needed human blood on a regular basis. At home, in a great city, it might be possible to satisfy his needs without fear of detection, but not in this small town.

His flight home was scheduled for Tuesday morning. He would be relieved to climb aboard that airplane and start the journey home.

But it takes off during daylight! he realized. I can't take the flight!

Venneman despaired for only a moment before remembering that vampires in movies could change themselves into bats. Can I do that? he wondered. I could fly home under my own power!

He concentrated on his body, frowning with effort. He imagined himself as a bat, a great, flying mammal, weighing as much as a man, his leathery wings beating the night air as he rose from the ground and soared through the dark.

For a moment, he thought he felt his bones changing, growing thinner and longer, and his flesh flowing into a new shape. For an instant, he imagined he could hear a universe of sound he had never heard before. But it was all imagination. Nothing had happened. He was still Richard Venneman, unchanged from his changed condition.

Wouldn't be much good, anyway, he told himself. It would take me days to get home, and I couldn't fly in the daylight. Every day, I'd have to land and find prey and a place to shelter until dark. It's not a practical approach to travel.

For an instant, he yearned to go looking for Elizabeth to ask her advice. Obviously she had come fully to terms with the vampire life. She would know what he should do. Then he shook his head. No, he told himself. I'll do everything for myself. I don't need her, and I don't want her. I'll think of something.

Venneman returned to his hotel room and started making telephone calls. He was able to change his flight home to one that left from Denver during Monday night and landed at Venneman's home city well before sunrise. The flight from Denver to the mountains had been a short one, so he was sure he would have no trouble finding a flight from the ski town to Denver that left the mountains after sunrise and would still get him to Denver in time to catch his flight home.

However, the reservations office for Rocky Mountain Ski Transport was closed for the night, and the message on the answering machine informed him that the company had flights leaving for Denver only between ten a.m. and four p.m.

Venneman felt tendrils of panic creeping in. This is the way it's going to be, he realized. Terror of the sun, love of the night, a life constrained by those two forces. Get used to it.

He tried to think calmly. Any other way of getting to Denver would require money—more cash than he had, and he had no credit card. I could kill someone and steal a credit card, he thought. For a moment, the callousness of the thought horrified him.

Impractical, too, he thought. It could link me to the murder.

And yet he was a creature of the darkness, an inhabitant of others' nightmares, an extension of the power and cunning of the Devil. Shouldn't he be able to use that somehow to solve such a minor problem?

He packed his belongings quickly into his single battered suitcase and went to the front desk to check out.

The night clerk's eyes flickered over the suitcase and Venneman's drab, bulky clothing, but his face remained impassive. "Do you need someone to carry that out for you, sir?"

"This?" Venneman lifted the case easily. "It's lighter than it looks. No, thanks." The case was in fact heavier than it looked, but to Venneman, it now seemed light. "What I do need is directions to the highway to Denver."

Venneman left the hotel and walked swiftly through town to the state highway the clerk had directed him to. He walked rapidly along the highway, his suitcase on one shoulder for convenience. Overhead, the sky was still dark. Venneman estimated he had four hours till daylight. He could have wished for more time, but that would be more than enough if someone came along soon.

For close to an hour he walked in utter silence unbroken by the passage of a car.

He could hear animals moving and breathing in the dark all around him. In his human days, he would have been unable to hear any of those sounds. If he had been able to, he would have been frightened by them. In those days, the dark alone would have made him uneasy, worried about something dangerous sneaking up on him and attacking him. Now he was enchanted and excited, and he felt a part of it—of the dark, of the animal life. He too was an animal, the greatest hunter of them all, just as Elizabeth had said. He belonged here.

No, he thought. The animals belong here because their prey is here. I belong in a city, where my prey is abundant.

Headlights swept around a curve behind him. They lit up the snow and the dark trees beside the highway. Venneman stopped and held out his hand, thumb extended. The car roared by him without slowing down.

Good decision, Venneman thought. Maybe the next guy won't be so smart.

The next guy was actually two men in a pickup truck, and they were not so smart as the previous driver. The truck slowed to a stop beside Venneman. A deep voice called out. "Where you going?"

"Denver," Venneman said.

"Hop in."

He threw his suitcase in the back of the truck. It landed with a soft thump instead of the metallic bang he expected. He pulled himself up into the cab, settled into the seat beside the door, and pulled the door to, slamming it loudly.

"Jesus, take it easy!" the man beside him said.

"Sorry." He was still delighted by his new strength, but he knew he'd have to learn to control it.

The truck's wheels spun on a patch of ice, and then the vehicle lurched ahead and moved along the highway.

The driver and his companion were beefy, middle-aged men. They both wore heavy boots and coats with the hoods thrown back, and they smelled of beer and tobacco and something else Venneman could not identify, something wild and exciting.

"What're you doing out here in the middle of nowhere on a night like this?" the driver asked.

"I was on a ski vacation," Venneman said, "and I got a call to come home right away. Medical emergency. But there's no transport to Stapleton Airport this late at night."

"Ski vacation, huh?" the passenger said, looking Venneman up and down quickly. "Hm."

Venneman laughed. "Okay. Truth is, my boss was on a ski vacation, and I was along to be his errand boy. He fired me when I got that phone call and told him I had to leave and go home. He said that wasn't covered in my contract."

"And how much of his stuff you got in your case?" the driver asked.

"None," Venneman said. He decided to drop his pose of affability. "You guys are pretty suspicious. What's your problem?"

The passenger shrugged. "Force of habit. We're Denver cops. Sorry. I'm Skip and this is Greg." He pulled off his right glove and held his hand out.

"Richard." Venneman shook his hand, which was large and soft, like the rest of the man. "So, Skip and Greg, are you up here looking for a bad guy from Denver?"

"No. We were hunting."

"In the dead of winter? I didn't know people did that." Venneman remembered the sound his suitcase had made when it landed in the back of the pickup. He twisted around and looked through the small window behind Skip's head, but he could see nothing in the dark. "What did you catch?"

The two men exchanged a glance. "Bear," Greg said. He turned onto a rising entrance ramp. The headlights picked up a sign reading I–70 East. Beneath it, on the same pole, another sign told Venneman that they were sixty miles from Denver.

"Don't they hibernate?" Venneman asked.

"Yeah," Skip said. "We got one in her den. You ever tasted bear cub roasted over a campfire?"

Venneman shook his head.

"Really good," Skip said, growing enthusiastic and losing the caution Venneman had sensed in him from the beginning. "A lot like pork, but real tender. Pretty fat, of course, this early in the winter. Got the grease on my jacket. Real good, though."

"Think you could take me to the airport in Denver?" Venneman asked abruptly. "Or is it too much out of your way?"

"No problem," Greg said. "See this highway we're on? It runs right by Stapleton."

"Good. So, tell me, Skip and Greg, is that legal? I mean, killing a hibernating mother bear in her den and then killing and eating her cub?"

Skip turned toward Venneman and glared at him. "Don't you worry about that, guy. We're the experts here on what's legal."

Venneman smiled disarmingly and nodded. "That makes sense. Say, either of you guys ever tasted fresh human blood?"

Skip's mouth fell open, and Greg took his eyes from the road for long enough to lean forward and look at Venneman around Skip's bulk. "What the fuck?" Greg said.

"You keep your eyes on the road," Skip said. "Dangerous tonight." He turned his glare on Venneman again. "Richard, you got something you want to tell us? We're the guys who can help you out, you know."

Venneman nodded. "Yes, I know you'll help me out. See, the thing is, I'm a vampire."

The other two burst out laughing. "A vampire, huh?" Skip said. "Okay, Richard. We thought you were going to say something that would make us take you to our district station and lock you up, but I can see that you need a different kind of facility."

Venneman joined in their laughter. "You mean an insane asylum, right? That right, Skip? Greg? Say, I wonder if crazy people's blood tastes any different. You think so?"

After a moment of hesitation, the other two laughed again. Then Skip said, "Richard, if you're a vampire, what happened to your fangs?"

Venneman had never thought about that before. "You're right! Vampires always have fangs in the movies. Maybe we could stop at a novelty store in Denver and I could buy myself a set."

The other two laughed again, but it was more forced this time. They were tiring of the game, Venneman knew.

He put his hands on his stomach and doubled over. "Oh,

man, I feel sick. Must've been the bad blood in that teenager I killed. I'm going to throw up."

Greg yelled, "Not in here! Get outta my truck!" He stepped on the brakes and the truck slid down the highway, turning slowly sideways. It came to a stop sitting at a right angle across both lanes.

"Asshole!" Skip yelled. "Get us out of traffic!"

Greg started up again and pulled off onto the shoulder. All three men piled out of the truck. Venneman shuffled bent over toward the railing at the side of the highway. The truck's headlights reflected off the snow beside the road, lighting up the immediate area, but beyond the railing the ground sloped downward and vanished into dark emptiness. Venneman leaned against the railing and looked into the blackness. He heard a metallic click behind him and turned around.

Skip was pointing a rifle at him. The muzzle looked enormous.

Greg came to his partner's side. "Skip, I don't think this is necessary."

Skip spoke quietly, calmly, in control of the situation. "I don't know how much of what he said was made up and how much was real, but I'm not taking any chances. We'll keep him covered from now on until we've got him safely locked up at the station."

Venneman said, "Skip, I'm just a harmless kook. I'm just a guy who thinks he's a vampire." He stepped forward.

Skip said, "Stay where you are, damn it."

Venneman looked at Greg. His movement had alarmed the other policeman. He shrugged—a disarming motion, he hoped. "Okay, Skip." And then he moved.

He punched Greg full in the face. He felt the bones of the man's head crunch and collapse under his fist, and it filled him with excitement. Greg gurgled and went limp, but Venneman caught him and held him up as a shield between himself and Skip.

Skip had scarcely reacted, so quick had Venneman's movements been. Now Skip yelled and fired wildly, repeatedly.

Venneman felt Greg jerking as the bullets tore into him. He felt two of the bullets pass through Greg's body and into his own, striking him in the chest. He felt his breastbone shatter. Pain exploded in his chest. He couldn't breathe.

He staggered back, dropping Greg. The policeman fell to the ground and lay unmoving. Venneman's legs hit the railing at the edge of the road and he tumbled over it backward. He seemed to be floating into the darkness and then down. He hit the sloping ground and rolled until he fetched up against a tree.

Venneman lay in the dark unable to move, filled with agony. Every attempt at drawing in a breath filled his chest with cutting pain, as though the pieces of his breastbone were sawing through the tissue around them. From above, he could hear Skip calling Greg's name and then shouting curses at Venneman.

Venneman's thoughts swam randomly. Elizabeth had been wrong about bullets. He was dying.

And then the pain faded away, and he could move again.

He rose to his feet ravenous with hunger, filled with strength, consumed by rage.

He ran up the slope and into the beams of the truck's lights. Skip saw him and began to turn his way, raising his rifle. To Venneman, Skip seemed to be moving in slow motion.

Venneman kept running, getting the truck between him

and the policeman. He kept moving, circling the truck.

He came around it and found himself facing Skip's back. The policeman was moving slowly, slowly, following Venneman, rifle pointed ahead of him.

Venneman slammed into him, knocking his rifle away. He bore the policeman to the ground, face down, yanked his head back, and sank his teeth into the side of his neck before the man had a chance to yell.

Skip regained enough breath to shriek once, and then the last of his strength deserted him. Venneman sucked eagerly, powerfully, draining the policeman's body of blood and life.

Venneman rose to his feet and bounded over to Greg. The other policeman was dead, his face smashed by Venneman's blow and his torso riddled by the bullets Skip had fired. But most of his blood was still in him, and it was still liquid enough to be drawn out. Venneman raised the corpse in his arms and lowered his mouth to its neck. He found the collapsing veins and bit into them and drew the corpse's blood into him.

When he was done feeding, Venneman carried Greg's body over to the railing at the edge of the road and threw it out into the darkness as far as he could. After a long pause, he heard it land far below and bounce twice, then roll further down the hillside. He went over to Skip's body, picked it up, and threw it after Greg's. His rage began to ease.

He walked back to the truck and looked in the back. His suitcase lay there, atop a tarpaulin. Venneman pulled one edge of the tarpaulin back, revealing the head and shoulders of a bear, its eyes open, its mouth slackly open, its tongue protruding limply. He pulled the cover back further. Now he saw just the head of a bear cub. He thought for a moment, then took out the cub's head and threw it after the two hunters' bodies. He threw Skip's rifle down the slope, too.

Finally, he covered the body of the bear sow up again and put his suitcase in the truck cab. Then he climbed in behind the wheel, restarted the engine, and pulled onto the highway. Only when he was underway did he realize how well he was suddenly able to see in the dark. The most recent meal, the blood of two full-grown men, had pushed him past some threshold.

He felt his chest. He pressed gently at first, then thumped vigorously. There was no pain, and there were no wounds from the bullets. He had thought himself a vampire before, but he had still been in the process of becoming one. Now the process was complete.

The eastern sky was growing pale by the time Venneman reached the western outskirts of Denver. The highway carried him eastward along the northern edge of the city. Traffic grew heavier as he drove, slowing him down. He gripped the steering wheel, fear of the day growing in him.

The light in the east was almost blinding him by the time he saw the sign for the airport. He followed the signs along a busy local street and headed into the airport's parking garage. Now he was under cover, safe from the direct light of the sun when it rose, although not from indirect light. The open sides of the parking garage were already impossibly bright to his eyes.

He left the truck in the first space he found, hurriedly wiped his fingerprints off the steering wheel, gear shift lever, key, and door handles, and then grabbed his suitcase and ran for the entrance to the covered ramp leading into the airport terminal.

Even the ramp had large windows along both walls. Venneman ran along it, ignoring the stares he drew. He kept his eyes almost closed, looking out through a narrow slit, and still the pain of the light lanced into his skull. And still the sun had not yet risen.

It's even worse than it was before, he thought. I can see better at night now, but the sunlight hurts me even more. Maybe, since I've become so much more a vampire, the sun can kill me now.

He pushed that thought away from him. He no longer wanted to die. Now he wanted to do whatever he needed to do to survive, for as long as his new nature allowed him to.

In this respect, too, Elizabeth had been correct.

Inside the terminal, he found it easier to stay away from windows. The fluorescent lighting everywhere bothered his eyes and felt unpleasantly warm on his skin, but it didn't feel dangerous, just uncomfortable.

He found an airport shop selling various tourist knick knacks. It was like tourist kitsch sold in other airports throughout the world, but each item was stamped with the Colorado state flag or a drawing of the Rocky Mountains. Venneman bought a garish pair of sunglasses and put them on. Now he found he could walk around inside the airport without discomfort. Through the dark lenses, the light inside the building seemed about the same as bright sunlight had seemed to him before, when he was still human.

For a few hours, Venneman walked around the airport, watching the crowds with distant curiosity. I can handle this, he thought. I can make it until tonight, when it's time for my plane to take off.

But then his face began to itch. He went into a men's room and looked at himself carefully in the mirror. Unlike the vampire of mythology, he had a perfectly normal reflection, and also unlike the mythological creature, he looked ruddy and healthy, not pale and corpselike. But the itching, he realized, was due to sunburn. The lighting in the airport was sufficient to do this to him.

Venneman looked around the restroom. No one else was there. There were two urinals and one stall, and there was a light switch on the wall beside the door. He flicked the switch off and removed his sunglasses.

In the dark, he relaxed, aware for the first time how tense and on guard he had been. He knew that the room must be pitch black to a human being, but to his eyes it was bathed in a soft, delightful, directionless glow. He took his suitcase into the stall and locked the door. Then he sat down on the toilet, set the alarm on his wristwatch, and tried to doze.

His sleep was uneasy and frequently interrupted. Twice, men opened the door and then, seeing the room dark, gave up and went elsewhere. But three other times, men came in, fumbled at the wall until they found the switch, and then spent what seemed to Venneman to be endless hours using the urinals. After each man had left, Venneman turned the lights off again and tried to go back to sleep.

He was deeply asleep when his alarm beeped.

He awoke feeling refreshed and vibrantly alive. Outside, in the terminal, the windows were dark except for manmade lights in the distance. The crowds were sparse now. Venneman was relieved to find that he could look at them without feeling hunger. He hoped he was already reaching the advanced stage

Elizabeth had mentioned and would no longer need to feed so often.

Venneman went through the tedious details of checking in and boarding. His airplane took off on time, for which he was thankful. Now he would be sure of arriving home before daylight.

When he was in the air, bound for home, he looked with interest at the two stewardesses assigned to the coach cabin. At first, they both reacted to him with the sexual interest he had become so familiar with and had always been so frightened by. But after a few seconds, they began to seem afraid of him and seemed to be hurrying by his seat, avoiding catching his eye. Now that he was interested in them for their blood, they shied away from him. The irony amused him.

He turned the overhead light off and put his seat back and relaxed. How nice it felt to be going home—home to peace and refuge and escape.

FIVE

Jill awoke with a gasp when he slid into bed beside her. "It's me," he said quickly. "It's okay."

"What?" she said, her tongue fumbling with the word. She sat up and turned on the light on the wall on her side of the bed. "Richie? Oh, God, you scared me!"

"Sorry, darling," Venneman said. "I left early. I couldn't stand the place, and I missed you. And I picked something up. A virus, maybe. I don't feel well." He pulled the covers up over his shoulder.

Jill drew away from him unconsciously. "You don't look right," she said. "Would you like me to make you something? Some tea?"

Venneman smiled at her. "Thanks, but I don't think tea will cure me. I think I need extra sleep. I think I'll just take the day off and sleep. I'm not expected back at work until Wednesday, anyway, so there'll be no problem."

Jill nodded. "Good idea. What time is it?" She leaned over Venneman and twisted the clock radio so that she could see the red numbers glowing on its face. "Three a.m. Oh, good, I don't have to get up for three more hours."

Venneman looked up at her nightgown and imagined the familiar breasts under it. He felt a stirring of desire and almost reached for her, but he knew that doing so would undermine his claim of being ill. Instead, he closed his eyes and lay still as Jill kissed him, told him she was glad he was home, turned the light off again, and slid back down beside him.

He heard her breathing become slower and steadier as she fell back asleep. He kept his eyes shut and lay without moving, but his mind was busily awake.

It had already become impossible for him to sleep during the night, he feared. And of course it was impossible for him to go outside during the day. At the same time, no matter how his new metabolism worked, he would need shelter and clothing. He wanted the trappings of normal human life. That would require money, and that would mean a job. He would be unable to stay at his old job, since there was no such thing as a night shift there. So that meant a change. But a change meant, among other things, interviewing. There were night jobs in the city, but he was sure the interviews for them were conducted during the day. He could see no way of resolving any of this.

A new problem intruded. As he lay beside Jill, her breathing seemed to fade away, replaced by her heartbeat and the pulsing of her blood.

Venneman clasped his hands together on his chest and held them tightly together. He pressed his arms against his torso, his legs against each other. He stared up at the ceiling, illuminated by the soft glow that, to his eyes, permeated the room.

She's not safe with me, he thought. Tears filled his eyes and rolled slowly down his cheeks on his pillow. I can't trust myself with her. I have to leave.

He would have to leave Jill for her own safety. For her to be completely safe, he would have to move to another city.

How could he tell her what he was planning without breaking her heart? Better to break her heart than to murder her, he told himself. And yet the prospect of hurting her, even for her own good, filled him with pain.

No, he told himself, that's a lie. It fills you with discomfort and guilt, but not pain. The truth is that you're eager to enter into your new life, and Jill is a trapping from the old one. You'll be happy to be free of her.

Was that part of the vampire's nature, too, he wondered—that coldness, that lack of feeling and commitment toward others?

But they're not *others* in that sense, he reminded himself. Not in the sense of being others of my kind. They're human beings. They are others in the sense of being something else, something utterly different from me.

He lay as still as he could, almost as still as a corpse, as the hours passed and his dilemma gnawed at him.

Eventually the radio turned on. Jill came awake with a moan. She turned over to face Venneman and smiled at him. "Feeling any better, Richie?"

He forced a smile in response. "A bit. Sleep helped. I'll make the coffee while you shower."

It was still dark outside.

Venneman stood with the coffee carafe in his hand, the tap still running, the kitchen light turned off, and stared out of the window. The dark drew him. There were millions of people out there, most of them still in their houses or apartments, but some of them walking the cold streets. And some of those streets were almost deserted. He could go out into the city at night and find prey everywhere. There were legions of the homeless and helpless whom nobody would miss. Indeed, the city would be grateful if their numbers diminished.

After Jill had left, Venneman stood again at the window. How much time did he have before daylight? Not enough, probably—not enough to find his prey in a deserted place, to kill, to feed, and then to hide the remains and to return here to shelter from the light.

He was aware of only the faintest feelings of hunger and thirst. He hoped he could go without feeding for at least another day.

He watched until the sun had risen and the street beyond the window was bathed in its light. The pain in his eyes had become intolerable. He turned the blinds over the window as far closed as they would go and retreated to the bedroom. Here, heavy curtains kept the room dark—darker to him, in fact, than during the night, for the sunlight had driven away the soft, directionless glow that now lit the night for him.

With daylight came sleepiness. Overcome by it, Venneman barely managed to climb into bed before he drifted into a dream of blood.

He swam in a red ocean. Slow, heavy swells buoyed him up and carried detached arms, legs, and heads past him. The smell of blood was overwhelming and nauseating. He was frightened only for the first few minutes of the dream. Then his fear faded and he felt invigorated. Something shifted in his sense of smell, and now the scent of the ocean filled him with delight. Above, the sky was black and filled with stars. The sea was warm, glowing with a light of its own, and a lazy current carried him along. As he rose on the swells, he caught glimpses of a jagged headland. The current carried him past it and toward a gentle coastline. Figures stood on the coast holding their arms out to him in welcome. He heard their voices calling him, melodious, gentle, loving.

Venneman swam toward the coast. His strokes were powerful, but the current became stronger, too strong for him to fight. No matter how hard he tried, the coastline and the welcoming figures receded. They were lost in a red mist, and Venneman found himself floating in the middle of the red ocean, with only a misty horizon in all directions.

He drifted still deeper into sleep, dreamless this time. Later, toward evening, the dream began again. Again he dreamed of the sea, the headland, the coast, and the beckoning figures. As he was trying to swim toward them, Jill entered the bedroom and tore him into reality.

She turned the light on. Venneman gasped and covered his eyes.

"Sorry," Jill said. She turned the light off again. "Have you been sleeping all day, Richie?" She came to the bed and sat down on it and gently pushed his hair away from his forehead. "Are you feeling better?" She leaned over and kissed his cheek softly. "You do feel hot."

Sexual desire exploded in Venneman, so sharp and intense that he gasped as if in pain.

"Richie!" Jill put her hands on either side of his face. "Richie, what is it?"

Venneman slid his arms out from under the covers and put them around her. He pulled her down beside him and kissed her.

Jill pulled her face away from his and held him off. "You need rest, Richie. Take it easy."

"I need you," Venneman said. He felt as he had when he first kissed Elizabeth, the way he had never felt before with Jill.

He realized for the first time that he was still fully dressed. Holding Jill easily with one arm around her, he pulled his trousers down clumsily with the other and then began undressing her.

"Richie, stop it!" She tried to push him away, but he scarcely noticed her struggles, and they had no effect on him.

He kissed her again, and just as he had absorbed that otherworldly sexual arousal from Elizabeth, Jill absorbed it from him. She slid her legs around him. She put one arm around his neck in order to hold his mouth against hers, and with her other hand she guided his penis into her.

She moved her pelvis wildly, back and forth, pounding it against his. She sucked and bit at his tongue.

They climaxed together, shouting, gripping each other. Venneman pressed his face against her shoulder and kissed her there. Jill groaned into his ear, "Jesus! Oh, Christ!"

As he emptied himself into her and felt her constricting around him, Venneman felt the pounding of her heart against his chest and heard the rushing of her blood through the artery only inches from his mouth. He could smell her blood through her skin and flesh.

The sound of her blood drowned out her cries of pleasure. He felt another kind of lust, and he was powerless to resist it.

Turning his face, Venneman buried his teeth in Jill's neck, his powerful jaws crunching through flesh and tendons, his teeth biting into her carotid artery.

He drank in her spurting blood, swallowing it and sucking out more, even while he continued to pump his own fluid into her. It seemed for a moment to be a cycle of some kind, liquid life passing from her to him, through him, and then back into her. And the blood had never tasted so wonderful to him before. None of his previous victims had filled him with such delight and life.

Jill struggled only briefly, cried out once in pain, and kept moving her hips under his as she died.

When he rose from her pale body, her eyes were closed, and he couldn't tell if she was grimacing in pain or smiling with pleasure.

Venneman sat on the side of the bed and wept. How could he stand an eternity of this? Oh, God, he thought, I'm cut off from everything. I'll never be able to love or be loved again. It will always lead to this.

Trying not to look at Jill, he pulled his clothes back on and went into the living room. There was nothing for him here, either. The apartment seemed empty to him in a way it never had before. It had lost the warmth and affection Jill had imbued it with.

Venneman sank onto the couch and put his head in his hands. He sat there for a long time, trying to think about the future, trying to come up with a way of avoiding the future.

I've got to try again, he thought. I've got to come up with a way to kill myself. I can't go through this again.

But how? he wondered. Bullets didn't work. I tried the sun,

and that didn't work. It just made me hungrier. Maybe I'm an exception to the rule, a vampire who can't be killed by the sun. Or maybe, he suddenly thought, I need something stronger than ordinary sunlight. Something more intense, something closer.

He had already found that starlight didn't hurt him, even though starlight was really sunlight, but at a vast distance. So perhaps even the sun itself wasn't close enough.

A sun close to me, he thought. Yes.

Venneman put back on the warm coat he had worn to Colorado, took the gloves from the pocket, and left the apartment. For a moment, he considered taking the bus, but it ran on a reduced schedule after rush hour, and he lacked the patience to wait for it. He decided instead to take the old car he and Jill used for shopping and evening trips. This late in the evening, there would be free parking at the university.

He parked in a free lot a short walk from Currigan Hall. It was close to nine p.m., and all the building's doors were already locked.

Venneman walked around the old building, trying to find a way in, an unlocked side door. At last he gave up and walked up the cracked concrete steps to the front doors.

The double doors were of heavy wood, with thick glass panes in their upper halves. Beyond the doors, the short corridor ended in a staircase, the left half leading up, the right half leading down to the lab where Venneman worked. The lights in the corridor were bright even out here. Venneman fished out of his coat pocket the sunglasses he had bought at the airport in Denver and put them on.

The night security man, Willie Gold, was supposed to be in

the building. Venneman pounded on the wood, making the doors rattle on their hinges. He knew he didn't have to wait for Willie. He was strong enough now to smash the doors open. But he also didn't want to alarm anyone and risk interference before he was finished.

Eventually, Willie came down the stairs toward the door, frowning. His frown eased when he recognized Venneman on the other side of the glass panels. Willie fumbled with his heavy key chain and opened the doors.

Willie Gold was a heavyset man in his sixties. He had retired from a local suburban police force and was supplementing his pension with the easy work of babysitting buildings whose daytime inhabitants were only too happy to stay away from them at night, and which local burglars knew contained nothing of interest to them.

"Hey, Richie! What're you doing here? I thought you were on vacation until tomorrow."

"I came back early, Willie. Got to get some stuff ready for Dinsmuir, so I thought I'd work on it this evening."

Will shook his head. "You're an idiot to put in extra time for that guy. You know that, don't you?"

Venneman smiled. "I should. You've told me often enough."

"Yeah, well, it's still true. What's with the shades?"

"Oh, I got a touch of snow blindness out there, on the ski slope. Got to protect my eyes for a few days."

"Jeez," Willie said. "You really should be home taking care of that, not here straining your eyes."

Venneman shrugged. "I don't have much choice this time."

"Guess maybe you'll get your reward in Heaven, huh?"

"Oh, yes," Venneman told him, edging past and toward the

staircase. "That's what I'm counting on."

As Venneman walked away, Willie called out to him, "You look good, Richie. The break did you good, except for the eyes."

Venneman raised a hand and waved acknowledgement. Oh, yes, he thought. It made a new man of me.

He was surprised at how calm and unemotional he felt, despite everything that had happened. It was the imminence of death and release, he decided, that had given him this brief moment of peace.

He went downstairs and let himself into the lab with his cardkey.

Automatically, he reached for the light switch beside the door. He caught himself in time and took off his sunglasses instead. Here again was the soft glow he was coming to love, the pale, directionless light that soothed his eyes and calmed him.

All the surfaces in the lab were clean and well organized. Dale had been keeping things in hand, as usual. He smiled at the imagined picture of her down here, quietly and competently maintaining control despite Dinsmuir's interference. He wished she were here now, so that he could tell her his problems. Surely Dale would have calm, rational advice for him.

Surely Dale would excite his blood hunger just as easily as anyone else might, alone here with him in the dark.

Venneman gritted his teeth and turned his attention to the reason he had come here.

Dinsmuir's experiment was unchanged, the great cylinder sitting quietly in the center of the room, steadily gathering data for the advancement of Dinsmuir's career. At least I'll be throwing a wrench into that, Venneman thought with some pleasure.

He took off his coat and went over to the cylinder and examined it.

It consisted of two shorter cylinders which had been bolted together, so that it could be easily opened at the end of the experiment for examination. But the seal was a tight one, for safety, because of the ferocity of the energy being generated within. The torque required to loosen the bolts was far beyond what a human being could generate by hand.

Venneman rummaged around in the tool cabinet until he found a wrench of the right size. He applied it to one of the bolts. He put his weight on the wrench, pushing down, grunting. His heels lifted from the floor, but the bolt did not move.

Venneman stepped back and thought for a moment. His strength had increased greatly now that he was a vampire, he knew, but as far as he could tell, his body weight was unchanged. He got from the tool cabinet another wrench of the right size for the cylinder's bolts. Then he put the new wrench on the bolt above the other one and, with one hand on each wrench, forced them toward each other. The movement was tightening the lower bolt, but the upper bolt began to move. Once it was loosened, Venneman unscrewed the upper bolt and dropped it to the floor. Then he moved on to the next pair of bolts and repeated the process.

Eventually he was left with only one bolt, with nothing to use as leverage against it. But the cylinder was unsealed except for that one bolt. Still the two halves sat firmly against each other, held in place by their weight.

Venneman stepped back again and paused, gathering his courage.

Slowly, he undressed. The more exposure, he thought, the

greater the likelihood of death.

When he was naked, he stepped forward again, put one hand against each half of the cylinder, and leaned forward, pressing as hard as he could.

One of the halves shifted slightly. A shaft of light shot out through the opening between the two halves, striking Venneman in the face and blinding him.

He dropped to the floor and curled into a ball, gasping in agony. His eyes were two spears of agony thrusting into his brain. He clapped his hands to them and felt only soft, jellied flesh. He knew that his eyes and much of his face had been melted away. He could no longer see that soft light that made the night so comforting and inviting.

Venneman forced himself to his knees and felt around for the cylinder. He felt the heat of its inner light before he touched the metal. But this was not enough. This would wound and cripple him, but it might not be enough to destroy him. Only the bar of sun imprisoned within the experiment could do that.

He groped up along the seam and found the opening. He managed to force his fingers into it, and he raised himself to his feet and struggled to pull the cylinders further apart. The light glaring out through the slit seared his chest and stomach, but Venneman persisted, exerting his new strength to separate the cylinders.

With a loud rasping squeak of metal sliding across concrete, the cylinders slid apart, and Venneman fell into the opening and inside the experiment.

He had only a brief moment of consciousness. He was bathed in agony as he had been when he had exposed himself to sunlight, but it was vastly more intense.

And then consciousness faded. He felt the world slipping away from him, and he was grateful for it. He welcomed real death at last.

SIX

"Richie! Richie!"

He became aware of the voice and of someone shaking his shoulder. The lights were on in the lab.

"Richie!" It was Willie Gold. He was on his knees beside Venneman. Willie's eyes were wide and staring, filled with horror. His face relaxed in relief when Venneman opened his eyes and looked up at him. "Jesus, Richie, I thought you were dead!" He rocked back onto his feet and pushed himself up. "Don't move! I'll call for an ambulance." Willie looked around for a telephone and took a step toward Dale's desk.

"No!" Venneman rolled over and pushed himself up onto his knees and elbows. "I'm okay. Minor accident, that's all." He could scarcely hold himself in position. His muscles were shaking with weakness. Can't alarm Willie any further, he thought. He struggled to stand up. "Help me out."

Willie jumped back to his side. "Of course, Richie." He put an arm around Venneman's naked waist, and Venneman put his own arm around the guard's shoulder and leaned heavily on him.

Venneman's head lolled forward. He felt scarcely able to

hold it up. "So weak," Venneman whispered.

"You sure you don't want an ambulance, Richie? What the hell happened in here?" He began to lead Venneman toward Dale's chair.

Venneman stopped moving and forced his head up and looked at Dinsmuir's machine. The two cylinders still stood apart, separated. The interior was dark, though, the plasma dead.

And I'm still alive, Venneman thought, despairing.

He could see without any trouble. His eyes must be normal again, healed. He raised a shaky hand to his face. The skin felt smooth and unmarred. The damage from the plasma might have been far greater than that done to him by the sun, but he seemed to have developed the ability to heal himself that much faster and more thoroughly. "How much time?" he asked Willie.

"Since you came in? About seven hours. I was finishing up my shift when I checked in here." He had followed Venneman's glance and now stared at Dinsmuir's experiment. "Shit," he said. "We're all in trouble now. Or was it Dinsmuir, Richie?" Willie grew angry. "Was that who it was? Did the bastard attack you, Richie? Is that why you're naked?"

Attack, his blood echoed. *Naked.*

"I've been reborn," Venneman said. "That's why I'm naked. And so hungry and thirsty."

He tightened his arm around the guard's shoulder and pulled the man him, chest to chest. His other arm went around Willie as well, so that Willie's arms were trapped against his side.

"Hey!" Willie shouted. "What the fuck? Richie, take it easy. Richie!"

His shout became a scream as Venneman bit deeply into his neck. Venneman found the carotid and began to suck eagerly.

But something had changed.

The blood burned in Venneman's mouth. It was acid in his throat, in his belly. He was filled with fire and pain. And Willie writhed against him, whining in delight.

Venneman sprang back, pushing Willie away violently. Willie flew backward, hit one of the heavy wood lab benches, and fell to the floor. He lay on the wooden floor and held his arms out to Venneman. "More, please! Richie, more!" Blood pumped from his neck, calling to Venneman with its lying promise of ecstasy.

Venneman needed more blood. He had not fed enough to repair and strengthen himself. He stepped forward, unable to resist the call of the blood.

"Yes," Willie said, "please."

Venneman closed his eyes and fought the song the blood sang. It burned me, he thought. Something about Willie. Something wrong with him. Have to find someone else.

He ignored Willie's moaned appeals and the whisper of Willie's blood and pulled on his clothes. I can murder anyone now, he thought. Good or bad, friend or stranger, lover or enemy. Anyone but myself. I have no soul and I've been cast out by God, so now I can kill without feeling. I only have to satisfy my own needs.

But Willie's voice persisted, and Venneman was filled with pain at the sounds of Willie's death.

"I'm sorry, Willie. It wasn't me. I didn't have any choice. I can't control it anymore. It controls me. It was your blood. It's the fault of your blood."

Willie's blood had stopped flowing. He was still alive. He sat up, balancing himself with hand on the floor. He swayed. He held out the other hand toward Venneman. "Please, Richie," he said, his voice weak and rasping. He sat in a pool of his own blood. It soaked into his uniform and into the old wood of the floor.

The wood is dry and thirsty, Venneman thought. It needs Willie's blood. He stepped forward again before catching himself and moving back. "No, Willie. I'm sorry I killed you for nothing. I can't use your blood."

But then he noticed that the wound in Willie's neck was almost closed. Willie had lost a lot of blood, but he wasn't losing any more, and he was neither dead nor dying.

Willie pushed himself forward onto hands and knees and crawled toward Venneman. "Richie, Richie, more."

Venneman backed away and pushed through the lab's double doors. He climbed the staircase hastily and left the building.

It was still dark outside, but he could already see a faint glow on the horizon. He stared at it for a moment in confusion, too stunned by what had happened in the lab to feel frightened.

Venneman climbed into his car and drove back to the apartment that had been his home.

Inside the apartment, Jill still lay across the bed as he had left her—unmoving, unbreathing, pale, the gaping wound in her neck as bloodless as the rest of her. She stared up at the ceiling, unblinking, uncaring. The blood Venneman had missed stained the sheet beneath her head.

My God, Venneman thought. My God. He repeated the phrase over and over as though it would save him, as though it would undo what he had already done, as though it could bring Jill back to life, as though it could at least save her soul.

Nothing changed.

He had destroyed Jill, but he could not destroy himself. And as he had already discovered, he could not resist the drive to feed. He was excluded from real human life, but he could not end his own. He could not even imagine what lay ahead of him, what kind of undead half-life he was doomed to endure until...

Until when? Until the sun died? Until the Second Coming?

Or would he survive even those? He and Elizabeth and whatever other vampires there might be on Earth—would they be left, in some unimaginably distant and terrible future, to wander the surface of a cold, dark, depopulated world, dying of hunger and thirst but unable to die, avoiding each other, unable to hunt even each other, growing ever weaker and hungrier and thirstier but enduring forever?

That will be our Hell, he realized suddenly, our eternal punishment. Eternal loneliness, eternal dark, eternal cold, eternal hunger and thirst. It would be even worse than the lake of eternal fire he had been brought up to fear.

Someone was pounding at the apartment's front door. Venneman left the bedroom, closing the door behind him, and went to the front door to see who it was.

Willie Gold stood in the hallway. He still had his right hand raised to knock, and he leaned against the wall with his left. He was panting with the effort of driving over from the campus and climbing one flight of stairs. His face was haggard, the lines deeper than Venneman remembered. His heavy body seemed to have shrunk, and what was left sagged more than before, yearning toward the earth. When Venneman opened the door, Willie let his right arm drop heavily to his side. He bent his head to one side, exposing his neck. A heavy scar had formed where Venneman had torn his neck open. He said nothing, but his eyes pleaded.

Venneman stared at him in shock, unable to move. Even the faint pulsing of blood beneath the scar tissue in Willie's neck lacked the power to make him move.

Willie fell forward against Venneman. He flung his arms about Venneman's neck and tried to drag Venneman's face down toward his neck.

Venneman turned and pushed Willie into the apartment. The guard staggered across the room, crashed into the closed bedroom door, and fell to his knees in front of it.

Venneman ran from the apartment, down the stairs, and out into the parking lot. He still had no idea where he should go or what his future would be, but he knew that this part of his life was forever closed to him.

The sun had risen. Venneman stopped moving and stood, suddenly breathless, in full sunlight.

It felt warm and pleasant on his skin. He could keep his eyes open and see without trouble.

Venneman looked around in wonder at the daylight world.

Willie Gold appeared in the doorway of the apartment building. He pushed himself away and weaved across the sidewalk toward Venneman.

Venneman shivered in horror and felt the taste of Willie's acid blood rising up from his stomach. He climbed into his car, started it up, and headed out into the street. In his rear-view mirror, he caught a glimpse of Willie Gold leaning against another car, fumbling with the door handle.

Pursued by that image, Venneman drove west.

Willie let his hand fall away from the handle. He sagged hopelessly against the side of the car. His guess that Venneman would head for home after what had happened in the laboratory had been a lucky one, but he had no idea where Venneman was going now, and Venneman's car was already out of sight. Even if Willie managed to open the door of his own car, he would be unable to pursue Venneman. He knew he couldn't drive in his present condition.

All he could think to do was wait here in hopes that Venneman would eventually return. The alternative was to give up all hope of ever again experiencing what he had felt when Venneman began to suck the blood from his neck, and Willie could not face that prospect.

Slowly, Willie made his way back into the apartment building.

He stood at the bottom of the long flight of stairs and looked up at it. He tried to recall the desperate energy, the desire that had driven him up those stairs only a few minutes earlier, but it had become a fleeting memory. At that time, he had been convinced without any logic that Richard Venneman was in his apartment at the top of the stairs, and that conviction had been enough to give Willie the strength to climb the stairs. Now he knew Venneman was not there.

Willie sat down heavily on the lowest step. For perhaps half an hour, he sat in a stupor. No one came or went, and Willie remained undisturbed and lost in both exhaustion and despair.

If only Venneman came back, Willie would promise not to be importunate, not to overwhelm him with his needs. Once a day—no, even once a week. He would demand no more than that.

But I've got to give him something in return, he realized. I've got to give him some reason to give me what I want.

More than want, he realized: need. That shock of supreme delight, part sexual, part spiritual, was already more important to him than food or air or love. Willie knew that his former self—the self he had been before Venneman attacked him—would have been horrified and repelled to know what he was thinking now, but the opinion of his former self mattered as little as anything else when set against what Venneman had given him and could give him again.

If he wants to, Willie thought. If I can talk him into it.

Suddenly he saw the solution.

I'll be his servant!

It was obvious, once it had occurred to him. He would do whatever Venneman and... and... What was her name? Jill, yes, Jill Kennedy. Whatever Venneman and Jill Kennedy wanted him to do—cooking, cleaning, laundry, buying groceries. Money, too. He didn't have much, but he'd share it with them. He'd do whatever he could to persuade Venneman to give him that ecstasy again.

And I'll keep myself healthy for him, too, he thought. Take much better care of myself, so I'll have a good supply of blood for him. If that's what he needs, if he's a...

Well, it was obvious enough what Venneman was. For a brief moment, a shiver passed through Willie Gold. Venneman was a vampire, and Willie was planning to make himself a vampire's slave. It was a disgusting and terrifying thought. Then he remembered what he had felt when Venneman had pulled his blood from him, and the disgust and terror both faded away.

I'll start right now, Willie thought. I'll clean up for them, and then maybe when Richie comes back, he'll be grateful enough to do it to me again right away.

Briefly energized by that image, Willie pushed himself to his feet and climbed the stairs.

At the top, faced by the open door to Venneman's apartment, Willie felt a moment of fear. Instead of the delight, he remembered the agony when Venneman's teeth first tore into his neck. He put a trembling hand to the side of his neck, half expecting to feel the wound Venneman had made. Instead he encountered a faint ridge of scar tissue. The skin was almost smooth and healed already.

All the movies he had seen were completely wrong, Willie realized. In them, vampire attacks meant terror and death, sometimes followed by resurrection as a vampire. But he had instead experienced something wonderful, he was still alive, and he hungered only for his usual food, not for human blood. Being a vampire's victim was only a positive thing. All he needed to do was talk Venneman into being gentler the next time, so that Willie would experience no pain at all.

Willie entered the apartment and looked around. It was fairly neat already. Not much need for him in the living room. He stepped into the small kitchen. Here, everything was put away and all the countertops were clean. The kitchen looked considerably cleaner and neater than Willie's own. Maybe the bedroom, he told himself. If Venneman and Jill kept even the bedroom clean and neat, then they wouldn't need his services at all. If that were the case, then what could he offer?

Depressed, he pushed the bedroom door open and stepped inside.

"Jesus!" he gasped. Jill Kennedy lay on her back on the bed, naked, the sheet beneath her head red with blood. Her eyes were closed, her skin scarcely less white than the pillow beside her head.

Now he understood what Richard Venneman was running from.

SEVEN

Venneman drove west.

As soon as he could, he switched over to the interstate highway system. From time to time, he looked in his rear-view mirror for signs of pursuit, but he saw none. The cars behind differed from time to time, and they passed him and continued away from him at high speed when he slowed down to see what they would do. When he needed more gas, he pulled off the highway and then sat for a while, parked beside the exit ramp, to see if anyone else would take the same exit. But no one ever did.

Willie must not have tried to follow him after all. Or if he had tried, he had lost Venneman's scent. The possibility remained that during his years as a policeman, Willie had learned techniques of following another car that enabled him to do so without the target of the pursuit being able to detect him, no matter how clever the target thought he was being. Venneman thought about Willie's personality and dismissed that possibility.

Perhaps Willie had gone back inside the apartment building and had discovered Jill's body. If so, Venneman would have to worry about a larger and more determined pursuit.

For a moment, the idea of that pursuit, and of the capture and imprisonment and condemnation to death that would follow, terrified Venneman. But then he imagined the weak bodies of human beings trying to hold him down and put handcuffs on him, and he laughed aloud. Why, he thought, I could probably pull the bars of a jail cell apart, even if they did manage to get me behind them!

And as for execution—no, he would no longer welcome that, he no longer wanted death. Not that he could be put to death, he knew. He had already tried to kill himself with part of the sun itself, and that had failed. Even the electric chair was a pale silliness by comparison with that.

Each time he filled his car, he paid with a credit card. Each time, the charge was accepted as valid. Surely, he thought, if the police knew about Jill's death and were chasing him, they would have had his credit cards canceled.

Jill's murder, he corrected himself. Call it what it is.

Evening found Venneman in northern Indiana, passing signs showing the diminishing distance to Chicago. He thought of the vast, spread-out city with its millions of citizens, its millions of walking sacks of blood, and his mouth watered.

Then he remembered that Jill's parents lived in one of the northern suburbs, and he gritted his teeth and kept driving.

He skirted the city, passing south of it.

The highway interchanges grew more frequent and complex for a while, the traffic denser, the drivers more casual about changing lanes. Venneman grinned fiercely at them and stepped on the gas, excited by the speed and danger, the high-speed dance of man and metal, the imminence of death—death for the other drivers, but not for him, who was immune to it. After a while, that very immunity to death made the game seem silly, and he slowed again and became, to outward appearance, just another weary, distracted commuter, driving unconsciously while dreaming of another world.

By dark, Venneman was in the western outskirts of Chicago and heading due west again. The buildings and the traffic were both growing sparser. Ahead of him lay the flat farmlands of western Illinois and, he supposed, ever fewer places to spend the night. He had little experience of America from this point westward, and he imagined that it was all empty wasteland, with only the occasional city to provide relief. From here to Denver, he thought, he would find nothing but snowy wilderness, like the place beside the highway in the mountains where he had waited for someone to pick him up and take him to the airport in Denver.

That image brought back the memory of the two policeman who had picked him up and whom he had murdered and drunk from. For a moment, he wondered if their bodies had been found yet, and if anyone had investigated the back of their pickup truck, which he had left parked at the airport. Then Venneman forgot those details and remembered only the taste of their blood. He smiled. He was still hungry and thirsty, and he still needed to find someone with normal blood, not like Willie's, to satisfy himself.

He began to look for a motel.

From the various lighted signs gleaming beside the highway, he selected one that had the word "economy" in it. Creature of the night and nightmare he might be, but certain old habits died hard. The night clerk was a plain, bored young woman who perked up when Venneman entered the office. He stared at the registration card she put before him, wondering whether to use a false name in case of police pursuit. No point in doing that, he realized, since he was using his credit card to pay for the room. He shrugged and filled in his name and the license plate number of his car, noticing in surprise how firm and bold his handwriting seemed now. I should sign it "Count Venneman, Prince of Darkness," he thought, amused at the idea.

"You're in 2B," the clerk said, handing him a key. "Go out the door and up the stairs. Real nearby." She turned the card around to read it. "Venneman?" she said. "That's a German name, right?"

No, he almost wanted to say, it's Transylvanian. "I guess so," Venneman said. "My folks never kept track of that sort of thing."

"My name's Anderson," she said. "Anita Anderson, but everyone calls me Nita. I'll be here for the next few hours, if you need anything."

The girl kept on trying to make idle conversation, and Venneman indulged her. One sack of blood was as good as another. If he was friendly now, it would be that much easier to return later and continue to the next step.

When he let himself into his room, Venneman stood in the doorway and looked at the double bed and the cheap furniture. He caught himself before he flipped the switch beside the door. With no light from the ceiling fixture or bedside lamp, the room was illuminated only by the last faint glow of evening shining through the thin curtain of the room's single window and through the open door. In this light, the room looked no better than it would have by electric light. I should have better, he thought. If I'm really some sort of superhuman being now, why am I spending my nights in a place like this? I should have a castle and wear a cape, like the vampires in the movies.

He smiled at the thought and closed the door behind him, but he couldn't easily shrug away the feeling that he didn't belong here. It was too mundane, too pedestrian. It was the sort of room in which traveling salesmen spent their nights. It was beneath him.

But how was he to obtain better? For that matter, what was he to do about his future? Where would he sleep, and how would he live? He tried to look into the future and could not make it take any definite shape in his mind. He had always been able to imagine his older self. In the future as he had always envisioned it, he was married and had children, then grandchildren, and so on. He had never gone so far as to imagine his own death, but he had accepted that it was inevitably part of the picture.

Now children and grandchildren were as impossible for him as death itself.

Or were they? He realized that he had no idea. He knew so little about the creature he had become! Could a vampire impregnate a human woman? Or a female vampire?

A female vampire! The image of Elizabeth filled his mind, and a kind of desire that had nothing to do with blood overwhelmed him. He sank down onto the bed, onto his back, and closed his eyes.

He had had sex with her the second time after his transformation from human to vampire, and the experience had been even more shattering and overwhelming than the first time, the time she had murdered him. What would it be like now—now that he had grown so much more into his new nature?

The only way to know was to find Elizabeth. He could wait until she called for him, assuming that she really could do that, as she had claimed. But she might decide never to call him. That might have been a cruel joke, the sort of cruelty he thought she must be quite capable of. So he must search for her.

Now his drive west had a goal at last.

He stared at the ceiling, thinking of Elizabeth. The last light faded away and the room turned dark.

But not to Venneman. The familiar glow was back, but now it was tinged with red and pulsed faintly with the beating of his heart. It was warm and soothing and enveloping. Venneman closed his eyes and gave himself to it.

And entered again into the sea of blood. Pulsating, rising and falling, living, it bore Venneman along, rushing him toward the dim shoreline where lovely voices sang to him and welcoming arms reached out to him, and then away again, out into the open sea. He floated endlessly under a red sky, sunless, featureless.

Venneman awoke shortly after midnight, hungrier and thirstier than ever, but refreshed by sleep. He left his room and stood for a moment at the railing outside, looking over the parking lot. There was a scattering of cars. Not many travelers at this time of year, Venneman thought. Or perhaps most others bypass the cheapest motels, like this one. Suitable for a vampire, though, he told himself, smiling at the oddness of the thought.

He looked right and left along the building. He couldn't see any lighted windows. Nor did he see any movement in the parking lot. The few people who had chosen this place to stop were all asleep, getting what rest they could before they rose early and drove away again.

At intervals, cars rushed by on the nearby interstate, and occasionally a truck roared past. Venneman thought he could catch the faintest hint of the drivers' blood flowing through their veins, over the sounds of their vehicles, but he told himself that must be his imagination. How could even a vampire's hearing be that acute?

Venneman wished it were still summer, for then he would also be able to hear the rustle of small animals in the grass beyond the parking lot, the whispery flight of bats above him, the struggles of insects caught by the bats in midair.

But perhaps, he thought, to us the sound of blood is a louder roar than any other.

He closed his eyes and concentrated.

A car passed on the interstate. Venneman heard the humming of its engine, the whine of its tires upon the road, the song of the wind flowing over and around and under it. And through all of that, beneath it, behind it, above it, he heard the rhythmic thumping of a heart.

The car receded into the distance. The noises of engine, tires, and wind faded with it. The heartbeat faded last of all, as though it lagged behind the car, reluctant to go away from Venneman, calling to him to follow.

Impossible! he thought. It can't be!

But now that he had caught the trick of listening for that sound, he could hear it with every car that passed, and even over the louder, more aggressive roars of passing trucks.

He turned his attention to the building, now, and he could make out the soft thumping of beating hearts everywhere. With that came the sound of the blood itself, rushing through arteries, whispering through capillaries, flowing slowly through veins. The sounds grew louder as he stood there listening, as though they had been waiting only for him to notice them, to learn how to hear them, waiting only for that to attack him.

Venneman staggered under the assault of the tide of blood.

It was too much. It was like being surrounded by a screaming crowd that would not stop. It was a nightmare, not a delight. Venneman clamped his jaws together and squeezed his eyes shut and concentrated on hearing nothing.

Slowly the song of the blood receded into the background. It was still there, but it no longer tortured him.

He realized that had been gripping the railing harder and harder. He released his hold and raised his hands. The metal bars were bent where he had been holding them. Venneman sighed. This new strength of his was one more thing he must learn to control if he was to keep his nature secret.

Venneman went downstairs to the motel office. The door was locked. Through its glass front, he could see that the desk was unoccupied. Behind the desk was a door, through which flickered the blue glow of a television set. Venneman closed his eyes and listened. He heard the voices of the actors in the movie on the television set, and beyond that, he heard a heart beating and blood pulsing.

He knocked on the door. The sound echoed across the empty parking lot, but inside the television must have been loud enough to drown it out. Venneman looked around nervously, but he saw no one in the parking lot or at the doors of any of the motel rooms. He knocked again and waited, but again no one appeared inside the office.

Venneman grasped the door handle, squeezing hard, and turned it slowly. At first, it resisted. He increased the force, and then something cracked and broke inside the lock, and the door surrendered and opened. He looked around again, quickly, and then entered the office and closed the door behind him.

He went behind the desk and stepped through the door, moving quickly to the side of the doorway so that he would not be visible to anyone outside the office. The room in front of him was simply furnished with a sofa, an armchair, and in front of the chair a small table with the television set on it. The young clerk, Anita, was in the armchair, sleeping, equally oblivious to the movie on the television and to the intruder in the room.

The girl had slipped down in the chair while she slept. Her hands were in her lap, and her head was turned to one side, with her hair concealing her throat. Even through the draping of hair, Venneman thought he could see the pulsing of blood in her neck.

He looked again toward the office, then moved silently, passing behind the armchair to the side away from the office door. He was sure that no casual passerby outside would be able to see him now. He looked down at the girl again to find that she had been awakened by his movement and now watched him, her eyes wide with fear.

Venneman stared into her eyes and smiled. "It's all right, Anita," he whispered. "You're safe."

She continued to stare at him, and the fear drained away. She nodded. "Yes," she said, sounding half asleep still. "Safe."

Venneman bent down toward her. He brushed the hair

away from her neck. There was the gentle pulse he thought he had seen before. He stroked her neck softly. "Safe," he repeated, bending further, leaning toward her neck.

The girl gasped and stiffened.

Venneman said, "Ssh." He kissed her neck softly, and she relaxed with a sigh.

He kissed her again, moving his lips up and down along the side of her neck. He put a hand lightly on each of her shoulders.

Then he gripped her shoulders tightly and bit into her.

For a moment, she cried out and struggled, but then his teeth sliced into her artery and he began to suck in her blood. She relaxed and bent her neck so that he could reach her even more easily. She put her arms around his head and pulled his face harder against her. She cried out and arched her body.

Venneman was in agony.

His need for blood had become so urgent that he could not stop feeding on her, but her blood burned in his mouth and throat and stomach as much as Willie's had. He tried to push her away, but for a moment, she was stronger than he was, as though his power had drained into her even as her blood flowed into him. He gagged on her foul blood but could not stop it from gushing into his mouth with every beat of her heart, could not keep himself from swallowing it, could not stop it from eating him away inside.

At last he managed to tear himself away from her. He staggered back, gasping for breath. He stumbled and sat down hard on the floor.

The girl pulled herself up in the chair to a sitting position and stared down at him, her face pale, her eyes wide in wonder. She held her arms out to him. "Again! Please!" The wound in her neck was closing as he watched.

She got out of the chair and stood beside it, swaying slightly. With one hand, she tugged at the collar of her blouse, fumbling with the buttons, trying unsuccessfully to open the blouse wider, to expose more of her flesh to Venneman. She held her other hand out to Venneman. "Please!" she said again. "Please! I want more! You've got to give me more!"

Venneman slid away from her and rose to his feet. The pain in his stomach was easing, although his mouth still felt burned. But he did feel stronger. The blood had done for him what it had before.

But when he looked at her and saw the trace of blood still on her neck, his stomach lurched in revulsion and he felt overcome by fear of her. "No more," he said. "Stay away from me." He wiped his arm across his mouth, rubbing away the last of her evil blood.

"I know what you are," the girl said. "I've seen it in the movies. I didn't know it would be so wonderful." She tried to come to Venneman, but her legs were too weak to hold her up. She went down on one knee. She looked up at Venneman pleadingly. "I need more," she said. "Please. Please let me have more!"

Venneman backed toward the door. "No more," he said. "Leave me alone." He spat on the floor, trying to get the last of the burning and foul taste from his mouth. He left the office and went back upstairs to his motel room, where he rinsed his mouth repeatedly at the bathroom sink.

It would be too great a coincidence for both Willie and this girl to be suffering from some affliction that made their blood such torture for him to drink, he knew. He was the one who had acquired an affliction of the blood.

Why had he chosen to stop here for the night? He felt more awake and alert now than he had during the daylight. That might have been the result of the girl's blood, though. Perhaps it had been some lingering trace of his human self that had caused him to pull off and check in for the night, like any normal man on a long trip. Or perhaps it had been the overwhelming need for blood.

He left the room and went down to the parking lot and into his car. He was pulling out of the parking lot when Anita appeared in the door of the office, barely able to hold herself up, staring at him. Her eyes were huge in a face grown suddenly skeletal. They blazed at him, glaring out her need, drawing him, filling him with fear. As he drove away, she stood unmoving, only her head turning, her gaze locked on his car, following the car until it disappeared into the dark.

Even as he pulled onto the interstate and accelerated, he imagined he could feel the pressure of her gaze on his back, as if she could follow him with her mind and find him again. Venneman shivered and stepped on the gas, speeding up still further, escaping. He fled into the red glow the night had become, escaping into its welcome cover.

Now he knew what he had done to himself when he used Dinsmuir's experiment in his suicide attempt. Modern science had not destroyed him. Instead, it had transformed him into a vampire unaffected by the sun but tortured by the blood of his human victims. At the same time, it had not released him from the need for that blood. He was as much a prisoner of his need and of his victims' blood as he had ever been. But his victims felt overwhelming pleasure at his bite. He had changed from a creature who caused agony in exchange for his own pleasure into one who suffered agony to survive and gave delight in return.

EIGHT

Venneman sat quietly at his table, his fork resting on his plate, and listened. Around him, the hum and chatter of human life filled the restaurant.

He let go of his fork and raised his glass of wine to his mouth instead. He sipped delicately from it, enough to enjoy the taste but not enough to sicken himself. He put the glass down and concentrated on the people around him again. Now and then he cut a small bite off the fish he had ordered and ate it—slowly, carefully, keeping each bite in his mouth for a long time before swallowing it. It was a small meal, although the price was absurdly high. He had finally learned to tolerate such small amounts of human food and drink. Light food, only—fish, sometimes chicken breast, vegetarian food, white wine, nothing heavier or darker than that. He could drink water in normal amounts now, although it had a hollowness that filled him without satisfying him. He put his fork down again and picked up his water glass. In the end, as always, he would eat little of his meal, small though it was. He was a generous tipper, and waiters at the better restaurants in town seemed quite willing to tolerate his eccentricity.

He came to restaurants not to eat, for only one food could now satisfy and nourish him, but rather to watch and listen to human beings. Surrounded by them but eternally separated from them, Richard Venneman drank in the sight and sound of humans as thirstily as he did their blood.

And yet the irony was that the food and drink he had trained himself to tolerate in small quantities no longer tasted foul to him. It made him ill if he ate or drank too much of it, and it passed through his body undigested, unchanged, exiting in a form more disgusting to him than feces had been in his previous lifetime, but he could hold it in his mouth and not feel compelled to spit it out. Human blood, on the other hand, burned his mouth and stomach, horrified and repelled him even as he drank it, and yet he had to have it to survive. He had tried again, as he had at the very beginning of his life as a vampire, to hold back and avoid blood, and again he had been unable to keep himself from taking a victim. Human blood ruled his eternal life and tortured him.

"Is everything all right, sir?"

It was Venneman's waiter, a tired man in late middle age trying hard to project the same youthful good cheer as the younger waiters did. Venneman wondered if his blood moved as sluggishly in his veins as he moved over the restaurant floor. That tired old blood would do Venneman's body less good than that of a younger man, as Venneman had learned from experience. Even so, it would do Venneman more good than the tasteless meal he had been mechanically chewing his way through. He smiled up at the waiter. "Oh, yes. Everything's perfect, as always."

The waiter responded to his smile, as everyone did. He

straightened and seemed momentarily more energetic. "Thank you, sir. Glad you're enjoying it." He walked away to another table, his back straighter and his step firmer.

I do give them something in return, Venneman thought. I take just a tiny sip of their blood, but they take a glimpse of something from me. What? Life lived at a higher, more vibrant level?

He had seen himself in such terms at first, but now he was coming to feel that his life was less than that of human beings. If he was a superior being, then why did he spend his days and nights so emptily and meaninglessly? Why was he so alone? Why did he yearn for human company? What kind of lion begged to be accepted as one of the lambs?

He became aware of the pressure of someone looking at him.

Venneman turned his head slightly and then glanced to the side. Across the room, a woman was staring intently at him. Venneman turned his head further to see her more clearly.

She was about his own age, he guessed. He thought she must normally be fairly pretty, but now her face was distorted by the emotions she was feeling. He knew what mixture of feelings must be possessing her, and he knew he should leave immediately.

The woman was sharing a booth with a man and another couple. She was ignoring them completely, seeing only Venneman, aware only of him.

How does she know? Venneman wondered. She can't have seen my face. I'm too careful nowadays.

But the way she stared at him was unmistakable. She was a former victim, someone he had caught in the dark, as he did all of his victims now—in the dark, from the rear, quickly and violently, giving them no chance to see their attacker. He had settled on this as a way to keep them from knowing who he was and pursuing him.

He was down to once every other month, now. He had learned to satisfy his physical needs without violating what was left of his conscience by killing any of his victims. For that matter, the foulness of their blood prevented him from taking too much at any one time. So they lived, but by not letting them see him, he was still free to move about his new city without fear of detection. And yet every now and then he ran into someone, a former victim, who sensed who he was.

The woman staring at him now must be feeling fear, he knew, remembrance of the pain and terror. And yet, like all of his victims, she must also be remembering the terrible ecstasy she had felt when he was feeding on her. He wondered if it was as intense and glorious as what he had felt when drinking human blood, during that short period before he had exposed himself to Dinsmuir's experiment. If so, then it was no wonder they all wanted it again.

Venneman gestured to the waiter. The man hurried over to him, concern on his face. He knew from experience that Venneman never ordered more than he now had before him. "Is something wrong, sir?"

"No, everything's fine. I need the check, though. I have to leave immediately."

"Certainly, sir. I'll be right back." He hurried away.

Venneman fidgeted impatiently while he waited for the man to come back. He tried to watch the woman without staring at her. She said something to the man beside her, and he heaved himself out of the booth, an annoyed look on his face. The woman slid across the seat of the booth.

Venneman pulled his wallet from his coat pocket and tried to calculate the total cost of meal, tax, and tip. He was gripped by panic and couldn't think clearly. He stood up, his napkin still in his lap, tipping his chair back so that it fell with a crash that brought instant silence to the room.

The waiter returned with the check. Venneman glanced at it and threw down some money—far more than enough—and headed quickly for the doorway.

The woman caught up with him before he could leave the dining room.

She grabbed his arm. "Wait," she said. "Please. I know who you are."

Venneman looked over her shoulder. The man she was with still stood beside the booth. He was watching her and Venneman with a surprised and angry frown. In a moment, Venneman guessed, he'd be coming this way himself.

"I'm sorry," Venneman said. "I don't know you."

"Of course you do," the woman said. "I was almost certain when I saw you across the room. Now I *am* certain. Please." She was almost crying. "Please! I've never begged a man before."

"Your husband," Venneman said. "He's getting very upset."

"Not my husband. Just a date. He doesn't matter. No one else does. Look." She bent her head to one side and pointed to her neck. The scar was faint and well healed, but it was still visible to Venneman, as was the pulse of acid blood beneath it. He could smell her blood. The smell was as beautiful as ever, belying the taste.

Venneman had never before been confronted so directly by

a victim. He had no idea how to deal with the situation. Denial seemed pointless. She was too completely convinced that he was the being who had attacked her to be diverted. "Where did it happen?" he asked her abruptly.

She was caught off balance for a moment, and then hope flickered. "Just off Seventeenth." She named a side street across from City Park. "It was about two in the morning. I was going to my car after visiting a friend."

Venneman nodded as though he remembered the incident. Perhaps he did. He wasn't sure. Even though he'd taken only seven victims since arriving in Denver, they all blended together in his memory. They had no individuality. "Be there tonight," he told her. "Same time."

The tension and fear disappeared entirely from her face. She smiled happily, beautiful at that moment.

For that moment, Venneman wished he could think of her as a fellow being, a companion, even a lover, and not as prey. Meaningless, he told himself. Silly. Too great a risk. You can't afford to think of them as being in any way like you. That's a trap.

He shook his head, as if warning himself to be cautious. The woman gasped as though he had struck her. "You're not changing your mind!" she said.

"No. No, I haven't changed my mind. Better go back to your table now."

Her date had finally lost his patience and was stalking toward them. His expression said *I'm going to have it out with this guy*.

Venneman grinned at him over the woman's shoulder. He waited until the other man reached them and then said, "You can have her back. For now."

He left the couple avoiding each other's eyes and walked from the restaurant feeling pleased with himself. But once outside, Venneman realized how foolish he had been to draw the other man's attention to him. Not drawing attention was at the center of his new lifestyle. He shook his head again. Too late to do anything about it now, he told himself. He would solve the problem presented by the woman during the small hours of the morning, and he would avoid the problem presented by the man by moving on to another city.

He walked slowly down the sidewalk, chewing over the problem. He had known that this time would come. Slowly as the number of his victims grew, it did grow. Every new human being who had come into Venneman's grip was another hunter looking for him afterward.

He stopped and looked up at the night sky. An early cold front had blown in during the day, dry air from the northern plains, clearing away the smog and what few clouds there had been. Despite the downtown lights, the stars shone brightly and steadily in the thin air. Venneman unbuttoned his coat and undid the top few buttons of his shirt, letting the cold air bathe his chest. He inhaled deeply, drawing it into him.

He felt someone watching him from behind.

Venneman spun around. No one. The sidewalk was empty.

Odd, he thought. He had learned to rely on that instinct, that awareness of being watched. But he also knew that he now moved so much faster than a human being that no one could have been standing on the sidewalk and managed to duck into hiding as he turned.

It was the incident with the woman and her date, he

realized. The awareness that he had made Denver inhospitable to himself was affecting him, making him imagine hostile eyes upon his back.

Why was he in Denver at all? Why had he chosen to stop here in his flight to the west, his flight from the body of Jill Kennedy? He had asked himself this before but could find no satisfactory answer. Something had told him to rest in this city. Not a feeling of security or refuge; even then, he had felt that this city was as dangerous to him as any other city of humans. He wondered if he had decided to stay in Denver because it was close to the place where it had all started for him, the town where he had been murdered, but not so close to it as to be frightening. Perhaps he was close to Elizabeth, if she was still in that mountain town. But not too close.

Venneman continued walking along the sidewalk toward his car. He had been in Denver for ten months already. Before tonight, he had managed so well to avoid his victims after feeding on them, and had lived so comfortably on the money taken from them, that he had foolishly begun to think of his present situation as permanent. He had begun to feel at home in the city. He was becoming increasingly familiar with its streets, especially at night. He had learned where and when he would be most likely to find wealthy young people walking alone in the dark—sources of both blood and funds for his new lifestyle.

He was, in a way, the ultimate thief. He took both his victims' lifeblood and their cash. The theft of blood no longer bothered him. Indeed, he had long ago ceased to think of it as theft. Money, though—why, that was simple thievery! Yet he was forced to live in these creatures' world, and therefore he must have the funds to live in it properly. And certainly he had lived well for these past ten months. If only blood still tasted like life instead of ancient death....

He reached his car and stood next to it for a moment, looking down at the ground, feeling for the keys in his pocket, aware again of the pressure of a gaze on his back.

This time, he suppressed the urge to spin around. Instead, he took the keys from his pocket and pretended to be fumbling at the door lock as though he were having trouble inserting the key and it was occupying all of his attention. He bent over as though to concentrate on the problem. Then he turned his head quickly to the right and looked over his shoulder.

No one. But had he seen just the final instant of movement, the corner of a piece of clothing disappearing around a corner?

Venneman shook his head in frustration. His imagination was playing tricks on him. *He* was the creature of nightmare, the evil that hid in the dark! How absurd that he should start fearing the dark and the imagined dangers that lurked in it!

At two o' clock in the morning, Venneman was leaning against the wall of an apartment building on a side street leading off 17th Avenue. All thought of dangers lurking in the dark—dangers other than Venneman himself—were forgotten. All he could think of now was this woman who knew who and what he was. She was danger enough, and she was not a figment of his imagination.

Venneman undid his coat and the top two buttons of his shirt. He wanted the chilly air against his skin—not so much to cool him down as to slow his heart, which was hammering. Tension, he told himself. Not fear. What do I have to be afraid of?

She came around the corner from 17th, a silhouette against

the lighted street. She stood at the corner, trying to see into the darkness of the side street.

Venneman stepped away from the wall and out onto the sidewalk. "Here," he said.

"Thank God!" the woman said. She walked quickly toward him. "I was afraid you'd change your mind. All this time, I haven't been able to think about anything else but you."

Venneman felt himself slipping into what he had come to think of as his feeding mode. Her could hear her voice less with every word, her blood more with every heartbeat. He stepped toward her.

"I didn't know how I'd ever find you again," she said. She breathed rapidly, having trouble speaking. "I thought I'd never experience it again. When I saw you in the restaurant, I—I didn't know what to do. I was scared. I didn't—I don't—I don't even know your name. What's your name?"

Venneman put his hand against her cheek and stroked it gently. "Richard."

"Richard," she whispered, almost reverentially. "Richard. My name's—"

"No," Venneman said sharply. He shook his head. "Don't tell me."

She stared up into his eyes, searching for something there. "Not my name? You don't want to know my name? But how can we get to know each other?"

Venneman smiled at her. "You have your whole lifetime for that." He slid his hand down her cheek and to her neck and bent slowly toward her.

She closed her eyes and bent her head to one side, exposing to him the faint scar she had shown him in the restaurant.

Before his lips could touch her skin or his teeth bite through it, Venneman raised his head suddenly and stood listening. Eyes. The pressure of someone's gaze. He had felt it again. And he thought he had heard something, too, this time, some slight movement, a breath, a muttered word.

"What's the matter?" the woman asked.

"Wait. Be quiet." Venneman closed his eyes, concentrating on his sense of hearing. If someone else were nearby, he should be able to hear the heartbeat and the blood. But the human heart now beating against his chest, the pulse he could feel beneath his hand, the heat of this woman's blood, the scent of it, all drowned out anything fainter.

"Nothing," he said at last. "Come." He took her hand and walked down the sidewalk toward his car. She came with him without hesitation or resistance.

He opened the car door and held it for her until she was in, then locked it behind her. He went around the car and stood beside the driver's door, looking up and down the street, listening carefully. Again there was nothing. But he couldn't shake the feeling that he was being watched—and what was worse, watched by someone he could not see. Despite the risk, he would take the woman to his apartment, he decided.

But when he got into the car and closed the door behind him, he was overwhelmed by the scent of her blood and her openness to him. It was as though the enclosed space of the car had magnified both. Waiting any longer was impossible. He reached for her, and she laughed happily and flung her arms around his neck and pulled his face down to her throat.

He waited only until he had a firm hold on her, in case she panicked and began to fight, and then he bit into her neck, roughly and without any attempt at delicacy, and began to feed.

She writhed against him, shrieking in pain and crying out in pleasure. She moved her pelvis back and forth, trying to reach him with it, to press her genitals against his.

He sucked hard, pulling the burning fluid into his mouth and forcing it down his throat. He was filled with the acid, but he kept drinking it in and swallowing it. He opened his mouth and bit still deeper, seeking some hidden core of being, some place within her where the blood was sweet again, some place where her soul dwelled.

Her movements were becoming more sluggish, and her moans of delight no longer came through her mouth but through the huge hole he had torn in her throat. The gaping hole was filled with pink foam, a froth of blood mixed with air from her lungs. Even as she died, her pelvis kept moving rhythmically.

Venneman wept as he fed. The tears burned down his cheeks and mingled with the caustic blood.

At last the woman moved no longer, and Venneman could draw no more blood from her body. He cradled her in his arms. He put one hand behind her head and moved it gently so that it rested on his chest. He stroked her cheek. He rocked her back and forth and kissed her forehead gently and whispered, "I'm sorry."

After all, he wished he knew her name. He wished he knew her. He wished she could have been allowed to live and that he could have learned to know her and love her. For those brief moments in his car, she was a person, an individual, and not just a prey animal. For that short time, now that she was dead, he felt in contact with her.

Venneman reached around her to her purse, which lay on the seat beside her. He opened it clumsily with one hand and took out her wallet. He flipped it open, exposing her driver's license. The glow of night, the red-tinged light of distant stars, revealed her photograph—smiling a bit too much, eager and nervous at the same time—and her name, Geraldine Travers.

Her friends must call her Gerrie, he thought.

"Gerrie," he whispered to her.

But she was immobile and unresponsive. She was a corpse, a bloodless corpse, thanks to him, cooling far more rapidly than a normal dead human body would.

Venneman let her slide from his arms onto the passenger seat. He got out, walked around the car, and opened the passenger-side door. He looked up and down the sidewalk quickly and saw no one. He pulled the woman's body from the car and carried it down the sidewalk, looking for a good place to dump it.

A bloodless corpse with a hole torn in its neck, he thought. Whatever I do with her, she'll attract attention. Good thing I was planning to leave the city anyway.

I could dump her in the river instead, he thought, hesitating. He wondered if the effect of water would mislead a coroner. Probably not, he realized. Absence of blood must be unmistakable, surely, even for human minds.

She felt so light to him. He had not killed since coming to this city. He had created seven victims who had yearned and hungered for him and therefore hunted him, but he had killed no one in all that time. If not for the threat this woman had posed, he would not have had to kill her. And yet, by creating victims who wanted him again, he had made this murder inevitable. This woman, this Geraldine Travers, had been consumed with the need to find him again, as all of his other victims were, and that had led her to recognize and confront him. And that had led him to kill her.

Venneman sighed. He was driven by what he was. He was defenseless against his own nature. But I always was, he thought. Even when I was human, I was the captive of my own nature. Everyone is.

He came upon an alcove formed by the meeting of the walls of two apartment buildings. There must be an alley somewhere, since this was an older part of the city, but he was growing nervous, worried that he would be seen carrying the woman's body. Gerrie's body, he corrected himself. Now you can afford to let her have her name, now that it's too late for her name to save her. He stooped and placed her light, lax body in the alcove and stepped back.

To his eyes, she was clearly visible, glowing faintly red against the red-tinged bricks, but he thought that human eyes would not be able to see her in this light. She would not be discovered until morning. Perhaps not even then, not right away. He had hours ahead of him during which to pack what he wanted, decide on a destination, and leave town.

He stood for a moment watching. Goodbye, Gerrie. He mouthed the words silently. I'm sorry. He said that again, knowing how pointless it was. She was clay, empty and lifeless and useless. He had taken everything from her and left nothing leaning against the brick walls.

Only now was he becoming aware of the sick, burning nausea in his stomach. Pity the woman though he might, her blood was simultaneously as nourishing and sickening as anyone else's.

He turned to leave and found himself facing another woman. She was almost as tall as Venneman, and she glowed with a light of her own, something beyond the red light that illuminated the nighttime world.

He knew her well, even in this light. She was the woman his soul had yearned for, and she was more beautiful than ever. Venneman gasped and stepped toward her, his arms held out. She must be a dream! How could she be real and here?

He was stopped by the scorn, the very real contempt in her face.

"You're as passionless as ever," she said. "You were an unfeeling man, and now you're an unfeeling vampire."

It was Jill Kennedy.

NINE

"How many bodies have you cluttered the city with, you cold-blooded fool?" Jill asked.

They were in Venneman's apartment.

"None, before this." Venneman was still dazed by her reappearance. On the drive here, he had asked her what had happened to her, why she was still alive, but she had told him brusquely to wait for her answer. Her force of personality and command of the situation had unnerved him.

He looked around his apartment, wondering what he could offer her and simultaneously aware how bizarre it was to be wondering that. He had no food or drink for humans in the place, of course. "Would you like a glass of water?" he asked her finally.

Jill snorted. "I don't drink water. Don't you get it yet, Richie? I'm what you are. I'm a vampire."

Venneman sat down abruptly on the couch. "A—? But..." He drew a breath and began again. "I don't understand."

Jill's face softened slightly. She came to the couch, sat beside him, and took both of his hands in hers. "I'm a vampire, Richie. Just like you. You made me one."

Venneman shook his head in denial. "It can't be," he whispered. "Oh, Jesus!"

Jill laughed. "You regret it? I don't, Richie. I don't regret it at all. It's wonderful!"

She stood up and spun around, her arms out wide, embracing the world. "I only thought I was alive before you killed me!" She looked at Venneman's horrified expression, and she laughed again. "I'm grateful to you, Richie. You did something wonderful for me."

"What about the others?" Venneman asked. "My God, do you mean I've been creating vampires all along? That's the way it is in the movies. Someone bitten by a vampire becomes one. But I thought I was avoiding that by not killing people. I've been so careful!"

"You mean you've never killed anyone except me?" Jill asked.

"Not *since* you," Venneman said. "At first, I had trouble controlling myself. I killed... I don't know how many I killed." He shivered. "I try not to think about that. My God, they're all vampires now! All of those people!"

"The world isn't overrun with vampires, Richie," Jill said. "Haven't you noticed that? Anyway, what you do at the beginning doesn't count. At that point, you were still rebuilding your body and gaining your new strength. It takes lots of blood for that. Did you have sex with any of your prey?"

"What?" Venneman was as shocked by the question as he was confused by it. "I don't understand you."

Jill stood before him, leaning forward slightly, looming over him. "I asked you if you had sex with any of your victims. While you were killing them, I meant. The way you did with me. Why is that so hard to understand?" She stood up and moved away. "Jesus Christ, Richie! You've become a vampire, and you're still as inhibited and moralistic as you were before!" She shook her head. "You're probably the only Calvinist vampire in the whole fucking world. You realize that?"

Venneman stared at her. "It's obviously changed you," he said at last.

"Thank God for that!"

"God!" Venneman looked aside. "I don't think God is due any thanks for what we are now."

"Didn't God make vampires, too?" Jill asked.

She sounded uncannily like Elizabeth at that moment. Venneman looked at her in shock. "God made man in his own image," he said, his voice husky. "Satan made vampires."

"Then Satan's a better craftsman than God," Jill told him.

She sat down beside him again, and again she took his hands in hers. "Never mind all that God and Satan shit, Richie. That's the sort of thing you always used to like to talk about. Hell, you used to go on and on about it sometimes. It drove me crazy."

"You liked that sort of discussion!" Venneman protested.

Jill frowned, as though trying to remember. "I suppose I did. Now it all seems pretty silly. You released me from all of that when you killed me." She watched Venneman's reaction to that phrase and repeated it. "When you killed me. When you made love to me and tore my throat out and drank my blood and drained me of life."

Venneman cringed away from her, retreating across the couch until he was pressed against one of its arms.

Jill moved after him. "Why are you denying it to yourself,

Richie? You never could deal with reality, but *now* you should be able to! You're a vampire, and you had sex with me and killed me, and that made me into a vampire."

"Why do you keep talking about sex?" Venneman said. He was aware of the whine in his voice. "What does that have to with anything?"

"That's what makes the difference between just killing your prey and making your prey into a vampire, Richie. Except that you probably say 'victim,' instead of 'prey.' You're still so scared of sex that you never even let yourself realize that."

She was right, of course. He could see it, now that she had pointed it out—could see both that Jill was right about the role of sex in the passing on of vampirism, and that she was right that he had avoided recognizing that role. Elizabeth had seduced him and murdered him, and he had become a vampire. He had done the same to Jill, with the same results. He had not had sex with any other victim, so that must mean that none of his other victims had become vampires.

Now he understood what Elizabeth had meant when he had come upon her with her latest victim, lying together in the snow, and she had told him that she had not made love to the man because she hadn't wanted him the way she had wanted Venneman.

She meant that she wanted to make me a vampire, Venneman thought. She did it to me cold-bloodedly, not because of some kind of overwhelming hunger, not the way I killed my early victims. She wanted me to be a vampire like her. She's worse than I am! I only do what I have to because I have no choice, and even then I do as little damage as I can. I made Jill a vampire because I didn't know what I was doing.

How, he suddenly wondered, did Jill know about this? Had she learned the hard way? Christ, what was he thinking—that Jill had had sex with many victims? Impossible! Not Jill!

He looked at her. He slid down on the couch so that he was resting on his spine, his legs splayed out before him. Jill was sitting up high, her back straight, looking down at him with a strange expression he could not interpret. It vanished and her face smoothed as he stared at her.

"Off in dreamland again, Richie? You spend too much time there."

"How did you find out about how vampires pass it on, Jill? I mean, how vampires are made?"

"You mean," Jill said, "what sex has to do with it? Can't you even say the word, Richie?"

"I can say 'sex,'" Venneman said. "I can also say 'vampire.' I just prefer not to say either one."

Jill sighed and turned away from him. "No, you really haven't changed. Too bad. I spent all of this time looking for you, listening to my blood, learning from it, imagining how much better it would be between us than it ever was while we were human. Instead, you're just the same." She turned back toward him and looked at him for a while, coldly, analytically. "I lived with someone for the last few months. A man named Henry. He's one of us, a vampire. But he's a very old one. He's been this way since around the time of the American Revolution." She grinned with fierce enthusiasm. "Can you imagine that? That's what's ahead of us, Richie! Anyway, he's learned a great deal about being a vampire in all that time, and he taught it all to me."

"You ... lived with someone?" Venneman said.

Jill laughed. "Good God, have you been alone all this time?

Yes, I suppose you have.

"Right," she continued, "I lived with someone. Henry and I recognized each other immediately. I can't say how, really, but it happened. You must know what I mean."

Venneman shook his head. "I've never met another vampire. Not since it began for me, I mean. Not until you, now."

"And you couldn't tell what I was until I told you," Jill said. "I guess it's just another aspect of what's always been missing in you, Richie. That animal side. You never had it when you were a human and you don't even have it now."

We were never all that tender and loving toward each other back then, Venneman thought. But we weren't vicious toward each other. We were always considerate. Kind, even. That's gone in her now. "If you're saying that I'm more like a human being than a vampire," Venneman said, "based on your extensive experience, I mean, then I'm complimented."

"Sarcasm!" Jill said. "I don't remember that you were capable of that before."

"And you weren't capable of sex with another man before," Venneman said. "Hell, you were scarcely capable of it with me."

She nodded. "I'm so glad I left that behind me. That last time with you, though, the time when you killed me, Richie—that was pretty amazing. I wanted you then. You did have that special animal power that one time. So it's really in you, too, just like every other vampire. Just like me. Just like Henry."

"The difference is that I fight it. Up to now, I've been fighting that side of me for ethical reasons. Now that I know what will happen if I make love to one of my victims, I'll be even more careful."

"But you didn't fight it all the time, did you?"

"What do you mean?"

"I mean," Jill said, "that even when you were still human, you must have had sex with another woman at least one time."

"Never!" Venneman said angrily. "I was always faithful to you."

"There was that girl at the lab you were always talking about."

"Dale Whitmer?" Venneman realized that he had not thought of Dale in all this time. Now he saw her face perfectly in his mind's eye, and he realized that he missed her soothing company. "She was a friend, Jill. There was never anything romantic between us."

"You never heard yourself talking about her. Anyway, that's not the woman I was referring to, Richie. I meant the woman who made you a vampire. You must have had sex with her for you to have been envamped. That's the word Henry likes to use. Envamped. The woman who envamped you."

"Envamped," Venneman muttered. What a ridiculous word. And a misleading one. It made the whole process sound magical, like the casting of a spell, whereas the truth was that he had been infected with something horrible and incurable.

"Did you try to kill yourself?" he asked suddenly. "When you realized what you had become, did you try to commit suicide?"

Jill drew back from him, frowning. "Have you gone crazy, Richie? I was confused about it all at first. I was physically weak, and I had trouble thinking clearly, but instinct took care of me. I made my first kill without really knowing what I was doing, but once I tasted his blood and felt his strength fill me and felt him weakening and dying against me..." She paused, breathing hard, her eyes shining. She turned her gaze on Venneman. He was struck again by the new force of her presence. "I realized at that point," she said, "that I hadn't really been alive before. I had been dead until you killed me and woke me up to real life. Why would I want to kill myself, even if I could? Wait a minute," she said, "you mean you did try?"

"I tried to save my soul, yes. It was the only thing to do, rather than go on the way I was."

"Theology, Richie. You keep seeing everything in those terms. Forget all that soul and Heaven and Hell shit. You're still a part of nature, just as you were before. You're just one step higher up on the evolutionary ladder, that's all. Henry taught me to see it that way."

"Up the ladder or down it?"

"Which do we admire more, Richie, the lion or the goat?"

"Is this argument something Henry taught you, too?"

Jill grinned at him. "Jealousy! Well, at least you're demonstrating some kind of feeling. Anyway, you're trying to change the subject. Look, you ran away and abandoned me. First you murdered me and used me and my blood for your own pleasure, envamping me in the process. Then you ran away. Moreover, before all of that happened, while you were away in Colorado on your vacation and I stayed home and worked, you were unfaithful to me. Just a little adventure—I suppose that's what you thought. Jill won't ever know, so why not? Have my little fling. Except that you picked a vampire to have your little fling with, right?"

"I didn't pick a vampire. The vampire picked me." But Venneman couldn't meet her eyes. "When I came home and I ... when I did that to you, you didn't want to at first, either, but you couldn't resist. Vampires have that power."

Jill put her hand on his chin and turned his face toward hers. She stared into his eyes. Venneman felt a sudden rush of sexual arousal. She seemed to be drawing it out in him, controlling it, heightening it, with her eyes alone. Then she released his chin and looked away, as though she had demonstrated what she wanted to.

"Was it a woman, Richie?" she asked. "I've just been assuming it was, but I don't really know that, do I? Maybe it was a man, up there in Colorado."

Venneman pushed himself up to a sitting position on the couch. "No! It was a woman!"

Jill laughed. "You're so horrified! Don't you realize that your power works on everyone? You could have a man just as easily as a woman, if you wanted to. You can have anyone you want to now, Richie. That's what's so wonderful about this! One of the things, I mean. You can draw someone to you, take just enough of their blood to take the edge off your hunger and thirst, and then you can call them back to you whenever you want to, for a second helping. Or a third. Or a fourth." She leaned toward him and whispered, "Just don't make love to them, because that's when vampires lose control and take everything."

He reached for her, unable to stop himself, and pulled her down, rolling on top of her. He undressed himself and her just enough to be able to enter her, his eagerness overpowering him. He pounded himself into her throughout the night, as she bucked and writhed beneath him, climaxing repeatedly, screaming up at him in her delight. And all the while, he thought she was laughing at him.

When the living–room window began to lighten with dawn, Jill asked him to pull down the blind, and they finally moved to the bedroom to sleep.

He noticed that Jill was reacting to daylight as he had at first—with a mixture of discomfort, fear, and overwhelming fatigue. Venneman lay beside her in the bed, listening to her breathing grow slower as she fell quickly asleep. He stared up at the ceiling, filled with restless energy. His body was tired from their exertions in the other room, but his mind was frantically wakeful.

This woman beside him was Jill but not Jill. Even physically she wasn't really Jill anymore.

She was of course stronger, but that mattered little because his own vampirish strength balanced hers, and so they seemed the same relative to each other as they had before. He thought she was taller and generally larger than before, but he knew that he had grown, too, as though a diet of human blood was more nourishing than any other kind of food, or as though it was the vampire's nature to be larger than its prey. So that change, too, left them relatively the same physically.

But other changes he could not ignore. Always beautiful, she was now even more beautiful, and beautiful in a deeper, more disturbing way. It was as though, he thought, her beauty had been proverbially skin deep before, but now it radiated from her soul. But surely her soul, which had been good and pure, was now evil, as his was!

Then there was her sexuality. Before her transformation, she had disliked and distrusted her own physical side as much as he had disdained his. Now she seemed to crave sex. What they had been doing on the couch was not lovemaking. It was sex, and it might just as well have been between two strangers. As they had writhed and risen and fallen together, he had looked at her face, looked into her eyes. He had concentrated on her touch, searching for some reflection of their old relationship from before his trip to Colorado. He had seen no sign of it. She was no different from Elizabeth, now—or from the uninhibited human beings he had encountered in that ski village.

He had also looked for the old affection. Instead, he had sensed hatred.

What did all this mean for the future? Were they supposed to try to live together again, two soulless creatures with only their lust for human blood in common, trying to build an undead life together for eternity?

You're thinking nonsense, he told himself. You're being melodramatic. This is Jill, whom you intended to live with for the rest of your life. So nothing has really changed.

At last he drifted into sleep and into his old dream of the ocean of blood.

The great red swells swept him to and fro, toward the shore of beckoning figures and away from it. Arms, legs, and heads were being carried past him. But this time, he was not alone. Someone swam beside him. It was a woman, breasting the waves with powerful strokes, moving ever closer to the shore and trying to pull him along with her.

"Jill," he whispered, feeling he ought to say that name. "Where are you going? Take me with you."

He managed at last to roll over toward the other swimmer. The naked figure was female, strongly built, stroking powerfully through the bloody ocean. The red fluid washed over her shoulders and down her gleaming back, over her solid hips and well-muscled legs. Her arms cut through the liquid confidently, setting a direction and keeping to it. Her hair was wet and red, and it stuck to her shoulders. Her face was hidden in the sea.

"Jill," he said again. His voice seemed weak to him. The rising ocean carried him up, high, into the heavy air, and away from the other swimmer. It bore him out, away from the shore. He shouted to her. "Jill! Help me!"

The other swimmer turned toward him at last. The face was Elizabeth's. Blood dripped from her hair and ran down her cheeks. She paused in her swimming and held both arms out toward him and smiled at him. "Come. Come with me. Come to the shore with me. You have the strength. Use it. Come with me, of your own free will."

Venneman opened his eyes and stared at the ceiling. Daylight was fading into night again. Prey was stirring outside, and Jill was stirring beside him.

Venneman thought suddenly of his first kill, that strong young man in the Colorado mountains whose name he did not know. The body had surely been found not long after Venneman had drained it of blood. Had it ended up on the coroner's table on which Venneman had come back to life not long before? Who had the man been, and whom had he left behind? Who had mourned him at the time, and did she still mourn him now?

He turned on his side toward Jill. "Who was the first human being you killed?" he asked her.

She stared into his face, examining it. "Who was yours?" she asked him. "Was I the first?"

"No," he whispered.

She frowned. "Of course not. You couldn't have lasted that

long. I remember that feeling at the beginning. Too much hunger and thirst."

"So who was your first?"

"That guy from the university," Jill said. "That guard. Willie."

"Oh, Jill!" Venneman rolled onto his back again and stared at the ceiling. The light on it had faded, and now it glowed red. "He was alive when I saw him. I was driving away from the apartment building."

Jill chuckled, a harsh sound. "Without looking back, right?" She reached over and stroked his chest. Her touch seemed to radiate down through his torso.

Venneman sat up and moved away from her. I've never stopped looking back, he thought. I have eternity to look forward to, but I can't stop looking back instead. "Why did you kill Willie?"

"I didn't have any choice, Richie. Not at that point. You know how it is. I was a newly minted vampire. I needed blood desperately, and Willie was there. He seemed eager for me to take him. Why was that, do you suppose? And why was he there?"

Venneman glanced at her and then away. Her expression said that she had guessed the answer to both questions and asked them only to torment him. "But you didn't have to kill him," he said. "You could have taken only part of his blood and let him live."

"He didn't have a full supply left in him, Richie."

The mocking tone made him look at her again. She was smiling at him, but there was no love in the smile.

"He was a good man," Venneman said.

"He was a sack of blood. A half-empty sack, and the blood was old and worn out. He didn't satisfy my needs."

Willie had stood in the doorway of the bedroom watching her. He knew he should use the bedside telephone to call for the police and an ambulance, but instead he stood unmoving, struck by Jill's pale, quiet beauty.

It was more than a matter of perfection of form. Willie had seen women with better bodies in nude photographs in his favorite magazines. But Jill, even close to death as he feared she was, radiated something beyond physical loveliness. Her face, her breasts, her stomach, her legs—they struck into his soul and held him.

Jill's eyes opened. She frowned in puzzlement. She looked at Willie. "Who—?" she whispered, her voice rasping and weak.

Willie moved at last. "It's okay, ma'am. Take it easy. You've been hurt. I'll call for help."

Jill moved her head slowly from side to side. "No. Not hurt. Weak. Help me up."

What Willie had suspected was now confirmed. Venneman had attacked her in the same way he had attacked Willie. Willie was overcome by jealousy. That's ridiculous, he told himself. They've been living together for years. She has more right than I have.

Jill was struggling to raise herself on one elbow. Willie went quickly to the side of the bed and helped her, supporting her as gently as he could. He tried to look at both sides of her neck without alarming her. "Jill, isn't it? You sure you're okay, Jill? No pain of any kind?"

Jill looked at him, frowning again. "You're Willie. From the lab. I remember you. Why're you here? Where's Richie?" Suddenly she looked frightened. She clutched at his shoulders. "Did something happen? Is Richie okay? Where *is* he?"

"Richie's fine, ma'am. Honestly. I came here to find him, actually. Do you know when he'll be back?"

"Back? He left." Jill stared into space as though searching for a memory. "I don't remember..." Her gaze drifted down and focused on Willie's neck. She touched the small, fading scar gently. "What happened to your neck?"

"It's nothing, ma'am," Willie said quickly. "Nothing at all. You'd better lie back and let me call someone."

He tried to push Jill down onto the bed again, but she grabbed his shoulders again and prevented him. She stared at his neck. "Did it hurt?" she whispered.

Willie hesitated. "A bit, at first," he said. "Listen, I'd better—"

Jill's fingers dug into his shoulders. "Thirsty," she said.

"I'll go get you some water, okay?" Willie was afraid Jill might be more badly hurt than she realized or appeared to be. He would scarcely endear himself to Venneman by letting Jill hurt herself. "Please, ma'am, Jill, you just relax and take it easy. I'll get you some water and then I'll call someone."

He tried to pull away, but he couldn't break Jill's grip.

She twisted to one side suddenly, and Willie felt himself being lifted off his feet and flipped over her. He landed on his back on the bed, and Jill landed on top of him. He could feel the blood-soaked sheet squelching faintly beneath his head. He could smell the sickeningly sweet smell of her blood. He stared up at Jill's face, stunned by her beauty and the animal strength that radiated from her. He felt weak again, unable to push her off and get away.

Jill lowered her head slowly and kissed the scar on his neck. She licked and mouthed the scar and sucked gently on it.

A thrill ran through Willie's body. She's going to do it to me, too! he thought. He relaxed and surrendered himself to the coming pleasure.

But when Jill bit into Willie's neck, her teeth crunching through the just-healed muscles and tendons and down to the carotid artery, all he could feel was agony.

Too late, he began to fight back. Jill's arms and legs were wrapped around him, imprisoning him. Her head was forcing his to one side, exposing his neck even more. He was weak and growing weaker. He tried to scream, but only a thin whine came out. She was tearing him apart, ripping his life away from him.

He was fading away. He knew, filled with despair, that he had lost and was dying. The sucking, slurping sounds of her feeding on him were the last sounds Willie ever heard.

Jill rose from Willie Gold's still body and stood beside the bed, looking down at herself. She walked across the room and closed the bedroom door so that she could look at herself in the full-length mirror screwed to the back of the door. She felt alive and vibrant, delighting in the beauty and strength of her naked body. Now she remembered everything and understood everything.

Willie had provided her with only half a meal. It was enough to give her strength and fully awaken her new appetite.

Now she needed far more.

"So I hunted for nights on end and slept during the daytime. But you must know all about that, Richie. Henry told me it's that way for everyone at the beginning. Every vampire, I mean." She sat up. "And now it's nighttime again, and I haven't fed in days. I was too eager to find you, once I sensed how close I was to you. But now I need to drink again. Don't you, Richie? Don't you need it, too? Come with me, Richie. Henry taught me how to hunt as a pair. Now I'll show you. Come, Richie." She smiled her predatory smile at him. "We used to do everything together, when we were human. Let's do this together now."

TEN

And so they hunted together through the night.

Watching Jill, Venneman realized for the first time that he had no hunting technique. From the very first, he had found his victims entirely by chance. When enough time had passed since his last feeding and he could no longer ignore the need for more blood, he would wander the darkest streets until he encountered a lone walker, and then he would strike. He acted from necessity and against his own wishes, driven by his need.

Jill entered into the hunt with enthusiasm. For her, it was something active and positive, an activity filled with pleasure, struggle, victory, fulfillment, a sense of accomplishment.

He told himself that this proved his moral superiority to Jill. But he could see that she was enjoying every instant of her eternal life, while he was managing only to endure the endless hours of his.

Jill insisted that they seek out the most heavily frequented sidewalks in the city. They strolled along arm-in-arm, past the theaters on 14th Street and the restaurants on Larimer.

There was enough light from the streetlights to overwhelm the red glow Venneman had come to rely on at night both for vision and for comfort. Its absence made him feel uneasy. The crowds were thick here on almost any evening, and noisy music blasted out of some of the doorways. It amused Venneman to notice how many of the younger revelers, with their pale faces and dark clothes, looked like the vampires of old movies, whereas he and Jill looked like ordinary mortals.

And yet not quite like ordinary mortals—not judging from the reactions of other pedestrians, anyway. The two of them drew the eyes of the passers-by, who stared at them with open fascination and interest. Jill squeezed Venneman's arm to her side and said to him in a low voice, "Remember how we were both frightened by the way people used to look at us? How stupid we were!"

Venneman looked down at her in surprise. Yes, she was smiling widely, delighted by the mingled fascination and unease of the human beings surrounding them. Her eyes were wide, as though to take in as much of it as possible.

"Look at them," she whispered. "Men and women both, they can't take their eyes off us. My God, Richie!" She squeezed his arm against her side again. "You sure it was a woman who envamped you?"

"Shit," Venneman muttered. "Yes, I'm sure." A woman who had chosen him deliberately, and who would perhaps be calling to him again, blood to blood, as she had said she would. He looked around, suddenly uneasy. No, there was no sign of Elizabeth. These were all human beings. Or so he thought. He wasn't sure, though, that he could tell the difference. "How do you recognize another vampire?" he asked Jill.

"I can't describe it. You just know it when you meet one. Can't you tell?"

"I don't know. I told you, I've never met another one before you. Not since the woman who made me into one." Perhaps I've run into endless numbers of them, he thought, and didn't know it. Again he looked around uneasily, looking for something different in the passing faces, but not sure what that difference would prove to be.

"It's too noisy and crowded here," Jill said. "Makes it hard to cut someone out."

"Cut out?" Venneman repeated. "That's what cowboys say about cattle."

Jill nodded. "That's the idea, pardner. That's what they are. Come on. Let's try a side street."

The turned on 15th and walked downhill toward Market Street. "What's ahead?" she asked.

"More of the same, I think. Not so many people walking, though."

"Good."

At first they ran into crowds of people on Market Street as well. But those passed by, and then there was a period during which they encountered only lone pedestrians.

"I thought you wanted the crowds," Venneman said.

"Not for the kill, just the warmup. It gets me juiced."

Juiced. Venneman turned the word over in his mind and decided he didn't like it.

They were now many blocks past the area of renovated industrial buildings that had been turned into restaurants and offices. Now they were in an area of old buildings badly in need of renovation, of broken sidewalks, of almost no traffic and no working streetlights. Venneman felt that he could see properly again. He straightened up, realizing for the first time that he had been hunching over defensively.

"The light is so lovely out here, away from the manmade lights," Jill said. "You see it, don't you? That grey light? Henry could see it, too. He said he thought it came from the stars."

"Yes," Venneman said, "I see it." But for me, it's no longer grey. It's the color of the blood that fills the world. If Jill and Henry were seeing by the light of the stars, then what light did he see by? Could it be the glow of the Earth's molten core, gleaming up through the layers of rock and dirt and roots and worms, shining up through the ground and from the walls of buildings and reflecting from the sky? The fierce sun hidden at the heart of the world, was he alone in seeing it?

"Here we go," Jill said. She was looking at another lone pedestrian coming toward them along the sidewalk. It was a young man, walking carefully and squinting at the ground, trying to see in the almost complete darkness. Jill stopped moving, and Venneman stood quietly beside her.

The young man almost bumped into them. He became aware of them at the last moment and gasped and stumbled back. "Jesus!" he said. "Sorry, folks."

"That's okay, no problem," Jill said. Her voice was silver in the darkness. "We're having trouble finding our way, too. Where are you headed?"

The young man was staring into the darkness, trying to see her face. To Venneman, his interest was obvious. He named a new restaurant on Larimer. "I'm supposed to meet some friends there. I couldn't find parking over there. I don't know how I ended up so far away."

Venneman sensed the attention Jill was focusing on the man. He realized that she was doing the same thing to the young man that Elizabeth had done to him, and it was having the same effect. The young man's breath was coming faster, and he seemed unable to look away from Jill's shadowy figure. He had ceased to notice Venneman's presence entirely.

Jill's hand slipped down Venneman's arm until she was gripping his hand. She held it tightly. With her other hand she reached out slowly toward the young man. She placed her palm lightly on his cheek. At the unexpected touch, he flinched momentarily. Then he grew still again, calmed by her touch.

Gentled, Venneman thought.

"Come with me instead," Jill said. She took her hand away from his face, reached down, and took one of his hands. She walked on into the darkness, Venneman on her right, the young stranger on her left.

Venneman opened his mouth to say something, but Jill squeezed his hand urgently, and he said nothing.

They walked for half a block before Jill found what she was looking for. They were in an area of old warehouses, some still in use, but most long abandoned. A row of the abandoned ones was being demolished. Fragments of walls still stood, with cranes looming over them.

Jill led the two men behind one of these partial walls. Still holding onto Venneman, she pushed the young man gently against the wall. He stood there still staring at her, still trying to see her, held firmly in place by her hand and her vampire strength.

For just a moment, alarm showed on his face. He grabbed at her wrist and tried ineffectually to shove her hand aside. "Who are—"

"Ssh," Jill said. "It's all right." She leaned forward and kissed him. He responded immediately, reaching for her.

Venneman wanted to look away but couldn't. He had felt aroused by their kiss, as though something had been transmitted through Jill's hand. He couldn't remember ever before watching two people kiss. On the screen, yes, but never in real life.

Jill had batted the young man's hands aside when he reached for her. Now she put her hand against his chest again. "We'll do this my way," she told him. "Keep your hands by your side and let me do all the work."

She moved her hand slowly down his chest and over his stomach to his trousers. She hooked her fingers over the waistband and with a quick, powerful jerk tore his trousers open. Still holding Venneman's hand with her right hand, with her left she yanked her victim's trousers and undershorts down to his ankles, handling him as roughly as his clothing. The young man said nothing in protest. He was breathing rapidly and hoarsely. His legs were shaking and goosebumps covered his thighs.

Venneman was astonished to see that the man had an erection. Why wasn't he wilting in fear? But he recalled his own reaction to Elizabeth before she had killed him, and he knew that his surprise was silly.

As Jill knelt down and leaned forward to take the man's penis in her mouth, she gripped Venneman's hand even tighter. By now, Venneman had forgotten all about the incongruity of his situation and any distaste at being a voyeur. He watched in astonishment as the penis disappeared into Jill's mouth and then appeared again. He was too amazed by everything Jill had done so far and too fascinated by what he was seeing now to say anything or to try to stop her.

And he was too aroused to want to stop her.

The young man was moaning. His knees began to buckle. Jill pulled away suddenly and looked up at Venneman. "Richie," she said quite calmly, "grab his hands and hold them behind him." She let go of Venneman's hand at last.

Her victim was halfway to a kneeling position when Venneman did as Jill had ordered him. The young man became aware of Venneman's presence only then and tried to rise. "Hey!" he shouted. "What the fuck—?" Venneman pushed him down all the way to his knees. The victim looked around wildly in the darkness.

Jill slapped him. For her, it was a light, careless blow, but it knocked the young man off his knees, and he would have fallen if Venneman hadn't pulled him back upright. He drew in a breath to yell again, but Jill put her palms against his cheeks and kissed him. Again he calmed down and relaxed.

Even remembering his own encounter with Elizabeth, Venneman was surprised. Did he have this much power, too, he wondered, or was Jill at some higher level of vampirism than he? Or some higher level of sexuality?

Again, the young man was visibly aroused. Jill lifted her mouth from his and whispered, "We're vampires, sweetie. We're going to suck the blood out of you. We're going to give you more pain than you've ever felt before."

"No!" It was a sigh, a faint sound, irrelevant against the force of the night.

"Yes," Jill said. She bent down and kissed his neck. Venneman watched her lips move over the young man's skin, watched her tongue lick him gently, and he imagined her doing that to him. He remembered how soft her lips were, how her tongue had felt in his mouth a few hours earlier. He watched her open her jaws.

Her lips drew back. She put her teeth firmly against her victim's skin and began to bite down, slowly, deliberately. She was deriving as much pleasure from the feeling of flesh and cartilage parting beneath her teeth and from her victim's drawn-out agony as she would from the taking of the blood itself, Venneman realized. Watching, he was simultaneously horrified and aroused.

The young man sobbed. "No! Please don't!" But Jill's jaws kept closing, driving her teeth slowly deeper and deeper into his neck. He began to struggle at last, but Jill put her arms around him, trapping his arms against his side, and she pulled him sideways to the ground, yanking his wrists from Venneman's hands, and twined her legs about his, trapping them. She rolled him over so that she was on top of him, all the while biting further into him.

At last she reached a major blood vessel and began to feed, sucking his blood in eagerly and swallowing it noisily. Blood ran out of her mouth and dripped onto the ground.

After a while, she tore herself away and looked around, her eyes momentarily glazed. Then she looked at Venneman. "Your turn," she said. "Not too much."

She released her victim and climbed to her feet. The young man thrashed about weakly, trying to push himself to his knees. Jill watched him for a moment. Then she smiled at Venneman and said, "Calm yourself down first, Richie. Remember, nothing sexual, or we'll be stuck with him forever."

Venneman scowled at her and dropped to his knees. He

grabbed the young man's shoulders and flipped him over, face up again.

"No!" the young man said again. "Please, no more!"

"Shut up!" Venneman growled at him between clenched teeth. He bent down quickly, putting his mouth over the ragged wound Jill had torn in the man's neck, and pulled in a mouthful of blood. The blood burned in his mouth, as it always did now.

The young man whined with delight, as Venneman's victims always did now.

Venneman spat the blood out and wiped the acid remnants from his lips. He flung the young man down on the ground and stood up. "Satisfied now?" he said to Jill.

She looked at him and then down at the young man lying stunned on the ground between them. "How could you waste it?" she said. "What's wrong with you?" She began to kneel down.

Venneman caught her shoulder and pulled her back up. "Leave him, or you'll kill him."

"So what? You've already ruined this city for us because of that woman you killed. Another one won't make it any more dangerous here for us."

"There's no need. You've had enough for one feeding. There's no need to kill."

Jill let him lead her away. She looked back reluctantly over her shoulder until their nearly unconscious victim was hidden by the partial wall. Then, as though a switch had been thrown, she turned her attention fully to Venneman. "Now you can see what Henry taught me," she said. "See how much better it is when two vampires work together? See how I was able to get sexual pleasure and get his blood heated up, and still not create another vampire?"

"What would you say about a human being who tortured his domestic animals while killing them for food?"

Jill laughed. "There probably are human beings who do just that, Richie. Why not, if it gives them pleasure?"

Venneman stared at her, searching for words. All he could think to say was, "I don't understand what's happened to you, Jill."

She put her arms around his neck and pulled his face down to hers. They kissed for a long, slow time. Her mouth tasted of blood, burning Venneman's tongue. In her mouth, though, it excited him.

When they drew apart, Jill whispered, "You happened to me, Richie. Don't you remember? Have you already forgotten that you killed me and made me a vampire?"

Venneman put his hands over his face to hide his sudden tears. "Why do you keep saying that?" he said. "Why are you torturing me with it?"

"Because I hate you for it, Richie. We all hate the one who envamped us. Henry taught me that, too."

Venneman lowered his hands and stared at her. "That's not true. I don't..." His voice trailed away as he realized that he did. That was the missing purpose in his new, never–ending life, the lack he had been unconsciously aware of all this time: the need to find and destroy Elizabeth.

"I can't do anything to you physically," Jill said. "So I'm stuck with the psychological part. I'm going to stay with you for the next few thousand years, and I'll keep reminding you just what you did and how evil you are for doing it. I'm also going to keep bringing out in you the sexuality you hate so much.

"So," she said after a moment, "now let's go do the same thing again, but this time with a woman. Just for you, Richie, dear."

Venneman shook his head. "I'm going home." He turned and began to walk away.

Jill caught up with him and linked arms with him. "Home," she repeated. "What a wonderful, sweet word that is. Something vampires don't ever really have. I'm coming with you, of course. I'm staying with you, Richie. Remember?"

ELEVEN

Venneman looked around his apartment. Home, yes—it had been that. He had done what he could to make it a home for himself—a real, human home. The television set and the newspaper on the coffee table symbolized his continuing contact with the human race. But now, even if the killing of Geraldine Travers hadn't made it necessary for him to leave Denver, the apartment would no longer be his home. Not with Jill Kennedy in it. Nor would she allow any other place ever to be home to him in the future. She had made that clear.

He stared at her silhouetted against the city lights. She was standing in front of the glass door that led to his balcony, looking out over the nighttime city and smiling. "So much healthy life out there, waiting for us to take it. Isn't it a wonderful thought, Richie? I like this city. I'm sorry you spoiled it for us."

He wondered how she had tracked him down. Perhaps it was something akin to what Elizabeth had talked about, the calling of the blood, victim's to vampire's, vampire's to victim's. Perhaps he had unknowingly been calling Jill to him because of his longing for the life he had lost when he had, as he had thought, killed her. Whatever it was, she seemed to think that she could always find him, that he could never escape from her. He assumed she was right about that. She seemed to know so such more about the vampire state than he did. She had had a teacher, whereas he had had to learn everything by himself.

"Why did you leave Henry?" he asked her.

Jill turned from the window and glanced at him, then turned back to the lights of the city. "You make it sound like a broken romance," she said. "You can't think in such terms anymore, Richie. When you're eternal, and you can only safely have sex with your own kind, and there aren't very many of you, then you can expect to spend time with the same few people over and over as the centuries go by. The problem is, vampires don't like to spend too much time with each other. We're solitary by nature. Solitary predators. We need each other sexually, but I think we don't really like each other. So I'll be seeing Henry again, and we'll spend another short time together. Someday, somewhere. For the moment, though, I had learned as much from him as I needed to know, and I was eager to find you and to start treating you to some hell on earth. I figure I'll devote the next two or three thousand years to that, and then before I get tired of the game, I'll move on."

Venneman tried to imagine thousands of years of the sort of conversations they had been having. He shivered. "You think you can stand living with me for that long, being the solitary predator you are?"

Jill laughed. "Being with you is a kind of hunting. Don't you get it yet?"

All too well, he thought. But she should have said that being with him was, for her, a kind of feeding. He tried another tack.

"Won't you get bored with tormenting me long before a few thousand years have passed?"

"That's a point," Jill nodded. "I'm already getting bored. While I was tracking you down, I kept thinking up cutting things I'd say to you, and it seemed to me that two or three thousand years might not be enough. But I guess I'd forgotten how boring a man you are. Maybe I'll only last for a couple of years before I move on again."

"Henry wasn't boring, I suppose."

Jill turned away from the window so that he could see and appreciate fully her wide, happy smile of reminiscence. "No," she said, "Henry was never, ever boring. I'm already looking forward to spending a long time with him in the future, after I've done all I can to you. Henry had done things with his life, Richie, unlike you. I mean, even before he was envamped, he had done things, interesting things—been places, broken laws, made love to many women and quite a few men. Then, when he was envamped, he embraced his new vampire state and started *really* enjoying life. I told you he's been a vampire for a long time, didn't I?"

"Since the time of the American Revolution, you said," Venneman replied, resigning himself to learning more about Henry than he wanted to know. He walked over to the couch and sat down heavily.

"His full name is Henry Hapgood," Jill said. "He was sent out to America to help manage his father's properties here, a few years before the Revolution. He was in trouble in England, and his father and older brother gave him the choice of going out to the colonies and staying there for the rest of his life, or going into the army. The alternative was to be cut loose without any money at all."

"Sounds like an utterly fascinating guy," Venneman said. "I can see why you like him—a man who was so despised by own family that they sent him three thousand miles away and told him never to come back home again."

Jill smiled slightly. "You should hear what he did in England to get himself into such trouble in the first place. He told me the most amazing stories. Anyway, Henry said that he didn't like the idea of wearing a uniform and having other people in uniforms trying to kill him. But he hated the idea of being cut off without funds even more, so he chose to come to America."

She came over to the couch and sat down beside Venneman before continuing. "Henry said that when he got here, the man working for his father managing some property in Boston expected Henry to sit behind a desk all day copying papers. Henry had different ideas, but he couldn't live without the stipend from his father, so he bore with it for a few months. Then he went to bed with a young man in Boston and woke up a vampire."

Venneman grimaced in disgust.

Jill noticed the gesture and laughed at him. "Which part bothers you more, Richie? Henry's being envamped, or his having sex with another man?"

Venneman refused to answer.

Jill waited for a few seconds, and then she shrugged and continued her story. "When fighting broke out, Henry did what he could to help the colonists. Not because he cared about the politics. He said it was because he couldn't look at a Redcoat without seeing his father and brother and all their friends, and he loved the idea of the child—the colonies—defeating and destroying the father."

"Except that England used to be called the Mother Country," Venneman pointed out, "not the Father Country."

Jill waved her hand in a gesture of irritation. "Never mind that. Anyway, Henry also liked the war itself, because he could roam around the battlefields at night after a battle, looking for men who had just died or were still dying."

"And help them along?"

Jill laughed. "Exactly. Help move them along on their passage. And of course when daylight came and whichever army had won explored the battlefield, they didn't bother examining the wounds to see what had killed the men. No autopsies in those days. They were more concerned with burying the dead. Henry said he's never again fed so well as he did during that war and the Civil War."

War. The idea of using the killing of man by man as a cover for the killing of man by vampire had never occurred to Venneman before. It was clever, he had to admit. Brilliant. And there was always war going on somewhere in the world. "It's worth considering," he said, thinking aloud.

"What is?"

"Going to wherever there's a particularly vicious war underway and doing what Henry did. It's the perfect cover."

"I thought about it," Jill said, nodding. "After Henry told me his story. But I decided I didn't like the idea. For one thing, it's hard to travel in the places where there are wars going on. Transport has been disrupted, so you have to walk a lot. Which makes for slow going, since we can only travel at night."

Venneman almost told her that that no longer applied to him, but at the last moment he decided to keep his secret to himself.

"Even if there were some way around that problem," Jill went on, "there'd be no thrill in it. No hunt, no chase, no seduction. Just helpless dead people. Or dying people, but also pretty helpless. I wouldn't get the charge out of it that I get out of drawing someone who's healthy and young away from the protection of the other human beings and then watching them while they realize what a big mistake they've made." She laughed, an expression of remembered pleasure. "Like that guy we took tonight. Did you see his face when I told him what we were going to do? Did you hear him?"

"I heard him," Venneman whispered. I heard his moan of pleasure when I drew his blood. He'll be haunted by me, too, another one roaming the city searching for me.

He tried to force the image away and said, "Henry only got the benefit of two big wars. He should have gone back to Europe. There's been so much more blood shed there during the last two hundred years than here."

"He did go back," Jill said. "Of course, he couldn't do it in the early days. He had to wait until the development of the Concorde, so that he could travel from here to England entirely during one night. When that became available, he did it."

"I wonder how the man who made Henry a vampire got here, then," Venneman said.

"You're assuming that man came over from England," Jill said. "Or somewhere in Europe, anyway. Or that the one who envamped *him* did, or someone back along the chain. That's because of those stupid old movies you used to like, the ones on TV where all the vampires had Transylvanian accents or whatever. I don't think you should assume that vampires came from Europe originally. I think they've always been around, evolving along with mankind."

"That's ridiculous," Venneman said. "If it were all part of evolution, then there'd be cat vampires to prey on cats, and dog vampires to prey on dogs, and monkey vampires to prey on monkeys, and so on."

"How do you know there aren't?" Jill asked him. "After all, until it happened to you, you didn't know there were human vampires, did you?"

"It's a meaningless discussion," Venneman said. "There's no such thing as evolution, anyway. Man was made by God in His image."

"Christ," Jill said, "here we go again. All right, look at it this way. However mankind originated, the Indians didn't originate here, right?"

"No," Venneman said. "Their ancestors came across over the Bering Strait land bridge. Supposedly."

"Right. So vampires came over here from Asia the same way, and at the same time, because some of those early Indians were vampires. So there've been vampires here in America for as long as there've been human beings."

"Henry could have gone back to Europe the same way. And found lots of wars along the way, as he walked from Siberia to England."

Jill glared at him. "The Bering Strait land bridge disappeared long ago, in prehistoric times, as you know. And there's water between France and England, as you also know."

"I bet Alaska and Siberia are connected by ice during the winter," Venneman said. "Even if they aren't, Henry could walk across under the water. Same thing for going from France to

England. A vampire should be able to do that, shouldn't he? For that matter, a vampire should be able to walk across the sea floor of the Atlantic, all the way from the East Coast of the U.S. to Britain."

"You're being a fool," Jill said. "We have to breathe, too. You know that. You're being a fool deliberately. For a change."

Yes, Venneman thought, we have to breathe. And we have blood circulating in us, and our hearts beat. They beat powerfully, far more powerfully than human hearts, and our blood pumps more vigorously, and we breathe more deeply and with more zest.

But why? If we're dead, why do we need any of those things?

And would we die without them?

If mankind ever achieved space travel, could Venneman find a way of going into space and thrusting himself into the vacuum and then die at last? Unlike his attempt to kill himself with sunlight, in his early days as a vampire, he could so position himself in space that he would not be physically able to run to shelter. He could go out on the surface of the moon, far from any space base, wearing a suit he had sabotaged. The suit would fail and he would be stuck out there, far from rescue, far from air and heat.

But would he die even then? Would he instead go into some kind of coma, perhaps, and revive as soon as he was discovered and brought back into normal air and heat? Would he revive as some even stronger, fiercer vampire creature? Needing more blood, perhaps, and less able to control his lust for it—and perhaps suffering even more when he took it. He told himself that his attempt to destroy himself with Dinsmuir's experiment should have taught him that the results of any further such attempts might be far worse than his present situation.

"Anyway," Jill said, "Henry flew back to England when supersonic flights first became available and headed for what had been the family's estate. He had cut off all contact with them as soon as he was envamped, of course."

"You mean he didn't send them yearly Christmas cards?" Venneman asked. "Having wonderful time. Wish you were here so that I could suck your blood."

"Henry felt that *they* had been sucking *his* blood during the years he lived in England. Anyway, the family mansion was gone. It used to be out in the countryside, but it's been swallowed up by London during the last two hundred years. Where the house used to be, there was a big, new shopping center. So Henry investigated further, and he discovered that the family had lost its fortune a hundred years earlier and they had died out. No living descendants. Except Henry, and he's not really a descendant."

"He's a descendant," Venneman said, "but he's not really living."

Jill looked momentarily startled. "Of course he's living!"

"We're the undead."

"Movie shit again," Jill said disgustedly. "We're obviously alive. I keep telling you, Richie. We're the next step in evolution."

"Evolution involves birth, not death," Venneman insisted.

"Evolution requires both. And we combine both."

"Can we have babies?" Venneman asked her. "Can we pass on our wonderful traits that way? Can you get pregnant?"

"I don't know. I didn't get pregnant by Henry, but that

doesn't mean anything. Maybe I'll get pregnant by you, Richie. Maybe we'll have a beautiful little vampire baby together."

"And it will suck its mother's blood while it's still in the womb," Venneman said. "Even when you were human, you never showed any love for babies. The way you are now, I can't see you as a loving mother. What would you feed a baby like that—bottles of warm human blood?"

"No, Richie. Bottles of *hot* human blood."

"Christ," Venneman muttered.

Jill frowned. "I have the feeling that I can't get pregnant, somehow. I know that doesn't make much sense, and I know that a human woman with any sense doesn't depend on a feeling like that. But this is different. It's more than a feeling. It's some kind of knowledge."

Venneman felt it, too: a deep knowledge of his own sterility. "So vampires can't procreate," he said. "We can only create new vampires by killing human beings. That's not evolution," he repeated.

"By killing them while having sex with them," Jill corrected him. "We're not killing them. We're giving them the gift of sex with a vampire, and many human beings would probably be willing to die for that gift even without hope of resurrection, if they knew how wonderful it is. But we're also giving them the gift of resurrection and eternal life. Not the religious fantasy you always befuddled your mind with, Richie. The real thing."

"Eternal life without love, without family, without children, without human contact."

"We have human contact," Jill said, laughing. "We contact them very intimately."

"You know that's not what I meant."

"I know. Look, Richie. Human beings are pack animals, and we're not. We're not dogs or coyotes. We're solitary hunters. We're tigers. We're bears. We're sharks. We're the top of the food chain. We come together in pairs occasionally for mutual pleasure, and then we split up again, just like the great hunters do. You have to learn to think in different terms if you're going to be happy as a vampire."

Venneman sighed. "I'll never be happy as a vampire. Why do you have so much trouble understanding that?"

"You mean you'll never *try* to be happy as a vampire," Jill said.

"I mean," Venneman said, "I'll never *want* to be happy as a vampire."

"What, you'd rather go back to being a human being?"

"If there were some way I could, yes, I would," Venneman said. He decided he would not tell her how he had tried to merge back into human society, both because he feared her scorn at his having attempted it, and because he feared her greater scorn at his failure.

"They hate us," he said. "It's not just cultural conditioning—the movies and books, the scary Transylvanian count, the bats, the creepy old castle. It's more than that. They know that we'll murder them with horrible pain and without hesitation. We want their blood and their life, and we don't care about them in any way."

"Of course we don't care about them," Jill said. "The lion doesn't care about the zebra's feelings. That's the way nature works."

"At least the zebra doesn't lie awake at night worrying about lions, or have nightmares about them. We're in the nightmares and waking thoughts of human beings all the time."

"Are we?" Jill asked. "How often did you think about vampires before you met your first one? Seriously think about them, I mean, as opposed to when you were watching those dumb movies?"

Ignoring her, Venneman said, "Another difference is that the zebra has a fighting chance. A lot of prey animals are pretty dangerous fighters when they're cornered, no matter how big and powerful the predator is. Humans have no way of defending themselves against us. All those superstitions are meaningless—crucifixes and garlic, whatever else."

"You've checked those out?"

Venneman nodded. "Yeah, I've checked them out."

"Well, see, that's because we're not magical beings. We're just part of nature, as I've been telling you, so magical charms aren't effective against us. Anyway," she added, "they aren't entirely defenseless."

Venneman looked at her. She was frowning, and the muscles in her jaw bunched. She rubbed her chest unconsciously. "What do you mean?" he asked her.

"One of mine, he came when I called him for another feeding, but he came with a goddamned wooden stake!" She laughed harshly. "Talk about watching too many of those movies! He thought he'd be able to kill me that way. Didn't work, of course, but it did hurt like hell. He was smart enough to come to me during the daytime, while I was still asleep. Well, that was my fault. I didn't think ahead when I called him. It was almost morning already. Anyway, he broke in while I was asleep and pounded the damned thing into me." She laughed again, a more genuinely happy sound this time. "But it was worth it just to see the look on his face when I woke up and pulled the stake out of my chest and the bleeding stopped right away. And then..."

"And then?"

"And then," she whispered, grinning fiercely, "then I made him pay for hurting me."

She glanced at the window. The sky was glowing faintly with the first hint of predawn light. "Day's coming, Richie," she said. She turned toward him. "It's time for bed." She reached out and stroked his cheek. "It's time for sex."

His need for her flared up at her touch, and he realized that it had never quite died away. Even during the most hostile part of their conversation, it had been there, still alive, waiting to be fanned to full blaze. Back in the laboratory, looking at Dinsmuir's experiment, he had wondered what it would be like to have sexual desire burning inside him like that manmade sun. Now he knew it was more terrifying than anything else about his vampire state.

Hours later, well into their protracted, violent lovemaking, the sound of Jill's heartbeat and the smell of her vampire blood suddenly hit Venneman like a physical blow.

It was like his reaction to human blood during his first days as a vampire, before his attempt to destroy himself with Dinsmuir's machine. But it was even stronger, just as the vampire heartbeat was more powerful than the human one and vampire blood more turbulent.

He had been holding himself up above her on straightened arms, staring down at her in fascination and watching the snarls and anger and hatred in her face as they ground their hips together. Now he bent his elbows and lowered himself slowly toward her, drawn uncontrollably by her blood.

But it's vampire blood, he told himself. You know what that means! Elizabeth showed you. Stop!

The song of her blood overpowered him. He lunged, opening his mouth and biting at the side of her neck.

"Richie!" Jill yelled.

The skin and flesh and muscle and ligament were stronger, harder than those of humans. Venneman bit hard, again and again, penetrating slowly.

Jill struggled beneath him, pounding her fists against the sides of his head. The blows dazed him, but he could not stop. He held her shoulders and clamped his teeth into her as hard as he could. Slowly the tissue parted between them.

"Richie!" Jill screamed in agony.

Venneman reached blood.

Pumped by her vampire heart, it shot into his mouth. It was electricity. It was pure life, pure vitality. It was sweeter and headier than anything he had ever imagined.

He sucked greedily at her, pulling her blood into him. Jill shrieked, but the sound was weak and muffled. She hit at him, but each blow was weaker and less effective. She tried to pull away from him, but he was far too strong for her now. All the while, their pelvises kept up their rhythmic movement against each other.

Eventually, Venneman could suck no more blood from Jill. She lay unmoving beneath him, her eyes open and staring up at the ceiling. Her blood released its hold over him, and Venneman pulled himself away from her.

He slid away from her across the bed and sat cross-legged, staring at her. He was stunned by what had happened. Elizabeth had taught him about the foulness of vampire blood, which protected vampires from each other. Dinsmuir's machine had changed even that, then.

Venneman reached out hesitantly and put his hand on Jill's chest. He held his breath and concentrated, dropping the guard he had erected months ago against the sounds of others' hearts beating and blood pumping. He began to hear the life of the human beings who lived in other apartments in the same building, but he could hear nothing from Jill.

Venneman put his head in his hands. The first time, he had taken away from Jill the eternal life of her soul, but at least he had given her another kind of eternal life in exchange. This time, he had taken even that away from her.

He raised his head slowly and put his arms down. Hypocrite, he said to himself.

His grief was artificial. He was making himself feel what he thought he ought to feel. The truth was that he had missed the pleasure he had experienced before his exposure to Dinsmuir's machine, before his suicide attempt had transformed him and made human blood a physically repellent necessity. Now he had found that pleasure again—an even greater pleasure. It had taken him this long to discover that Dinsmuir's machine had given him something in return for what it had taken away. He had become a creature that fed with delight on vampires.

Venneman slid back down onto his side facing Jill. He put his hand across her unmoving chest and pressed his face against her cooling shoulder and drifted into sleep.

He drifted with her all day long on the sea of blood. In his dream, she was as lifeless as in the waking world. Her limbs floated up and down on the red swells, under the control of the living ocean. Venneman floated beside her, at peace for the moment, letting the current take them where it wanted. He heard the voices calling but didn't bother raising his head to try to see them. He and Jill floated side by side, both on their backs, and Venneman held her hand.

One of the calling voices became stronger than the others. It was a woman's voice, and it was calling his name over and over. "Richie! This way! Richie!" He knew it was Elizabeth's voice.

The current surged, pulling Venneman and Jill apart. He grabbed for her hand as it slid out from under his, but he could no longer see her. He was alone on the sea with only Elizabeth's distant, calling voice for company.

He awoke to see Jill standing with her back pressed against the bedroom wall, staring at him in wide-eyed terror.

"You pervert!" she screamed.

Venneman jumped from the bed. "You're alive! Thank God!" He stepped toward her, his arms out toward her. He wanted to embrace her in relief and in gratitude that he hadn't killed her after all. He wanted to feel her against him, warm and living again.

Jill's knees buckled and she slid down the wall into a sitting position. "Stay away from me," she whimpered.

"I'm so glad you're okay, Jill," Venneman said. He reached down and pulled her gently to her feet.

"No, don't hurt me again!"

"I'm not going to hurt you, Jill. I don't know what came over me. I'm just so relieved! But I guess I should have known you'd be okay. You can't kill a vampire that way, right?" He forced a laugh.

She looked up at him, afraid to meet his eyes. "You're not supposed to be able to feed on a vampire at all," she said. Her voice was weak and rough, like that of someone barely recovered from a draining illness. "I tried it with Henry, because he said to, and I had to spit it out."

"Yes," Venneman said, kneading her shoulders. "I guess I'm different."

And so was Jill. She was shorter and thinner than she had been the night before. Venneman looked down at her, looked her body over, and frowned at the strangeness of this change. "You remanufactured your blood," he said suddenly. "That's what it is. You used up energy and tissue to make new blood for yourself. That's why you look so different!"

Jill pushed his hands away and slid away from him. "I'm not smaller, you bastard, you're bigger. You took my blood and grew."

"Jill." Venneman stepped toward her again, raising his hands placatingly. "It won't happen again, I promise."

"Damned straight," she muttered. She collected her clothes from the floor, where she had scattered them the morning before, and pulled them on. "You'll never get another chance. I'm getting the fuck out of this place and away from you. If I spend time with someone else again, it'll be someone normal like Henry." She paused, breathing shallowly and rapidly, then forced herself to resume dressing. "I'm so damned hungry and thirsty, I feel like I'm dying. It's your fault."

Venneman watched her dress. She was shaking. He couldn't tell if it was from fear or weakness.

She headed for the apartment door. He could hear her

blood and heartbeat again. They were not as strong as before, but they were still stronger and more seductive than any human's, and he felt them drawing him toward her. He didn't want her to leave. He wanted her to stay with him and give him that unearthly pleasure again. He searched for something to say, something that would spark enough of her hatred and desire to hurt him that it would overcome her fear. "So Henry's a normal vampire, is he?" he said.

Jill stopped at the door and turned to him. "You were never much of a man," she said scornfully, "and now you're not even much of a vampire."

It was such a ludicrous perversion of badly written lines from second-rate movies that Venneman burst out laughing. Jill glared at him, but when he stepped toward her, the glare changed again to fear, and she yanked the door open and ran from the apartment.

Bloodlust raged in Venneman. He stepped forward, intending to run after her and drag her back.

He caught hold of the doorway and held on, warring with himself.

No, he told himself. You've done enough to her.

TWELVE

Venneman closed the door and looked around his apartment. It was his again. "I left her once," he said aloud, speaking to his apartment, "and now she's left me. Now we're even."

He was free of her and of the psychological torture she had planned for him.

Venneman stood in the middle of his living room and breathed deeply. He felt alive and vital as he hadn't in months.

It wasn't just because of Jill's leaving him alone and free again, he realized. It was also because of her blood. Because human blood was now so disgusting to him, he had been half starved all this time. He had been at far less than his potential strength and health. Vampire blood, he now understood, not only filled his needs and gave him exquisite pleasure in its taking. It also gave him more pleasure than human blood ever had and filled him with far more strength and vitality.

And size and height? Was Jill right about that?

He went into the bedroom and looked at himself in the mirror screwed to the back of the door. Perhaps he was slightly taller, judging as best he could by how close the top of his reflected head came to the wooden border at the top of the mirror. He went to the doorway and stood in it, looking up at the lintel. But he had never bothered doing that before, so doing it now told him nothing.

Venneman shrugged and put the question aside. What difference did it make? What counted was the way he felt now: stronger than ever and more alive. And more hopeful about the future.

He went back into the living room and picked up the newspaper. Because of Jill, he had not yet read this edition. The truth was that he usually threw the paper away unread. It was more the act of having a paper delivered every day that counted for Venneman, not the reading of it. The presence of the new newspaper at his door every morning, like the television set he so rarely turned on, were signs of his continuing attachment to the human race. Or at least of his attempted continuing attachment to it.

And now I don't even need to force myself to feed on them, he thought. Now I really can start trying to think of them as people again, as individuals, instead of just as prey.

Because now vampires are my prey.

He would have to learn to identify other vampires in the mysterious way Jill had said she could. And he would have to hope that there were more of them around than he had been assuming.

He unfolded the paper and sat down on the couch to allow himself a pleasant hour or two of reading it. He tried to concentrate on the great events shaking the world, reported under bold black headlines on the first page, but he found his attention wandering. These really were the little doings of little creatures, weren't they? Perhaps Jill was right about that. The paper's portentous tone seemed so silly to him.

He shook his head. No, he was just mentally tired after the emotional events of the last couple of days and nights.

No, he contradicted himself, I'm more alert and awake than ever.

He tried the second page instead, but the news on it seemed even less important than the major stories reported on page one. He went on, trying to absorb what he was reading, stories of disasters caused by nature or created by man, tragedies on an individual scale or a national one, but it became a stream of words without meaning, curious black marks without content.

When he was somewhere in the middle of the paper's main section, on a page headed *Science and Technology*, Venneman realized he was reading about Harold Dinsmuir. He stopped and began the article again.

Dinsmuir had called a press conference, bypassing normal peer review journals and going straight for glory. No surprise there, Venneman thought. What was surprising was, first, that the experiment Venneman had stopped prematurely in his attempt to destroy himself had been restarted, and, second, that despite the setback Dinsmuir had managed to collect enough supporting data to go public. Venneman read:

Professor Dinsmuir explained that his device is only big enough to prove the validity of his theories. To produce commercially significant quantities of power, Dinsmuir said, will require much bigger versions of the machine. He added that discussions are now underway with various private corporations and government agencies concerning funding for the construction of commercial power plants using his discovery.

When asked to describe the importance of this development, Professor Dinsmuir likened it to the discovery of fire. "Not even the Manhattan Project or the harnessing of steam or electricity compares to this," the physicist said. "None of those changed society the way my success with this experiment will. Hold on to your hats, boys and girls. We've been through the Steam Age and the Electricity Age, and those were pretty exciting, but now we're entering the Dinsmuir Age, and it's going to be the most exciting one of all."

Questioned about a series of mishaps that have dogged the project, Professor Dinsmuir brushed the questions aside and said that the incidents were coincidence and unimportant. He dismissed a reporter's suggestion that the incidents were proof that someone was trying to sabotage his experiment. "You've been reading too many thrillers," he quipped. Professor Dinsmuir then left for a meeting with the Secretary of Energy in Washington, leaving his assistant, a graduate student named Dale Whitmer, to deal with reporters' remaining questions.

Ms. Whitmer concurred with the professor's statement that the incidents of almost a year ago had not disrupted the project, although she expressed her sorrow at the mysterious disappearance of another assistant, a technician named Richard Venneman, whom she described as "a good friend."

Venneman's fiancée, Jill Kennedy, disappeared at the same time. A campus security guard named William Gold was found murdered at the apartment shared by Venneman and Kennedy. Police are searching for both for questioning in the case. Professor Dinsmuir's experimental device was reportedly disabled at about the same time, although it proved possible to restart the experiment with only minimal loss of data.

There were no photographs with the article, but reading the familiar names brought their faces back sharply to Venneman. Once again, he felt a pang of sadness at not having seen Dale in all this time, and he yearned to talk to her. She was perhaps the only person he knew who would be able to listen calmly to his story of what had happened to him, to believe him, and then to offer wise advice.

He shook his head at the impossibility of the idea. He went into the kitchen and rummaged around in the drawers until he found a pair of scissors, which he used to cut the article out of the paper. He folded the piece of newspaper carefully and put it in his shirt pocket. It was a link with the past, even if he could never go back to it.

He sat down on the couch again with the newspaper in his lap. He wasn't thinking of anything in particular; he was reveling in a feeling of melancholy. The loss of his past life no longer seemed to cut into him as fiercely as it once had. The pain had receded somewhat, declined to an ache rather than a sharp agony. Better to let it keep going in that direction, he thought. Let it keep fading away until I no longer notice it.

But I could call Dale, he thought suddenly. I could go to a public phone and phone her up. I remember both the lab number and her home number.

And what would you tell her? he asked himself. Would you tell her your story over the phone? Even Dale couldn't handle that. She'd call the police, and they'd find out where you called from, and then you'd have to deal with that.

On the other hand, he was planning to leave Denver

anyway.

He wrestled with the problem for a few minutes but could come to no resolution. Idly, he picked the paper up again and looked at the section that contained society news, gossip columns, advice columns, comics. The section was called Lifestyles.

I should start a newspaper for vampires, Venneman thought idly. I could call it Deathstyles. Wonder how I'd get the word out to potential subscribers, though. Leave flyers in graveyards?

He was amused at the off-center course of his own thoughts. It was, he thought, a reaction to his release from Jill. Short as their most recent time together had been, it had been long enough to oppress him and fill him with a dread of their future together as she had painted it.

He opened the Lifestyles section and found himself staring at a large photograph of Elizabeth.

Even in a photograph, her eyes held his gaze. He felt the strength flowing out of his hands and could barely hold onto the paper. She seemed to call him through the photograph. He could hear her voice in his mind. Richie, I need you again. Come to me, Richie.

He tore his eyes away from the picture and read the story underneath it eagerly.

Bestselling historical romance writer Elizabeth Vallé addressed a gathering of her fans in Denver by telephone last night from her mountain estate. The reclusive Ms. Vallé, who rarely ventures far from her retreat, has authorized this one photograph for use on her books and all other publicity. Unlike other bestselling writers, Ms. Vallé has never appeared on television talk shows or in person at dinners in her honor. She does, however, frequently speak to such gatherings via telephone.

"A writer!" Venneman said aloud, amazed. Well, it was probably a safer and easier way of getting money than the one he had chosen—stealing from his victims. And maybe she didn't have to do any research. Maybe she wrote from her memories of eras she had lived through. Just how old was she? When had she become a vampire, and how much history had she seen at first hand?

Her mountain estate, Venneman thought. That covers a lot of territory. Her retreat, from which she rarely ventures very far. But I know that she does occasionally venture a bit, and if she doesn't venture very far, then it's a pretty good bet that her home is near the town where...

His thoughts froze at that point, as if unable to confront the reality of the event. "Where I was envamped," he said aloud, forcing the words out. Where she envamped me. Where I lost my humanity and my soul and became what I am now.

Now he had a good use for a public telephone after all.

He picked up his keys and left his apartment, locking the door carefully, as he always did. Outside the building, the air was crisp and clear. Venneman paused to breathe the cold air deep into his lungs and to stare up at the night sky, filled with stars and awash in red. The distant suns were brilliant pinpoints of glaring red in the warm pink of the sky. He reached up toward their friendly light and stood for a moment with his arms up.

He lowered them slowly, then got in his car and drove to a

nearby convenience store to use the pay telephone.

He gave the information operator the name of the ski town where he had been envamped, and the name Elizabeth Vallé. What a beautiful name it is, he thought, struck by the sound of it when he spoke it aloud. And struck, too, by how much hatred he felt for her.

"I'm sorry, sir," the operator said, "that's an unlisted number."

"Oh, I see," Venneman said. "Must be a problem with all those bloodsucking fans. Okay, thanks."

So she does live in or near that town, he thought as he hung up. Good, that's a start.

His first impulse was to drive up there immediately and begin his search for her. But then he realized how great an advantage his ability to endure the sun gave him, and he decided to spend the night saying goodbye to the city he had lived in for the past ten months. He had grown fond of it during that time and regretted the need to move on.

I'll be back someday, he thought. It was a pleasing realization. The human beings who could recognize him, the former victims who wanted to be his victims again, would die off as the years passed, and in time Denver would be safe for him again. He could wait for twenty or fifty years and then come back.

He spent hours driving around the parts of the city he had frequented during his ten months of living there. The buildings and streets glowed at him with their own inner red light, brighter than ever before. It occurred to him that if the increase continued, the night would become as bright for him as the day, with only the color and source of the light being different.

He found himself near Larimer Street and decided to park and walk along the crowded sidewalks. Perhaps Jill would be there. Perhaps she hadn't yet left the city. She had complained about her hunger and thirst before leaving his apartment, and Larimer was the only area of the city that she knew where she could satisfy herself. He wasn't sure why he wanted to see her again, so soon after having been freed. Partly, perhaps, he wanted to reassure himself that she would continue to avoid him.

But he saw no sign of her among the crowds of human beings.

He walked slowly up and down the length of the block-long area where most of the restaurants and bars and people were, fascinated by their energy and the desperation of their search for pleasure and escape. Most of them were young. He wondered if they feared they would grow old before they had experienced everything the world had to offer.

There was one experience he could offer them, the existence of which they did not even suspect. Were he to describe it to them, they would react with fear and horror. Were they to experience it, they would spend the rest of their lives hunting him, wanting to experience it again.

A few hours earlier, he had lowered his guard against the sound of heartbeat and blood in an attempt to see if he had indeed murdered Jill a second time. He had not yet managed to reestablish the barrier fully. Now he became uncomfortably aware of the lives around him. Their excitement because of each other's presence, their hopes for entertainment and sex with each other that evening, elevated the volume and caused the pounding to leak through the barricade Venneman had built within himself. He stopped walking and closed his eyes for a moment, concentrating on rebuilding that wall, sealing it carefully.

The sounds faded away slowly, receding to a faint background pulsation, low enough to be pleasant instead of unsettling.

And he felt someone staring at his face.

Jill! he thought. His eyes snapped open.

Standing in front of him, staring up at him with longing, was the young man Jill had attacked the night before. "I know what you are," he said.

Venneman looked around quickly, but the hurrying crowds were ignoring them. He turned back to the young man. "You know very little, and you're better off that way. Forget what happened."

He turned away, but the other man caught his sleeve.

"Wait, please," the young man said. "I—I can't forget about it. I can't think of anything else. The woman said she was going to kill—"

"Shut up!" Venneman said. "For God's sake!" He looked around again, but fortunately no one had been listening to them. "Come on." Gesturing to the other man to follow, he hurried down the sidewalk to the end of the block and turned north on 15th, downhill. He could feel the other man close behind him. It made him nervous, as though he had become the hunted.

Away from the lights and crowds of Larimer, Venneman stopped and turned around. "Don't you have any sense?" he said angrily.

The young man shook his head. "Not anymore. Not since last night. You took it away from me."

Pity welled up in Venneman. "I'm sorry for that. But you'll do yourself no good following me. You'll have to go back to your normal life."

The young man shook his head again. He looked up at Venneman searchingly, pleadingly. "It won't mean anything to me anymore. It was like I was only half alive. I didn't really wake up until you ... until you..."

"You can't even say it," Venneman said scornfully. "How can you long for something you can't even name? She would have killed you if I hadn't stopped her. Then you wouldn't even be half alive, would you?"

"When she did it, it hurt me. It was awful. But you—that was different. You're vampires, both of you, aren't you?"

"She's a vampire," Venneman said. "I'm ... something else. Tell me your name."

"Larry," he said eagerly. "Larry Driscoll." He stepped even closer and bent his head. "Look, it's all healed! I'm ready again. You could do it to me again right now." He clutched at Venneman's clothing in his desperation. "Please! I have to have that again!"

Venneman pushed him away and watched him stumble from the force of the blow. "Larry," he repeated. The name had no power over him. Now that humans were no longer his natural victims, their names meant no more than anything else about them. They had become insignificant in every way. Jill had pretended to see human beings that way, and Venneman remembered that he had gone through a period of adopting the same pose, but he and Jill had both lied. To Venneman then and to Jill now, humans were an obsession. Rather, he corrected himself, their blood was an obsession. It was like water to a man in the desert. But now, for Venneman, other vampires and their blood had become the obsession.

Driscoll was keeping his distance, but he still stood with his neck exposed and a pleading look on his face. In the red glow of night, Venneman could see that the man's wound had completely healed. That was the only real good I did him, Venneman thought. I speeded the healing of the hole Jill tore in him.

"I don't want your blood," Venneman said. "It disgusts me. All human blood disgusts me."

"But—I don't understand! That's what you are! And last night—"

"Last night was her idea," Venneman told him. *"She* needs human blood."

"Then I'll have to find her," Driscoll said sadly. "I only found you by accident. I stayed around here, just in case, but I didn't know if you'd really be back."

"You won't be able to find her," Venneman said. "You might find someone else just like her, but if you do, you'll be in for more pain, like last night, and maybe death."

"But what am I going to do?" Driscoll cried. "How can I live without you?"

"Deal with it," Venneman said, turning around and walking away rapidly.

Driscoll was right behind him, hanging onto him. "No, please!" He was crying and stumbling, trying to hold Venneman back, trying to keep up with him.

Venneman turned, picked the man up, and threw him down the sloping street. "Leave me alone!" he screamed.

He ran, heading for his car, moving as fast as he could,

hoping that Driscoll would not able to get up in time or run as fast.

He reached his car without seeing any sign of the other man. He drove back to his apartment by a circuitous route. As far as he could tell, no one was following him.

What a waste of time his months in this city had been, he thought. He had spent them trying to become a human being again, or at least to act like one. This was the second time he had tried this, and he had failed both times. It was futile and silly. He was not a human being, and as he had told Larry Driscoll, he wasn't even a vampire. Following Jill's logic, he was something better than either, an even further step along the evolutionary road. But the only one of my kind in existence, he reminded himself. Some evolution!

All that his upward movement in the great chain of being had accomplished so far was to make him more solitary than any other being on earth, and at the same time more hunted.

During his human days, he had been pursued by men and women who wanted to use him for their pleasure despite his revulsion. Now he was being pursued by men and women who wanted to use him for their pleasure despite his pain. He had changed himself from a being hunted by those who wanted to destroy his soul to one who was hunted by former victims yearning to be his victims again. They pursued him and hungered for him. They were vampires to him.

No, he thought, their memory of me is a vampire to them, draining away their ability to enjoy normal human life. Larry Driscoll proves that. And Geraldine Travers. The ones who survive will keep looking for me. If they're unlucky, they'll find a vampire, and then they'll find violent and painful deaths. Some of them might even come back after death as vampires themselves! I thought I was choosing the more moral path by not killing my victims, but instead I've condemned them to lives of emptiness, dissatisfaction, and longing. Or to terrible deaths, followed perhaps by the curse of life after death as a vampire.

He reached his apartment and began the sad task of throwing away the human belongings with which he had surrounded himself during the previous months.

By morning, he was ready to leave behind him the pretense at life he had tried to create and take shelter in.

THIRTEEN

Venneman drove west on Interstate 70. Across the median, the eastbound lanes were heavy with morning rush-hour traffic. Occasionally he glanced over at the rows of slowly moving cars, each containing one or two half-awake, disgruntled human beings bound for another day of drudgery. Venneman drove swiftly westward on his nearly empty side of the highway, liking the symbolism of the difference between him and the human drivers heading the other way. His car contained only him, two suitcases of clothing in the trunk, and the morning newspaper, as yet unread, lying on the passenger seat.

The city was cold but sunny. It had been snowing heavily for days in the mountains. He would be leaving sunny skies behind him.

It struck him that he was leaving the city by the same route he had first entered it. That had been only a few days after his envamping, in a pickup truck belonging to the two off-duty policeman he had killed. He regretted that he had made no effort, during his months in Denver, to find out how much uproar had been caused by the discovery of their truck and the bear carcass in it. Surely their bodies had also been found, where he had flung them in the mountains, although he didn't really know that. What were their names? Venneman frowned, trying to remember, but could not bring them back.

He shook his head in momentary annoyance and then put the matter out of his thoughts. Anyway, he told himself, he regretted the death of the bear and her cub far more than that of the two men who had killed her.

He accelerated, hoping to make as good time as possible at the lower elevations, where the highway was still clear, hoping also to fill his mind with the business of driving the car and thus to drive away thought. He raced along the interstate, traveling backward to his vampire origin.

After a couple of hours, he began to encounter patches of ice on the highway. Snow was piled beside the road, and the fields to either side were solid white. He passed through road cuts where small frozen waterfalls hung from rock faces. The sky grew hazy, and the haze thickened into cloud cover. The light dimmed. Now the road itself was covered with a layer of hard-packed snow, the substrate the plows had not been able to scrape away.

Venneman turned off the interstate onto the state highway his road map indicated. Now that he was on it, he recognized it as the highway down which the two Denver policemen who had picked him up had driven to reach the interstate. He frowned, trying again to remember their names. Skip and ... Greg. Skip and Greg.

Had they had families? Had they left behind grieving widows and children? He had never thought of that before. Venneman sighed and shook his head. Pointless to worry about that now. He had been, in effect, young and naive at the time, the equivalent of an adolescent boy with too high a level of hormones and too low a level of social awareness. A newly minted vampire was just that impulsive and careless. He had learned a great deal since then. He had matured.

I'm a mature vampire, he thought. Henry Hapgood's a normal vampire, but I'm a mature one. So I'm much better than he is. He chuckled, in good spirits for the moment.

Snow began to fall. The familiar red glow appeared. The sun was shining above the clouds, and yet the night glow lit up the world down below. So it does come from the earth itself, Venneman reasoned, and not from the sky.

He drove by that light for a while, but then he realized that the world was growing dark to the human eyes of other drivers, and he turned on his headlights and windshield wipers. He opened the driver's-side window all the way, reveling in the cold air that washed over him. His body temperature had been rising as he drove, and he welcomed the wind blowing in the open window. He was in his true element again, in the wild, where the other predators played their eternal, terrible game with their prey, away from the artificial world built by humans.

Then he remembered that he was driving in a car, on a highway, headed for a very high-priced town, and he smiled at his own pretentiousness. There's nothing romantic about any of this, he thought. That's the mistake Jill makes—to think that we're exotic and wonderful beings. She kept saying that we're just another form of life, and that's all, but she didn't really believe that. But she was right, in a way. Whether we're magical or not, we're still part of God's creation, because even the Devil was created by God.

Just what part of God's creation vampires were, and what

role Venneman was supposed to play in that creation, he still did not know. Perhaps in the future, after he had done what he was here to do, he could devote more time to trying to discover the answer to that question.

Venneman slowed down, squinting through the driving snow and the glare from his own headlights, looking for the street he had walked down to get to the highway he was now on. He turned off his headlights with an annoyed twist of his wrist and searched instead by the gentle, directionless red glow that was always there when the sun's brightness didn't mask it.

There it was: the place where he had begun walking beside the highway, wondering if anyone would ever stop to pick him up. Perhaps his memory for places was also more acute than it had been during his human years.

Indeed, he found as he drove down the deserted street that he remembered the tiniest details along the way with almost disturbing precision. A leafless tree, the wooden rails along the edge of a pasture—as he passed them, he remembered each one and remembered walking past them in the opposite direction, carrying his suitcase and wearing his shabby clothes. He remembered this town, where he had spent only a few days, far better than the city where had lived and worked for years.

And why not? he asked himself. That was just a place where I spent time. This is where I was born.

He drove to the motel where he had stayed before on Harold Dinsmuir's credit card. The man behind the desk was not the one who had been on duty when Venneman had checked out of the place the year before, but that had been at night, and now it was daytime. He filled out the registration card and paid for one night ahead in cash. "Guess I'm lucky you have room at this time of year, right?"

"Yes, sir," the desk clerk said. "It's been pretty slow here this year, for ski season. People are avoiding the place a bit, I guess. Because of the safety problems on the runs."

"Safety problems?"

"Well, yeah. I guess I shouldn't have said anything. There've been some problems, fatal accidents on the ski runs. You, uh, still want your room?"

Venneman smiled at him. "I'm not here for the skiing. But what did you mean about accidents? There are always accidents at these places, aren't there?"

"Yeah, but not this many. And they can usually figure out what happened. We've been having trouble with people skiing alone at night, which is pretty stupid to begin with in a place that doesn't have special lighting, and then being found frozen in the morning."

"Sounds as though it serves them right," Venneman said.

"That's just what I say! And some of them were local people, who really should know better. You expect a couple of assholes to come up here from Denver every year and kill themselves, but—Oh, I'm sorry, sir!"

Venneman laughed. "That's okay. I'm from Denver, but I'm not one of the assholes from Denver. So what do the police think happened to these people? Had a bad fall, knocked themselves unconscious, then froze to death?"

"That's what the sheriff says. Or else they got drunk in one of the local bars and then stumbled out too far into one of the fields and went to sleep." He checked himself, drew back, then asked, "You're sure you're going to keep the room, sir?"

Venneman nodded. "As I said, I'm not here for the skiing.

And even if I were, I wouldn't be doing it at night by myself. I'll be here for at least one night. It may even take more than that to take care of my business."

Looking relieved, the desk clerk gave him his key. He had retreated into his professional persona, and Venneman sensed there'd be no more unwise confidences forthcoming.

He took his suitcase into his room, changed into clothing that would fit in with the standard dress for the ski crowd, and left the motel, headed for the few–block stretch of bars and restaurants he remembered. It seemed the best place to begin his search.

There did seem to be far fewer people on the sidewalk than he remembered, although that had been evening and this was morning. Some of the tourists might already be up and out on the slopes. Perhaps many others were still in bed, sleeping away the excesses of the previous night. Or exerting themselves in bed because of the successes of the previous night. Venneman smiled at that thought, aware that the image would once have shocked him. The idea of promiscuity still shocked him, but the fact of it seemed to have lost its power to disturb.

The bars were already open. Reading the signs posted in their windows, he realized that they doubled as restaurants. He walked until he found the one where he had met Elizabeth.

"Elizabeth Vallé," he whispered, delighting again in the sound of the name. He was glad that he knew her full name, now, and perversely happy that it was a beautiful one.

The place was almost empty.

Venneman sat at the bar and ordered toast and coffee from the young woman tending the bar. Her name tag said "Kelly." He smiled warmly at her and used her name and was almost surprised by how strongly she reacted to him. Jill had been right about that, anyway. He could attract someone he was interested in even more easily than when he was a human. He found the ability curious and interesting, rather than frightening as he had in the past.

She brought his toast and coffee and stayed nearby, watching him. Venneman took his time adding cream and sugar to the coffee and stirring it. He slowly opened one of the plastic packages of jelly, divided its contents evenly between his two slices of toast, and carefully spread the jelly on each of them, taking care to cover both surfaces completely. Then he put the coffee cup to his lips and let the hot liquid touch his lips. He put the cup down and smiled at the girl. "Not many people here, Kelly. Is it too early in the day?"

Kelly put her hands on the bar and leaned toward him. She smiled broadly at him. Her teeth were large and even but stained. From the powerful smell of tobacco on her breath, he guessed the stains were due to nicotine. The human urge for death was surprisingly strong, Venneman thought. Perhaps his fellow vampires weren't really giving human beings anything they didn't in fact want.

"Yeah, it's early," Kelly said. She ran the fingers of her right hand through her curly hair, brushing it back from her face. The gesture gave Venneman a generous view of her large breasts. "Doesn't usually pick up until after dinner. How long you up here for?"

"Oh, for as long as it takes me to do my business here. Then I'll be heading on. You live here?"

"Yeah. Well, I share an apartment with a couple of other girls. I'd love a place of my own, but I can't afford it. Not in this town. Where're you staying?"

Venneman named his motel.

"Nice place," Kelly said.

"You've been there?"

She grinned at him. "I've met people who were staying there."

Venneman grinned back at her, but it was a forced grin. Even now, this game felt unnatural to him. "I've only been here once before," he said. "Last winter. Seems to me there were more people on the streets back then."

Kelly nodded. "Yeah, it's been pretty slow this year."

"Some kind of accidents, right? I think I read about it in the paper in Denver. Must be scaring people away."

Kelly drew back slightly. "Are you some kind of investigator?"

Venneman laughed. "You mean, a private eye? You want to see my gun?"

"Is it a big one?"

"It does the job."

"Yeah, I bet it does. No, I meant like someone from the government or something."

Venneman shook his head. "I'm just a private citizen. I'm here on private business, nothing to do with skiing, but I heard about those accidents, and I was just kind of curious."

She leaned forward again. "So you're not scared by the accidents?"

"No reason to be. I never expose myself to accidents, Kelly."

"You've never had an accident in your life?"

Venneman lowered his gaze and looked at his coffee. Accident, design, or malice? What had happened to him, he would once have said, was the result of human malice—rather, of vampire malice. Certainly it had not been an accident. Vampire design? Higher design? If there was a purpose to all of this, then where did the purpose and design originate?

He looked up at Kelly again. "Not in recent years. Someone told me that the people who died froze to death because of their own carelessness. That the sheriff said they got drunk and fell asleep outside, or went skiing at night and got knocked unconscious."

"Maybe," Kelly said. "Of course, that's the kind of thing Karl always says."

"Karl?"

"Karl Jergens, the sheriff. He's a lazy s.o.b., and saying that's the easy way out for him. Whenever anyone dies up here, he says they got drunk and fell asleep outside and froze to death. Or something like that."

"Isn't there always an inquest?"

Kelly looked around quickly. A few more people had drifted into the bar during their conversation and had been trying unsuccessfully and with increasing annoyance to get her attention. "Oops," she said. "Be right back."

She hurried around the room taking orders. Venneman turned on his stool to watch her, admiring her walk and her body. She must, he thought, do a fair amount of skiing herself, and the results were pleasing to his eye. It surprised him somewhat to realize that he was beginning to react to her as a human man might, not as a predator would to its prey. It was the effect, he realized, of his discovery that his natural prey was no longer human beings but other vampires. He was also interested to note how many of the orders Kelly delivered to the other customers included, or in some cases consisted only of, alcoholic drinks. Destructive a creature as he had become through no act of his own, these creatures were still more destructive. And in their case, it was entirely through their own actions.

Finally Kelly was finished and went back behind the bar and came over to talk again to Venneman. She resumed her former position, hands on the bar, leaning forward to create intimacy. "Where were we? You know, I don't even know your name, and you know mine."

"Richard. I was asking you about inquests on the bodies of the accident victims."

"Oh, right. Wouldn't you rather talk about something more pleasant, Rich?"

"Richard. Just humor me for a few minutes, okay, Kelly?" He put his hand on one of hers and squeezed gently. He smiled at her, looking into her eyes, and saw the response there. "Tell me what you were going to tell me before."

She stared at him, saying nothing. He could smell her blood with increasing intensity and feel its heat.

"Kelly?"

"Oh. Yeah. Well, I've got a friend who works part-time at the funeral parlor, where the bodies are taken. He says the man who runs the place does the inquests, and he's pretty sloppy about it. Just cuts the bodies open and rummages around inside for a few minutes, just so he can say he's done it and it's all official, and that's it for the inquest. Uh, that's kind of disgusting, isn't it? Sorry."

"That's fine," Venneman assured her. "It fascinates me." I've done a bit of that rummaging myself, he thought. He remembered his awakening and now understood where he must have been.

"Well, anyway, according to my friend, the corpses didn't smell of alcohol at all, and some of them looked awfully pale to him. He said he thinks maybe they actually bled to death. He thinks we've got a problem with some sort of animal attacking people at night. And of course no one wants that story to get out."

"How interesting," Venneman said, working to keep his tone even. It was an effort to speak normally. He feared that Kelly could hear his pounding heart. "What sort of animal would bite someone badly enough to make them bleed to death but not leave obvious wounds?"

Kelly frowned. "I don't know. My friend doesn't know, either. Nothing big, like a bear or a wolf or a mountain lion, because those would take chunks out of you."

"Not to mention that bears would be hibernating now," Venneman pointed out. "And there aren't supposed to be any wolves around here nowadays. Has your friend discussed his theory with anyone else besides you?"

She shook her head. "He doesn't want to get in trouble with the funeral parlor. He needs his job. Hard to get work around here, especially this year, with business down."

"How good a friend is he?" Venneman asked.

"Doesn't matter," Kelly said. "That's my problem, not yours. Now, let's talk about more pleasant things."

"What time should I come back?"

"I get off at four," she said. "Should I meet you here around six?"

"Right, six," Venneman said, his thoughts elsewhere. He put

enough money on the bar to cover the cost of his uneaten toast and undrunk coffee, plus a large tip for Kelly. Then he left and walked back to his motel.

There were still few people on the sidewalk. Those he passed stared up at him with interest, but Venneman didn't notice. Elizabeth surely wouldn't be that careless, he was thinking. Someone else? Does that mean that this has become someone else's territory and Elizabeth has moved on? The possibility made him feel frantic.

By the time he reached the motel, he was walking slowly and wearily. The charge of energy he'd gained from Jill's blood was fading at last, he realized. Perhaps vampire blood had less staying power than the human kind. Perhaps it burned more briefly as well more brightly. Or perhaps he simply needed much more of it, to counter the effects of so many months of taking small amounts of human blood.

He let himself into his room and fell heavily onto the bed. His outstretched arm landed on something that crackled.

Venneman rolled over to look, and saw that his arm was resting on the unread newspaper he had brought with him. He pushed himself up to a sitting position, spread the paper on the bed, and glanced over the first page. Below the fold he saw:

Death in Lower Downtown

Larry Driscoll told his friends he was going to Larimer Square to meet someone new, someone he had met the first time only a few days before. Now his friends are wondering about the darker side of Larry's lifestyle, a darker side that left him dead last night.

Witnesses told police that they heard sounds of a loud argument in the 1300 block of 15th Street in lower downtown Denver late last night and witnessed an altercation between two men. One of the men left in a hurry, walking south on 15th. When witnesses investigated, they found Driscoll, 26, lying unconscious on the sidewalk. He was rushed to a hospital, where he later died. Police say the cause of death was massive head wounds. They are searching for the man seen leaving the scene of the murder.

The killer is described by witnesses as being a tall, powerfully built Caucasian male in his thirties. Police say they have not yet detained any suspects.

But I didn't kill him! Venneman thought. I just pushed him away! It must have been someone else, later, after I left.

No, I didn't just push him away. I ... *threw* him away. Maybe it was hard enough for him to hit his head against something and be killed by the blow.

Even when I tried to save someone, he thought, I killed him. It's just part of my nature. I'm a destroyer of life.

He reread the last paragraph. "The killer was tall and powerfully built," he said aloud.

He pushed himself off the bed and went into the room's small bathroom, where a full-length mirror was attached to the back of the door. He stood in front of it, examining himself. He looked much the same to himself as he always had, except for the extra glow of health and vitality in his face compared to when he was human. Any difference must be in the eyes of human observers.

But when I was human, he thought, I never killed anyone. I never destroyed any lives, let alone damned any souls.

He staggered back to the bed, fell onto it, and rolled onto his back. He lay for a long time, exhausted beyond measure but unable to sleep, staring up into the red haze that obscured the ceiling. He willed himself to relax, willed his mind to dream, but he remained tensely awake.

I don't want to be a killer anymore, he thought. I don't want to destroy anything.

Except for the destroyers themselves. I want to destroy them.

Slowly, his mind calmed. The haze above him changed into the hazy sky above the red ocean.

The sea of blood was less tranquil than usual. The swells had become waves, breaking in pink froth all around him. The body parts that floated on the sea were flung against him, stinging him when they struck him, clinging to him. The detached hands seemed to clutch at him. He hit at them, filled with horror.

He realized suddenly that he wasn't floating as easily as before. His chest and head were on the surface, but his hips and legs were below it, deep in the blood, and it was numbingly cold beneath the hot surface layer.

A red wave broke over his face. Blood filled his mouth. It was the sour, nauseating blood of humans, and he choked and gagged on it. He paddled furiously, coughing, gasping for air. The blood blinded him. He knuckled it from his eyes, desperate to see and to escape.

He heard the calling voices and tried to swim toward them. Above the rest, he could hear Elizabeth's voice. The sea was fighting him, holding him back, sucking at him, washing him away from the welcoming shore.

Hands grasped his ankles and tried to pull him under. Venneman kicked downward desperately. For a moment, the hands let go. But then they were back, grabbing his knees, his thighs, his waist.

Venneman fought to stay above the surface. Something rose from the sea beside him. It was a human form, a man, a distorted figure with long hair plastered down either side of its face and scabs covering its forehead. Then he recognized the face. It was his own.

Venneman screamed and hit at the figure. It grinned at him, caught his arms, and pulled him to it. "Let me kiss you," it said hoarsely, in Venneman's own voice. It lowered its face toward his, opening its mouth hugely, protruding a scab–covered tongue.

Venneman awoke, lying quietly on his back on the bed in his motel room. The sheet covering him was neat and unwrinkled, as though Venneman had lain in that position all day without any thrashing about.

He looked toward the window. It was dark outside.

Venneman closed his eyes, but only to try to relax for a moment. He was afraid to sleep again.

FOURTEEN

Venneman stumbled about his room, trying to wake up fully. The red ocean pursued him even during waking hours. He had thought the background noise he was sometimes aware of was the collective pulse of all the humans in the world, the many-billion-fold beating of a heart. Now he understood that it was instead the heaving of the sea he swam upon in dreams. It was the reality underlying the world. All of this—the seeming solidity, the rushing about of humans and beasts, even the movements of the sun and moon and stars—was a mask, a thin layer of existence, appearance without substance. The vast sea of blood was reality. It had risen from its hiding place beneath the veneer of the world and broken out into the open. It had come to claim him.

This is crazy thinking, he told himself. You're thinking crazy thoughts. It makes no sense. Reality is what you see, and the sea is what you dream about. You mustn't confuse the two. You're just tired. It's your fatigue that's confusing your thoughts.

I need more vampire blood, he thought. That's the only real food for me. That's what makes my brain work properly.

He got into the shower and turned on only the cold water.

Here in the mountains, it felt as though it was just barely above freezing. He stood under it for fifteen minutes, thirty, waiting for some effect. At first it chilled his skin, but then it felt pleasant.

He emerged dripping wet and still tired.

He dried himself off, dressed, and headed out the door. Outside, it was dark, and the air temperature was well below freezing. Venneman unzipped the coat he had just zipped up, undid the top few buttons of his shirt, and breathed the cold air in. It had no sting and no effect.

Walking down the street, he staggered and had to pause every few steps to recover his strength. Once, crossing a street, he fell to one knee and was almost unable to rise to his feet again. Fortunately there was no one around to see him. When he reached the other side of the street, he leaned against a wall for a few seconds before trying to walk. He walked with one hand touching the wall, trying to draw support from its solidity, even though he was starting to fear its red glow.

He thought he could hear ocean waves behind him, but every time he turned around to look, he saw only the empty street and sidewalk.

It's hiding around the corner, he thought. Waiting for me to drop my guard.

He tried walking backward, but the sound moved so that it was still behind him.

It was everywhere, he realized, despairing. It permeated the world. It was the world, the real world. He wanted to weep, but he would not give it that satisfaction.

He straightened his back and turned about and walked slowly, carefully, erect toward his goal. He refused to look behind him. He refused to be weak.

It was seven when Venneman finally reached the bar, and his legs were shaking.

The bar was full. Despite what he had been told about the decrease in the tourist business this year, the bar looked as crowded to his eye as it had on his last evening visit to it, the winter before, the night he had met Elizabeth Vallé.

He stood in the doorway for a moment, feeling the wave of human vitality radiating from the crowd. It drowned out the sound of the heaving ocean. Leaning against the doorway and watching and listening to the crowd of humans, Venneman felt some of his strength returning. After a few minutes, he felt able to walk normally again, and his mind was less confused. He saw Kelly sitting at the bar and looking angry, and he headed across the room toward her.

The stool to her right was empty. Venneman slipped onto it. "Hello," he said. "Sorry I'm late."

Kelly tried to maintain her anger, but it melted before his smile. "Hi, Richard. That's okay. I'm just glad you're here."

Her reaction filled Venneman with guilt. He wasn't interested in her—neither in the way a human man would be nor in the way another vampire would be. She represented only information to him, and it was likely that he had already gotten from her all the useful information she had.

Based on what he had heard from Kelly and the hotel desk clerk, Venneman was now sure that a vampire was on the hunt here and that he must be a newly minted one, still driven by the need for large amounts of blood, still lacking in caution and self-control. Given his own history, it seemed likely to Venneman that the new vampire had been created by Elizabeth Vallé. Venneman wanted to find this vampire in the hope that he could point him toward Elizabeth. Perhaps Kelly knew something more that would prove useful, some bit of information that would lead Venneman to the vampire. Or perhaps Elizabeth herself would show up in the bar. Perhaps it was her usual hunting grounds.

Either way, Venneman had decided to spend the evening here and see if he gained anything from it.

Kelly drank steadily as the evening wore on. Venneman sipped water and paid for her drinks. He listened to her increasingly disjointed conversation and made occasional, monosyllabic replies which seemed to satisfy her. She seemed to want to tell him the story of her life, what there was of it so far, but the story got harder and harder to follow as the hours wore on. He gleaned from what she said that she had suffered more than her share of disappointment and ill treatment, but he got little more than that out of it.

Venneman's eyes roamed over the crowd, which by now seemed as large and closely packed as it had on his previous visit to the town. Perhaps everyone who had come up here to ski had ended up at this bar. Perhaps the other bars in town were empty.

He saw no sign of Elizabeth, and he saw no one else who seemed to him to be a vampire. For a moment, he regretted that Jill wasn't with him. He could have used her ability to tell whether or not someone else was a vampire. For all he knew, the man he wanted was already in the bar—or had been in there and had left. Perhaps he had been in, selected his victim of the evening, and left with her.

Venneman gritted his teeth in anger. Kelly's words receded, drowned out by his own pulse. How dare the man play with him! Once he found him, he would do to him what he had done to Jill.

He recognized that overpowering, irrational anger. He remembered that it had possessed him frequently at the beginning of his vampire life, but he had been free of it for a long time. Was Elizabeth's nearness drawing it out in him again?

Again he looked around carefully. This time he also listened, trying to tell if a powerful vampire heart beat among the weaker human ones filling the place. No. When he dropped his guard, he was stunned by a cacophony of thumping hearts, but they were all the same, all human.

He reestablished his mental guard against the sound and resigned himself to waiting and watching. He tried to pay more attention to what Kelly was saying, but by now her sentences were fragments and he could get little out of any of it. He noticed, though, that she was also looking around. She was growing nervous, and she looked at the door repeatedly.

"Outta here," she said. "Let's get. Do it. Get outta here."

"Why?" Venneman asked her. "What's the matter?"

"It's ... late. Getting late. Friend getting off work. Go home."

"It's getting late, your boyfriend will be getting off work soon, and you want to get home before he does. Spending the evening with me suddenly doesn't seem like such a good idea. Did I miss anything?"

Kelly stared at him. She grabbed at the edge of the bar suddenly and held on tightly. "Sick."

"Everyone in this town is," Venneman told her. He sighed. "I'll get you home and tuck you in. I owe you that." He stood up and gripped her elbow. He was about to pull her off the stool and to her feet when he felt a pressure move down his spine and then up again. He let go of Kelly and turned slowly around until he was facing the door. Karen Belmont stood there, staring at him uncertainly.

When he turned and she saw his face, she came forward slowly, threading her way between the mostly empty tables. When she reached him, she stood in front of him for a few seconds, staring at him, still unsure. "Richie? Richie Venneman?"

He nodded slowly. "Hello, Karen."

"I don't understand why you're here," she said. Her gaze traveled over his face, examining, analyzing. "You've changed."

"I know. You've hardly changed at all."

Kelly pulled herself up onto the stool Venneman had just vacated. The bartender—another young woman of about the same age as Kelly—came over and asked, "Can I get you something, Ma'am?"

Karen looked at her briefly and then back at Venneman. "I think I've found what I wanted."

"You really haven't changed, have you?" Venneman said.

Kelly said, "Richard?"

Karen turned slightly and looked at Kelly over her shoulder. "Sorry, girl," she said. "This is the way Richie operates." She turned back to Venneman. "Isn't it, Richie?" She reached up and stroked his cheek. "Are you waiting for your fiancée again, Richie?"

"Fiancée?" Kelly said. She sounded much more sober.

"Life's a lot more complicated than you seem to think it is, Karen," Venneman said.

"Oh, I know how complicated it is," Karen said. "You're here alone, then?"

"I was, but we can talk about that. Actually, I came here to find someone."

The slight frown that had remained on Karen's face disappeared. "Oh! Now I understand! You felt you had no choice, is that it? That you had to come here? You were being called back?"

"Well, well," Venneman said. "Perhaps you *do* know how complicated life is."

Behind him, Kelly muttered, "Fucking foreign language." She levered herself off the stool and moved away, walking unevenly. She made it as far as the first table, which was occupied by three men. Kelly sat down heavily in one of the two vacant chairs. The men seemed delighted.

"Good, she's finally given up," Karen said. "Now we can talk more easily."

"I hope we're talking about the same thing," Venneman said. He was looking over her shoulder at Kelly, feeling guilty and responsible for her. "Look, can you wait here for me? I think I'd better see that she gets home safely."

Karen laughed, a harsh sound. "Forget it. Girls like that sleep in a different bed every night in these towns during the season. It's part of what brings the tourists up here. Everyone's happy."

Venneman switched his gaze to her. "Except that some of them end up dead, isn't that true? Mysteriously dead. It's been happening to a few people around here, I understand."

Karen smiled at him. "They don't count, Richie. Unimportant." She reached up again and put her hand against the side of his face. "It's hot in here, Richie. Too many people. Too much noise. Come outside." She slid off the stool, grabbed his hand, and pulled him toward the door.

Venneman spared one last, guilty look at Kelly and then let Karen pull him out onto the street.

Outside, she again put her hand against his cheek and repeated his name. This time, Venneman bent down and kissed her. Karen pulled away and set off down the sidewalk, drawing Venneman with her. She was following the same route Elizabeth had months before. Venneman was surprised at the tingle of fear that arose in him at the realization.

Her grip grew tighter as she walked rapidly down the alley, with Venneman close behind her. They reached the snowy meadow beyond the limits of the town where Elizabeth had killed him, and she stopped and began to undress. "Quickly, Richie!" she said.

For the first time, Venneman became aware of the bitterly cold wind blowing across the field. He looked up at the night sky, with its field of red stars blazing brilliantly through the red haze. He looked back at Karen, who was already almost naked. He grabbed her upper arms and held her still.

She struggled against him for a moment and then stopped when she realized how much stronger he was than she. Her eyes went wide with apprehension.

"You thought I was still human, that Elizabeth let me live," Venneman said. He shook his head. "She did the same thing to me that she did to you."

Karen stood looking up at him. The fear mounted in her face and then faded. Tears filled her eyes and ran down her cheeks. She collapsed against him, weeping. "I hate that bitch!" she sobbed. "I hate her! I hate her! She keeps using me!"

Venneman held her against him. He stroked her hair and her naked back, admiring the shape of her body and the texture of her skin under his hands. I could have had this last year, he thought, back when we were both human. And then I wouldn't have fallen in with Elizabeth, and everything would have been so different. Different for Karen, too, perhaps.

He felt her growing calmer. Her sobs died away, and she stood quietly, leaning against him, her arms around his waist. Then he said, "You were ready to use me."

Karen drew back slightly and looked up at him. "Yes. I did think you were human. I was going to kill you and leave you out here. I'd have been doing you a favor—freeing you from her. I'm supposed to bring people to her, but I didn't want to do that to you. I wanted your blood for myself. I'm so hungry all the time, Richie. She keeps me so hungry."

He could see in her now the same deep weariness he felt in himself. "You can tell me about it later," he said. He helped her get dressed again, and they walked slowly toward his motel, hand in hand.

When they were safely inside his motel room, Karen again clung to him, crying. Venneman was astonished at the change in her. She was neither the cocky, self-confident woman he had first met almost a year earlier, nor the predatory vampire of the bar that evening. Her weakness and need made her seem more human to him than she ever had before.

He lifted her up and sat down on the bed with her, cradling her in his lap like a child while she wept.

"I hate her," she said over and over. "I hate her so much."

"We all hate the one who envamped us. Someone explained that to me. It's natural for us."

Karen's tears finally stopped. "It's more than that," she said, her voice hoarse. "At first, I didn't hate her at all, in spite of the pain. That first time—I'd never experienced sex like that with anyone else. I used to go up to her house, and we'd make love, and it was always wonderful."

Venneman felt himself stiffening with revulsion and tried not to let it show.

"That was while I still had to keep feeding," Karen continued. "At the beginning. You know how it is then. I quit my job, and I stayed here. Elizabeth said something about making someone else into a vampire before me, but he managed to get away from the town." She looked up at Venneman. "That was you! I just realized."

"Yes," Venneman said. "But you couldn't get away?"

"I didn't *want* to get away! I was happy here! And I probably wouldn't have been able to figure out any way to do it, even if I did want to. How did you manage it?"

"It doesn't matter. I'll tell you later. So how did you come to hate Elizabeth?"

Karen sighed. "When I started slowing down a bit, not needing so much blood, she ordered me to keep picking up victims but not to feed on them. I have to bring them up to her house. Then she feeds instead. She takes most of their blood, and I only get what's left. I finish them off, but it's never enough. She never allows me to be fully satisfied. I thought I'd be able to feed fully on you, but now I can't even do that, since you're a vampire too."

"Why didn't you ignore her?"

"I couldn't! You know that! No," she added, "you don't know that. You left before she had time to fully establish her control over you."

Venneman remembered the control Elizabeth had been able to exert the second time he'd been with her, in the snow beside the body of her victim, and thought he understood. If he had stayed with Jill, it would have been that way between the two of them. He would have been able to control her will in the way Elizabeth evidently controlled Karen's. The image aroused him to a degree he found disturbing.

Something struck him about Karen's story. "Why does Elizabeth need the blood? I thought vampires don't have to feed very often after the initial period."

"I don't know. I think it's something that started happening only a few months ago. Some kind of change in her. Maybe it's some kind of cycle. Maybe it's something that happens when you've been a vampire for long enough. I don't know." She pushed herself away from him suddenly, sliding off his lap and onto the bed beside him. "Why did you come back? You escaped. You were free. She called you, didn't she? I know she keeps control over all her victims, the ones she lets live."

"No," Venneman said. "She didn't call me. I came deliberately, looking for her. I came here to kill her."

"Then you're an idiot," Karen said sharply. "We can't be killed. You should know that by now."

"I know a few things the rest of you don't." But he thought of the many times he had dreamed of Elizabeth's voice calling him, and he wondered if he really had come here of his own free will, or if he had indeed been under Elizabeth's control all along. "Where does she live?" he asked Karen.

Karen hesitated, then said, "If you really do have some way of killing her, then I don't know if I want you to. I ... I still need her. She stopped making love to me about the same time she started needing lots of blood again, but maybe she'll change back in the future and want me again."

Venneman stared at her in contempt.

Misinterpreting the cause of his revulsion, Karen said, "I guess you're right, though. That's pretty cowardly of me. She just got tired of me, that's all. I guess—oh, Richard, I just don't know!"

She thought for a few minutes. "Okay," she said at last. "We'll help each other. Maybe you do know some way of killing Elizabeth, and then I'll be in control again. Hell, you can leave the way you did the first time, and then I'll be able to stay here and really start to enjoy my life for a change." She told Venneman how to find Elizabeth's house. "But when you get there, I bet you'll find out she's been expecting you."

You'll never know, he thought. It was time to begin the necessary experiment. Briefly, he had had second thoughts about it. He had felt, for a few moments, that Karen deserved better. But she had gone on and said more, had said too much, and he had put his doubts aside.

Now he put her arms around her and pulled her toward him. He pressed her down onto the bed, lying half on top of her. "When we were both humans, you wanted me," he said.

Karen laughed. "And you were afraid of me."

"Not anymore."

He lowered his face to her neck and kissed her. She bent her head to the side. He kissed her again, and she gasped. "Oh, it's good, Richie."

"As good as with Elizabeth?" he asked her.

"No one's as good as Elizabeth."

Venneman opened his mouth wide and bit down, forcing

his teeth through the tough skin and tendons of her vampire neck, seeking the vampire blood.

"No!" she shouted. She struggled against him, trying to free her arms, to push him off, to pull her neck away from his teeth. Her strength surprised him, but he was far stronger and heavier, and he held her pinned down while he gnawed deeper. He reached the powerful stream of blood and began to feed.

It filled him with delight, sexual pleasure that flooded his body. He could feel her vitality and strength flowing out of her and into him. He could scarcely hear her faint and fading scream.

Her strength gave out suddenly and she lay helpless under him as he sucked and sucked with all his strength at the diminishing flow. She made a faint noise. Perhaps it was a word, but he could not understand it. She died for the second time.

All of his earlier weakness and sleepiness had vanished. Once again, as he had after feeding on the envamped Jill, Venneman felt filled with strength. He felt extraordinarily awake and alert.

He watched Karen for a few minutes, but she lay unmoving, her eyes open and staring up at the ceiling. The ragged wound in her neck was pale and bloodless.

No, he realized, not entirely bloodless. A faint sheen of blood colored the edges. He bent over her and licked the flesh repeatedly, getting that last hint of her blood, feeling its faint electric tingle against his tongue. Then he left the room and went to the front desk, where he paid for another night.

By the time he came back to the room, the wound in Karen's neck had closed almost entirely. It healed itself as he watched. Karen looked even smaller than before, and he was sure she was shrinking slowly as he watched her body.

Slowly, her pale face took on a touch of pink. The stillness of the room gave way to a faint pulse. It grew stronger as he stood beside the bed, watching her. He could see it beating in her neck again. Her eyelids fluttered. She moved slightly, moaned, licked her lips.

Venneman lay down beside her and waited, watching her sleep.

She shrank a little bit more and then stabilized when her blood was completely replaced. She slept for a couple of hours and then awoke with a start.

"What?" she said. "What—"

"Ssh," Venneman said. He put his arms around her and pulled her to him. He rolled over on top of her. "I'm sorry, Karen," he said to her.

"You mustn't!" she shouted.

She was smaller and weaker this time, and he had gained both mass and strength from her blood. It was even easier this time. Again he bit into her neck and drank until she was dead.

Forty-eight hours later, Karen was less than six inches tall. He held her clutched in one hand while she struggled and squirmed, hitting and biting at his hand, blows he could scarcely feel. Her shouts of anger and terror were small and faint, like the squeaking of a mouse.

"Now what?" he asked her. "This is what I planned to do to Elizabeth, you see. I was experimenting on you, Karen, but I hadn't really thought this far ahead. If I let you go now, you'll force yourself to catch and feed on small animals. Or maybe you'll sneak into babies' cribs. Either way, you'll not only survive, but eventually you'll be back up to your normal size. I bet that's the way it works. Although no one really knows, do they? I mean, you can't go to a library and find a book on this subject, can you? *The Biology of Vampires*, or maybe *Medical Problems of the Undead*." He laughed. "How about those titles, Karen? What do you think?"

She struggled and screamed and hit at his hand even more vigorously. He wondered if she could hear his voice properly, given the difference in their size, and, if so, whether she could understand him. He wondered if she were still sane after what she had just been through. He wasn't sure that he was.

"So you see, the experiment isn't complete, is it? I mean, the whole idea was to see if my ability to drink vampire blood—my *need* for it, in fact—would enable me to feed on another vampire until she died. That's what I planned to do to Elizabeth. But I didn't take this size thing into account, even though I should have, because I saw it happen before. Anyway, Karen, now you're too small for me to feed on properly, and you're still alive. So how do I finish the job?"

He sighed. "Well, I have thought of something. I'm really, really sorry about this. You don't deserve it. But Elizabeth does, and I know you'll die happy knowing that you're contributing to killing Elizabeth. So, here goes. Get ready."

She stopped moving suddenly, staring at his face with her eyes wide in horror. So she had not only understood him, he realized, she had even guessed what he intended to do.

"The quicker the better, for both of us," he told her. He brought her up to his mouth and, with a powerful crunching of his teeth, bit off her head. Blood spurted from the tiny stub of her neck and ran down his hands.

He tried to swallow her head, but it was too big. He rolled it around in his mouth, not knowing what to do next. He could feel her tiny mouth and eyelids moving against his tongue. She can't still be alive! he thought. He had to put an end to this.

With his tongue, he pushed her head between his molars and bit down. The skull resisted, as hard as a stone. Venneman squeezed his jaws together as hard as he could. At last, the pressure was too much even for vampire bone, and Karen's skull collapsed. Venneman's mouth was filled with something slippery. He coughed and gagged, but managed to swallow.

He gasped. Her head was stuck in his esophagus, the jagged pieces of bone keeping it from going down. But blood was still spurting from her neck. Venneman sucked greedily at it, using the liquid to help force her head down. At last he felt it sliding down into his stomach, and he sighed in relief. Her body still twitched slightly in his hand, as though her vampiric vitality had actually increased in inverse proportion to her body size. What an amazing form of life we are, he thought admiringly.

Laboriously and with mounting distaste, he bit pieces off her body and swallowed them. It took him longer than he had expected because of the toughness of her vampire bone and muscle, but finally there was nothing left.

He lay down upon the bed, feeling bloated and heavy. Indeed, he filled the bed as he had not before, and his clothes had become too tight to wear. He had gained all of Karen's mass, he realized. Effortlessly, he tore his clothing away, dropping the pieces onto the floor. He closed his heavy eyelids.

He knew he should hate himself for what he had done, but instead he felt a vast sense of accomplishment.

He had killed a vampire at last.

FIFTEEN

The sea was calm again.

Venneman floated on it peacefully, as he had so often during the months before it turned hostile. It was welcoming and comforting, soothing him with its unspoken assurance that the terrible thing he had done to Karen Belmont had been justified and he need feel no guilt. He was alone on the sea. No parts of human bodies floated near him, and no voices called. He floated without effort, and nothing pulled at him from below. The sea supported and healed him.

Until he felt eyes upon him.

He rolled over in that direction, squinting against the harsh brightness of the eternal haze. Something huge floated on the sea an indeterminate distance away. It grew larger, moving toward him.

Suddenly it was moving fast, churning the bloody surface. Red spray flew to either side of it. He could see its huge eyes fixed on his face and the coils of its body rising into the air and then plunging back beneath the surface behind it.

Venneman floated as if paralyzed, watching the serpent ploughing through the sea toward him.

The reptilian head rose high above him. The face changed to Karen's, but the head was still narrower than hers had been, as though it still showed the effect of having been crushed between Venneman's teeth. Her mouth opened wide. It was full of sharp, pointed teeth. Her head plunged down toward him.

Venneman held out his hands imploringly. He screamed. "No!"

The mouth grabbed him about his middle and crunched down. Agony tore through Venneman. He tried to scream again but had no breath.

He awoke writhing in agony. The room pulsated with red light. His abdomen was torn open and blood fountained from it. A small, human figure clawed its way through the opening and stood, its feet planted within Venneman, and stared down at him. It was covered with blood, and Venneman could scarcely think because of the pain, but he recognized it as Karen Belmont. She was bigger, almost a foot in length.

"Bastard!" she screamed at him. She climbed out of him and hopped off the bed.

Venneman struggled to sit up, but he could scarcely move. He could feel his life slipping away as his blood pumped from the huge wound in his abdomen. He fought for only a moment and then gave up the struggle. Elizabeth had won after all.

Venneman was not entirely surprised when he awoke again.

The pain had faded to a dull ache suffusing his abdomen. As he lay on his back, his thoughts unfocused, the ache faded away to nothing. He tried to lift his head to look down at himself, but all he had the strength to do was roll his head slightly from side to side. He tried to lift his hand, but it felt as though it were weighted down. Straining and grunting with the effort, Venneman managed to lift it off the sheet and let if flop onto his stomach. His sense of touch was numbed, but as far as he could tell by moving his fingers back and forth across his skin, the hole Karen had torn in him in her escape had healed completely.

He slid his arm further across his stomach and chest and tried to use its weight to roll himself onto his side. He couldn't do it, and the effort left him exhausted and gasping for breath. A lot of blood, he thought. Drained out of me.

He turned his head until he could see the door. It stood partly open. The opening was just wide enough, he thought, for a one-foot-tall woman to have exited through it. He imagined her jumping up and grabbing the handle, holding onto it, swinging from side to side so that she could turn it and open the door. Vampire strength had served her well.

Faint daylight showed around the opening. Got to close the door, he thought. Not safe, this weak. But he could not move his body, no matter how hard he tried.

He lay with his head turned, watching the door. He was too mentally numb and physically weak to do anything else.

The daylight grew brighter, driving away the red light of night. Venneman could see now that the bed was soaked in blood. His blood, he realized.

He forced his head further to the side, until he could touch the pillow with his tongue.

His tongue tingled where it touched the cloth of the pillowcase, vibrated with the electricity of his own blood. He pressed the corner of his mouth against the pillow and tried to suck blood in. Something came into his mouth, some kind of liquid. He wasn't sure what it was, but it had hints of the vitality of vampire blood to it, mixed with other things he could not identify. Cleaning fluids, he thought. Traces of who knew what. None of that mattered. He was immune to damage from any of it.

The small amount of blood gave him more motivation than strength, but it was enough to enable him to roll onto his side and move his mouth over the pillow and the sheet, hungrily sucking in the blood that still glistened on the surfaces.

It gave him enough added strength to slide off the bed and onto the floor. He dragged himself to the door on hands and knees and fell against it, forcing it shut.

The effort had drained him completely. He lay huddled against the door, shivering in the slight draft of cold air leaking in along its bottom, a cold he hadn't been able to feel in almost a year. He drifted into sleep.

For once, Venneman didn't dream of the red ocean. He didn't dream at all. When he awoke, he felt immeasurably better—virtually normal, although filled with raging hunger and anger. He needed blood to recover his strength and grow back to normal size. He needed vampire blood.

By the clock, it was noon. He knew he had no time to waste. It had been night when Karen had escaped, but he had no idea what the hour had been, how many hours of night she had had left when she got away. Where would she have gone? She needed blood to rebuild herself to normal size, but how would a one–foot tall vampire get blood? Venneman was almost amused by the image.

Much as Karen hated Elizabeth Vallé, she might have decided that Elizabeth's house would be her best bet for shelter and protection and also that Elizabeth would be willing to help her get the blood she needed. She had been Elizabeth's faithful little servant for some time, after all, and she might be betting on some sort of return of the favor, now that she needed it. A foolish chance for her to take, Venneman thought. Small as his experience of other vampires was, it was enough to have taught him that they were by nature solitary, greedy, vengeful, and violent.

The vampire movies Venneman had seen and loved as a boy and young man, and the novels he had read on the subject, all seemed to hypothesize some sort of vampire subculture. They even depicted ages-long liaisons between vampires, and the transmission of vampiric knowledge from one generation of vampires to the next. This was sentimental nonsense, he now knew. It was a dreamy-eyed invention by people who had never encountered real vampires. But Karen might believe it.

If she knew better and was avoiding Elizabeth, then he had nothing to worry about from that quarter. But if she had gone to Elizabeth for help and had told her what Venneman had done and what he had said, Elizabeth would be forewarned.

A foot-high woman would travel slowly on foot, but she might have managed to get to Elizabeth's place during the night. For that matter, he realized with a shock, he might have been asleep for two nights. Or three. In which case, the odds increased that Karen had reached Elizabeth and warned her that Venneman was hunting her. Elizabeth would be expecting him.

Or she might have fled.

He would have to assume that she was still in her house. There was no alternative for him at the moment. But he also had to assume, for the sake of his own safety, that she knew he was coming, and that she also knew what he intended to do to her. The only edge he had was the one she had no way of knowing about: his immunity to sunlight. He had to get to her while it was still day.

He showered and dressed in clean clothes. The clothes hung loosely on him. The arms of the shirt and the legs of the trousers were inches too long. He had to tighten the belt three holes further along than usual. The trousers bunched around his waist. The shirt, once he buttoned it, hung in folds on him. Quite a contrast with the suave European count of the movies, Venneman thought. But everything in his life since Elizabeth's attack had been different—different from those movies, different from his human life before, different from the lives of every other human being.

And since my attempt to kill myself with Dr. Dirtbag's machine, he thought, my life has been different from that of every other vampire.

Presumably. Perhaps there were others like him. But how would they have become converted to what he was now? If it required a bit of sun trapped on Earth, then Dinsmuir's machine was the only available tool.

But perhaps there's some other way of becoming what I am now, he thought. Or perhaps someone else is conducting an experiment like Dinsmuir's, and some other vampire tried to use it to commit suicide, just as I did.

The idea that he might not be unique after all disturbed him, to his own surprise. But the idea that Dinsmuir's experiment might not be unique brought a smile to his face.

He finished dressing and put on his coat. He didn't need it—indeed, he felt hot in it and welcomed the cold air of mountain winter on his eternally flushed skin—but he didn't want to draw unnecessary attention to himself, and walking around outside in this climate without a warm coat would certainly draw attention. When he got into his car, he found he had to pull the seat forward a notch or two. Just how much size had he lost? A couple of inches in height, judging by his trousers and the car seat. More to the point, would it cause him problems when he tackled Elizabeth?

He drove with all the windows open. It was just too hot, too stifling with the windows rolled up. Even this might draw attention to him, but he had no choice. He would suffocate if he kept the windows closed.

If not for the open windows, he would not have heard the dog snarling.

The sound came from an alley off to his right, and there was something about the sound, some quality in it, that held his attention. The hairs on the back of his neck stood up, and he felt himself breathing harder and snarling in response.

Venneman pulled over to the curb, turned off the car, and got out. He stood for a moment listening, and then walked cautiously into the alley. The dry snow crunched under his shoes. He sniffed the air and caught something wild in it. He moved over against one of the walls that formed the boundaries of the alley and moved on into the alley sideways, his back to the wall, trying to make himself as unobtrusive as possible. He could sense two heartbeats ahead, one of them faint and rapid, the other stronger and not quite so fast.

The snarling stopped.

Now he could hear a voice, high-pitched and speaking at a low volume. It seemed familiar. He stopped and concentrated on it, straining to hear it more clearly. "Come on, come here," it was saying. It was Karen Belmont's voice—her voice as it now was, the voice that had cursed him as she had arisen from the hole she had torn in his stomach.

He edged closer. The alley was dark. Not quite so dark as at night, but sheltered enough from the sunlight that Karen must have crept in here for protection when the sun rose. The ground and buildings radiated a fainter version of the red glow Venneman saw by at night. He took a few more cautious steps, and saw movement.

Venneman stood still, holding his breath, hoping she would not be able to hear his heart as he could hear hers.

But she was too intent on something else to notice him. She stood in a half-crouch, sideways to Venneman. She was still naked, and every muscle stood out on her slender body, quivering with tension. A small dog faced her, also crouching. Its ears were flat against its head, its eyes wide and fixed on her, its tail down between its legs, its lips drawn back to show its teeth.

It was too small to be a threat to Venneman, but it must have been a monster to Karen. She held her hand out to it and spoke to it soothingly, but Venneman could smell fear radiating from her. The dog seemed confused by the human voice and words coming from something so small. He moved a step toward Karen and then backed away, drawn to the potential prey but frightened by it at the same time.

He should be frightened, Venneman thought. Karen must have been sleeping in this sheltered spot, waiting for night, and been discovered by the dog. Perhaps it had already tried to attack her, thinking her some small animal it could kill and eat. Venneman looked but could see no wounds on the side of

Karen's body toward him. Perhaps she had been awakened in time by her vampire senses.

The parallel with his own killing of a dog and feeding on it the previous winter struck Venneman. The blood had been foul, but it had worked for him, given him strength. Was Karen strong enough right now to overpower this animal, which Venneman guessed must weigh more than she did? At best, the dog would be able to fight her off and would run away. At worst, she would suffer still more injury in the process, meaning more loss of blood, meaning more loss of size and overall strength.

To his surprise, Venneman felt an impulse to help her—not just to save her from the dog, but to rescue her completely, to take her back to his car and help her find a human being to feed on.

It's just guilt speaking, he told himself. She's a threat to you and a danger to your plans for Elizabeth Vallé. Leave her to her fate and keep on your way to Elizabeth's house.

But he couldn't leave. He was fixed in place, watching the strange miniature drama in fascination.

The dog's manner changed slowly under the influence of Karen's voice and hand gestures. His ears and tail came up partway, and he rose to a normal position. He still stared at Karen intently, but he no longer seemed on the point of attacking her. Karen, too, straightened and relaxed a bit. "Come here, boy," she said. "I won't hurt you."

We can't tell the truth, Venneman thought. It's as though our nature requires us to lie to other creatures, to our victims.

The dog was getting an erection. Karen relaxed still more and grinned at it. "That's right, boy. Come on, boy. Come closer."

Venneman stared in amazement. Was vampire sexuality so

strong that even a member of another species sensed it and reacted to it? Was that how Karen hoped to get the animal to come close enough—and let down its guard enough—for her to attack it?

The dog stepped cautiously closer to her, looking at her sideways. It seemed to still be struggling with the decision between approach and flight. But now the desire to approach was the need to couple, not the need to kill and eat. It stopped a foot or two away from her, just out of her reach, and wavered back and forth.

Karen cursed softly. Then she dropped to her hands and knees on the thin layer of ice and snow that covered the ground in the alley and turned so that her buttocks were toward the dog. She waited motionlessly.

The dog's desire overcame its fear. It leaped onto Karen's back, gripped the back of her neck between its teeth, and thrust itself into her. Its haunches moved back and forth like a piston. It grunted loudly with each stroke.

Venneman heard a groaning sound and thought it was coming from the dog. But he realized that it was Karen making the sound. Jesus, he thought, she's enjoying it! She's reacting to a goddamned animal!

Suddenly Karen twisted her upper body around. Her arm swept the dog's snout from her neck, and now she was holding its head tightly with both arms, keeping its mouth shut, and she was biting into its neck.

The dog squealed and tried to pull free, but she was too strong for it. Somehow, she must have been holding its penis trapped inside her. It could not even pull its haunches away from her. Its attempts to do so seemed to excite Karen all the more, for she groaned and writhed in pleasure as she tore at the dog's neck and sucked at its blood.

It was by now an old drama for Venneman, and yet this time it horrified him as rarely before. He had been forced by his own nature to accept the need of the vampire for human blood. He could even, intellectually, accept the transference of that need to an animal victim's blood under certain circumstances. But sex with an animal was beyond the pale.

Yet he watched. He watched, unable not to watch, as Karen fed until sated and the dog ceased moving. He watched as she thrust her buttocks one last time against the dog's now unresponsive torso and then pulled away from him. He watched the dog's still-erect penis against the ice and snow and the drop of colorless liquid that slowly squeezed its way out of the pointed glans. He watched Karen rise to her feet, look down, and kick the dog's carcass.

She looked up suddenly in alarm, and her eyes met Venneman's.

Karen gasped, turned, and ran deeper into the alley.

Venneman knew she could not go far before encountering sunlight. She would find more places to hide because of her size than he could, but even so, he could probably catch her if he wanted to.

But she might elude him and, when night fell, make her way to Elizabeth. She would have the dog's life in her. She could run through the wild places, finding her way in a manner he would never be able to.

Venneman turned and hurried back to his car. Daylight was the only sure ally he had.

The house was on a mountainside with a lovely view of the town in the valley below. It was on a north-facing slope of the mountain, so that the house was in perpetual shade. Elizabeth, Venneman realized, need never fear being touched directly by sunlight even in the daytime. A clever idea, and he gave her full credit for it. Then he turned his thoughts to getting inside.

Venneman had driven up the hillside on a hardtop county road which snaked back and forth in a series of rising hairpin curves. At intervals, he passed mailboxes, and beside each box was a dirt road that disappeared into the pine forest. He had turned off at the one Karen had described and had driven at least a mile before reaching the house. The county road had soon disappeared, thanks to the curve of the ground and the pine trees. Now he was parked on the leveled dirt that served as the house's driveway, examining the house from inside his car.

Fortunately, the owners of the expensive houses on the hillsides outside town valued their privacy as well as their luxury. From the car, at least, no other houses were visible.

He got out of the car, closing the door as quietly as he could, and walked slowly around the house, again quietly. He knew, though, that if Elizabeth were awake for some reason, her vampire hearing would render his caution pointless. He had to count on her following what seemed to be the normal vampire day-night cycle and being asleep.

He paused for a moment to admire the view of the town and to savor the smell of pine trees. The wind soughed in their tops, a steady, soft sound like the muted roar of a distant ocean. This was not an ocean that pulsated and heaved and had its hidden currents. This one was peaceful.

There were bars on all the windows. He could test his

vampire strength against them, he supposed, try to rip them out of the wall. But they were surely designed to withstand humans using tools, so they might well stand up even against him. For that matter, he suspected that at the moment he was not all that much stronger than a large, healthy human male. At intervals around the house, he encountered small signs implanted in the ground, telling him that the house was protected by Langston Security, Inc. and that any attempt to break in would trigger an alarm in the local sheriff's office as well as the offices of Langston Security.

As he had long ago, he wished he could transform himself as fictional vampires did, could become a bat and fly down the chimney and into the house.

But even if he could, wouldn't the bat be the same size as he was now? And that was still too big to fit down a normal chimney.

The chimney idea wasn't a bad one, he decided. Or wouldn't be, if he were small enough. And he could make himself small enough. He knew how to, now. All it required was massive loss of blood. He could take care of that by cutting himself open and letting the blood drain out, and cutting again every time his fast-healing vampire flesh healed itself. He tried to make himself accept the idea and imagined himself hiding in the woods near the house, cutting open the veins in his arm and watching the blood spurt out and splash on the pine-needle-covered ground. The flow of blood would stop quickly, he imagined, and the wound would close. Then, another quick cut. Venneman shivered. The images horrified him and made him feel faint.

I don't have anything to cut myself with, he thought, and

abandoned the idea.

Maybe there really isn't any alarm system, he thought. Maybe it's just a gimmick to scare off any would-be burglars. Maybe the doors aren't even locked.

He was at the rear of the house at this point. There was a door there, and he walked boldly up to it and tried to turn the handle. But the handle wouldn't turn. He went to a nearby window and tugged at the bars covering it. They were immobile.

The stupid woman, he thought. What would she do in case of a fire? Probably be completely unbothered by it, he realized. A fire would be insignificant compared to sunlight, and he already knew that even while it would injure and weaken a vampire, it could not kill one.

He had no strength to try anything else. He was still too weak from the blood he'd lost when Karen tore her way out of him. He might fantasize about the chimney, but even the act of climbing to the roof was beyond him now.

He had lost whatever advantage daylight might have given him. There was no point even in ringing the bell at the front door, since he was sure that Elizabeth wouldn't answer the door during daylight. Nor would there be anyone else there—a human being to take care of things during daylight. Venneman knew that from some deep instinct that arose from his non-human nature. He knew that no vampire would trust a human prowling about the vampire's home while the vampire slept.

Venneman went back to his car, started it, and drove it carefully into a narrow space between the trees, beyond the cleared land of the house. As far as he could tell, it was hidden from both the house and the dirt road. Then he left the car and retreated into the woods, where he sat down in the snow with his back to a tree. He leaned against it, supported by its unyielding strength, and waited for nightfall.

SIXTEEN

When dark came, Venneman grabbed the trunk of the tree and pulled himself to his feet. He made his way to Elizabeth's front door, and he had no need to pretend to be weak. He could hardly walk, could hardly stand. He leaned against the door and looked for a button to push. There was none. He pounded on the door with his fist. He could scarcely hear the sound himself. It was more a faint padding sound than a knocking. He felt dazed and scarcely able to think.

Suddenly, he sensed Elizabeth on the other side of the door.

The door opened. She was there, smiling at him. Smiling down at him. "Hello, Richard," she said. "I've been calling you for a couple of months, now. I'm surprised it took you so long to get here."

In the months that had passed, she had rarely been out of his thoughts, but the details of her appearance had become blurred. When he had thought of her, he had seen her only as a vague, threatening, hated image. How could he have forgotten how beautiful she was and what a powerful, magnetic physical presence she had? He remembered thinking, that first night in the bar, that she was handsome but far outshone by both Jill and Karen. Now he could see how blind he had been.

Venneman straightened slowly. She was still taller than he.

Elizabeth's welcoming smile gave way to puzzlement. "What happened to you? You look terrible! Come inside."

She put her arm around him and helped him into the house. Venneman leaned against her, excited despite himself by her greater size and strength. And worried by it. How could he carry out his intentions the way he was now, the way they were relative to each other?

Elizabeth helped him down a hallway lined with what Venneman took to be antiques. There were paintings on the wall that he assumed were expensive, although he lacked the background to identify them. "Now I can see why you didn't come earlier," Elizabeth was saying. "You must have lost a lot of blood, and you're still not recovered. How did it happen?"

Yes, it really was her voice and her image in his dreams of the ocean of blood. That had been the way he had heard her call, he realized. And yet it hadn't controlled him, the way she evidently thought it had. That must have been another effect of the change wrought in him by Dinsmuir's machine, Venneman realized. The control Elizabeth was used to exerting effortlessly over the souls of those she had envamped had no power over him. Little power, he corrected himself. I *am* here, after all.

When he didn't reply, she asked again. "What happened to you, Richard? How did you get so hurt?"

They had reached a small sitting room. It, too, was furnished with antiques. The red light washed out all colors, but as far as Venneman could tell, everything was in perfect condition. "You live well," he said.

"I've always liked to," Elizabeth said. "And I can afford to buy what I want when I see it."

"Elizabeth Vallé, famous romance author, who only shops at night," Venneman said.

She laughed. "I have agents who purchase my things for me. I window-shop at night, and they buy it for me by day. Delivery is more complicated, but I'm not interested in talking about that. Sit down over here." She led him to a couch, a graceful thing with curved, narrow legs. She helped him sit down and then sat beside him. There was scarcely room for both of them on it.

"This thing's old," Venneman said. "Is it safe to sit on it?"

"It only looks old," Elizabeth said. "It's a replica of a piece from 17th-century France, but it was made here in America just a couple of years ago. Carefully crafted to look like an antique."

"You like old things. Is that another vampire characteristic you didn't have a chance to tell me about?"

Elizabeth stared at him for a moment, weighing something. "There were a lot of things I didn't have a chance to tell you about vampires. I'm sure you've already discovered many of them on your own. No, I don't like old things. I don't like being reminded of age and death. But I do like beautiful things, whenever they were made. I especially like the way this sort of furniture looks in nightlight. It lets you just make out the colors. Beautiful. Don't you think so?"

Perhaps she was right, Venneman thought, looking around him, but he had no way of knowing. He could remember the pearl-grey glow she called nightlight, but even that memory was fading for him. The red light in which he saw the room and everything in it, the light which glowed from every surface, coming from no particular direction, washed out all color except for the color of blood.

"You still haven't told me what happened to you," Elizabeth said. She leaned slightly toward him. For a moment, she became a looming, menacing figure.

Venneman tensed, trying not to shrink away in visible fear.

"You seem to be avoiding the subject," Elizabeth said.

Because I can hardly tell you the truth, he thought, and I need to make something up. "My fiancée tried to kill me," he said, suddenly inspired. "I made her a vampire, after I left here and got back home. I ... envamped her. I didn't know what I was doing. I didn't realize. It just happened."

Elizabeth nodded understandingly. She put her hand against Venneman's cheek. He was pleased at how little effect the gesture had on him now. It had not affected him when Karen had tried it, either. He pressed his face against her hand, though, hoping the motion would make her think she was still in control.

"You tried to make love to her, didn't you?" Elizabeth asked.

Venneman nodded.

"But you were still in the early stages and very hungry and thirsty, and you lost control and took her blood during the act of love."

"The act of love," Venneman repeated. "There wasn't much love in it."

"No." Elizabeth shook her head. "There never is for us. Mutual need, mutual gratification, mutual hatred. That's the combination we feel. So your fiancée—what was her name?"

"Jill. Jill Kennedy. Was her name and still is."

"And always will be until the end of time. You'll be meeting her again, you know. Over and over."

No, Venneman thought, she'll be avoiding me until the end of time. "Yes, I realized that afterwards."

"So she woke up as a vampire," Elizabeth continued, "and of course she hated you. That's natural for our kind, too—to hate the one who created us."

"Created us?"

"Made us a vampire. I'm your creator, and you were Jill's. You hate me, but it doesn't matter, because you also need me so much and because I control you so completely. Anytime I want to, I can exert control over you. You realize that by now, don't you, Richard?"

"Influence, maybe. Not control."

Elizabeth smiled. "You'll see. If you had stayed, I'd have shown you how completely I can control you whenever I want to. I'd also have trained you to do the same to your own creations. Then your Jill wouldn't have been able to attack you. What did she do?"

"She pounded a wooden stake into my chest while I was asleep."

Elizabeth burst out laughing. "A movie fan!"

Venneman nodded. "Jill always watched vampire movies. She was addicted to them. So of course she did to me what worked in the movies. And it did hurt. A great deal." He had a flash of physiological memory, a brief return of the awful pain he had felt when Karen had torn her way out of him. "It was terrible, and very bloody." He noticed Elizabeth's surprised and skeptical look, and he added, "I yanked it out of me right away, of course, and the wound started to close up, but she grabbed it and rammed it into me again and kept it in there, working it back and forth to keep the blood flowing."

"Hmm," Elizabeth said. "And she was already a vampire, so she had the strength to do that. Sometimes the strength is temporarily greater right at the beginning."

"I was weakened by pain and loss of blood. And I couldn't bear to hit at her, not after what I'd already done to her. Making her a vampire, I mean."

"But all this was months ago, almost a year!" Elizabeth said. "You look as though it just happened to you."

"Oh, it did just happen. I env—made Jill into a vampire back then, right after I got away from here. Then we lived together for a brief time, but we separated. I couldn't handle her open hatred of me. I moved to another city, but she tracked me down and got into my apartment while I was asleep. That's when she attacked me."

"She tracked you down because you were calling to her without realizing it," Elizabeth said. "You could have avoided that, if you'd known how to. That's another thing I would have shown you. But I'm puzzled. You were sleeping during the day, of course. How could she have broken in during daylight?"

"Why, you're right," Venneman said. "I never even thought of that. She must have broken in during the night, while I was away, and waited for me. I still haven't adjusted my thinking, I guess. I tend to think of other people sleeping during the night, even when they're vampires. Well, that's a detail. It doesn't matter."

"How did you get away?"

Venneman frowned. "I can scarcely remember. I can remember the pain and fear, and trying to push her away without hurting her. I guess I must have managed to throw her off and get out the door. Anyway, I headed straight for my car and started driving here. I wanted to stop and feed. I needed it desperately. But I couldn't, somehow. All I could think about was getting here, to you."

"Of course," Elizabeth said. "You don't have to worry about anything, Richard. I'll get you what you need. I even have someone who helps me in that regard nowadays. I think you may have known her in your previous life. Together, we'll feed you back up to your normal size. And then I'll take up your education where we left off."

Elizabeth stood up and pulled him to his feet. "She won't be back for a few hours. We'll be able to begin with the feeding then, using whatever she's brought back with her. In the meantime..." She bent suddenly, put one arm around his shoulders and another behind his legs, and lifted him up. She held him tightly and effortlessly. "In the meantime, we'll use the hours in another way."

She carried him from the room, down the hallway, and up the stairs at the end. Venneman was too frightened of her to even try to resist.

Venneman awoke with a start, amazed to realize that he had fallen asleep for a few seconds during Elizabeth's violent lovemaking. He managed to respond until she had finished, even though he felt that he was suffocating under the weight of her body. When she was done, she stayed on top of him. He tried to move out from under her, but she kept him tight in the steel grip of her arms and legs.

"I think I like you like this," she said. "Smaller and weaker than me. I don't think I want to feed you back up to where you were before. What do you think of that idea, Richard?"

Before he could answer, she covered his mouth with hers. Then she raised her head again and said, "Yes, I like this. I'll let you feed on whatever Karen's bringing us tonight, but a limited amount."

Elizabeth had been referring to Karen all along! Of course. This made it certain that Karen would be trying to reach the house. It also meant that Elizabeth would become suspicious if Karen didn't show up.

Venneman felt a rising sense of panic. There was no way he could attack Elizabeth. His diminished size and strength compared to hers made the idea a joke. He couldn't wait until she exhausted herself with sex and fell asleep, for she showed no sign of doing so. He didn't know how many hours remained until dawn, but he was sure it was too many.

He tried desperately to think of something. Elizabeth lowered her face to his again. Her tongue shot into his mouth. It seemed immense to him, filling his mouth, choking him. Even thinking about how to overpower her was impossible. He could think of nothing other than Elizabeth's tongue.

He bit deep into it and swallowed the blood that suddenly filled his mouth.

Elizabeth made a strange, loud sound deep in her throat and hit the side of his head. He was stunned by the blow but kept his hold. She grabbed his head and tried to force him away. He wrapped his arms around her head and held on desperately, sucking as hard as he could and swallowing rapidly. But she was far too strong for him. He could feel her head slipping out of his grip and her tongue pulling out of his mouth, tearing away from between his teeth.

He bit harder, sucked harder, hoping only to weaken her enough. He could feel his own strength growing again at last, but how fast was hers diminishing?

She pulled free of him, sat up with one hand clapped over her mouth, and slapped him twice with the other hand, back and forth, knocking him first to one side and then the other. Elizabeth growled out some words, but they were indistinguishable through the hand covering her mouth and the blood running between her fingers. She glared down at him. Venneman stared at the blood leaking down her hand, fascinated by it, yearning for it. He raised his eyes to hers and froze, terrified by the desire to destroy him that he read in them.

Then Elizabeth made her mistake. Instead of using her still superior physical strength, she kept staring into Venneman's eyes, trying to exert the control over him that she assumed she still had.

Venneman lay quietly, staring back at her, trying to convince her that she was succeeding.

She seemed satisfied. She rose to her knees, letting him fall out of her, then swung her leg over him and climbed out of bed. She leaned against the wall for a moment with her free hand, her other hand still covering her mouth. He could hear her swallowing repeatedly.

She's cheating me, he thought. That blood belongs to me. I should be the one swallowing it.

He hadn't swallowed enough, he thought, despairing. I'm still too weak and small, and she's still too big and strong.

Elizabeth turned to look at him again. She stood beside the bed, staring down at him thoughtfully. "Too eager for blood," she said. Venneman could barely understand the words. They were muffled, as though her mouth were filled with something large and inflexible. "Should have foreseen it." She raised her hand slowly and pointed at his face. "Don't move. Stay."

Like a dog, Venneman thought as Elizabeth turned and left the bedroom. Which is all I would ever have been to her, if I hadn't used Dinsmuir's machine. I'd be what she's made Karen into.

He waited until she had left the room and then slipped out of bed and followed her. He was heartened by the new energy he felt in his body. It might not last, and it might not be enough, but he had gained more from that small amount of Elizabeth's blood than he had realized. The blood of an older vampire, he thought. Distilled, thickened, more vital than the blood of someone like Jill or Karen. The lives of all her victims are circulating in her blood, and now I'm benefiting from all of them.

Elizabeth was at the end of the hallway, looking out a window. Watching for Karen and tonight's supply of blood, Venneman realized.

He crept down the hallway toward her, his naked feet silent on the carpeting, but of course she heard him—heard his heart pounding in fear and excitement.

She spun around. She froze when she saw him, amazed that he was free to move about in defiance of her order.

Venneman ran the last few feet and threw himself on her, flinging his arms around her chest and burying his teeth in her neck, biting.

They staggered back together and crashed through the window, tearing the bars from the wall. They fell through the red night air, Elizabeth striking at him, Venneman sucking eagerly.

They landed on the cleared dirt of her driveway, Elizabeth on the bottom. Her back hit the ground, Venneman's forearms underneath her. Venneman could feel the bones in his arms shatter and the crackle of some of her ribs snapping. But the bars from the window had landed under both of them, impaling them, pinning them together on steel stakes.

For the few seconds before both of them healed, he was the master. Before those seconds were over, he had taken enough of her blood to remain the master.

At last he pulled himself off the bars that penetrated his chest and rose to his feet, sated, filled with the energy of Elizabeth's blood. He bent his head and watched the holes in his chest close. Elizabeth lay dead on the ground, not breathing, not bleeding, seemingly already shrunken.

Venneman hadn't even felt the bars pulling through his body as he stood up. He held up one arm, made a fist, relaxed it. There was no pain in his forearm. Elizabeth's blood had filled him with life and energy and made his healing even faster than usual. Was this how she felt all the time? Was this how he would feel, eventually? And how much more intensely this way would he feel by morning?

He felt eyes on his back and heard a familiar light, rapid heartbeat. He spun about quickly, just in time to see Karen's frightened face pulling back into the forest.

She must think I can't see her hidden in there, he thought. But he could. She showed up clearly in the red light glowing from the trees and the earth.

He turned and looked back at the house. He remembered Elizabeth locking the front door again after letting him in. Karen would have no way of getting in, given her still reduced size and strength, and he'd better keep things that way by doing nothing to breach the house's security. He bent and picked up Elizabeth's flaccid corpse, held it up over his head, and threw it upward with all his strength.

Arms and legs flopping in the air, Elizabeth's body sailed upward through the red night, arced over, and fell through the open window through which she and Venneman had crashed moments before. He heard her land inside and roll briefly across the floor.

Venneman turned and looked toward the woods. Karen still stood there, watching, her eyes wide and her mouth open. Venneman grinned at her. Then he turned again toward the house, took a few steps back, ran forward, and leaped.

His fingers scraped the broken edges of the window and slipped off. He grabbed wildly at the wall. He caught the jagged holes where the bars had been anchored. He hung for a moment, his fingers jammed into two of the holes, his feet dangling, brushing against the rough brick. Slowly, he pulled himself up until he was in a crouching position, knees against the wall, fingers gripping the insides of the holes left by the bars. Only his hands' grip was keeping him up.

He was exhilarated. My God, he thought, it's so easy! I'm so strong! He looked over his shoulder, down and toward the woods again. Karen had come to the edge of the driveway and was staring up at him. "Go away!" he shouted to her. "Elizabeth is mine, now!"

He let go with one hand, cautiously, and found he could still hold himself in place. With the free hand, he reached up and knocked out the remaining glass in the window, pushing it into the house. Then he grasped the window frame and pulled himself up and crawled back into the house. He stood barefoot on the broken glass covering the hallway carpet. Elizabeth lay a few feet further down the hallway, motionless. Venneman turned and leaned out the window. Karen was still standing where she had been before, still staring up at him. The look of wonder on her face had been replaced by one of open hatred. "Go away!" he yelled to her again. "You can't do what I just did. You can't do anything."

After a moment, she lowered her eyes and turned and walked into the woods, her shoulders slumping.

What a ridiculous little manikin she is, he thought, trying to hide from himself the pang of pity he felt for her.

He turned back to Elizabeth and began his night's work.

By dawn, Elizabeth was less than three feet tall, while Venneman had grown accordingly.

He had spent the time between each feeding watching Elizabeth come back to life. She revived far more rapidly than either Jill or Karen had. The strength of her vampire life force must be greater than that of the other two women, Venneman speculated, just as her blood was more powerful than theirs. He knew that each feeding on her had invigorated him more than his feedings on them, and he had gained more weight and height and alertness each time. It was a good thing for vampires, he thought, that the rest of them couldn't feed on each other.

On and off through the night, he heard sounds from outside that he knew must be Karen Belmont trying to find a way in. For the most part, he ignored the sounds. As he grew and Elizabeth dwindled, his worry about what Karen might do to interfere with him faded.

When he could see the sky growing light through the broken window at the end of the hallway, Venneman left Elizabeth dead on the floor and went downstairs. He unlocked the front door and stepped out into the daylight. He left the door open behind him, knowing that Karen, wherever she was, would not cross the open space to get into the house. Strong and large as he now was, he had no more fear of her, no matter what she did. He retrieved his car from where he had parked it the day before and drove it in reverse up to the house, parking with the trunk against the door. He got out, opened the trunk, and went back into the house.

Only then did he realize that he was still naked.

He went upstairs and checked Elizabeth again. She was stirring already.

He hesitated for a minute, wondering if he dared take the time to get dressed. No, he thought. She had recovered too quickly the previous few times during the night. Each time, she had come back to life and immediately attacked him. The first time, she had almost escaped. So he must hurry with her, and there was no need to spend time dressing her. No one would see her.

He picked her up, went quickly downstairs with her and out to his car. He put her into the trunk and lowered the lid partway, completely shading her. Altogether, she had been exposed to the sun for only a few seconds. Even that had been enough to make her moan in pain and for blisters to appear on her skin.

Elizabeth opened her eyes and stared up at him. She tensed for a moment, as though she planned to attack him again, but then she squinted her eyes at the brightness of the light outside the car trunk, and she touched her blistered face gingerly.

"That's right," Venneman told her, "it's daylight. You should be safe in there, but you know what it would be like if you got out. I don't know if you're still strong enough to break out of a locked trunk. Probably not." Thinking of Karen tearing her way out of him, he wasn't so sure. But Karen, after her body had managed to reconstitute itself, had probably drunk his blood inside him as she worked to chew and claw her way through his tissues. So perhaps she had been stronger at that moment than Elizabeth was now. Besides, the metal of the car was a much harder barrier to break through than vampire flesh and muscle, tough though those were. "Even if you can somehow," he went on, "I'll just stop the car and feed on you again, and then you'll be dead for a while again, so I can keep on driving. So every time you try to escape, you'll just end up being made smaller and even weaker. Not to mention the pain you'll have to endure while I feed. Save yourself all of that by just lying quietly in there for the next few days."

He started to close the lid, but Elizabeth stopped him by saying, "Are you still blaming the Devil for what you've become?"

"What are you talking about?"

"I made you a vampire, but you made yourself a rapist and traitor. That must have been in you all along, Richard."

He slammed the trunk lid angrily and stalked to the front of the car. He got in, but then got out again and walked back to the rear of the car. He unlocked the lid and held it open a few inches, enough to allow him to yell at Elizabeth, "I've never raped anyone! And what I did wasn't treason, it was self-defense."

He slammed the trunk lid again and went back into the

house and dressed quickly. He came back outside and opened the trunk a crack to make sure Elizabeth was still there. She lay on her back, as he had left her, her arms crossed protectively over her breasts. She stared up at him unblinkingly despite the brightness of the sky behind him. Venneman glanced at her naked body, still beautiful and womanly and desirable despite her shrunken size, and at her blistered face. Then he lowered the lid, pressing it down until he heard it click. He got back into the car and started the engine, trying to suppress his feelings of guilt. Rape and treason, he thought angrily. Meaningless. None of that applies to me.

He raced down the dirt road through the pine forest. Off to his left, he thought he glimpsed a small, human figure running between the trees, trying to keep up with him. Karen.

He wasn't sure if he had really seen her. Perhaps he merely had a guilty conscience despite his brave defiance of Elizabeth's words, and that had made him imagine seeing Karen. Nor could he be sure that he had seen, rather than imagined, the canine shape winding its own way between the trees behind Karen, perhaps following her, perhaps hunting her.

Venneman kept his speed up all the way to the county road, then to the town, then through it, then along the state highway, and finally to the interstate. There he headed east, back toward Denver.

All along, he saw no one, no human beings, no other cars, no animals. He was alone with the vampire in the trunk of his car and the beast of self-loathing in his mind.

SEVENTEEN

By sunset, Venneman was far to the east of Denver, on an almost empty interstate highway, surrounded by rolling farmland that was snow-covered in the shadowed low places and brown and dead on the high ground. A red glow lay over all of it—from the setting sun behind him, this time, not from the bloody light of nighttime. Ahead of him lay Kansas and many more miles and hours of empty highway.

Venneman kept glancing in his rear-view mirror, watching the lid of the trunk, half expecting to see it begin to bulge upward as Elizabeth tried to force her way out. But it remained smooth and normal. Gradually, he began to relax.

After dark, when he was in Kansas and the few other cars on the highway had their headlights on, Venneman judged it safe to pull off the road and have a look in the trunk.

He almost chose a rest stop built and maintained by the state, but it was brightly lighted and there were other cars there. One of them was a Kansas state trooper car. He drove on for a few miles and then pulled off on the shoulder. He would have to be quick in order to avoid attracting the attention of any would-be Good Samaritans.

He stood beside the car for a moment and breathed in the clean night air. It was filled with the smells of the wildlife hiding in the fields or sleeping beneath the surface of the ground. For a few seconds, he let his sense of hearing become more sensitive so that he could listen to the many small, fast heartbeats. He felt filled with happiness and peace for the first time in almost a year. He had not undone what had been done to him, and he had finally become resigned to the fact that he never would be able to undo it. But at least he was beginning to have his revenge.

Venneman walked to the back of the car, listening with fascination to the faint crunching his shoes made on the gravel with which the shoulder of the highway was covered. He unlocked the trunk lid and raised it slowly, carefully, fully on his guard.

Elizabeth lay on her back just as before, her arms still across her chest. Her eyes were closed and her face was tranquil. She might have been asleep, or perhaps laid out in a coffin for public viewing before burial. The blisters were entirely gone. Venneman listened to her strong heartbeat and the powerful rushing of her vampire blood and felt reassured. He had done her no permanent harm, of course, and he could safely continue as he had planned. He stood for a moment looking at her, admiration warring in him with hatred. After all, she had been driven by her nature to do what she had done to him, not by malice. The world glowed red as always at night, but Elizabeth glowed with a light of her own, a purer, brighter red.

Car headlights washed over him and stopped, lighting up Venneman and the back of his car. A male voice called out, "Everything okay, sir?"

Venneman looked over his shoulder. A police car had

pulled up behind him. He cursed himself for letting his fascination with Elizabeth make him so unwary.

"No problem," he called out. "Just thought something was shifting in the trunk."

Suddenly both troopers were out of the car and pointing guns at him.

One of them yelled, "Hold it, don't move!"

The other trooper, his gun still on Venneman, strode forward, shouting, "You've got a kid in there, you motherfucker!"

Venneman turned back to the car. Elizabeth was sitting up, wearing a lost and woebegone expression. "Damn you," Venneman muttered.

She chuckled softly, a sound only he could hear.

He could kill both troopers in a moment, he knew, and with any luck, no passing motorist would see it happen. But what if they had already called in where they were and what they had seen, including a description of his car and his license plate number? He was trying to avoid complications, not create new ones. He had wanted to make this trip unnoticed, and now this had happened practically at the start. "Damn you," he said again.

Something pressed against the back of his head. The trooper bellowed in Venneman's ear, "Put your hands behind you, motherfucker!"

"Such language in front of a child," Venneman said. But he put his hands behind him and let the trooper click the handcuffs on.

The other trooper had joined them and was leaning over the trunk, reaching for Elizabeth. "There, honey, you're okay now. You're safe."

Elizabeth rose to her knees. Fully illuminated in the squad car's headlights, her arms by her side, still naked, she stared at the state trooper.

The trooper drew back and turned to his comrade. "Uh, I don't think she's a kid," he said.

Elizabeth lunged. She gripped the back of his shirt and pulled him backward, off his feet. With a yell, he fell over the back of the car and into the trunk with her. Before he could yell again, she was at his throat.

The other trooper yelled and grabbed at his partner, trying to pull him away from Elizabeth.

Venneman hesitated for only a moment. The decision about what to do had been taken out of his hands, and he knew he must not waste time.

The moment he had already spent thinking about what to do was an infinitesimal fraction of time to a human being. The trooper in Elizabeth's grip was still gurgling and fighting against her and his partner was still tugging at the dying man's shirt. Venneman pulled his hands apart. The links connecting the two cuffs snapped immediately. He leaned over the second trooper, swung his arms out and brought them together again, the broken links on the cuffs meeting at the man's head with a loud crack. The trooper dropped limply onto the edge of the car trunk and slid to the ground, blood gushing from his head.

Elizabeth cried out and flung her victim aside. She scrambled from the car and pounced on the trooper on the ground. "Don't waste it!" she shouted. She fastened her mouth on the side of his head and sucked vigorously.

Venneman glanced at the man in the trunk. He was still moving, and blood was spurting from his torn neck. "You're wasting the other guy's blood," Venneman said calmly.

Elizabeth pulled away from the trooper's shattered head long enough to say, "Help me! Drink it, store it for me!"

Venneman shook his head. "I only feed on vampires nowadays."

Frantically, Elizabeth flung the trooper away and jumped back into the trunk to resume feeding on the first victim. She was crying with frustration while she drank.

Venneman left her at it. He picked the trooper up from the ground and carried him back to his squad car and flung him inside it. He paused for a moment, listening to the chatter over the car's radio, trying to make out any messages addressed to this car, any indication that others might be on the way to help. But he could make no sense of the welter of voices and the arcane, abbreviated messages. He shrugged and returned to his own car.

He was just in time to catch Elizabeth as she rose from the still body of the state trooper and tried to escape. She jumped out of the car trunk and ran toward the fields beside the road, but Venneman took two long steps and caught her.

He tucked her under his arm, her back toward him. She squirmed and twisted, trying to get at him with her teeth, but to no avail. He noticed that she felt a bit heavier than before, thanks to the gallon or two of blood she had had time to swallow.

Venneman pushed the dead trooper all the way into the trunk and shut it. Then he carried Elizabeth to the side of the car facing away from the highway and crouched down. He put her on the ground and held her there, his arms straight. "Now you're going to be stronger again," he told her. "And I can see that you'll keep trying anything to get away. So I'm going to have to feed on you again and kill you again. That way, you won't come back to life until morning, and when you do, you'll be even smaller and weaker." He bent toward her.

Elizabeth struggled desperately. "Richard, no! Please!" She burst into tears.

Venneman drew back in surprise.

"It hurt so much last time, Richard. Please don't do it to me again."

"It hurt that state trooper you just killed," he told her. "It hurt me when you murdered me a year ago. That didn't stop you."

She stared up at him. "But this is different."

Irrationally, he found himself agreeing that it was.

"Don't put me in the trunk," Elizabeth said quickly. "Let me sit in the car with you. I won't try to escape. I give you my word. I want to be able to see the world, and I want to be able to talk to you."

Venneman knew she was trying to exert the control she was used to having over those she had envamped. Perhaps it would be a good idea to let her think she still had that kind of control over him. Slowly, he nodded. "And if you do try," he said, "you know I can catch you, and you know what I'll do. Come with me now. Stay right by my side."

Venneman opened the trunk again and carried the trooper's body off the road, into the darkness. He pulled the uniform off the corpse and then took the undershirt off. He handed the undershirt to Elizabeth. "Put this on. It'll be long enough to cover you entirely, and I won't have to worry about anyone seeing us and thinking I've got a naked young girl in my car."

"There's blood on the back of your car," Elizabeth said. "Aren't you going to wipe it off before we leave?"

"I hadn't noticed," Venneman said. At night, to his eyes, everything was covered with blood now. He could no longer distinguish smears of real blood. He took a handkerchief from the rear pocket of the dead man's trousers and held it out to Elizabeth. "You wipe it off while I do something about the other car."

They waited beside Venneman's car for a few minutes while a huge truck passed by, followed by three or four passenger cars. Then the highway was dark and empty again. Elizabeth bent over, looking at something on Venneman's car that he could not see. He walked quickly to the state trooper car and stood beside it on the highway side. He glanced at the body in the front seat, and then squatted and gripped the car frame just under the driver's door. He straightened his legs slowly, and the police car rose up onto two wheels. Venneman heaved, and the car flipped over away from him, rolled once, and then rolled a second time off the highway and into the darkness beyond. He turned to find Elizabeth watching him.

"You could have just driven it off the highway," she said.

"I wanted you to see what I can do now," Venneman said.

Elizabeth nodded. "I'm proud of you, Richard."

He walked back to her. "Did you wipe the blood off?"

She raised her eyebrows. "You can't tell? It's gone. I didn't wipe it off. I licked it off." She pointed down. "And off the ground, too."

"You have a real problem," Venneman said. "Have you ever thought about a twelve-step program?"

Elizabeth smiled. "The likable things about you haven't changed at all, Richard. I'm glad about that."

Venneman felt uneasy at the speed with which she seemed to be regaining her self-control and equilibrium. "Get in the car. We've been here too damned long already." When they were both inside and he'd started the engine, before he pulled back onto the highway, he told Elizabeth to fasten her seatbelt. That sent her into a long peal of laughter, but she did it and then sat grinning at him.

They drove in silence for hours.

Venneman stopped to fill up at an all-night station on the western edge of Kansas City. He pulled up beside one of the full-service pumps so that he could stay inside the car with Elizabeth. He searched her face, but he couldn't tell if she was disappointed at his not leaving the car. Perhaps she really wasn't planning to escape, he thought. Then he told himself not to be foolish. He must keep his guard up.

The young attendant wiping the windshield seemed fascinated by Elizabeth. She stared at him, encouraging his interest. Venneman rolled down the window and held out two twenties. "Take this and get lost," he told the young man. The attendant looked into Venneman's eyes, and his cocky grin faded. He took the money and busied himself at the pump. Venneman waited until the gas cap had been replaced, and then he pulled back quickly onto the highway and accelerated.

More hours passed silently on the highway.

Elizabeth finally broke the silence. "What happened to change you?" she asked. "You can tolerate sunlight, you drink vampire blood, and you have no ethical or moral standards at all. What did you do to yourself?"

Venneman glared at her briefly and then turned his attention back to the highway. "No ethical or moral standards," he repeated. "And you're capable of infinite hypocrisy. It's your fault if I'm less moral and ethical than I used to be. As for the sunlight and the vampire blood..." He paused and then decided not to continue. Let her wait.

After a few minutes of silence, Venneman said, "When I came to your house last night, you were waiting for Karen Belmont, weren't you?"

"Yes, I was," Elizabeth said. "How did you know that?"

"Because I met Karen in town, and she told me. More or less. Right before I killed her."

Elizabeth said, "You're lying, of course. You must have already discovered that you can't kill a vampire."

"I can," Venneman said. "Because of my special abilities, which other vampires don't have. You know I can drink your blood, right?"

"Obviously," she said.

"And you know what happens as a result. You saw how you shrank in size when your body tried to replace the lost blood, right?"

Elizabeth said nothing.

"Right," Venneman said. "Well, that's what I did to Karen. Except that I did it repeatedly, until she was small enough." He glanced at Elizabeth. "Small enough," he repeated.

She was pressed against the door, looking at him with a horrified expression. "Small enough for what?" she whispered.

"Small enough to eat," Venneman said. He turned his attention to the road again. "I chewed her up and swallowed her." He took one hand off the wheel and patted his stomach.

"She's a part of me, now. And she's dead."

He thought he heard a sob, and he looked quickly at Elizabeth. She was staring ahead at the onrushing roadway. There was no sign of tears in her eyes or grief on her face. Perhaps he had imagined the sob. He looked away. "She's dead," he repeated. "I killed a vampire."

"Why haven't you done the same thing to me?" Elizabeth asked.

Venneman pondered the question, searching for a plausible answer. "Too quick and easy," he said at last. "I think you deserve something much more special. Karen wasn't the one who made me a vampire. She was your victim, too, just like me. I was doing her a favor, really. I was saving her soul from further pollution. Well, maybe she wouldn't have agreed with me, but that doesn't matter now."

The road ahead rippled and heaved. It tore apart and waves of blood washed out of the jagged openings and flooded across the roadway. Venneman gasped and gripped the wheel hard. This couldn't be happening!

He slowed down, creeping slowly toward the sea that had spread across the world, its red waves breaking on the short stretch of solid highway that remained.

"What's the matter?" Elizabeth said. "What do you see?"

A car came up behind him, its horn blaring, and swerved into the passenger lane. Despite the closed windows of both cars, Venneman heard shouted curses as the other car sped by him. It plunged ahead into the bloody ocean and was swallowed up without slowing down. There was no visible sign of its entry, no waves, no surf surrounding it.

Venneman gritted his teeth and accelerated.

"Richard," Elizabeth asked again, "what do you see?"

"Nothing," Venneman said. "There's nothing there."

The highway had reformed itself, stretching like a floating bridge across the surface of the ocean, which heaved beneath it and sent thin washes of red foam over it. As Venneman drove on the seemingly solid road, the ocean surface froze in place, becoming the normal surface of the world. Venneman understood now that the rolling hills and valleys of the farmland around them were in actuality the momentarily hardened waves of the ocean, disguising themselves as firm ground. Then even that illusion became more convincing as the landscape slid, stretched, became flat. Now he could see endless stretches of winter-frozen farmland in all directions.

But the ocean was still there. He could sense it, hungry, eager, just beneath the unstable skin, the illusion of the world. Stay down there long enough, he pleaded with it. Just until I'm finished.

He relaxed slowly and drove in a normal way. He could feel Elizabeth's eyes on him. "Maybe you're losing your mind," she said suddenly. "Maybe feeding on vampire blood does that to a vampire. I wouldn't know, because you're the first vampire I've ever known who could drink the stuff. Maybe you've had so much of it already that it's destroying your brain."

"Or maybe it's the effect of eating another vampire," he snarled at her. "You haven't forgotten what I did to Karen already, have you?" He rubbed his stomach again. "Just pretend she's still with you, sitting right beside you, Elizabeth."

Elizabeth said nothing.

After a while, Venneman said, "Looks like it's starting to get light. Time for you to get back into the trunk."

She shivered and licked her lips. "I was..." She tried again. "I was buried alive a long time ago. I really don't—Please don't, Richard. Look, let's stop somewhere for the day. At a motel. We could just sleep together for a few hours. Wouldn't you like that, Richard? Wouldn't you like to make love to me again?"

The image made Venneman shiver with desire. "You think I'd take the chance of falling asleep next to you?" he asked her. "Why do you think I'm such a fool?"

"Richard, maybe you don't need to sleep, either, the way you've changed. But I still do. I'm already feeling tired because daylight's coming, and also because of what I've been through. And I'm hungry, because of what you did to me. I need human blood. Those state troopers weren't enough. I've got to feed and sleep. That's all I can think of now."

Venneman looked at her. She seemed haggard, suddenly. He suppressed the pity that rose in him. "That's all you can think of?" he said. "What about making love with me?"

Elizabeth shrugged. "Whatever you want. I'm completely in your control now. Whatever price you want, I'll pay it."

"I'd never ask anyone to pay that sort of price," he snapped. "What do you take me for?"

"A completely evil being," Elizabeth said.

When Venneman turned off the highway, Elizabeth stiffened in fear. "Don't worry," he told her, "I'm not going to put you in the trunk. We're stopping at this motel."

Not until he pulled up in front of the office did he realize that it was the one he had stopped at before, during his trip west the previous year. He had fed on the young female night clerk here, his second victim since his transformation, his first after

Willie Gold. Was his stopping here now a coincidence, or had his unconscious chosen this place? Venneman tried not to think about it. What difference did it make, anyway?

He turned to Elizabeth. "I'm taking you at your word. Just sit here and don't try to run away while I go inside and get us a room."

Elizabeth nodded. It was almost, Venneman thought, as though she were too weak to speak.

As he got out of the car, Venneman wondered what had happened to the young woman who had been working at the motel the year before. By now, she would be physically completely recovered from what he had done to her. He hoped she was psychologically recovered, too, hoped that she had managed to forget about it, to put it behind her. His vampirism had destroyed his own life and dominated his thoughts every waking moment, but there was no reason it should do the same thing to his victims.

She had probably moved far away from this place right after her encounter with him, he guessed. He would have.

The office door was locked. A sign on it directed him to press a button beside the door for service after business hours. He couldn't remember the sign or the button being there the last time.

He pressed it and waited, staring at the ground. He felt the pressure of someone's gaze and looked up. A small video camera was mounted above the door. It was aimed down at him, and the light on it glowed red.

The door was yanked open. A young woman stood in the doorway, staring wide-eyed at him. Her face was gaunt and there were dark shadows under her eyes, but he recognized her and remembered her name. "Anita! You're still working here?"

She nodded. "Waiting for you. I stayed on the night shift. I knew you'd be back. I tried going away, but I couldn't forget the way it felt, so I just stayed here."

Venneman stepped backward, shaking his head. "No. We'll go somewhere else."

"He fed on you," a familiar voice said, "and you liked it?" It was Elizabeth, standing beside him. The top of her head reached almost to his elbow. She had grown more from feeding on the two state troopers than he had realized.

Anita stared at her in fascination. "What are you?"

Elizabeth laughed and then smiled at her. It was a thoroughly charming performance, and it seemed to entrance Anita. "I'm just like him," Elizabeth said. "Did he feed on you, and did you like it?"

"Yes, he did. And it was wonderful."

"I could do that for you, too," Elizabeth said. "Let's go inside, and I'll show you."

"She's lying," Venneman said. "Don't believe her. She's not like me at all." He gripped Elizabeth's arm and started to pull her away. "Come on, we're going somewhere else to find a room."

"Richard, we don't have time!" Elizabeth said urgently. "Look at the sky!"

Venneman could see the greyness of dawn warring on the horizon with the redness of night. She was right. For Elizabeth, there wasn't time to go back on the highway and search for another motel. He hesitated, not knowing what to do.

"You owe me this," Elizabeth said, keeping her voice low. "I haven't recovered from what you did to me. You have an obligation, Richard."

He owed something to Anita, too: to leave her in peace. And yet Elizabeth had a point. Perhaps if she fed sparingly on Anita—and it would be sparing, because of Elizabeth's diminished size and therefore diminished capacity—she would be all right for the rest of the trip. Reluctantly, Venneman let her lead him inside the motel office.

Anita was holding out a key. "2B," she said. "Same room as before. I always try to keep that one free to the end, even when the place is filling up, just in case."

"How sweet!" Elizabeth said, reaching for the key. "Isn't she sweet, Richard? What's your name? Mine's Elizabeth."

"Richard," Anita repeated in a soft whisper. "Uh, Anita. Nita. Call me Nita."

"Nita," Elizabeth repeated. Venneman could sense the seductive control she was aiming at the girl. It was the power she had exerted over him when they had first met in the mountains, and it was having the same effect on Anita. "Come, Anita," Elizabeth said. "Come with us to the room."

Elizabeth moved backward slowly, and both Venneman and Anita followed her. She turned and walked away, confident that they would stay behind her, and they did.

She's not back in control, Venneman told himself. But she's controlling Anita, and I have to stay with them.

He went back to close the office door and then followed the two women up the stairs toward the second-floor balcony, marveling at the strength Elizabeth's small body exuded and the way she dominated the much larger girl who walked behind her and towered over her.

Nightfall.

Elizabeth stretched slowly and awoke. She had been lying on her side with her back to Venneman. Now she rolled over and looked at him and at Nita's corpse.

The dead girl lay against Venneman, her head on his shoulder, her arm across his chest, as though she were sleeping. Venneman shifted, burying his head in Nita's hair so that Elizabeth would not see the tears in his eyes.

"That's very touching," Elizabeth said. If she intended sarcasm, Venneman could not detect it in her voice. Perhaps she was being sincere.

She vanished into the bathroom, and Venneman heard the shower running for a while. Elizabeth came out, naked, her hair wet, toweling herself. She went to the window and drew the curtains cautiously aside so that she could look out. "Good, it's dark. I think I'll wear her clothes now. They'll be too big for me, but that'll be better than that stupid T-shirt you took from the policeman. Come on, Richard. The night is young, and we'll always be young."

Nita will always be young, Venneman thought. The dead don't age, either, just like the undead.

He slid his arm out from under her head and moved her gently aside so that she lay on her side on the bed. Her body was flaccid. If there had been rigor mortis, then it must have come on her and then passed away again while he and Elizabeth slept their profound vampire sleep. Had he dreamed of the sea of blood? He didn't think so. He thought that for once he had slept without dreaming. He had fatally misjudged Elizabeth's capacity and the depth of her need for blood. He had helped her murder this innocent girl. Yet he had slept more peacefully, even with the dead girl's head on his shoulder, than he had in a long time.

He went into the bathroom and began to shower. He turned the water temperature as high as it would go and stood under it, thinking about Nita and her death.

He had held her wrists so that she would not be able to struggle once Elizabeth bit into her neck and she experienced agony instead of the delight Venneman had given her. She had looked at him while Elizabeth fed, her face filled with bewilderment as well as pain, her eyes pleading with him. At the end, he had tried to push Elizabeth away, but he had tried too late. Satiated, Elizabeth had fallen asleep, while he had lain cradling Nita, stroking her hair and face, trying to soothe and comfort her, hoping she would live, but listening to her faint heartbeat dwindle to nothing.

Now she was nothing.

He could have saved her right up to the end. He could have made love to her and sucked what little blood remained in her, quickly, while she still lived, so that she would die and reawaken as one of them. It would have been a kind of rescue. But it would have been worse than what he had already done to her, so he had done nothing.

Venneman came out of the bathroom to find that Elizabeth was pulling the dead girl's clothing off. She put it on herself. The clothes hung on her, looking foolish, but they were not so loose as he had expected them to be. She was right, he thought. This would look better when she was sitting in the car than the trooper's undershirt had.

He put his own clothing back on. "What are we going to do about the body?" he asked.

Elizabeth shrugged. "Why should we bother doing

anything? We'll leave it here."

"Drained of blood?"

"Do they do autopsies automatically in this state? Maybe they do. But you know, the first thing they'll think, when they see her throat, is that some maniac stopped in here and decided to rape and murder the night clerk. By the time they examine her more carefully, we'll be long gone."

"They'll check the register."

"You didn't have to register, Richard. Don't you remember? Nita had the key all ready, and you didn't even have to sign in. There's no trace of us."

No trace, Venneman thought. Our kind leaves no trace except for the ruined lives of our victims. Or the lives we've taken from our victims, he thought, looking at Nita's corpse, now lying naked and pale on the bed.

Elizabeth noticed his glance. She pushed Nita's feet under the covers and pulled the covers up over the girl's body, tucking them in under her chin. "There," she said. "Now she looks like she's just someone sleeping in late. Maybe that'll delay things a bit further."

"You didn't have to kill her," Venneman said. "You could have stopped sooner."

"No, I couldn't have," Elizabeth said. "I needed all the blood I could get, thanks to you. And I was helping you, protecting you from her. She knew your name and your license number. I bet you did register the previous time you were here, didn't you?"

When Venneman didn't answer, Elizabeth chuckled and set about wiping various surfaces with the undershirt she had been wearing when they arrived.

"Fingerprints?" Venneman said. "Do vampires leave them?

Dead people don't sweat, do they?"

"I don't know about you," Elizabeth said, "but I still sweat. We're not dead, Richard. I've explained it to you before. We're living beings. We're just a higher form of life than we were before. I don't know if your prints are recorded anywhere, but I know mine are. Mine were among the very first ones ever recorded, I think. I suppose those records may have been lost, but maybe not, so I'm always very careful about this. I can just imagine the questions it would generate if someone did match my prints to those early ones, given the dates involved."

"What are the dates?"

She reached up and stroked his cheek, and a shiver ran through him. "Oh, Richard, don't you know that an older woman always likes to hide her true age from the younger man she's involved with?"

Venneman turned away and headed toward the door.

"Wait a minute," Elizabeth said. "Do you have the room key?"

"In my pocket."

"Leave it in here. And put the DO NOT DISTURB sign on the outside handle. That'll slow things down a bit more."

"You think of everything," Venneman said.

"Yes," Elizabeth said. "You're lucky I'm with you."

EIGHTEEN

Venneman entered the city he had spent most of his human life in. He drove down a city street with boarded-up stores on both sides and loose papers stuck to the glaze of ice that covered the road. He drove slowly, cautiously. It was alien territory, now. It seemed dangerous to him.

Elizabeth sat up looked out the window with interest. "I haven't been back to this part of the country in about fifty years," she said. "It hasn't improved."

Venneman would have said something in the city's defense, but it looked seedier and less appealing than he remembered. What had happened while he was away? It had been less than a year. Could there have been an economic collapse in such a short time?

He drove around aimlessly, marveling at the unfamiliarity of the place. Was it the red light illuminating everything that made it seem so different, he wondered, or was it something else, some real change in the city or in him?

"It'll be daylight again in only a couple of hours," Elizabeth reminded him. "I hope you have a hiding place already picked out. You see, Richard, this is why vampires tend to avoid unfamiliar places! I don't know this city at all—not the way it is now, anyway. I wouldn't know where to go to spend the day safely. But I'm sure you've planned ahead carefully, haven't you?"

He ignored her heavy-handed sarcasm. In fact, he hadn't thought about such details at all. He had come here with only a vague plan, forgetting about the problem of daylight. Soon, according to that vague plan, daylight would cease to be a problem for Elizabeth. But in the meantime, he had to deal with it.

They were only ten or fifteen minutes away from the apartment he had once shared with Jill. Yearning for that lost past overcame him briefly, the wish to drive there and somehow magically bring that past back into being. But strangers would be living in the apartment now, and the past lay on the other side of an uncrossable gulf, the chasm separating life from death. He had lost a life that had been satisfying and safe, no matter how unexciting it had been. Elizabeth had taken that away from him when she had robbed him of his humanity.

He needed time to think out his next steps in detail. Was there anyone he could call on for help?

How few friends he and Jill had had! It hadn't seemed to matter before, but now the realization struck him forcefully and made him feel even emptier and more cut off, made the city seem even more alien and unfriendly. It wasn't that we had each other and therefore didn't need friends, he thought. It's that we were both frightened of other people. We used each other's company to justify avoiding our fellow human beings.

"If you don't have something specific in mind," Elizabeth said, urgency in her voice, "then maybe you'd better find another motel. And quickly."

"The sunlight doesn't bother me, and I don't feel tired," Venneman said. "Perhaps you should just spend the day in the trunk of the car." He glanced at her and then away. "Never mind. I've got a better idea."

Venneman headed north to Jefferson Avenue and turned east. When he glimpsed the administration building, the university's only highrise, he pointed it out to Elizabeth. "That's the campus where I used to work. That's where I acquired my tolerance of the sun. An enlightening experience. You'll get a chance to see it and learn all about it later."

Elizabeth was looking at him instead of at the distant building. She wore a puzzled expression.

Venneman smiled at her. "Don't worry. All will become clear."

They drove past the campus, past the lights of downtown to their left, and kept on as the city gave way to semi–rural suburbs.

Ahead of them, the sky was growing lighter. To Venneman's eyes, Elizabeth looked tired as well as worried. "We'll make it," he told her. "Don't worry. You have nothing at all to worry about. You're in good hands."

Elizabeth gave him a scornful glance. "Good hands! You've already murdered Karen. How are you planning to kill me? The same way?"

"Kill you? No. I'm not going to kill you. I wanted to at first, but then I came up with something better. You'll see."

They lapsed into tense silence as Venneman threaded his way through the curving streets. He had driven over here only once before, and he wasn't sure if he was remembering the way correctly. The houses here were small and widely separated from each other. It was a neighborhood of large, old trees, now bare of leaves, and lawns that, in the summer, always seemed near death.

At last Venneman parked the car and turned off the engine. "This is it, I think. Come on." He got out and waited on the sidewalk for Elizabeth to join him. The sidewalk was cracked and parts of it had been pushed up by the roots of the huge trees that lined the street.

"How quaint," Elizabeth said.

"Well, there aren't any famous, wealthy romance writers living here, that's true. Or vampires. So it's a good place to raise your kids. If you had any kids. If any kids would ever want you as a mother."

Elizabeth smiled up at him, unaffected by his attempt at wounding her. "My life has been more complicated and full than you can imagine, Richard. I wanted to make you a part of that and show you how wonderful life can be for our kind. I'd still like to."

"I thought you said I was a completely evil being."

"I've changed my mind. You're just embittered and lonely."

"You mean all I need is a good woman to reform me? I wonder where I'd find one of those. Maybe in this house. Let's go find out."

He strode up the pathway to the front door, leaving Elizabeth to run to try to keep up. Each of his steps equaled two of hers.

Venneman knocked on the front door and waited.

"Who lives here?" Elizabeth asked.

Venneman ignored her. He could hear footsteps and a

heartbeat within the house. He had never listened to that heartbeat before, but he knew instantly that it belonged to the person he wanted, that he had come to the right place. He could not have said how he knew whose heartbeat it was. Somehow, it matched the personality.

The door opened, and Dale Whitmer stood there. She stared at Venneman, her eyes wide. "Richie! What are—" She stopped suddenly, leaned out the door, looked up and down the street quickly, and then pulled him inside the house. "Get inside! The police have been looking for you since you disappeared!"

Only then did she notice Elizabeth, who had followed Venneman inside the house quietly. "What—" Dale corrected herself. "Who are you?" she asked Elizabeth.

"A friend of Richie's," Elizabeth said. She reached up and hooked her arm through Venneman's. "A really, really good friend. My name's Elizabeth. What's your name, dear?"

Dale looked her up and down, puzzled. "Dale," she said automatically. Then she shook herself, as though to rid herself of Elizabeth's disturbing influence, and looked up at Venneman. "Where's Jill? Richie, you've got a lot to explain!"

He did, but he still wasn't sure how much of it he could entrust to Dale. He had always known intuitively that she was a fundamentally trustworthy person, even though he had never before presumed on that trust or asked her for help with personal problems. Still, asking her first to believe the story he had to tell and then to help him with what he was planning was probably expecting too much. "I don't know where Jill is," he said finally. "She may be back in town, but I don't know. We're not together any more."

"Did you kill Willie? That's what the police said."

Venneman shook his head. "No, of course not." He paused, then took the plunge. "Jill killed him. She's a vampire."

Dale stared at him, her mouth open. "A vampire? You mean like in the movies? Have you gone nuts?"

Elizabeth said, "That's a good question. Richard, are you insane?"

Venneman yanked his arm away from Elizabeth's hand angrily and said to Dale, "I'm not crazy. Look, do you know how Willie died?"

Dale shook her head. "All I know is, Willie was found dead in your apartment, and you and Jill had vanished. The police were looking for you for months, and there were stories on the news about the two of you, how you killed the poor guy and then took off. Some sort of weird cult murder pact, or something. I don't know. I did ... I did hear from one of the other campus policemen that Willie's blood..." The words trailed away. She stared up at Venneman, her eyes filled with bewilderment and remembered fear.

"That all the blood had been sucked out of his body?" Elizabeth asked.

Dale glanced at her and then away, returning her gaze to Venneman's face. "Yes. All of his blood."

"Well, there you are," Elizabeth said brightly. "Sure proof of a vampire hanging around, wouldn't you say? You've seen all the movies, haven't you? Some dark, brooding fellow in a cape, a saturnine man with slicked-back hair. Have you seen anyone like that?"

If she had hoped to undermine Venneman in his attempt to convince Dale, Elizabeth miscalculated. The image she evoked elicited horror in Dale. "A vampire!" she said. "Richie, do you really mean it?"

"Yes, Dale," Venneman said. "I mean it literally. Jill became a vampire, and she killed Willie by draining his blood from him. I wouldn't have believed it either, but it's true. Anyway, I had to run to escape from her. She was after me, too. She probably still is. I think I know—" He broke off, then turned to Elizabeth. "Stay here." He bent down and whispered to her, "It's probably already too light outside for you to go anywhere, so just relax and do nothing."

He straightened and went to the window that looked out over the street. "Yes," he said, "it's dawn."

Venneman took Dale's arm and led her out of the room. "The back door," he said. "Let's go outside, in the back yard."

When they were outside the house, standing close to each other in the grey-lit, snowy back yard, he said quietly, "I don't want Elizabeth to hear us talking. Here, take my coat." He took it off and handed it to Dale.

She put it on gratefully. "Won't you be cold?" she asked him.

"I'm too keyed up to feel it." He looked at her for a few seconds, considering his next words. She was slightly shorter than he. Hadn't she been taller before? Or at least no shorter? He couldn't quite remember. He said, "That woman, Elizabeth. She's one of them. She's a vampire."

Dale drew back and stared at him, saying nothing. After a moment, she leaned forward again, ready to listen.

"You can see how small she is," Venneman said. "I think she was a normal midget before she became a vampire, and so she stayed small that way. Fortunately, it makes her a lot less strong than other vampires, so I was able to overpower her. She's a ... a friend of Jill's. I'm pretty sure Jill is chasing us in order to kill me and free her friend. I came here because I think I know how to use Dinsmuir's machine to kill both of them."

"Kill them!"

Venneman put his finger over his mouth. "They have much better hearing than humans," he said. "Than we do. Speak very softly." His own hearing was sensitive enough that he was monitoring Elizabeth's heartbeat all the while, alert to any indication that she was trying to leave despite the sunlight. So far, she had remained in Dale's front room. She was near the door, but she had not moved.

"How can you even talk about killing people, especially Jill?" Dale asked.

Her anger surprised Venneman, and her hostility saddened him. He had never felt anything but warmth and friendly concern from her. He put his hand softly against her cheek and stood there, saying nothing, waiting for the expected effect.

Dale's emotions changed. She leaned into his hand and stared into his eyes. He could hear her heart and the growing intensity of the rush of the blood.

Venneman withdrew his hand, feeling vile. Dale was the one human being he had not wanted to lie to or manipulate. She was the one person whose blood he did not want to hear.

Over Dale's shoulder, in a distant corner of the yard, something moved.

Venneman stared, frowned, concentrated. Against the white snow, a small pool of red glistened in the light from the dawn sky. It bubbled, a spring of blood. Suddenly, it gushed out of the ground and spread across the yard toward them.

"No!" Venneman yelled.

"What? What's the matter?" Dale turned around. She gasped and backed up against Venneman. "Richie, what is that thing?"

Oh, God, she sees it, too! Venneman thought. It's real!

He stared fiercely at the approaching arm of the bloody sea, concentrating, gritting his teeth. "Go back," he muttered. "Go away."

The pool of blood stopped spreading. Its surface froze and turned white. The bubbling spring died away and turned to ice.

"Dale, what did you see?" Venneman asked her.

Still staring at the now normal corner of her back yard, Dale shook her head. "I don't know. Something—something I imagined, probably." She turned back to Venneman. "I haven't been able to sleep well since you left. Sometimes I think I see things, but they aren't really there."

She sighed. "Things seemed normal and on track before. Everything's been screwed up since you left. And now you're back with this amazing story, and you've got that woman with you, and you claim she's a vampire! Richie, I don't know what's real and what isn't!"

She looked at his face and then stepped back and looked him up and down. "You've changed a lot. You're bigger and stronger. I'm scared of you, now, and I don't even know why. You'd never hurt me. That's what I'd say, if anyone ever asked me. And yet you're talking about committing murder!"

"I've had a lot of strange experiences since I left here," Venneman said. "A lot of them had to do with Jill and her vampirism. And with Elizabeth and her nature. Look, it's not that I'm happy about the idea of killing the two of them. I'm doing it to save my own life, and also the lives of their future victims. I'm like a soldier in a war. I'm doing what I have to do." He put his hand on her cheek again. "You must trust me, Dale."

They stood there for long moments, Dale softening. Her pulse calmed, slowed. "Yes," she said. "I trust you. What do you need?"

"Dinsmuir's machine, his experiment. It's running again, isn't it?"

Dale nodded. "Yes. He got funds from the government to fix it up and restart it after whatever it was that happened to it."

"I happened to it," Venneman said. "I was trying to use it to cure Jill at that point. You know how sunlight is supposed to kill vampires? At first, Jill tried to kill herself, after she discovered what she had become. She tried standing in the sun. It hurt her, but it didn't kill her. But it seemed to me that it had made her a bit more human again. So I persuaded her to let me try exposing her to the light inside Dinsmuir's machine. The way you explained it to me, it's a form of sunshine, but much more intense than what we feel when we go outside in the sun."

"Yes, I guess that's true, in a way," Dale said.

The light had increased while they had been talking. Nearby, a stretch of ground was illuminated by a shaft of weak sunlight. Venneman pointed at it. "Let's go stand over there and get a bit of warmth."

He noticed a subtle relaxation in Dale when they were standing in the sunlight. He knew that she was taking his lack of reaction to the light shining on him as proof that he was as human as she. He knew she had feared otherwise.

"We went to the lab during the night," Venneman said. "Willie was there. He let us in. Jill was so strong that she was able to pull the machine apart, open it up. Willie tried to stop her, but she knocked him out. Then she opened the machine and stepped into the light from inside it."

"Where were you during all of this?"

"I was waiting outside. Jill made me wait outside with Willie. To watch him and make sure he was okay, but also to stay away from any possible danger. When nothing happened after a while, I went into the lab. I found the machine open and dead, turned off, and Jill lying on the floor. She looked dead to me at first, but when I shook her, she woke up. And then..." He paused. "And then she attacked me. She went for my throat. Tried to kill me."

"Oh, Richie!" Dale put her arms around him and held him. Meant to comfort, the gesture filled Venneman with guilt.

He pushed her away, but gently, and went on. "The light from Dinsmuir's machine hadn't cured her, obviously. It made her worse, more thoroughly a vampire. I managed to break away from her just in time and run. I didn't know where to go, so I went back to our apartment. Pretty stupid, but I wasn't thinking straight."

"I can understand that," Dale said.

"Yes. Well, a short time later, Jill showed up there. She was carrying Willie. She made me watch while she tore his neck open with her teeth and sucked his blood until he died. He was fighting her, and I was trying to pull her off, but she was stronger than both of us. I came to my senses enough to run while she was still finishing up with Willie. I got in our car and headed west. I've been on the run ever since."

"My God!" Dale said. "I never thought any of that stuff was real. I thought it was just movies and books, you know?"

"I know. So did I. And I'm the guy who used to watch those

movies and read those books all the time. It turned out that Jill was hunting me. I don't know if it was some strange perversion of the love she had felt before, while she was human, or if she just wanted to get rid of me because I knew what she was. Anyway, she kept showing up wherever I was. A couple of times, near the beginning, she almost got me."

"And Elizabeth?"

"She introduced herself to me at a bar one evening. She—well, she picked me up. She was interesting. Fun. We went back to her place, and Jill was waiting there for me."

"You mean they were working together?"

Venneman nodded. "They almost got me, too. Then I found myself running from both of them. I finally figured out that Elizabeth was also a vampire, and that she was probably the one who made Jill into one in the first place. I think—" He paused, swallowed, went on. "I think they're lovers."

"Oh, Richie! I'm so sorry."

"Yeah. Anyway, I finally managed to turn the tables on them. I was able to get to Elizabeth when Jill wasn't around, and I overpowered her and brought her back here. I just know Jill will be following us. Then I'll get both of them, using Dinsmuir's machine."

"But if it didn't work the first time with Jill, why do you think it'll work this time?"

"I've been thinking about what happened when Jill pulled the machine open. She didn't know enough about it to keep it running. I bet that it stopped working almost immediately and she only got a small dose. Just enough to make her even hungrier and to change her attitude entirely—make her happy with being a vampire and all the more murderous."

"How awful!" Dale said. She frowned in thought. "The experiment had cutoffs engineered into it from the beginning, of course. You could be right about what happened." Suddenly she looked excited. "But Dinsmuir was in such a hurry to get it restarted and get his career back on track that he ordered us to bypass the cutoffs when we restarted it. It was quicker that way. Oh, Richie, I think we could do it! So how will we? Just wait until Jill tracks you here?" She shivered in sudden fear.

Venneman put his arms around her and held her tightly. "I'd never expose you to that, Dale. No, I don't plan to stay in your house or to keep Elizabeth there. I just had to go somewhere quickly to protect her from the sunlight."

Dale pushed him away. "Just a minute ago, you were talking about murdering her, Richie. But at the same time, you're protecting her from the sunlight because it would hurt her. Don't you see that you can't really kill anyone? It's not in your nature! You know you can't do this. It would be too awful. You do see that, don't you?"

"I think we're all capable of killing in self-defense, Dale. Or to defend those we love. That's no sin. That's all I'd be doing. That's not murder. Anyway, what I want to do is wait in the lab with Elizabeth, with Dinsmuir's machine all ready to open up the minute Jill shows up.

"And she will show up," he said. "I don't know how she does it, how she tracks me. Some kind of power that vampires have, I suppose. Whatever it is, she seems to be able to find me, eventually, wherever I try to hide from her. And she's really been hunting me seriously since I kidnapped Elizabeth. So she'll show up at the lab eventually—probably pretty soon. I'll have the machine set up so that I can open it quickly and push her into it. And Elizabeth with her."

"But you said she's very strong now, didn't you?"

"If I have to, I'll jump in the machine myself, carrying Elizabeth, so that Jill will follow us into it." He held up his hand to prevent Dale from speaking. "She's made my life not worth living, Dale. If I can't destroy her, both of them, then there's no point in surviving."

Dale looked away. "Are you going to ask me to help you kill yourself?"

"I'm still hoping it won't come to suicide, Dale. The only help I'm going to ask you for is to get me in and out of the lab. I don't have my cardkey any more, and even if I did, I'm sure I've been shut out of the security system. I wanted to go to the lab with you this morning, just to look it over and try to come up with some way of setting things up for whatever happens. We can leave Elizabeth here by herself. She won't even think of stepping outside during the day." He paused and concentrated on Elizabeth's heartbeat. "In fact, I bet she's asleep right now. They have to sleep during the day. Vampires, I mean."

"They really are like in the movies!"

"In a lot of ways. No fangs, though. And no feelings, no ethics, no morals, no souls. They'll use anyone, kill anyone, lie to anyone if it'll help them." He turned abruptly toward the house. "Come on, let's get going."

Elizabeth was indeed sound asleep. She was curled up on the couch in Dale's living room, her face pushed into the space between the cushions and the back, her eyes completely shaded from the light shining through the crack in the curtains over the front window. Dale walked softly to the window and fiddled with the curtains until she had eliminated even that light. Then she fetched a spare blanket from her bedroom and spread it over the tiny woman.

Venneman watched her in amazement. Dale gave him an apologetic look and went back into her bedroom to get ready to leave.

They arrived at the lab about half an hour earlier than Dale's normal time for starting work. People were walking along the campus pathways, and a small knot of junior faculty and students entered Currigan Hall with Venneman and Dale. But the others all headed upstairs, talking loudly to each other and paying no attention to Venneman and Dale, who headed down. Venneman relaxed. He had no idea what he would do if he were recognized. He certainly had no idea what he'd do if someone tried to apprehend him. For the moment, he was tired of violence. And it would interfere with his plans.

He relaxed even more when Dale opened the door of the lab with her cardkey without any difficulty. On some level, he realized, he had been expecting the computer that controlled access to magically know whom she was with and to sound an alarm.

The stepped inside the lab and closed the door behind them. Venneman sighed in relief. Dale fumbled briefly for the light switch.

Light flooded the laboratory. A woman screamed, and a man yelled "Shit!"

Professor Harold Dinsmuir rose up from behind the wooden bench that had concealed him. A young woman rose, too, and ran past them and out the door. She was holding her clothes pressed against her breasts. Venneman wondered idly if she intended to put her clothes back on in the hallway or to continue naked all the way out of the building and into the winter morning. Perhaps she hadn't considered the details at all, he decided.

Dinsmuir yelled at them, "What the fuck are you—" Then he recognized Venneman. "Richard Venneman! Holy shit!"

Venneman said, "The coeds get younger every year, don't they, Dr. Dirty?"

NINETEEN

"What do you want here, you fucking murderer?" Dinsmuir said.

"Asked the fucking professor," Venneman said. "I want your Nobel Prize."

"What? Listen, you idiot—"

"You're still naked, Dirty," Venneman said.

Dinsmuir grinned suddenly. "Does that make you uneasy, Richard? Does my nakedness disturb you?" He spread his arms wide.

"This man," Venneman said to Dale, "will be a sophomore all his life." He concentrated on Dinsmuir, listening to his heart and his breathing, smelling him, watching the faint, tiny movements of his body, the contractions and expansions of his skin.

Dinsmuir's heart rate increased and his smell grew stronger. He looked down at himself, muttered angrily, and picked his trousers up from the floor and pulled them on. "Cold in here," he said, and finished dressing.

Venneman smiled, feeling his power and control. I don't even need to take their blood first, he thought. I've grown so strong, I can manipulate them ahead of time, all of them.

"All right," Dinsmuir said, "what did you mean about my Nobel Prize? And Dale, I hope you've already called the police."

"No, Dr. Dinsmuir," Dale said. "I didn't see any reason to."

"Reason to? This man's a murderer, Dale! And now he's also a trespasser. You'll tell the police that he forced you to let him in here, that he gave you no choice. Don't worry, I'll take care of you."

Dinsmuir's way of manipulating people seemed silly and inept to Venneman now. And it seemed to be having no effect on Dale, he was pleased to see. Perhaps his own manipulation of her had inoculated her against Dinsmuir's.

"We don't have time for your blustering," Venneman said. "I was referring to the Nobel Prize you thought you were going to get because of your wonderful machine." It was at the other end of the lab, behind Dinsmuir. To Venneman's eyes, it looked unchanged.

Dinsmuir moved protectively in front of the huge cylinder. "No one's going to mess with this a second time!" he said loudly. "I had a hell of a time recovering from that setback before." A thought struck him. "Did you have something to do with that, Venneman?"

"I'm not Richard anymore? I'm hurt. I had everything to do with what happened, Dinsmuir. I cracked that drum, and I'm going to have to do it again."

Suddenly Dinsmuir was running around the bench and toward the door of the lab.

He certainly has kept himself in good shape, Venneman thought. Give him credit for that.

With ease, he caught Dinsmuir a few feet away from the

door and flung him across the bench. Dinsmuir crashed to the wooden floor and lay dazed. After a moment, he struggled to his feet.

"Nothing broken, I hope," Venneman said. "But I won't let you interfere." How am I going to keep him from interfering? he asked himself. Kill him?

"You shithead," Dinsmuir said. His voice had lost its force, and there was fear in his eyes now, instead of the usual arrogance.

Dale was staring wide-eyed at Venneman. "You're awfully strong, Richie. You couldn't have done that before."

Venneman read the suspicion in her pale, frightened face. "I've done a lot of weightlifting during the last year, Dale. Had to do what I could to protect myself against ... you know." He locked gazes with her.

At last she relaxed again and the fear left her face. She nodded. "Yes, I guess I understand."

Too much at one time, Venneman thought. Too many people to control. He had the feeling that events were getting ahead of him, that he was trying to control too many separate strands. They were diverging, making it impossible for him to keep his hands firmly on all of them at the same time.

Dale came to Venneman's side and beckoned him to lean forward. She whispered to him, "What are you going to do about him? You might need his help, but as soon as we leave, he'll call the police."

"I'm more worried about what he'll do to you after I leave," Venneman whispered back.

Dale smiled at him and squeezed his hand. "I'm past that point. I've got some good friends on the faculty now. He just doesn't know that. Don't worry about me."

"Okay, then. I'm going to have to give him what he's always wanted from me. That might do the trick."

Dale read the look of disgust on his face. "Oh, Richie!"

"It's a matter of life or death," Venneman told her. She was still holding his hand. He gave it a quick squeeze and then raised his head and looked at Dinsmuir again.

The physicist was busy feeling himself all over, reassuring himself that, indeed, nothing was broken in the precious Dinsmuir body.

"Everything in working order, Professor?" Venneman asked.

"Shithead," Dinsmuir muttered.

To Dale, Venneman said, "Stay here just in case anyone else shows up. Keep them occupied and away from the supply closet."

"Okay, Richie. I still don't think—"

"It's all right!" Venneman said sharply. He stepped around the bench and grasped Dinsmuir's upper arm. "Come with me, Harold." He began to pull Dinsmuir toward the rear of the lab.

"Richard, what are—"

Venneman stopped and stared into Dinsmuir's eyes. The man was still taller than Venneman, but not by so much as before. "Dinsmuir, I'm going to give you something you've always wanted, whether you want it at the moment or not." He squeezed Dinsmuir's arm harder. "Do you want it rough or gentle?"

Dinsmuir relaxed. "Richard, I don't—I never—" He stared back at Venneman for a while and then smiled. "I won't be able to get you your job back, if that's what you're thinking."

"I have a different calling now, Harold," Venneman said. He led the now cooperative Dinsmuir into the supply closet at the back of the lab and closed the door behind them.

Dinsmuir looked around the cramped space with its shelves full of stationery supplies and electrical components and down at the pail and mop on the floor beside his feet. "We could go to my house after my evening classes, Richard. That would be so much more comfortable."

"Oh, I'm much too eager for this, Harold." Venneman put his hands on either side of Dinsmuir's head and pulled him forward. "Just relax, now."

"Uh, Richard," Dinsmuir said, "I prefer to be in control."

"I could tell," Venneman said. He bent Dinsmuir's head to the side and put his lips against the man's neck. He bit the skin, just enough to make it bleed slightly. He looked at the tiny flow of blood, steeling himself.

"Ouch!" Dinsmuir said. "Hey, I'm not into pain!"

Venneman sucked the trace of blood into his mouth. Dinsmuir gasped in surprise. Resisting the urge to spit out the acrid blood, Venneman swallowed it and pressed his tongue against the small wound. The skin tore, parting under the pressure of his powerful tongue. The flow of blood increased.

Dinsmuir struggled briefly, but again Venneman sucked and Dinsmuir gasped in surprised pleasure. He wrapped his arms around Venneman and tried to pull him closer. Venneman ignored what was to him the man's weak grasp and sucked harder.

Dinsmuir sagged, held up mainly by Venneman's grip on his head. "Oh, my God!" Dinsmuir said. "I've never..." He gasped, unable to continue speaking.

Venneman thrust Dinsmuir away and stood with his eyes closed, supporting himself with a hand on one of the shelves, concentrating on not vomiting.

He felt a hand on his shoulder and looked up at Dinsmuir's stunned, pleading face. "Again, Richard, please! I don't understand what you were doing, or how you were doing it, but I want to feel that again!"

The nausea and burning were fading. Venneman concentrated on Dinsmuir. "That was nothing, Harold—just the biggest hickey of your life, that's all. I could give you a lot more than that, much more pleasure, more intense, much longer. But your Nobel Prize is more important to you, isn't it?"

Looking as though he hated himself for saying the words but could not keep from speaking them, Dinsmuir said, "Nothing is as important as this. Nothing. Please. Please, Richard!"

Venneman nodded. "Later. Help me use your machine for my own purposes, and then I'll reward you."

Dinsmuir looked at the floor and nodded.

On their way back to Dale's house, Venneman said, "When we were driving over this morning, I didn't have a firm idea what I was going to do. But with Dinsmuir's cooperation, everything's working out much better than I could have hoped. I'm getting optimistic about this at last."

"You're that confident about Dinsmuir?" Dale asked. "You don't think he might change his mind now that he's alone and has a chance to think about what he'll be doing to his career? You always hated the way you attracted sexual attention, but you've obviously changed. Now you're overestimating the power of your sexual attraction."

Venneman was surprised at the sudden anger and hostility in her voice. "It's a lot more complicated than that, Dale. It has nothing to do with the way people used to be attracted to me. I mean, it does," he said quickly, annoyed at himself for having said too much, "but there are other things involved. I can't tell you right now. Maybe when this is all over, I'll be able to explain."

"I suppose I won't ever be able to really understand it," Dale said quietly, a lifetime of sadness in her voice. "No one was ever attracted to me—especially the people I was attracted to."

"You have more important qualities, inner qualities," Venneman said, knowing full well how foolish he sounded. He tried again. "Having other people drawn to you physically isn't all that great."

"So you always used to say. I never really believed you. Not really and truly and fully. You and Jill. I can't imagine what it would be like to look like her. She's so beau—" She stopped in mid sentence. "Good God!" she said. "What does she look like now? Like a corpse, or something?"

"That would make it easier to recognize them, wouldn't it? Well, no, they don't look like corpses. You've seen Elizabeth Vallé. And Jill's even more beautiful than ever."

"Elizabeth Vallé," Dale repeated. "I know that name. Isn't she a writer or something?"

"A writer *and* something. A writer and a vampire. I'm surprised you recognize the name. You never struck me as the sort of woman who reads romances."

"More the sort of woman who reads physics journals and great works of literature, right?"

"I didn't say that, Dale."

Dale sighed. "You thought it. Yes, Richie, after a long, hard day of smashing atoms and reformulating mankind's basic understanding of the fundamental structure of the universe, there's nothing a gal likes better than to relax with a good romance novel. Historical romances—*that's* what she writes! Now I remember. I think I've read something by her."

"Was it any good?"

"It pales next to a good physics journal, of course. I don't really remember the book all that well. Something about a romantic young English nobleman going to the colonies and ending up joining the American Revolution."

"Henry Hapgood," Venneman said automatically.

"Why, I think that was his name! You read the book, too?" Dale said, laughing.

"The guy gets around." And why not? Venneman asked himself. He has eternity to indulge in the fleshly pleasures he loves. Whereas I'm using eternity to agonize over questions of Heaven, Hell, and sin.

"I read those books pretty quickly," Dale said. "Then I exchange them with a friend of mine. She was supposed to be bringing over a box of them this morning. Maybe there'll be an Elizabeth Vallé in there, and I can have her autograph it."

"Yes, maybe," Venneman said, scarcely listening. Then he realized what Dale had said. "This morning? What time?"

"No definite time," Dale said. "While I'm at work. She'll just leave them in the living room. She's got a key to the house."

"God damn it!" Venneman said. He stepped on the gas pedal.

What little traffic there was on the street was mostly on the other side, headed downtown. Venneman ignored traffic laws and Dale's protests as he sped along.

Dale shouted at him, "Richie! What the hell are you doing?"

"Trying to save your friend's life."

"What?" Then it sank in. Dale sat quietly, holding onto the dashboard with one hand and the door handle with the other.

There was a strange car parked in front of Dale's house. Venneman parked behind it and ran up the path toward the front door. Dale ran behind him, trying to keep up. Even from outside, from the porch, Venneman could hear the sound. The door was unlocked. When Venneman opened it, the sound was unmistakable: the noise of a vampire feeding greedily.

The sound stopped when Venneman stepped into the house. Across the living room, Elizabeth rose to her feet. An unmoving body lay on the carpet before her.

Dale screamed and ran past Venneman and dropped to her knees beside the body. "Laurie!" she shouted. "Oh, God, Laurie!"

Elizabeth watched for a moment as Dale cradled the dead woman against her and rocked back and forth, crying. Then Elizabeth strolled across the room to Venneman and said, "She was one of my fans. My fans keep me going. But now I think I'll go back to sleep. That woman, Laurie, woke me up, but it was worth it. I feel bigger and stronger already. Do I look bigger to you, Richard?"

In fact, she did. Venneman said, "You look more evil to me."

Elizabeth glanced again at Dale. "Your friend Dale looks big and strong, too. I bet she has a lot of blood in her. I wonder how much I'll grow after I've drunk all of hers. Or were you planning to take her yourself, Richard, and leave nothing for me?"

"Don't touch her!" Venneman snarled at her.

"I see," Elizabeth said. "You *are* planning to save her for yourself. Good night, Richard." She went to the couch, lay down, and seemed to fall asleep immediately.

Venneman went over to Dale and stood behind her, wanting to comfort her but not knowing what to say. He was acutely aware of his guilt in bringing Elizabeth to the house. He knelt beside Dale and put his arm over her shoulder. To his relief, she didn't shake his arm off or accuse him of guilt in Laurie's death. Instead, she leaned against him and put her tear-stained face against his shoulder.

Laurie's eyes were open, staring sightlessly up at them. Her neck was almost gone; he could see the bones of her spine. Such fury, such hunger! Why couldn't Elizabeth have let the woman live?

Because of what I did to her, he thought. Perhaps she couldn't restrain herself, because of the hunger my feeding on her induced. So this terrible thing is doubly my fault.

Elizabeth slept without moving. Venneman sat facing her in one of Dale's two rickety armchairs and watched without moving. He was listening even more than watching.

Almost imperceptibly, Elizabeth grew as she digested Laurie's blood. It would be far too little to make her anything near Venneman's size or strength, but she would be that much more able to fight against him and, perhaps, to escape.

Venneman was aware of Dale moving aimlessly about the house, distracted by the terrible death of her friend and by her friend's body. The body still lay in the living room. Venneman had forbidden Dale to call the police or to move the body before nightfall. Reluctantly, she had seen the wisdom in what he said.

For a few hours, Dale tried to nap in her bedroom on the

second floor. Venneman could hear her through the ceiling, tossing about on her bed, unable to sleep, trying to stifle her sobs. He wondered how long it would take her to recover emotionally from what she had seen, and if she ever would.

As the light faded outside, Elizabeth's heart rate and breathing speeded up. But still she lay unmoving. Venneman tensed and waited. The window grew dark.

Elizabeth changed in an instant from stillness to motion, leaping from the couch and running toward the door.

But Venneman had been waiting for exactly that. He caught her halfway and fell with her to the floor.

Her eyes blazed fury at him and she hit at his head and kicked him repeatedly. The blows dazed him. He struggled to grab her wrists or to pin her arms to her side, but she was already too strong for that. He managed at last to wrap his arms around her, trapping her arms, and his legs around hers, and to roll on top of her.

She twisted and bucked frantically in an attempt to break his grip or throw him off. Venneman held on and pressed his mouth to her neck. Elizabeth redoubled her efforts. She threw her head from side to side, pounding her cheek against his head. Venneman bit in desperately, chewing through the leather-tough skin and steely tendons, finding at last the honeyed blood.

When she was dead and he could suck nothing more from her, Venneman relaxed at last and lay atop her, gasping in release. He raised his head and saw Dale watching him.

Her hands were over her mouth and her eyes were enormous. Vomit dribbled between her fingers. She choked out unintelligible words.

For a moment, Venneman saw himself through Dale's eyes:

not a mighty predator taking what was his, but a man–sized rat. He said nothing. He lay where he was, looking up at Dale.

She swallowed repeatedly, dropped her hands, and said, "You lied to me."

"I'm not like them," Venneman said. "They made me this way. I had no choice."

Dale said, "You're lying to yourself. Are you going to kill me, now, the way she killed Laurie? And the way you killed her?"

Venneman pushed himself away from Elizabeth's body and stood up slowly. He avoided any sudden motion that might startle Dale into flight. "I'd never harm you, Dale. You're my friend."

Dale stared at him in horror. "My friend's dead! I don't know who *you* are!"

Venneman's senses were overwhelmed with the electricity of Elizabeth's blood inside him, suffusing him, becoming part of his ever larger, ever stronger body. He could scarcely hear what Dale said, could scarcely understand her words. It was like some faint, meaningless animal noise. He shook with sudden anger. She was making impertinent demands upon him, delaying him! He raised his hand.

What's happening to me?

He changed the motion of his hand and smoothed back his hair, hoping that Dale didn't realize that he had been about to strike her. That unreasoning vampirish anger—where did it come from? I was suppressing it, he thought. It was always there, waiting for its chance. I can't ever get rid of it. It's part of my nature now.

"I'm the same Richard Venneman, Dale," he said. "Except for one thing. Yes, I lied about that. They managed to get to me and change me into one of them. I knew if I told you that, you'd act the way you're acting now and refuse to help me. But can't you see from the way I've been behaving all day that I haven't really changed, that I'm the same as I was?"

He pointed at Elizabeth. "You think I killed her? Well, I wish it were that easy. She's still alive, unlike your friend Laurie. Elizabeth can't be killed, not this way. That's why I want to use Dinsmuir's machine, and that's why I want to step inside it with her. I want to kill myself as well as her."

"What about Jill?"

Venneman shrugged. "Her too, if she shows up. I'd like to kill all of them, all the vampires in the world, but I only know three of them. Anyway, Dinsmuir's machine is hardly portable, is it?" He snorted. "Maybe I should make Dinsmuir work on coming up with a portable version! Then I could take it around the world and try to kill all of them."

"How come you're able to go outside in the daylight?" Dale asked suddenly.

"You always were great at catching the little details," Venneman said admiringly. "You never let anything get away from you. You'll make a great physics researcher."

"Don't patronize me!" Dale snapped. "Answer my question!"

"I told you I'm not like them. I'm different from the rest of them physically, as well as psychologically. Being able to tolerate sunlight is one way. Another is that I can't drink human blood."

"Damn you," Dale said, "can't you tell me the truth? I know what I saw!"

"You saw me feeding on a fellow vampire. That's the only

kind of blood I can drink—vampire blood. I hunger for it the way they hunger for human blood. But human blood tastes like acid to me. I can't stand it. I can't force it down." A little lie, he thought, and excusable under the circumstances. And almost true, almost not a lie.

"How do I know if I can believe you?" Dale asked sadly.

"You don't. I'm trying to demonstrate my trustworthiness by my actions. One additional fact for you." He told her how humans reacted to his bite. "I don't know what they feel," he added. "I don't know if it's sexual or some kind of spiritual ecstasy. Whatever it is, they can't seem to live without it. That's why I know that Dinsmuir will do what I told him to. I took one mouthful of his blood, and that was enough. I spat it out immediately." His face twisted in disgust at the memory of Dinsmuir's human blood in his mouth. He imagined for a moment that he felt it burning in his stomach again.

The look on his face seemed to dispel Dale's remaining doubts. She came to him and put her hands on his shoulders. "Poor Richie. What did they do to you?"

"They destroyed my life. I'm not a human being any more, and I'm not even a real vampire!"

"You could try to live a normal life," Dale said. "You're not driven to attack humans, so that wouldn't be a problem. As for what you are driven to attack—well, they deserve it, don't they?"

Venneman smiled at her. "I'm surprised to hear that coming from you. You're right, though. They do deserve it. But there aren't enough vampires in the world. And I have trouble recognizing them when I do find them. Jill told me she could tell instantly, but I guess that's another way I'm different from the rest of them. I've spent the last ten months being hungry and thirsty and weak most of the time. I tried living among humans and being one of them, but it never worked. I was always cut off from them. I'm tired of it all, Dale. I'm tired of being alone and so different. I just want to put an end to it all. I want revenge, and then I want to stop it." He realized how true the words were, and he let his head fall forward onto Dale's shoulder.

She put one arm around him and the other around his neck. She rocked him slightly, like a child she was comforting. "It's okay, Richie. We'll do... this thing you need to do, and then we'll talk some more about it." She stroked his head.

Venneman felt more at peace than he had since his envamping. He put his arms around Dale and held onto her.

But he knew this taste of peace was a lie for him. A brief taste was all he could ever have. Perhaps Dale thought that she could save him. Perhaps she had fallen prey to the myth of the tortured, noble, larger–than–life outsider whom only she could understand and help. She could have no idea how completely outside all help and love Venneman had placed himself.

Was placed, he thought. No fault of mine. It was done to me, and no one asked my permission.

Humans could hold onto the illusion of a loving God and admission to Heaven at the end of life. Vampires could not afford illusions. No god worth worshipping would have allowed one of his faithful followers to be tortured and metamorphosed as Venneman had been. If God did exist, He must be an evil being with an evil plan for His creation. How could Venneman continue to let himself be used by such a deity? What was left for him to believe in? Better to cease to exist inside Dinsmuir's machine than to have to continue to deal with these dilemmas.

Perhaps what he had said to Dale really was the truth, and the machine would destroy him if he exposed himself to it a second time. He found himself hoping it would.

"Richie, would you..." Dale's voice trailed off, and then she tried again. "Would you show me what it feels like? I mean, I understand that it's disgusting to you, but just a little bit? I'd really like to know. To feel that, whatever it is, just once."

Venneman turned his head so that his face was against her neck. He watched the pulse beating there, sniffed at the warm blood rushing through her. He kissed her neck and then straightened up and put his hand against her cheek, this time with no desire to control her. "When we get back to the lab, look at Dinsmuir's face," he told her. "It may be some kind of pleasure to them, but it's also torture. I'm not going to do that to you. I'll never hurt you in any way."

To his astonishment, her face was suffused with love. She pulled his face to hers and kissed him quickly, then stepped away from him. "Don't you see how human you still are underneath, Richie?" she said. "I think what happened, what made you so different from the others, is that you didn't really become one of them. You're trapped in the middle—part vampire, part human. All you need is the right environment, and you can be healed. Let me help you. We'll do it together."

Venneman yearned for what she was offering, in spite of everything he had learned during the past ten months.

And then he heard Elizabeth's heartbeat and breathing begin again behind him. Dale disappeared from his thoughts. All he could think of now was Elizabeth and the task ahead.

TWENTY

Dinsmuir was waiting for them in the lab. He was sitting at Dale's desk, his shoulders slumping, his head forward, his chin resting on his chest. When Venneman entered, Dinsmuir's head snapped up and he jumped to his feet.

"You're back at last!" Dinsmuir said. "I've been waiting here all day. Why, I had a class to teach, and I forgot all about it until now!" he said wonderingly. "I've never done that before."

"Physics 101, perhaps?" Venneman asked. "Filled with juicy little freshmen with elastic skin?"

"Yes, I think that's was it." Dinsmuir was staring fixedly at Venneman's mouth, and he spoke vaguely, as though the class he had been momentarily alarmed about missing had vanished from his thoughts again.

"You do have some kind of control, after all," Elizabeth said suddenly. She stood in front of Venneman with her arms behind her, her wrists held tightly in Venneman's grip. He had been holding onto her all the way from Dale's house, while Dale drove. She had made no attempt to escape, instead sitting quietly in the car and looking out the window, as though interested in the way the city had changed and looking forward with interest to whatever Venneman planned.

"You fooled me, Richard," Elizabeth continued. "Good for you." She was squinting against the bright overhead lights, but other than that, she was remarkably cool and relaxed. She examined Dinsmuir's slack face. "It's different from what I've seen before, though. How interesting. You'll have to explain to me what you've done to him."

Dinsmuir tore his eyes away from Venneman's face and looked down at Elizabeth. "Who's this, Richard?"

"This is the subject of our experiment, Harold. Meet Elizabeth Vallé. She probably has more publications than you."

Dinsmuir didn't rise to the bait. "Oh," he said in a dull tone. Then his gaze drifted upward from Elizabeth's face and back to Venneman's, where it remained fixed.

"This is something else, isn't it, Richard?" Elizabeth said. "There's some other kind of control going on here, isn't there?"

"You'll find out," Venneman told her. "I don't plan to keep you in the dark."

Dale came into the lab. "Okay, Richie," she said. "I stuck my badge into the slot out there and bent it back and forth until it broke. It's not likely that anyone would come down here this late at night, but just in case, they'll probably get discouraged and give up when they can't get their cardkey into the slot. This may make the doors inoperable. I don't know. We'll deal with that when we're ready to go."

"Everyone's so willing to help you, Richard," Elizabeth said. "That's impressive. Really. Of course, they don't know you as well as I do. Oh, pardon me. I should have said, everyone's willing to help you except your former fiancée. She is the one who stuck the stake into your heart, isn't she?"

Dale gasped and put her hands to her face. "Richie! You didn't tell me about that!"

"It doesn't matter any more," Venneman said. "We heal quickly." He turned to Dinsmuir. "Harold, I want you to unseal the two cylinders. Then we'll open up the machine."

"I'll have to power it down," Dinsmuir said, speaking slowly. He raised a hand sluggishly to gesture, let it drop limply to his side. "Power it down first. Take a while to do that."

"No," Venneman said, "you don't understand. I want the power on. It's the energy inside it that I need. I need to have it open and in operation."

Dinsmuir frowned, trying to understand. He shook his head. "Can't do that. That'll kill you."

"This is a different kind of science, Harold. Just do what I tell you to, without arguing, and I'll..." Venneman hesitated and glanced at Elizabeth. She was listening with fascination. Why hide it now? Venneman asked himself. "And I'll do it to you again," he said to Dinsmuir. "I'll give you your reward."

Dinsmuir's face lit up, and he hurried away.

Dale said, "But aren't you going to wait for Jill to show up?"

Venneman frowned at her and shook his head, warning her to keep quiet.

"Now this is really interesting," Elizabeth said. "Obviously, that man wants you to feed on him instead of being terrified by the idea, and big full-blooded Dale says you're supposed to wait for your former fiancée. Why, this is a mystery."

Ignoring her, Venneman said to Dale, "I just realized that it would make things too complicated and dangerous if Jill were here. We'll do it one at a time. First Elizabeth, and then Jill when she shows up. And as for you," he said to Elizabeth, "you're going to have to cooperate with me. Harold isn't strong enough to crack the cylinder. It's going to take my kind of strength. Which means I'll have to let go of you. Now, you can just stand here and wait, or you can try to run. But you should know by now that I'll catch you easily if you try to escape, and you know what I'll be forced to do then. I'd rather have you alive and conscious."

Elizabeth disappointed him by becoming thoughtful rather than frightened. She stood quietly for a while, considering the options he had given her. Finally, she said, "Obviously you're planning something nasty for me, Richard. Given that, it might be in my best interests to try to escape, despite your superior speed and strength. At the worst, I'd be no worse off than if I didn't try. However, I also want to be conscious so that I can see what happens here. I have a strong intuition that it's going to be a more interesting evening than you intend."

"You never stop trying to manipulate, do you?" Venneman said, marveling at her. "It's too late for that, Elizabeth. So you'll just stand here and not try to run?"

Elizabeth nodded.

"I don't believe you for a minute," Venneman said, but he released her wrists. "However, I do need my hands. So I'll have to keep watching you. Dale, please go over to the control panel and stay there, so that I'll be between you and Elizabeth. You can help me by keeping your eyes on Elizabeth all the time. Yell if she moves an inch."

"You know she's not fast enough to do that, Richard," Elizabeth said. "I could be at her throat before she made a sound. If you're willing to wait for twenty-four hours, you could make her fast enough. I know you know how to do that."

Dale said to her, "You mean, tear out my throat and make me into one of you?" She straightened her back and said proudly, "Richie would never do that to me."

Elizabeth raised her eyebrows. "My, my." She smiled at Dale. "Perhaps you aren't aware of all that's involved in the process, Dale, sweet sack of blood."

"That's enough," Venneman said. "Dale, please. The further away you are, the safer you'll be." He motioned with his head, and Dale went hurriedly across the lab to the control panel at the rear of the cylinder.

"Just give up, Elizabeth," Venneman said to her. "Just leave these people alone and stop trying to control them. They don't deserve this. They've never hurt you."

Elizabeth stared at him expressionlessly for a moment. "They're nothing to me, Richard, except as a way to get at you."

Venneman threw his hands up in disgust. He turned his back on her and walked over to Dinsmuir's machine.

Dinsmuir was there with a random assortment of tools in his hands. He was looking confusedly from the tools to the cylinder and back again. He looked up as Venneman approached. "I don't know how to do this, Richard. I tried to loosen the bolts, but nothing happened." His eyes filled with tears.

"Christ, Dinsmuir," Venneman said, "I sucked out some of your blood, not your brain cells! Wake up." He wondered what was the matter with the man. What had happened to his brilliance and sharpness? The way he was now, he'd be of little help.

"Go over there with Dale, by the control panel," Venneman told him. "I'm going to open the machine, and I want you and

Dale to make sure the energy keeps flowing all the time. That'll be your job."

Dinsmuir let the tools drop from his hands and fall clanking on the floor. He wandered toward Dale, not following a straight path.

"On second thought," Venneman called out, watching him, "Dale can handle it. You just stand there next to her and keep her company." He shook his head in amazement.

Venneman bent down and rummaged among the tools. He chose a wrench that looked the same to him as the one he had used to open the cylinder the previous time. He had needed two of them then, but he could only find one in the pile of tools Dinsmuir had fetched. "Shit." He straightened up and held up the wrench. "Dale, go into the supply room and look for another one of these."

"I could help you, Richard," Elizabeth said. "May I approach the king?"

"What is it?" Venneman barked. She was doing it after all—regaining control. Not in the way she was used to, the supernatural control of a vampire over its former victims, but in a very human way, by making him feel silly. "All right, come here."

Elizabeth stood too close to him, staring up into his face. "I'm a lot stronger than a human being, despite my size, Richard. As you know. Since you don't want to enjoy my strength, why not take advantage of it? You want to undo these bolts, right?" She gestured toward the cylinder. "Together, we could probably do it a lot faster. I'm getting tired of all of this, Richard. Now I just want to get it over with."

"Here, Richie." It was Dale, holding the wrench he had

wanted.

Venneman took it and waved her away—away from Elizabeth. He waited until Dale was back at the control panel and then gave the wrench to Elizabeth and gestured at the cylinder. "Give it a try," he said.

Elizabeth's attempt at loosening a bolt was as ineffective as Venneman's had been the first time he'd tried. She pushed down on the wrench until her feet began to lift from the floor, but the bolt did not move.

"See," Venneman told her, "it's not just a matter of strength, but how you use it." He took the wrench from her and used the two wrenches together, the way he had learned to do the first time. He put one on each of two adjacent bolts and then forced the wrenches toward each other, tightening the lower bolt while loosening the upper one. "Like that," he said.

"Oh, Richie," Elizabeth said, "you're so strong and smart. When I'm big again, I hope I can be as smart as you."

Venneman scowled at her and returned to his work, laboriously loosening one bolt after another. Something was loosening inside him, too, as he worked. He told himself that that was because he was freeing himself from the captivity in which he had been trapped for almost a year. At the end, he would still be a vampire, but he would have taken control of his life and fate.

"About now," Elizabeth said, "you should be boasting about what you're going to do to me when you get this thing opened up."

Venneman stopped working and said, "God lives in here. I'm going to show you the face of God."

Elizabeth sighed. "You're the first utterly mad vampire I've ever known. I've always assumed our kind was immune to mental disease, but now I know better."

Venneman chuckled and returned to work. He kept Elizabeth within his peripheral vision, but she made no move. She stayed near him and watched with apparent interest.

At last the cylinders were unbolted and stood sealed only by their own weight holding them in place. Venneman turned to Elizabeth and opened his mouth to speak.

Over her head, he could see the lab doors. The hallway beyond them was dark to human eyes. To Venneman's eyes, it glowed red through the glass. As he stood watching the red-tinged glass of the doors, the red light began to ooze through the glass and slide down the inside surface of the door. It reached the floor and piled up thickly on it. Then it began to move toward him, slowly, taking its time.

"You're seeing something again, aren't you?" Elizabeth said. "What is it, Richard?"

Venneman steeled himself to ignore the encroaching redness. "Nothing," he said. "It's getting late. Get undressed."

"Sex now, Richard? In front of your two friends?"

"Not sex, Elizabeth. Salvation. Hurry up."

Elizabeth shrugged and took her clothes off. She stood in front of him, as if inviting his admiration. As before, she was diminished in size evenly, her proportions unchanged.

Venneman refused to look at her. "Help me," he said.

This time, he knew better than to force the cylinders apart while standing in front of the seam between them. He crouched in front of the rightmost cylinder and slid his hand as far under it as he could. Then he began trying to simultaneously lift it and push it away, so that the seam would open. "Help me!" he said again.

Elizabeth hesitated visibly, her mask of self–assurance slipping for an instant. Then she crouched beside Venneman and did as he was doing.

The cylinder shifted a fraction of an inch.

The lab was bathed in brilliant light.

Elizabeth fell to her knees and covered her eyes with her hands. "Richard, what is that? Help me, Richard!"

The seam between the two cylinders had become a gleaming split. A fierce white light poured out of it, a shaft that stretched from the cylinder to the far wall of the lab. A smell of burning filled the air.

"Richie!" Dale shouted. "We've got to turn it off!"

"Not yet! Just a few more seconds!"

Venneman grabbed Elizabeth's shoulder and pulled her to her feet. "I told you, Elizabeth. God is in there. You're going to meet Him now. That light is the face of God. No, wait a minute, that's not right." Venneman frowned and tried to remember what he had worked out for himself almost a year ago, back in the mountains. "That's it!" he said, pleased with himself for managing to recall the idea. "It's the light of creation. It's like the sun, but it's right here. It's here for us. For me. So that I can use it."

Elizabeth's eyes were shut tight. "It's too bright, Richard. I've got to get away from it." She squirmed in his grasp, but she was unable to break free of him.

Venneman picked her up and tucked her under his left arm, holding her tightly and trapping her arms against her sides. Clumsily, he bent over and searched the pile of tools with his right hand. He fished out a crowbar.

The white light pouring from Dinsmuir's machine was changing slowly to red. Venneman glanced over his shoulder. The light from the doorway lay thick upon the floor. It was spreading throughout the lab; it was only a few feet away from him now. Its approach was speeding up, he was sure. Its surface rippled as it spread toward him. It had changed from light into liquid—he knew what liquid.

Gritting his teeth, Venneman turned back to the cylinder. Standing to one side, out of the brilliant light, he shoved one end of the crowbar into the opening. He leaned backward, using his weight to pull on the crowbar.

For a moment, nothing happened. Then the cylinder he and Elizabeth had managed to move slid suddenly, friction briefly overcome, and the crack between the cylinders widened to a few feet at its center.

The scarlet light of creation gushed out. Venneman was almost blinded by it. He squeezed his eyes almost shut, looking out through a slit.

The tip of the crowbar had been vaporized. What remained of it glowed white hot. Venneman's hand sizzled against the metal. He dropped the crowbar, gritted his teeth against the pain, and used both hands to hold Elizabeth. The pain didn't matter, he told himself. The injury would heal itself in a matter of minutes, as always. He gripped Elizabeth's upper arms tightly and held her in the air front of him, using her to shield his eyes from the light. Venneman slid his feet forward.

"Richard!" Elizabeth shrieked. "It's burning me!"

"You're going to God, Elizabeth. You'd never get there any other way. Say hello to God." He held her up and kept moving forward cautiously. This time, he would avoid the light himself.

He would thrust Elizabeth through the opening. His hands might be injured, but nothing else, and they would heal quickly enough.

Elizabeth twisted desperately in his grasp. Venneman's damaged hand wasn't working properly, and she managed to free her right arm. She twisted again, reached down with her free arm, and picked up the glowing, shortened crowbar.

Venneman grabbed at her, but his hand failed him, and Elizabeth got one foot on the floor and drove the crowbar up into him, into his left side, into his heart.

Venneman stood frozen. He felt his heart jerk convulsively, once, and then stop. He felt the glowing bar of metal burning deep within him.

Elizabeth stood still, her hands by her side, watching him.

Venneman moved. He yanked the crowbar from his side and flung it away. He grabbed Elizabeth again, this time in a grip she could not break. He tried to say something to her, but there was no breath in his lungs.

He pulled her to him, wrapped his arms around her, lifted her off the ground, and stepped calmly and steadily into the cylinder.

He could hear Elizabeth's screams, feel them against his chest, and he heard Dale shout his name, but he could think only of the light that was consuming him.

The inside of the cylinder was no longer filled with white light. It was filled with blood, and Venneman was drowning in it. He screamed, but the sound was choked off by the red liquid filling his mouth and nose and lungs. Venneman writhed in agony beneath the boiling ocean of blood and died.

The light had become orange, and it flickered through a haze of smoke. Something hissed, and the orange faded away.

Tears filled Venneman's eyes. He blinked repeatedly to clear them and raised his head.

Harold Dinsmuir and Dale Whitmer were using fire extinguishers to put out the flames that raced across the painted walls. Venneman watched stupidly until they were finished. He looked around the lab in wonder and noticed Elizabeth Vallé's unconscious body lying beside him. Why is she naked? he wondered.

Suddenly Venneman remembered everything.

He sat up quickly. He gasped at a sharp pain in his left side. He looked down at himself. He too was naked, except for a few charred remnants of his clothing, and those slid off him and fell to the floor. He put his hand to his side and brought it away bloody. He felt himself gingerly. He could feel a short, ragged wound in his side, painful to the touch, wet around the edges. He snatched his hand away in horror.

Elizabeth stirred and sighed and opened her eyes. She sprang to her feet and looked around wildly. Venneman was relieved to see that she was as diminutive as before. And yet her presence filled the room.

"I'm alive!" Elizabeth said. She laughed in delight. "Richard, you failed!" She looked at herself and ran her hands over her body in delight. "As good as ever, Richard. Better than ever. You failed," she said again.

Venneman shook his head. "I did exactly what I set out to do. I wasn't really trying to kill you. I had something much better in mind. That machine is what changed me. Now you've been changed the same way. You can tolerate sunshine, but you can no longer tolerate human blood. The tiniest sip will be agony to you. But it will be ecstasy to your victims, and they'll pursue you for all eternity, eager victims, hordes of humans, more and more of them every year. Now you're a prisoner of their blood, just like me.

"And your dreams," he added. "Well, I'll let you find out about those on your own."

Dale had come to Venneman's side. She crouched beside him and helped him to his feet. She was sobbing. "Oh, God, Richie, I was sure you were dead! I turned off the machine. I'm sorry, but I just couldn't let you die. I panicked when you stepped inside." She noticed the wound in his side. "Richie, you're hurt!"

"It's okay, Dale," he told her. "We heal quickly, remember. That'll be gone in a few minutes, probably."

He noticed the way Elizabeth was staring at Dale. He said to Elizabeth, "Hungrier and thirstier than ever, aren't you? You're going to have to spend eternity half-starved, because of the way their blood will feel to you."

Elizabeth's eyes were fixed on Dale's throat. She took a step toward Dale.

Venneman put his arm protectively around Dale and held his other hand up warningly. "Uh-uh," he said to Elizabeth. "I told you before, stay away from her."

Elizabeth's hand shot out, faster than Venneman's eye could follow. She struck him on the side of the head, knocking him away from Dale. He landed on the floor a few feet away, stunned. Through the ringing in his ears, he could hear Dale scream his name once, and then her voice was cut off.

Venneman struggled desperately to get to his feet. He

couldn't think properly, and the wound in his side was like a burning spear into his heart. He made it to his hands and knees and stopped at that point, feeling nauseated, swaying, fighting for balance. He raised his head and blinked over and over, trying to clear his misted vision.

He saw Dale lying still on the floor and Elizabeth standing above her. On Elizabeth's face was an expression of disgust. She spat repeatedly, as though trying to rid her mouth of an awful taste.

Venneman knew what that taste was. She would taste it again. Oh, yes, she would be forced to taste it again and again, for all time.

Dale sat up, clutching at her throat. The wound had already healed. She put her hands down, an expression of wonder on her face. Then she held her arms up to Elizabeth. "Oh, Elizabeth!" she said. "Please! Again!"

Elizabeth snarled at her and backed away. She noticed Venneman, still kneeling, laughing silently at her. "I'll starve, damn you!" she screamed at him.

Venneman shook his head. The movement increased his nausea and dizziness. "Not as long as you find vampires to feed on," he said. His voice was a croaking sound in his own ears. He cleared his throat and said, "Now you're able to do what I did to you and Karen. In fact, you'll have to do it. It's the only real nourishment there is for you now—the blood of other vampires."

"Then I'll start with yours, you bastard," Elizabeth said. She leaned down, gripped him by the shoulders, and pulled him easily to his feet.

He tried to push her away, but it felt like fighting against a brick wall. She ignored his childlike blows and lowered her face to his throat, snarling, her mouth opening.

It was agony, just like the first time she attacked him. But it was only agony at first, during those first moments as she bit furiously into him. When she reached Venneman's artery and sucked in a spurting mouthful of his blood, his body was filled with a new kind of delight. It radiated from her mouth and filled him, all of him, his limbs, his torso, his head. He was overcome with sexual excitement, greater even than what he had felt before with her. It was something he had never imagined possible. It was worth giving up life for.

But it stopped almost as soon as it had started. Elizabeth jumped away from him, coughing and gagging.

Released by her, Venneman dropped heavily to one knee. He watched her in bewilderment.

As she had with Dale's blood, Elizabeth spat repeatedly to get any remnants of Venneman's from her mouth. She stopped suddenly and turned to Venneman, her eyes and mouth both wide in surprise.

Venneman saw his blood still on her chin, and he was sickened by the sight.

Elizabeth laughed. "Don't you realize yet what you've done to yourself, Richard? My God, whatever you've managed to do to me, it was worth it, just to see this!"

Venneman touched his throat, where the hole she had torn was already closed and healing, and then his side, where the wound she had made earlier with the crowbar was still open and oozing blood. He shook his head. "No!"

"Yes!" Elizabeth's laughter filled the room. "You kept saying you wanted your old life back again. Now you've got it, Richard.

That light burned away your vampire nature. You're human again. And I..." Her face was filled with wonder. "I can live in daylight again! Oh, Richard, you've given me the best of both worlds! I'll be thanking you forever for this, Richard. I'll still be grateful to you long, long after you've died of old age and rotted away to nothing under the earth. Pardon me. Gone to your Heavenly reward."

Leisurely, lithely, Elizabeth strolled over to the clothes she had taken off earlier. She drew them on slowly, seeming to delight in the feeling of the cloth against her skin and in the physical sensations of her own body. "I'll need new clothing for my new life, won't I, Richard? Smaller sizes until I can grow back into my old things."

She stopped and looked at Dale's pleading eyes and Venneman's averted ones. "It's terrible stuff to me now, your blood. You were right about that. But I think I could learn to tolerate small quantities of it and survive that way when I'm unable to find other vampires. The way you both want me to feed on you again—why, it's wonderful! What a gift, Richard! Hordes of eager sacks of blood following me about all the time, begging me to sip from them." She laughed. "It's a vampire's dream come true! Richard, Richard, you had all this and you threw it away!" She shook her head. "You're an object lesson to all of us. I'll think about that lesson for the next few thousand years, you may be sure."

Elizabeth finished dressing. Without a glance back at Venneman, she strolled to the lab doors and pushed on them. They were locked shut because of Dale's sabotage. With a negligent blow of her hand, Elizabeth broke them open. She stepped through the doorway and vanished from Venneman's sight. She slipped into a night that was again black.

Venneman dragged himself painfully over to Dale, who was now standing up and looking at the broken lab doors. "Dale," he said, "what am I going to do now?"

Dale ignored him. Her attention was fixed on the doors and the night beyond. "Elizabeth," she whispered. "Elizabeth."

TWENTY-ONE

The first and last time Dale asked Venneman to help her in any important way was when she disposed of Laurie's body.

As soon as they felt physically able to, Dale and Venneman left the physics building and drove back to Dale's house. They left Harold Dinsmuir behind in the ruined lab, sitting in the chair in front of Dale's desk and staring blankly at the silent, darkened machine that had once been his ticket to fame and fortune.

Together, a couple of hours before dawn, they carried Laurie's body out to her car and put it in the trunk. Dale went back into her house and called the police. She told them that she had just received an incoherent call from Dinsmuir, during which he had said something vague about a fire and an attack in the basement lab of Currigan Hall on the university campus. Then Dale drove Laurie's car to the university, with Venneman following her in his car.

Dale parked Laurie's car well away from Currigan Hall and the jumble of flashing red and blue lights. She left Laurie's keys in the car and got into Venneman's car, and they drove slowly into the parking lot adjacent to the physics building.

A policeman approached them immediately. This was not a

city policeman, but rather a member of the campus security force. He gestured to Venneman to roll down his window. The cold night air flowed in, making Venneman shiver.

The guard bent down to look in. "Sorry, folks, building's closed." He stared at Venneman, frowning, as though trying to conjure a name from memory to match the hauntingly familiar face.

Dale leaned across Venneman, toward the window. "Hi, Steve. What's the problem?"

Steve's face lit up with the kind of pleasure Venneman had always felt when seeing Dale. "Hi, Miss Whitmer! Well, it's pretty strange. Remember what happened to Dr. Dinsmuir's experiment a year ago? Same thing's happened again. And now Dirtbag—" He broke off and glanced at Venneman. "Dinsmuir's sitting in his lab babbling about..." He took a deep breath and tried again. "Vampires!" He burst into loud laughter. When he got himself under control again, he said, "What are you doing here so late? Dinsmuir got you overworking again?"

"No, Steve, not this time," Dale said. "I was supposed to meet a friend here. She was going to go out for a hamburger with us tonight. She's..." Dale looked around, as though afraid someone might be listening to them. "Well, I probably shouldn't tell you this, but she's been dating Professor Dinsmuir, and she was supposed to be visiting him in the lab tonight."

The guard stared at her for a long time. Finally he said, "Miss Whitmer, I hate to say this, but maybe you'd better go on inside the lab and tell the city cops about your friend. I've got a bad feeling about this."

Dale smiled at him. "Steve, you watch too many cop shows on TV."

Dale and Venneman did a good job of acting bewildered and surprised when they entered the lab and saw the broken doors and the charred walls, even though they had left the place in the same condition less than an hour before. Dinsmuir still sat in Dale's desk chair, but now he was surrounded by policeman, both in uniform and wearing civilian clothes, and he was indeed babbling about vampires.

"They suck your blood," he was saying, "and it feels so wonderful, you can't imagine. It's not painful, the way you'd expect. Well, okay, it was at first. In fact, it hurt like hell for the first few seconds, but then it became like... like..." He paused, frowning, trying to come up with the right analogy. "Like all of the best fucks you ever had in your life combined and then increased by two orders of magnitude."

The policemen listening to him exchanged puzzled glances.

"I'll explain what I mean," Dinsmuir said, frustrated by their lack of understanding. "Where's a blackboard?" He looked around wildly, but instead of a blackboard, he saw Dale and Venneman watching him. He jumped to his feet. "There he is!" He pointed at Venneman. "That's the guy who sucked my blood! He's the vampire!"

The policemen whirled around, drawing their guns and pointing them at Venneman. Slowly, uncertainly, Venneman raised his hands.

One of the policemen approached Venneman cautiously, gun held ready. "Pardon me, sir," he said, "would you mind opening your mouth?"

Venneman did so.

"No fangs," the policeman called out. "I'm sorry, sir," he said to Venneman, "but you've been accused of being a vampire.

Could I see some identification?"

"Richard," Dinsmuir said, "where's your girlfriend, the other vampire?"

Dale said, "Officer, this is ridiculous. My friend here has been with me all evening. We just came to the lab to pick up a friend of mine who was supposed to meet us here. She was supposed to be..." She paused, then she put a slight emphasis on the next words: "...spending some time here with Dr. Dinsmuir. Dr. Dinsmuir has been very stressed out because of his experiment. He's been talking about vampires quite a bit lately, but I've never known what he meant by it."

The policeman looked at Dinsmuir for a moment. Then he said to Dale, "Tell me about your friend."

Dale described Laurie. "I introduced her to Dr. Dinsmuir a couple of months ago. They've been dating since then. I'm worried about her. She should have been here."

"What?" Dinsmuir yelled. "I don't know anyone named Laurie. I'm not dating anyone right now. I've been too busy with my work."

"Dr. Dinsmuir," Dale said, horrified, "how can you say such a thing? You told Laurie you loved her. She said that when she cut her finger a couple of days ago, you kissed away the blood, because you said everything about her was precious to you, even her blood. Especially her blood."

All the police became very interested.

It took them an hour to find Laurie's car in the distant lot where Dale had parked it. In the trunk, they found Laurie's bloodless corpse with its ruined throat.

Within two more hours, Dinsmuir had been charged with both Laurie's murder and the previously unsolved but very similar murder of Willie Gold.

The evidence linking Dinsmuir to either crime was flimsy and circumstantial. The evidence that he was a stereotypical mad professor was solid. The story he had told a large gathering of policemen about Richard Venneman and his midget female vampire companion, coupled with the results of a physical examination of Venneman conducted by an apologetic doctor under contract to the police department, might have been enough by itself to lead to Dinsmuir's institutionalization. The readiness of so many of his academic colleagues, a fair number of them cuckolded husbands, to testify to his frequently irrational behavior was icing on the cake.

Dale treated Dinsmuir's removal from the campus as a victory. To Venneman, it seemed unimportant. His own exoneration and consequent freedom to fully rejoin human society were, he thought, its only positive aspects.

If only he could have taken advantage of that freedom.

He had never done well at socializing with other human beings. His ten months of being a vampire had not improved matters.

There were times when he thought that his period as a vampire could not really have happened. Surely he was imagining all of it. Surely Jill's disappearance had some other explanation. He had simply lost the memory of yet another tedious, uninteresting ten-month period in his life, and Harold Dinsmuir was indeed crazy.

Then Venneman would have a flash of tactile memory, sharp, achingly clear and detailed: the way it had felt to tear into a throat, the way blood had spurted into his mouth, the way his victim's life had flowed so gloriously into every part of his body.

The way vampire blood had tasted!

And now human food might as well have been cardboard. Nothing had any taste, nothing had color. The nights were dark and empty, and the light of day was dull and washed out. Now he would be able to kill himself easily, if he really wanted to, and he often thought about doing it.

No permanent replacement had ever been hired to fill Venneman's job at the physics lab. He might have applied for the job again if the lab had still been in operation. But with Dinsmuir gone and his experiment permanently shut down, the basement of Currigan Hall had been left to gather dust instead of data. Someday, no doubt, the physics department would have the money and interest and need to put the space to use again. There was no sign of that happening, however.

Venneman stayed with Dale, contributing nothing, supported by her. The physics department had awarded her the largest fellowship in its power, eager to hold onto one of its most promising graduate students in years. She had other, meager sources of income, concerning the nature of which Venneman never inquired.

He felt guilty at forcing her to stretch her slender resources still further. He looked for work and found an occasional menial job.

None of the jobs lasted very long. Even when the work itself was physically easy, Venneman found himself unable to do it adequately. He was subject to unpredictable fits of daydreaming and detachment from reality. His employers always interpreted this as laziness. Twice he took a job involving some strenuous work. Both times, the wound in his left side tore open and bled for hours before closing again, despite stitches put in and dressing applied in a hospital emergency room.

That stab wound never really closed. A scab would form over it, and then what looked like a layer of scar tissue. But Venneman could always tell, when he moved, that there was still a hole inside him beneath the layer of skin. He imagined it constantly filled with blood. The surface layer, seemingly solid flesh, hid the reality of freed blood, rippling back and forth within his chest, rotting.

Venneman's unhealing wound terrified him. Rationally, he feared infection. Irrationally, he feared that all his blood would leak out through it, as though sucked slowly from him by an invisible vampire.

At first, Venneman slept on Dale's couch, the same couch on which Elizabeth had slept. After a few weeks, he moved to Dale's bed. He wasn't sure whether she had invited him to make the move or he had invited himself.

There was no sex involved. They shared a bed, but nothing else. Dale was cordial toward him, but no longer warm. She seemed to feel obligated to shelter him. Venneman could detect nothing more in her than that sense of obligation. He could detect nothing warmer in himself than gratitude and obligation.

And yet one night they did make love. It was a joyless and mechanical coupling. Dale achieved orgasm after long, strenuous effort. She cried out "Elizabeth!" twice and then pushed Venneman off her, rolled onto her side away from him, and fell into a troubled sleep.

Venneman watched her for a while. She twitched and moaned occasionally while she slept. He felt no desire to comfort her.

He had not managed to climax while inside her. He had been able to feel little sensation, as though Dale wasn't really there, as though she had turned into something wispy—smoke in the shape of a woman. He turned away from her and masturbated. He was overcome by a fantasy of making love to Elizabeth while floating on the ocean of blood, and then he finally climaxed.

Afterward, Venneman lay quietly, unable to sleep. Tears rolled down his cheeks and onto his pillow.

The next morning, Dale told Venneman she wanted him to move out.

"I could move back to the couch," Venneman said, offering the only sacrifice within his power to make.

"The problem isn't where you sleep," Dale said. "I just don't want you in my house anymore. I'll be on the campus all day. Please be gone when I get back."

"But what about my belongings?" Venneman said, hearing himself whine. Then he realized that he had no belongings other than the clothes he was wearing. There would be no trace of him after he had left, and he had had no real impact while he was there. It was he who was made of smoke, of emptiness, not Dale.

Spring had arrived early. No, not spring, Venneman thought, but the false promise of spring. This warm evening, so fortuitous for him now that he had no bed to return to, would surely be followed by weeks of cold, snow, dampness—misery for a suddenly homeless man.

He was driving around the city aimlessly, using up the hours of daylight and the gas in his tank. He had no idea what he would do when both were gone. Perhaps he could sell the car. It would fetch little, but it might be enough to buy a bus ticket to a warmer climate and a few days of cheap shelter when he got there.

And what then?

I'll sleep in my car tonight, he thought, and decide what to do tomorrow morning.

But nothing would have changed during the night. The situation in the morning would be no better than the situation now. He thought about cold, about shivering in an unheated car throughout a chilly night. It might be warm for this time of year during the day, but the temperature would begin to drop once the sun had set.

He had been a vampire for less than a year, and yet it seemed strange to him to have to worry about air temperature. It would take him far longer, he thought, to become reaccustomed to being a human being than it had taken him to adjust to being a vampire. Perhaps vampire existence was more natural for him than being human. Maybe it's more suited to my soul, he thought. Maybe it's my nature to live as a parasite on the human race and to be cut off from God and salvation.

Such theological speculation suddenly struck him as silly and as an inappropriate way for a grown man to expend his mental energy.

Venneman counted his money. He had a total of thirty-five dollars in his pockets. That included the twenty-dollar bill Dale had given him before she'd left the house. He had almost refused to take it, but fortunately common sense had triumphed over pride.

He decided to be foolish and spend some of the money right away. It was the sort of decision he would never have made during his first human life. He would have been horrified by such irresponsibility and contemptuous of the man exhibiting it. To be so irresponsible now was his way of declaring his independence of that other Richard Venneman. He might be human again, he told himself, but he could try to avoid being the same kind of human being he had been before.

He drove to a coffee shop he had liked before, but that Jill had found distasteful. Because of her opinion of the place, he had rarely been able to talk her into going there with him.

It was within walking distance of the campus, at the edge of the downtown business district. The clientele were a diverse lot—students from the university, theatrical types from the small theater district not far away, reporters from the daily paper, and anal-retentive young businessmen and women from downtown gawking at all of the preceding with envy poorly disguised as contempt.

Venneman had always found it an exciting place. He had been attracted to the youthful sexuality of the students, drawn to the flamboyance and self-conscious loudness of the theater crowd, intrigued by the hard-boiled act of the reporters, and envious of the ostentatiously displayed wealth of the yuppies. Jill had been simply repelled by all of them. Now, he thought, he could spend as much time in the place as he wanted to. Or as much as he could afford to.

Venneman was lucky enough to find free parking along the street just in front of the restaurant. It was late afternoon by now, after the lunch crush but before the after-work crowd, and business was slow.

He went inside, bought himself an overpriced sandwich and a cup of coffee, and sat down to watch what customers there were. At this time of day, most of the tables were empty, but there were enough other people there to capture his interest.

He thought about nothing—not Dale, not Jill, not Dinsmuir or Elizabeth or Karen, not vampirism or blood, not God. He tried to live through his senses instead of thinking. He concentrated on the texture of the sandwich in his mouth as he chewed it slowly, on its taste, on the smell of the coffee and the feel of it on his tongue. He let his gaze linger on a coed at a nearby table, talking animatedly to her friends.

She wore a woolen skirt with a bulky sweater. She had dark tights on her shapely legs. The sweater disguised her form above, but the short skirt and the tights emphasized her shape below. She was probably little more than half his age, Venneman realized. He reveled in the shock he imagined his earlier human self would have felt at his interest in the girl now and the open way he stared at her. Jill would have been even more shocked.

And he was shocked to realize that he had missed the most important difference between himself now and himself then. The earlier human Richard Venneman would not have stared at the girl because he would not have wanted to, but also because he would have been terrified of drawing her attention to himself and perhaps arousing her sexual interest. Now he was staring at her with sexual longing as well as visual delight. And she was oblivious to him.

Had he lost it at last—that ability to inspire sexual desire in others, that unwanted ability that had always frightened him so and bedeviled him all his life? If so, it was yet another loss he now mourned, one more in a lifetime characterized by loss.

At another table, a group of foreign students were drinking their coffee, smoking, and talking in a language Venneman didn't recognize. Studying them, he decided they must be from North Africa and were presumably speaking Arabic. How utterly foreign they must feel, he thought. How cut off from everyone around them. It was understandable that they would seek out each other's company, would yearn for a touch of something familiar in a foreign land. Whom would he ever be able to speak to with that feeling of the familiar? Who would ever understand the strange language his experiences had led him to speak? With whom could he ever be his true self, whatever that now was? It would have been possible with Elizabeth—a realization that came to him much too late.

Venneman sat at his table, watching the other customers and drinking cup after cup of coffee, as the day wore into evening and the restaurant filled up. He could see through the front doors that it had grown dark outside. He began to feel hungry again and wondered if he should spend still more money on another sandwich.

He decided to do so.

It took quite a while to get the food this time, thanks to the customers filling the place and lining up at the counter. He was away from his table for perhaps a quarter of an hour. He carried his tray back to his table with a feeling of relief. His side had begun to ache again from standing so long, waiting to be served. He sat down and put his hand gently to his side, comforting himself, until the pain had faded to a level he could ignore. Maybe I'll get used to it eventually, he thought.

He took a small bite from his new sandwich and a small sip from his refilled cup of coffee and began to chew slowly, determined to make both food and drink last. He let his gaze drift over the room, examining the crowd of newcomers.

At a table in a far corner, leaning across the table to stare into the eyes of a handsome young man, was Jill Kennedy.

Venneman froze with his coffee cup halfway to his mouth. He stopped chewing the bite of sandwich in his mouth.

My God, she's beautiful! he thought.

His heart pounded and he felt short of breath. Now that his eyes had chanced on Jill, he could scarcely tear them away.

Did I really live with that woman, that goddess? he thought. Sleep with her, make love to her?

He drank her in with his eyes. Her profile, the way she held her hand, her hair, her smile, the curve of her back and her breast—all were perfect, all were as far above an ordinary woman as the angels were above mankind.

And she's a vampire, he thought.

She's a vampire, a predator, a lioness. She's not an angel, she's a killer.

The young man she was stalking was probably not much older than the girl Venneman had been watching earlier. He was a weightlifter, Venneman thought, judging his physique as well as he could through the bulky clothing he was wearing. Venneman wondered if men who lifted weights had more blood than men who didn't, or if their blood flowed more vigorously through their veins, or if it tasted better or imparted greater strength to the vampire who drank it. What was undeniable was the young man's good looks—and his total fascination with the beautiful woman across the table from him.

Watching Jill hunting her young prey, Venneman had one of those flashes of memory. He could almost feel the boy's blood flowing into his mouth, his strong young body wilting in Venneman's grip, giving up its fight to live. For that instant, Venneman could smell and hear the blood flowing powerfully through the boy's neck.

Then it was gone, and all Venneman could hear was the hum of conversation from adjacent tables, and all he could smell was his sandwich and coffee. Shaken, he put the cup down hard, slopping coffee into the saucer. He forced the bite of food down with an effort, disgusted by its taste.

There was a third party at the table, another handsome man, but older than the boy. Jill's age, Venneman thought, although he realized that it was hard to say just what that age was. The older man sat back in his chair, a smile on his face, watching Jill at her work with amusement and interest.

Venneman examined the man. He was tall and slender, and he relaxed in his chair in a way that for the first time made the word "lounging" meaningful to Venneman. Was it Henry Hapgood? Indeed, the man's type of good looks and his manner suited him to be the rake in a Regency romance. Venneman could imagine him wearing a lacy, ruffled shirt and playing idly with a dueling sword.

The man had experienced two hundred years of American history and would live many centuries more of it. Venneman slumped in his chair. While I, he thought, have experienced nothing and threw away the chance of experiencing more.

The two vampires stood up. Jill's and Hapgood's chairs scraped slightly against the coffee shop's wooden floor as they pushed them back. Their young victim jumped to his feet so quickly and with such eagerness that his chair toppled over backward and hit the floor with a crash.

Conversation stopped throughout the place as patrons looked for the cause of the noise.

The young man himself, however, seemed oblivious to what he had done. His eyes were fixed on Jill's. He could see nothing but her, could think of nothing but the promise of her body. He was unaware of Hapgood, standing next to him and grinning a predatory grin as he looked over the healthy young body.

Jill put her arm through the young man's and pressed it tightly against her side. The boy looked dizzy; his knees seemed about to give way. With her other hand, Jill reached out for Hapgood's hand. She led both men away from the table and toward the front door. Hapgood walked casually and easily beside her, a smile on his face. The young man was having trouble walking. His eyes were fixed on Jill's face and he stumbled. Jill jerked on his arm, pulling him along. To Venneman, it appeared that she was half holding her victim up.

They passed Venneman's table on their way out.

Jill was concentrating too much on her prey to notice Venneman, but Hapgood's eyes were wandering. For a few seconds, they lingered on a trio of female students at an adjacent table. Then they drifted to Venneman's face.

Hapgood slowed down and stopped. He and Venneman stared at each other, each with a different kind of interest.

Venneman examined the aristocratic face, looking for some visible sign that this was a vampire, not a human being—and searching too for whatever it was that had made Jill find Hapgood so much more exciting to be with than she had found him.

Hapgood's interest was frankly and openly sexual.

Venneman was surprised at that. He was even more surprised to feel something inside him reacting to Hapgood's stare.

Jill turned to see why Hapgood had stopped. She gasped in horror. "What are you doing here?" she asked, her voice rasping.

"Everyone has to be somewhere, Jill," Venneman said quietly.

"And this is?" Hapgood asked Jill.

Venneman stood up and held out his hand. "Richard Venneman. Jill must have told you about me, Henry."

Hapgood smiled broadly at him. "Oh, indeed." He took Venneman's hand and held it gently for a long time. His hand was warm, almost hot, and Venneman felt the heat from it racing through his own body. Hapgood's hand was slender, but Venneman could feel the strength in it, vampire strength. He remembered from his encounters with Elizabeth during his human phases just how much greater that strength was than his own was now, but the thought of Hapgood's physical power excited him rather than frightened him.

Jill was pale and looked as though she might be about to throw up. "For God's sake, leave me alone!" she said to Venneman. Then she rushed from the restaurant, dragging the two men with her.

Just before they passed through the door, Hapgood stopped again and looked back at Venneman. They held each other's gaze for a moment before Hapgood disappeared.

On Hapgood's side, it was a look that held only the promise of mutual pleasure. He could not have known how much more promise it held for Venneman.

Venneman felt a sharp stab in his side and realized that the pain of his unhealing wound had disappeared completely when he caught sight of Jill and had not reappeared until she and Hapgood had passed out of sight.

Venneman sat down slowly and resumed eating his sandwich and drinking his coffee. There was no hurry. He would give them all the time they needed with their healthy young prey. Then he would leave this place and follow them with renewed hope.

About the Author

David Dvorkin was born in 1943 in Reading, England. His family moved to South Africa after World War II, and then to the United States when David was a teenager. After attending college in Indiana, he worked at NASA in Houston on the Apollo Project, then at Martin Marietta in Denver on the Viking Mars lander project. His aerospace career ended in 1974. Thereafter, until 2009, he worked as a software developer and technical writer. He and his wife, Leonore, and their son, Daniel, have lived in Denver since 1971.

In addition to non-fiction, David has published many science fiction, horror, and mystery novels. For details, as well as quite a bit of nonfiction reading material, please see David's website: http://www.dvorkin.com/

David is on Facebook at
http://www.facebook.com/DavidDvorkin
and on Twitter at http://twitter.com/David_Dvorkin
His blog is http://eyeblister.blogspot.com/

For information about the self–publishing service that David operates with his wife, please see https://www.dldbooks.com/

David in 2019

www.ingramcontent.com/pod-product-compliance
Lightning Source LLC
Chambersburg PA
CBHW060601310726
48982CB00008B/1199/J

* 9 7 8 1 7 3 4 5 6 3 6 9 6 *